The
WELSH WARRIOR'S
INHERITANCE

Second volume in The Welsh Warrior series

by

Arianwen Nunn

ISBN 978-1-962465-82-3

HISTORUM PRESS

NEW YORK, NY / MACON, GA

2024

Dedication

Without my husband's amazing support, this book would not have reached publication. He knows the books and the many characters by heart! Thank you also to my family and friends who have shown such enthusiasm and encouragement.

Acknowledgments

Many thanks to the many friends who have read and discussed the events and characters portrayed in this book. Thank you also to Darrell Wolcott who has offered many interesting insights into the period depicted.

About the Author

Arianwen Nunn was born in Wales in 1958. After spending her early life between Wales and England, she studied English Literature at Swansea University and post-graduate studies at Bristol University led her to take up teaching. Moving to Papua New Guinea with her husband, she discovered a very different world. Four years later, Australia became home for Arianwen, her husband, two children and, now, two grandchildren. Arianwen is passionate about history and all things Welsh.

CONTENTS

Alphabetical List of Characters

Aeddan was one of Gruffydd ap Cynan's longest-serving men at arms.

Angharad, wife of Gruffydd ap Cynan, King of Gwynedd, was the daughter of Owain Fradwr, Owain the Traitor. She was considered one of the noblest queens in Wales. She was beautiful, kind-hearted and intelligent. Angharad was the mother of eight children with Gruffydd, and her main concern was that Gwynedd had peace. She had seen the horrors of war firsthand and wanted to avoid war at all costs. She was much younger than her husband but a loving wife.

Annest was a daughter of Angharad and Gruffydd ap Cynan.

Arnulf de Montgomery was the younger son of Roger and Mabel de Montogomery, who were the most powerful and wealthy barons in England. Arnulf was made Earl of Pembroke and took over the old Welsh lands of Dyfed. He was as brutal as his parents and changed sides many times in the Norman wars between King Henry I of England and his brother, Robert Curthose, Duke of Normandy. Arnulf was married to Lafracoth, daughter of the king of Leinster, High King of Ireland. Arnulf was exiled from England by Henry I.

Bethan was Angharad's maid. She had a son, Rhys, out of wedlock with Angharad's brother Gronwy. She had never married but had a soft spot for Hywel.

Bishop Richard, also known as **Richard de Belmeis**, was King Henry I eyes and ears to Wales as chief agent in the Welsh Marches. He was appointed Bishop of London in 1108. He lived in Shrewsbury and thought he could control events among the Welsh kings and nobles.

Cadwgan ap Bleddyn was a King of Powys and came to power when his brothers, Madog and Rhyrid, were killed fighting against Princess Nest's father, Rhys ap Tewdwr. He was a worthy nobleman yet hard-drinking and a womanizer. He was also a noted warrior who allied with Gruffydd ap Cynan to fight against the Normans between 1093 and 1098.

Cadwallon ap Gruffydd was Angharad and Gruffydd ap Cynan's firstborn son. He was good-looking but a touch arrogant.

Cadwaladr ap Gruffydd was Angharad and Gruffydd ap Cynan's third son. He had a mischievous streak.

Davydd was Uchdryd's man of arms.

Dyddgu ferch Idnerth was the wife of Llywarch ap Trehearn. She was a good mother and sensitive about her oldest child Cadafael who was simple.

Gilbert Strongbow, Earl of Strygill and later lord of Ceredigion. Gilbert married Adelaide de Clermont. He led action to subjugate the Welsh.

Gladwys ferch Llywarch was the lovely daughter of Llywarch ap Trahearn and his wife, Dyddgu.

Gogan was one of Gronwy's men.

Griffith ap Rhys was Princess Nest's brother and a prince of Deheubarth. He had been in exile in Ireland and wanted to return to reclaim Deheubarth.

Gronwy ap Owain was a lord of Gwynedd and Angharad's brother. He resented Angharad and Gruffydd ap Cynan and was determined to oust them from power. He was married to Genilles ferch Hoedlyw ap Ithel and had a daughter Cristyn.

Gruffydd ap Cynan, King of Gwynedd, was considered the foremost king of Wales. He was intelligent and cultured but a fierce and clever warrior and strategist. He had brought Gwynedd from ruin to wealth. He loved music, supported his bards, built churches, funded the building of Bangor Cathedral, spoke many languages fluently, and had wonderful alliances with other monarchs and nobles. He was a loving but strict father. He was a man in his prime but aware that age was creeping up on him.

Gwenllian ferch Gruffydd was Angharad and Gruffydd ap Cynan's eldest daughter. She was beautiful, intelligent, and an impressive fighter.

Gwir was Dyddgu's old maid.

Henry I, King of England, also known as **Henry Beauclerc**, was a younger son of William the Conqueror. He took the throne in 1100 when his brother was killed by an arrow when hunting. Rather than attend to his brother's body he rode at speed to Winchester to take charge of the treasury. He spent much of his time and England's money fighting in

Normandy principally against his brother, Robert Curthose who, as firstborn of William the Conqueror, had a valid claim to the English throne.

Hova was one of Gronwy's men.

Howel ap Rhys was Nest's brother who had been imprisoned and castrated by Arnulf de Montgomery.

Hunydd ferch Einudd was the wife of Maredudd ap Bleddyn. She was an ambitious woman who knew how to scheme.

Hywel was the leader of King Gruffydd ap Cynan's warband. His love for his queen, Angharad was unrequited. He was a loyal and worthy warrior who respected Gruffydd ap Cynan to whom he owed his life.

Ina was Meilyr ap Owain's wife. She was beautiful but unpleasant with expensive tastes.

Iorwedd ap Bleddyn was a brother of Cadwgan ap Bleddyn, King of Powys. He was a worthy warrior but his scheming led to his changing sides from supporting the earls who rebelled against Henry I. Perhaps Henry felt he was too much of a liability and threw him into prison for seven years.

Ithel ap Rhyrid was Madog ap Rhyrid's brother. His father was killed fighting Rhys ap Tewdwr. He was warlike and greedy.

Lafracoth, daughter of King Murtagh, High King of Ireland, was unhappily married to Arnulf de Montgomery.

Llywarch ap Owain was Angharad's youngest brother.

Llywarch ap Trehearn was a lord of Arwystli. His father once ruled both Gwynedd and Powys. He supported the Normans and hated Owain ap Cadwgan, who killed his brothers when they 'overreached'.

Lleuci was the wife of Rhydir ap Owain, Angharad's brother. She was a breath of fresh air and always happy.

Madog ap Rhyrid was the son of Rhyrid ap Bleddyn, a king of Powys, killed in a battle with Princess Nest's father, Rhys ap Tewdwr. Madog was ambitious but wild.

Maredudd ap Bleddyn was Cadwgan ap Bleddyn's youngest half-brother. His five years as a hostage, given to King Henry by his brother Iorwedd, marked him. He became a wily scheming statesman driven on by his wife Hunydd.

Marged was a daughter of Angharad and Gruffydd ap Cynan.

Meilyr ap Owain was Angharad's favourite brother. He had mixed loyalties but needed to support Gronwy to maintain his standard of living.

Meirion was one of Gruffydd ap Cynan's longest-serving men-at-arms.

Nest ferch Rhys, Princess of Deheubarth. As a young girl, her father was killed by the Normans, and she lost everything. She was sent to be brought up at an English court and there caught the eye of Henry, Prince of England. They became lovers, but he did not consider her enough of a match to marry. She bore him a child, Henry Fitz Henry. Henry, who then became king, married her to Gerald of Windsor, who was one of his main lords in Wales.

Owain ap Cadwgan was Cadwgan ap Bleddyn's son. His father despaired of his wildness and what he felt was his irresponsibility, yet to many, he was a Welsh nationalistic hero. He hated the Normans and the Flemings who settled in Wales, pushing out the Welsh landowners.

Owain ap Gruffydd was Angharad and Gruffydd ap Cynan's second son. He was well-liked, a thinker, and mature for his age.

Rainaillt was a daughter of Angharad and Gruffydd ap Cynan.

Rhoddri was Gruffydd Cynan's chief bard.

Rhydir ap Owain was Angharad's brother. He supported Gronwy who was his older brother.

Rhys was the bastard son of Gronwy ap Owain and lived at Gruffydd ap Cynan's llys, and had been taught to read and write. He trained the royal children in battle skills.

Rhys ap Tewdwr was the father of Griffith ap Rhys, Howel ap Rhys, and Nest ferch Rhys. He was the ruler of Deheubarth and died in 1093.

Robert Curthose, Duke of Normandy, was the eldest son of William the Conqueror and felt he had the right to the throne of England. He spent long years at war with his brothers William 11, also known as William Rufus and Henry 1. He had a son called William Clito.

Robert de Belleme was the son of Roger and Mabel de Montgomery. He was the third Earl of Shrewsbury. Robert was a supporter of Robert Curthose, Duke of Normandy, and led the magnates against William II and Henry I along with his brother, Arnulf de Montgomery. He was known for his cruelty. Robert was exiled from England by Henry I.

Susanna was the youngest daughter of Angharad and Gruffydd ap Cynan.

Susannah was Angharad's maid. She had been with her mistress since she was a child.

Uchdryd ap Edwin was Angharad's uncle and the chief of Cadwgan ap Bleddyn's warband. He was a schemer but a decent man with a wonderful sense of humour. He was well-liked and a great leader of men. The Normans had great respect for him.

Weasel Face was one of Owain ap Cadwgan's men. He was a cousin of Owain, and his real name was Merddyn.

William II of England, also known as **William Rufus,** was the second son of William the Conqueror. He was killed in 1100, by an arrow while hunting with his brother who became Henry I.

William Clito was the son of Robert Curthose, Duke of Normandy. He was born in 1102 and much of his life was spent avoiding the threats from his uncle Henry I who regarded him as a threat.

Wyon was Gronwy ap Owain's leader of the warband.

Understanding a little about
Welsh Pronunciation

The Welsh alphabet has 28 letters made up of seven vowels: A, E, I, O, U, W and Y and twenty-one consonants: B, C, Ch, D, Dd, F, Ff, G, Ng, H, L, Ll, M, N, P, Ph, R, Rh, S, T, and Th.

Ch is pronounced as in Ba**ch**: **Uchdryd** is pronounced **Uch-drid**

Dd is pronounced as the 'th' in Pa**th**: **Gruffydd** is pronounced **Griffith**; **Robert of Rhuddlan** is pronounced **Robert of Rith-lhun**

F is pronounced as the 'v' in **V**inegar: **Angharad ferch Owain** is pronounced **Ang-har-ad verch O-wain**

Ff is pronounced as the 'f' in **F**inger.

Ll doesn't have an English equivalent, but it sounds a bit like **Thl**: **Llewelyn** is pronounced **Thl-well-in**.

W, as a vowel, is pronounced like in S**oo**n or B**u**ll. W is also used as a consonant as it is in English: Town

Rh is pronounced as in **Rh**ino

Y at end of a word is pronounced as the 'ee' in Fl**ee**: **Gronwy** is pronounced **Gron-wee; Rhys** is pronounced **Reece.**

Y in the middle of a word is pronounced as the 'u' in Flutter or as the 'i' in Din: **Rhydir** is pronounced **Rud-deer; Meilyr** is pronounced **My-Ler.**

U is pronounced as the 'ee' in **Deep**: The Welsh word for Wales is **Cymru** and is pronounced **Cum-ree.**

A few other names and their pronunciations to get you started:

Einion: Ay-knee-on

Hywel: Howell

Cadwgan-ap-Bleddyn: Cad-oo-gan ap Blethin

Robert of Rhuddlan: Robert of Rith-luhn

Maredudd: muh-rit-ith. The English would have pronounced it Mare-dith.

Historical Notes

This book is a work of fiction but draws on some real characters whose story is dimly hinted at by the few documents which survive from the time. Most of the events which took place are real but I have interpreted them in a way that makes sense to me. I am hoping that the below elaborates on my thinking in putting together the fragments of history that exist and explain some of the unfamiliar terms used.

Welsh Names.

In Wales, a son or daughter was given a first name and then further identified as being the child of their father so Gruffydd ap Cynan is Gruffydd son of Cynan, Angharad Ferch Owain is Angharad daughter of Owain. The Welsh word for a son is 'mab' but it becomes 'ab' or 'ap'. To keep it simple although the convention is to use 'ap' before consonants and 'ab' before vowels I have used 'ap' meaning 'son of' throughout the book. Similarly, although the word for daughter is usually 'ferch' in modern Welsh but 'verch' was used in the Middle Ages, I have chosen to use 'ferch' to mean 'daughter of'.

Gruffydd ap Cynan.

After his death, a book about his life was put together. In Latin: Historia Gruffydd vab Kenan. The intention of this history was to establish the right of Gruffydd's heirs to the royal throne and it was a marketing exercise setting out the character of Gruffydd as Arthuresque. After doing some research I felt that Darrell Wolcott presents a very compelling argument in his essay 'History of Gruffudd ap Cynan- A New Perspective' in which he suggests that the history tells the life of two men both called Gruffydd ap Cynan. One is the nephew of Iago and one is the grandson. I have chosen to make the hero of my story the grandson.

Owain ap Edwin, Angharad's Father

Owain ap Edwin was also known as Owain Fradwr or Owain the Traitor. His relationship with the Normans was unusually good and it seems strange that he decided to marry his daughter to Gruffydd ap Cynan unless he was wanting to have a foot in both camps. This is the view that I have taken in the story.

Uchdryd ap Edwin.

Owain ap Edwin's brother, leader of Cadwgan ap Bleddyn's warband. There is confusion over why Uchdryd was so respected by the Normans. I have suggested a reason although there is no written evidence supporting that reason.

Marriage date of Angharad ferch Owain and Gruffydd ap Cynan and therefore age of children.

There is some confusion over the date of the marriage of this couple. Some theories suggest that the return of Gruffydd from Ireland to retain Anglesey was linked with the marriage of Owain ap Edwin's daughter in 1098. I have taken the view that their marriage was likely in 1095 allowing for more time for the birth of their children in line with what happened in their lives subsequently.

Maredudd ap Bleddyn

It is not clear why Maredudd ap Bleddyn stood in the shadows for so many years. I have crafted my version of why this was.

Princess Nest

Although some sources claim that Princess Nest had her son, Henry Fitz Henry, by Henry 1 of England in 1103 and married Gerald Constable of Pembroke and Windsor Castles in 1105 I have preferred earlier dates to suit the plot of this novel.

Griffith ap Rhys

I have slightly adjusted the timing for Griffith's likely return to Wales to fit in with my story.

Cantref/ Cantrefi

Anglesey at the time of Gruffydd ap Cynan was made up of three cantrefi (the plural of cantref). These were Aberffraw, where the king's llys was; Cemais and Rhosyr. The division of land in Wales in the Middle Ages was based on a cantref or an administrative centre which was made up of several commutes. Cant means one hundred and Tref means a town but originally a cantref might be made up of one hundred settlements some being as small as a couple of houses. Each cantref would have its own court.

Llys

A llys is a royal court where judiciary matters would also be settled. http://ardal-wales.co.uk/english/local-history/royal-courts/

Teulu

Kings of Wales would have an armed retinue who were called the teulu. There were very strong relationships formed between the king and his teulu. The king was responsible for looking after them and the greater his teulu the better his reputation. The teulu in return would fight to the death for their king against an enemy.

Normans.

The Normans were often referred to as the French at this time in history but I have chosen to call them the Normans.

The Welsh

The Welsh rulers were united with common culture and language and saw themselves as the Britons. Since a movement to unite Wales and Welshmen was happening at this time I often have my characters refer to themselves and their countrymen as Welsh.

The Laws of Hywel the Good: Cyfraith Hywel Dda

The Welsh laws were codified by Hywel the Good in the mid-tenth century. They are very different from the Norman laws. They include laws on capital punishment which were rare as the Welsh preferred the system of compensation to families, inheritance and laws for women. The Laws for women stated that on marriage an AMOBR or fee was to be paid to the woman's lord. On the morning after the marriage, a fee was payable to the woman by her husband for taking her virginity and this was called a COWYLL. During the marriage, the DOWER was a common pool of property that was due to the woman if they separated before seven years. After seven years the woman was entitled to half the common pool. Another law that was different to the Norman laws was that when a landowner died his land was to be divided up between his sons equally and even including illegitimate sons if their father had acknowledged them.

Anglesey

I have chosen to call the island of Anglesey by the name it was known to Vikings and Normans. The Welsh would refer to the island of Anglesey as Ynys Mon.

Eryri

This is the Welsh name for what we know as Snowdonia.

Welsh words.

I have used a few Welsh words in this book. Some commonly used are:

Brychan: a coarse cloth used as a blanket.

Cariad: an endearment meaning 'love'.

Cawl: a thick soup.

Hafod: Haf means 'summer' and Hafod was the summer pasture for cattle or summer dwelling for people high in the mountains.

Chapter 1: Night Flight (December 1109)

The fifteen riders wore mail, hooded dark cloaks, swords at their sides, and carried round willow iron-edged shields on their backs. They had hurried through the night, heavy hooves flinging clods of earth behind them. As they came to the muddy track hard against the thick wood beside silvered fields, they slowed to a walk. A doe, lured by hunger into the open, froze, then darted back into the cover of the trees, startling the lead stallion, which skittered sideways, ears back, eyes rolling. Only superb horsemanship brought the huge beast under control. The riders stopped, alarmed by the noise of the big animal crashing through the undergrowth, and their subsequent murmur of relief betrayed their own nervousness.

They continued, hugging woods to where the trees thinned into a clearing. Beyond was the River Teifi, mercury water snaking through a gorge towards the sea. In front of them, below the firmament of stars, the castle gleamed in ghostly moonlight, seemingly floating on a thin mist that had risen from the water. As they gazed up at the vast palisade, some of the men touched the crosses at their necks, shivering involuntarily, eyes wide. None of the men liked being out in the shadows of the night, which turned trees into monsters and heightened the innocent animal calls into the cries of ghouls. Neither did they like the stretch of open ground ahead that held no cover from archers who might have them in their sights, but they could not turn back now. Their russet-haired, chisel-faced leader held a gloved ringed hand to stop them as he twisted in his saddle. He was a tall, powerfully built man on a grey stallion, riding with a straight back and, though young, he had the air of someone used to command. The moonlight glinted on the silver of his harness, spurs, and sword hilt. An owl, white-faced, flew across in front of them, shrieking as it went, and a few trembled. The owl was not a good omen, but the russet-haired swordsman was set on the task ahead.

'Gethin, we will dismount here, but your job is to keep the horses still and safe.' He spoke in an urgent but low, deep voice. A blond-haired, lanky youth with soulful eyes slithered off his horse and, as each of his companions dismounted, started to tether their horses to the branches of an aged oak. He did not want to be left there alone, but he said nothing. He was more frightened of the wrath of his lord.

The tall man led his men forward confidently on foot, their steps crunching over the mud and frosted, rotting leaves underfoot. The leader silently congratulated himself that all had so far gone to plan. His father, Cadwgan ap Bleddyn, storied King of Powys, had reacted exactly as he predicted he would, giving him good reason to storm out into the night from his father's Christmas feast, unquestioned, at a time when everyone would be celebrating or recovering from the celebration. Not even the ever-vigilant Uchdryd ap Edwin, head of his father's warband, had thought to stop him.

The fortress was silent. They scrambled up to the edge of the high shadowy walls of the oak palisade, solid trunks sunk deep into a bank of earth. Owain ap Cadwgan cast his eyes around cautiously, but seeing nothing to alarm him, made his way determinedly towards the eastern edge where undergrowth grew thickly, gesturing for his men to follow him. His wide mouth broke into a white-toothed smile. He hacked into the brambles with his sword and standing back, the moonlight revealed a place where the wooden structure joined a rock wall. He pushed himself towards it and started to pull at a boulder. 'Come on boys, move this rock,' he said and grinned.

The boulder was already loose, and three of the men were able to roll it away, creating a gap the size of a small man where someone's carelessness or laziness meant that the wooden planks had not been taken to the ground.

'So much for Norman workmanship!' he hissed scornfully. 'Not enough to hold back Welshmen, eh? We'll easily get through here.'

His men crowded around as he examined the gap in the fortification where he intended they pull themselves through.

'What about the sentries, my lord?' a wiry, thin, and pock-faced, older member of the group with restless eyes asked dubiously. He had voiced the uneasiness that gripped the others of trapping themselves on the wrong side of a well-fortified Norman stronghold.

The leader tapped his sword and casually assured him, 'We'll have no issues, Merddyn. You worry too much, cousin!'

Merddyn shook his head disbelievingly and rolled his eyes. The gesture was caught by Owain, who glared at him, his eyes narrowing to slits of jet, before challenging them irritably: 'Anyone else have doubts?'

Merddyn shifted uncomfortably. There was some shuffling, but nobody else spoke. Owain scanned their faces for dissent, knew their fears, and felt sure they would not let him down despite the awkward clearing of throats. He held his hands out to them, cocking his head to give them a last chance to speak, but there was still silence. He dropped to the ground and was the first to pull himself through. His voice gave the signal from the other side, and the party slithered into the enemy fortress one by one.

Inside the palisade was a deserted courtyard across which was a guardhouse, the door open. Owain crept forward, flattening himself against the outside wall, listening before his swift inspection showed nobody inside. They could also make out a collection of neat outbuildings, including kitchen, dairy, byres, smithy and stables. The only noises were horses moving and whinnying quietly, and the heavy breathing and gentle lowing of cows in the byre.

As the last men wriggled through the fence, Owain indicated to two solidly built men charged with unbarring and opening the broad, heavy wooden gates that were strengthened with iron. They could hardly credit that there was no sentry on duty or that nobody rushed at them as the gates groaned open.

Owain accelerated his commands.

'You four, drive the animals outside the palisade. Merddyn and Ieuan, quickly get all the horses to Gethin. I want four of them saddled up. They need to be gentle but fast.' Then, pointing at three young warriors, he gave his order, 'We'll take the door, and when you get to the fire, you know what to do. Wait until I give you the signal. If they are waiting inside, no heroics! We back out and ride like devils.' They nodded that they understood. Then he indicated to two men holding longbows. 'Get up onto the palisade and cover us as we enter. Kill any men coming out with weapons.' He waited as they got into position.

The door to the main building was also heavy wood and iron but opened easily, if noisily. Again, Owain was first in, and although they proceeded cautiously, there was nobody to bar their way.

Owain paused for a moment, hardly believing his eyes. A fire lit up the hall where a feast had been held. The air was thick with the combination of ale, wine, grease, sweat and smoke. Tables were littered with uneaten food scraps and overturned drinking vessels. Unarmed men sprawled, sleeping, oblivious to all. There was not a stir from any of them, even the dogs around the table, except for the movement in their bodies as they breathed. His spearmen looked at Owain in wonder. He smiled exultantly and scanned the room, lighting on the stairway to a chamber above. He moved across the room, first prodding a dog and then an old soldier, yet elicited no response from either. Owain shook his head and let out a soft oath. Open-eyed, still marvelling at the scene of slumber before them, his men followed Owain across to the bottom of the stairs. A log dropped in the fireplace, and they swung round, muscles tense, then relaxed as they saw there was no danger. Owain paused a moment on the first step, waiting with his group of comrades, his sword drawn and their spears at the ready.

At his signal, two men went to the fire, lit burning torches, and quietly made their way back outside. Others went into the hall with shields held high and swords brandished, ready should the slumbering men and dogs awake. They could scarcely believe that they were inside a Norman fortress uncontested.

'Hurry,' urged Owain. The men ran to the empty outbuildings, hurling the torches to light the thatch and wood. The night air was suddenly filled with the tell-tale crackle of fire spreading, the smell of burning wood, as flames greedily devoured everything in reach. The horsemen had brought the destruction that terrified. Every child had grown up fearing waking to smoke that killed, charred, and left black sooty residue where once a home had thrived. Despite all the devastation, the castle's occupants slept on like enchanted characters from an old fairy tale. The eeriness of it was as unsettling as the conflict Owain had anticipated.

Finally, as the blaze took hold, someone shrieked in the upstairs chamber. There were footsteps, and a woman's voice screamed, 'Whoever you are, take what you wish, but if it is my husband you have come for, he is not here. I beg you, do not hurt the men, women and children here.'

Owain's eyes shone. He snorted, shook his head, and bounded up the stairs with athletic grace, two at a time, his laugh wild. He was invincible. The night was his.

***

'He did what?' King Gruffydd's voice bellowed across the llys so that his oldest four children, who were in the chamber next door practising their Latin with their mother, looked at her with alarm.

'Why is Father shouting at Uncle Uchdryd?' asked Owain earnestly as the raging continued.

'I do not think he is angry with Uncle Uchdryd,' explained his mother, Angharad. 'I think he is frustrated by some news Uncle Uchdryd has brought him.'

Gruffydd exploded again. There was a mighty crash, followed by the sound of pottery smashing. Angharad winced. In the almost thirteen years since she had married Gruffydd, his outbursts had lessened, but he could be volatile when pushed. It was not surprising that he was a formidable warrior.

'I think that was the jug,' commented Gwenllian, her rich copper hair swinging about her as she turned her head to give her mother a cheeky grin, her clear, sparkling blue eyes full of merriment. As a sister to three lively brothers, confrontation did not upset her unduly.

Cadwallon, the eldest, pushed his hand through his thick golden waves, gasped dramatically, and screwed up his handsome face into a look of pain as further objects were being shattered. 'And there's the goblets. But, have no fear, for the King of Gwynedd has plenty of goblets to replace them!'

The children giggled but quickly quelled their mirth when their mother's eyebrows raised, her voice resonating with potential punishment.

'Cadwallon, you are the heir to Gwynedd, and you must behave with decorum. You are setting a bad example for your siblings. What is more, when your Great Uncle, who is the head of Cadwgan ap Bleddyn's warband, comes to speak with your father, you should not take it lightly!'

Cadwallon coloured and gave a tiny nod of acceptance, but his deep blue eyes glowered at his mother when she turned away. He did not like being chastised. His younger brother, Owain's hazel eyes caught his look and shot a warning glance. Owain, fiercely loyal to his parents, would not brook any disrespect from his siblings. Cadwallon's face sneered as he shook his head in disgust at his sanctimonious brother. The raised voices in the hall next door continued. The children knew well that their father was essentially a reasonable man, very patient and considerate, but on the odd occasion, they had seen his temper flare and knew well to avoid him at such times. They also knew he would never hurt them, although his punishments were stringent if they misbehaved.

'Mother,' said the opportunist Cadwaladr, youngest of the four, twisting his slender frame away from his work and smiling charmingly, 'it is very hard to concentrate with all the noise going on, so please could we come back to this later?'

Angharad felt increasingly tense at the escalating disruption in the hall and thought she needed to smooth the waters. She let out an aggrieved sigh but agreed to let the children leave their studies for an hour. Getting them to apply themselves was hard enough, as they all preferred being outdoors, even on a freezing wintry day like this.

'Boys, go to find Rhys and ask him if you can practise your swordcraft.'

Rhys was the son of Angharad's maid, Bethan, born out of wedlock. His father was Angharad's brother Gronwy ap Owain, now Lord of East Gwynedd and ally of the Normans. He had never acknowledged Rhys. Now sixteen years old, Rhys had been brought up in the family with Angharad ensuring he was literate, while Gruffydd undertook to ensure he was a solid warrior. He had inherited Gronwy's stocky, short frame, red hair, and freckled fair face. Like his mother, Bethan, he was diligent, keen to please, working hard to learn his swordcraft and to master the other tools of war, but he did not have natural talent. Everything he had learnt he had perfected by repetition, and now he had been given the task of tutoring King Gruffydd's heirs in those same skills. It was supposed to be an honour, but sometimes it rankled with him.

Eight-year-old Cadwaladr shot through the door, leaving his quill and ink precariously balanced on the edge of the table he had been working on. Gwenllian, only a year older but far more mature, caught the ink pot before it fell, tidying her quills, ink and parchment, and his, before following him out.

'Gwenllian, find Susannah and continue with your needlecraft,' Angharad instructed her as she watched her daughter stride out the door.

Gwenllian turned, smiled cherubically, her unusual bluebell-coloured eyes twinkling, then dashed out after her brother. Owain, his thick brown hair flopping over his forehead in mimicry of his father's, finished what he was doing first, carefully sanding what he had written to avoid ink spots, while his older brother Cadwallon, who was eleven, urged him to hurry up. There was only a year difference between the ages of Owain and Cadwallon, but Owain was much more responsible than his older sibling. Owain was always the one organising the games and was very serious about everything he did. He was the most advanced of her children when it came to learning, being well ahead in Latin and fluent in Welsh, French and English. Owain was usually even-tempered, whereas his brother Cadwallon was fiery and quick to anger. It was rare, but if Owain was pushed too far, he had a fearsome rage like his father. The siblings had learnt to run if they had driven him to that point!

The roaring next door had reduced to hot discontent. Angharad could hear her husband and Uncle Uchdryd still arguing but with less heat. Gathering her skirts, she went through to a small area off the hall where Susannah was minding the younger children.

Susannah, sturdy-framed, and whose faintly lined, ruddy face framed by wispy pale hair always looked on the edge of a smile, had practically brought up Angharad when her mother died, even though she was only a few years older than her mistress. She had been Angharad's confidant when her father had thought to marry her to the Earl of Chester, Hugh the Fat, and when, unexpectedly, her mistress had won the love of the handsome Gruffydd ap Cynan. She had been at her mistress' side while waiting for Gruffydd to return from warring against the Normans, winning battle after battle to his fiancée's relief. She had also felt sorrow as she farewelled Angharad to her new home in Anglesey. Yet her most profound distress had come when Angharad's own father had led the Norman forces to Anglesey, watching while they killed and maimed Welshmen and laid waste to the lands. For this, the lord she had so admired had earned the nickname Owain Fradwr, or Owain the Traitor.

She had not understood how such a thing had happened, for her respect for her lord had been bedded in years of watching his quiet achievements and consideration for others. She could only reconcile herself by supposing that anyone might suffer madness that muddied their thinking. She had prayed for him and, when he eventually died, feared that his error might not be forgiven. She knew that her relief when her mistress and husband returned from exile in Ireland, and her pride when her mistress persuaded her father to intercede successfully on Gruffydd's behalf, meant a lot to Angharad.

When old Owain had died, Susannah had left the manor now owned by Gronwy and joined her married mistress in Anglesey. She and Bethan, who had been with Angharad since she had married, had a special relationship with their mistress and loved their lives at Aberffraw.

Although King Gruffydd owned other llysau and castles, such as the huge one in Caernarvon, once a Roman fort and then made strong by the Norman baron, Hugh the Fat, Gruffydd and his family preferred the more modest llys at Aberffraw. Aberffraw was the historic royal palace of the Kings of Gwynedd, and Gruffydd had himself been born here. Whenever they visited the other parts of Gwynedd they ruled over, they were pleased to return to the island of Anglesey with its milder climate, rich fertile lands and wild, untamed seas.

Angharad saw that Gwenllian had not joined Susannah and the younger girls as she had been instructed. Annest, Rainaillt, Marged and baby Susanna had made a pretend house under the table and were playing with dolls and carved wooden animals. The little girls whooped with joy to see their mother's face appear under the draped cloth that formed their pretend walls.

'This is our llys, Mamma,' explained Annest proudly, 'and Baby Susanna is our bard. Listen!'

There were squeals of laughter as the baby gurgled incoherently. The mother's heart filled with pride and love. Every day she felt gratitude that she and Gruffydd had eight healthy, beautiful children, sharp and full of life, all of them. This was no small thing when childbirth was hazardous, and plague or sickness might strike at any time. She cherished her children, finding each one beguiling. Gruffydd, she knew, was equally captivated. It was apparent to her that he preferred the company of Gwenllian and Owain, yet he had endless love for all his children. Reflecting on this, she counted her blessings again: her husband was no ordinary man, no typical king.

Angharad, extracting herself from the world of make-believe, looked out of the window. Gwenllian ran into the practice yard after her brothers with a wooden sword. She could see that even in the minutes since he had left the study, Cadwallon had managed to upset Rhys and was giving him cheek. She grimaced. She needed to take that boy in hand: he had his father's short temper, which needed curbing, and she feared he was becoming arrogant. She had probably spoilt her firstborn, she admitted.

Gwenllian came up from behind her brother and flicked his sword out of his hand, diffusing the situation with Rhys but invoking her brother's ire. He chased her across the courtyard, but she spun quickly, defiantly holding her wooden sword and stopping him in his tracks.

'How can a girl who looks so innocent, so feminine enjoy fighting better than anything else?' Angharad asked herself out loud.

Susannah's chuckle was deep and earthy. 'She is as good as them, my lady, and I have often watched her beating her brothers to the ground. She is a strong girl and fast. She dances around them, never afraid of a bruise or a blow.'

'Look at her! She is her father's daughter, sure enough!' said Angharad shaking her head and sighing. That was not a problem to tackle today.

Bethan entered the room with a tray of freshly baked bread, golden butter, white crumbly cheese, and thick bean stew in pottery bowls for the young children who pleaded with her to allow them to eat it in their table llys. Despite having a sixteen-year-old son, Bethan was still very attractive with a heart-shaped face, thick dark curly hair always escaping her cap and a shapely figure. She had been asked for her hand many times, but she was happy with Angharad as her mistress, especially knowing that her son was having opportunities he most certainly would not have if she had stayed on her parent's farm.

'I see the Lord Uchdryd has come, my lady. I saw him go into the hall with King Gruffydd,' she remarked, hoping to prise some gossip from her mistress. Usually a forlorn hope, but when being well-informed provided infinite kudos in a llys, she always kept her ears open.

'You will have seen and surely heard! I am going to find out what the commotion is all about now,' Angharad returned.

Angharad knelt down to the children under the table and played for a few minutes before straightening her fine blue woollen gown and making her way into the Great Hall. It seemed quiet. They kept the interior limewashed so that it always seemed light, even in winter. The colourful tapestries, rugs and cushions gave warmth to the long room with its oak beams. The furniture was solid, made from oak from the vast forests of Anglesey. Warm bear skins and animal furs were draped over chairs and benches, and piles of blankets were in each corner. The floor was covered with fresh reeds and herbs, and Angharad's eye automatically checked whether there was a need to change the reeds. Both she and Gruffydd believed that dirt led to sickness, and so were fastidious about such things. An enormous fire crackled and sparked; their hounds had gravitated towards the warmth. It was there that the two men stood, and tension bristled.

Most of the teulu had returned to their own homesteads after the Christmas festivities. King Gruffydd was generous in allowing them time to deal with the administration that always arose from owning land. Winter was not a time for war, and they could easily be assembled if there was a threat. Anglesey was not such a big place, but caution was a priority. Gruffydd always kept some men at arms and rotated a few of the most senior members of his teulu at the llys during the cold months. The dull thuds and ringing of metal outside confirmed that those of the teulu who remained were in the practice yard, and the two men who had accompanied Uchdryd were stabling their horses. It crossed Angharad's mind that they must be cold and hungry after their long journey but perhaps too timid to barge into the llys kitchen. It was unlike Uchdryd not to ensure his men were comfortable; perhaps this attested to the gravity of the news he had brought.

Angharad noticed that her bear of an uncle looked older and uncharacteristically troubled. He still stood straight-backed and tall, but the lines around his eyes and mouth had deepened, and his face looked worn. His moustache was grey now, and his skin was more weather-beaten than she remembered. Gruffydd looked at her as she entered the hall, his face showing exasperation. The passing of time had been kinder to him. He was still an impressive figure. His broad shoulders were even broader, his waist a little fuller than in his youth but still trim. He was a handsome man, but right now, his blue eyes flashed darkly in his strong face, and his fists were clenched. He swept back his blonde hair and, in answer to her raised eyebrow, thundered, 'Owain ap Cadwgan! That ill-bred idiot has abducted Nest!'

'Nest?'

'Nest,' he spat out, 'Princess Nest that was, Nest the daughter of Rhys ap Tewdwr, Nest the wife of Gerald the Stewart of Pembroke Castle, Nest the mother of King Henry of England's bastard son. Of all the Nests in Wales, she is the Nest he kidnaps!'

Angharad stared at her husband in amazement for a few seconds, her mind racing with questions, her stomach already cramping, but she quickly recovered herself. She had learned to keep calm and silent to get a full grip on the facts before reacting.

Her uncle looked embarrassed but came forward to embrace her. 'You are looking lovelier than ever, Queen Angharad.'

'There is no need to be so formal, Uncle,' she smiled warmly, 'I am the same niece you cradled in your arms soon after I was born!'

'It is fit and proper to address you as the title Queen of Gwynedd demands,' he replied seriously and then, with a sideward glance at King Gruffydd, puffed out his cheeks. 'I am afraid that I have brought you unfortunate tidings.'

Gruffydd's ire was not yet spent.

'That idiot, Owain ap Cadwgan, has endangered a truce we have with King Henry of England. I worked so hard to negotiate a peace for all of Wales, and now that fool takes the wife of one of Henry's loyal officers in flagrant disregard for propriety. Worse than that, much worse than that, he also absconds with the King of England's son. It will bring the wrath of all England upon us and an excuse for the Normans to start pushing into Wales again.'

His tirade was curtailed by the appearance of two serving maids who came in, eyes lowered, carrying a pottery pitcher of ale and a platter with cheese, slices of cold sliced meat and freshly baked bread. They glanced at the broken pottery on the floor and sidestepped it, looking to Angharad, who gave an almost imperceptible shake of her head.

Gruffydd gestured to the table, and he, his wife and her uncle sat at the far end nearest to the roaring fire.

'I have never thought much of Owain,' admitted Gruffydd, bristling. 'He is a good fighter, I will give him that, but he is arrogant and lacks common sense. Even back when the Normans were fighting us here in Anglesey, I am certain he did some fancy negotiating when he went to Ireland to get help from the Norse mercenaries. He cheated them or some such nonsense. I am sure that caused them to change sides when they got here. Why else would they fight with the Normans against us after years of sound relationships? We lost good men because of him.'

'Lord King, you cannot be sure of that,' protested Uchdryd vehemently.

Gruffydd slammed his fist on the table. 'I had no issue with those Irish mercenaries before that. We could have lost Anglesey, lost Gwynedd, lost Wales, because of him.'

'That was over twelve years ago, Lord King,' argued Uchdryd, 'and he was young then. We all made mistakes when we were green.'

'And he is as slippery and stupid now as then. If Magnus Barefoot had not sailed in with his troops and killed the Earl of Shrewsbury, we would still be hiding in Ireland twelve years on, and Anglesey, in fact, the whole of Gwynedd, would be Norman lands. The cost has been years of hard toil for all of us here. Now he has endangered everything we have worked for yet again.'

Angharad put her slender hand over her husband's paw to still him.

Gruffydd stabbed at a piece of meat from the platter with his knife but left it on the side of his plate.

'What happened, Uncle?' asked Angharad gently. Her heart was already thumping, and she had the sick feeling and breathlessness she always felt whenever there was a chance of conflict. Even from the little she had heard, she knew that the might of Norman wrath might come down on them. The thought of what that meant was sobering. She still woke shivering from nightmares as she remembered the carnage a dozen years before when the Marcher Earl of Chester, Hugh the Fat, and Hugh Montgomery, Earl of Shrewsbury, led massive forces against her husband and his staunch ally, Cadwgan ap Bleddyn. She had been little more than a child then, a young pregnant bride with no idea about the horrors of battle. She had learnt quickly with a brutal initiation into the reality of war. The bloodshed and destruction had given her an insatiable drive to give her people peace. Now it seemed, Cadwgan's son, Owain, had threatened the tranquil harmony that her husband in Gwynedd, and Cadwgan in Powys, had worked so hard to forge.

Uchdryd was a great raconteur and would usually jump at the chance to recount a tale, but now he seemed reluctant to relate this one. He glanced up at Gruffydd, and Angharad saw that her uncle knew the retelling would irritate Gruffydd further. He had heard enough. Uchdryd drew a breath through his teeth, and without his usual gusto, low voiced, he started to brief his niece.

'As is the tradition, Cadwgan ap Bleddyn had a feast at Christmas in Ceredigion. He invited all the nobles from thereabouts, so, of course, Owain, being his son, was there with all his companions.'

'We were invited, Uncle, but we always have a feast in Caernarvon for the teulu and the nobles hereabouts as well,' Angharad explained. Feasts at Christmas, New Year, Easter and Whitsun were an opportunity for the royal families to renew loyalties, show their strength and power and keep an eye on what was going on. They were also good fun with food and drink, bards, music, performers, and dancing. It was also an opportunity for marriages to be arranged and news to be passed on.

'Well, I was there. I had to be there as leader of Cadwgan's warband, and the mead was flowing. Very, very good mead at that.' He glanced quickly at Gruffydd but, seeing his mood was still dark, returned to the story keeping any levity out of the telling.

'Cadwgan was on good form, everyone in good spirits, but somehow the conversation came around to the castle close by that scoundrel Gerald of Windsor had built at Cenarth Brychan for his wife, Nest. The lands had formed part of Nest's dowry, being her mother's lands. Owain had had a fair bit to drink. You know he has never had time for his stepmother. I am not sure if you have met her, but she is the daughter of the Norman lord, Picot di Say. A formidable lady, let us say, and leave it at that. Well, Owain started saying that he would have been married to Nest if not for the Normans killing Nest's father in cold blood. He was doing it to inflame his stepmother, but what he said was true, of course. They were indeed betrothed.'

'I had heard that,' said Angharad, but what she knew of Owain made her feel that Nest might have escaped a bitter marriage.

Her uncle continued, and Angharad noticed that he had not touched the ale or food, which was unusual for a man with a hearty appetite. He looked down at his knife, remembering and twirling it back and forth in his large fingers.

'Things were getting heated, and Cadwgan told Owain to get outside until he had cooled off. Outside he went, along with a group of his men, but the next thing we heard were horses being whipped out of the courtyard at speed. Of course, we did not know at the time where he had gone. We thought they had ridden back to his own manor or an inn, so the feast continued with nobody alarmed. Later, we discovered that Owain and fourteen of his followers had taken off for Cenarth Brychan, fully armed.'

'Hot-headed idiots!' muttered Gruffydd.

'Next day, no sign of Owain but one of his cousins, Merddyn, who has always had issues with Owain, had returned to Cadwgan's llys and what a story he had to tell. They had broken into Gerald of Windsor's castle at Cenarth Brychan. Nest had helped her husband escape through the privy while she remained with her children to meet the attackers. Apparently, Owain took her and the children, stole their livestock, set the castle alight, and headed off to his father's hunting lodge, Plas Uchaf in Eglwyseg.'

Angharad gasped, her dark blue eyes widening as she asked, 'Where were the sentries? How could they have broken in so easily?'

'There are many things about the abduction that do not make much sense and that I cannot answer. Nevertheless, the situation occurred.'

'And what has Cadwgan done about it?'

'Father and son have ever had a tumultuous relationship, as you know. Cadwgan pleaded with Owain to release Nest and her family.'

'And?' growled Gruffydd

'It seems that Nest has agreed to stay with Owain but asked for the return of the children to Gerald, to which Owain agreed, and they were returned in safety but....'

'But?' scowled Gruffydd

Uchdryd looked extremely uncomfortable, closed his eyes, and took a deep breath.

'They are here. Owain and Nest are here.'

'What?' bellowed Gruffydd, jumping to his feet. 'Why in God's name would you bring them here? Why would you implicate us in all this?'

Uchdryd looked shamefaced.

'My Lord King, you of all people know what it is like to be outlawed, and Cadwgan jumped to fight with you when you were trying to regain the throne of Gwynedd. You are one of the only people Cadwgan can trust. This is his son despite everything! He cannot even trust his own family: you know how they would leap at the opportunity to take Owain's land in Ceredigion and to undo Cadwgan himself.'

Gruffydd was so angry that he was white and shuddering with fury.

'My family could lose everything if we are found to be harbouring a fugitive from the English king and being complicit in the kidnapping of King Henry's mistress.'

'Nobody will know....'

'Nobody will know. Are you mad? Henry's spies are everywhere! I have eight children, six of whom speak well enough to incriminate us if asked. I have a teulu with eyes and ears, and who know Owain. I have servants and regular visitors to the llys. How can you say that nobody will know? Word will leak out. If I am seen to be involved in sheltering Henry's enemy, we will have the Normans here in Anglesey, pillaging, ransacking, maiming, and killing our good people. Have you forgotten the last time?'

Angharad paled. She remembered the torture inflicted on the Welsh, the burning and destruction of their lands. Even now, twelve years later, there were families where children had grown up fatherless or their menfolk had been maimed. That King Henry, in his anger, would send his troops from England against them, she had no doubt, yet she put a gentle hand on her husband's arm to calm him, then turned to her uncle.

'Where are they right at this moment, Uncle?'

'In the stable. They came under cover of being my servants.'

Gruffydd threw back his head, breathed deeply and cursed.

'So already the stableboys will be aware.'

'They are well disguised, Lord King.'

'Uchdryd, please, do not think I am a fool.'

'Nobody would recognise them. There was only Rhys in the stables. We told him we could manage, and he was taking one of your horses to be shoed, so he did not pay attention.'

Angharad looked up at her husband and spoke carefully.

'What is done is done! They are here. If I may suggest that Uncle Uchdryd fetches them from the stable. With luck, nobody else will have seen them. We can put them into your chamber. They can stay there until we have decided what to do for the best.'

Gruffydd looked at his wife, then Uchdryd, and reluctantly nodded. Without hesitation, Uchdryd leapt up and made his way out quickly.

'Come into your chamber,' said Angharad, and the two made their way from the hall into a finely furnished room with a large bed, a beechwood chair, four stools, and intricately carved chests to hold clothes. A small table held Gruffydd's writing materials and the seal of Gwynedd. On the walls hung rich tapestries depicting hunting scenes and one religious scene of the parting of the Red Sea. A small brazier was burning applewood logs against the cold. The noise of the men keeping up their battle skills and the high-pitched cries and squeals of the children drifted in through the window. She could hear Rhys's voice. 'We stick to the basics until you have mastered them. Now, first block, then cut, followed by a step forward and a lunge. And again!'

Gruffydd threw himself into the chair, and Angharad sat on the edge of one of the chests.

'We have to help them, Gruffydd. We cannot abandon them. You can persuade Owain to return Nest; that way, you can win favour with Henry. Meanwhile, we can keep Owain safe at least.'

'You do understand what this means if we are all caught?'

'How would we be caught if we can keep it quiet that they are here? You know if you make an enemy of Owain, soon we will have war in Wales again. Cadwgan is not in the best of health, and this could help you in the future. Better we take the risk of covering things up and helping them. We can surely help Owain to get to Ireland. Nobody needs to know it was with our help, and we can return Nest to her husband. We could say that she escaped Owain and made her way to us for protection. Surely, they can stay here until we can arrange something.'

'They can stay here just tonight, but then we need to have Owain on a skiff on the sea to anywhere and Nest on her way back to her husband.'

At that moment, Uchdryd knocked quietly at the door and entered, shadowed by two figures in coarsely woven hooded cloaks. As the door closed, they threw back their hoods, and there stood Owain and Nest, clasping each other's hands.

'Oh, dear God,' murmured Gruffydd as Owain bowed and Nest fell into a curtsey. With one look at the pair, he realised they were smitten, and the proposed separation would not be an option.

Chapter 2: Plots and Plans (January 1110)

At fifty-nine years old, a man might be considered old, but Richard de Belmeis was as fit as a man many years younger with all the ambition of one in his twenties. He was wiry, with silky grey hair fringed above narrow pale blue eyes that darted suspiciously, missing nothing. Richard's talent was reading people, and he had an extraordinary ability to unearth the truth. He knew, by the clench of a hand, the nervous touching of a face, the quick movement of an eye, when someone was telling a lie. That is why he had been summoned to see King Henry of England.

As Henry's confessor, Bishop Richard knew much that the world would like to be party to, but his silence, his absolute loyalty, had stood him in good stead. He had hoped to be Archbishop of Canterbury but, in truth, that was a poisoned chalice. Now that he was the most senior ecclesiastical power in Wales and the Marches, he had already established a significant reputation for himself. He smiled inwardly, wondering what his humble Norman parents would have made of his rise to Viceroy of Shropshire and Warden of the Marches! He was now immensely wealthy. The position had earned him the estates of Tong and Donington, which the Montgomery family had previously owned, but they had forfeited their lands after their revolt against King Henry. How satisfied he was to know that all his years of working himself to the bone for the Montgomery family, whom he despised, had resulted in such a rise in fortunes. He was not afraid of hard work; he thrived on it and was a great believer that effort brought success. Yes, he was undoubtedly testimony to that: he was a magnate now with vast estates in Shropshire and Sussex. His parents had told him he was a fool to leave Normandy to support a bastard's ambitions, but William the Conqueror was more than a bastard: he was a force of nature.

Richard was only sixteen years old when he left his small family home in Beaumais sur Dive, Normandy, and came with the Conqueror to seek his fortune in a new land. God had been kind, and he had found favour with the Montgomery family, where he became clerk and steward to Earl Roger of Shrewsbury. On Earl Roger's death, he served Earl Hugh, and then when that earl was shot through the eye by Magnus Barefoot, King of Norway, he became useful to Earl Hugh's brother, Robert de Belleme. He had listened to the family's machinations as they had plotted and rebelled against King Henry, but he had been loyal to the king, who had continued to reward him.

The bishop took a mouthful of the velvety, smooth wine and swirled it around inside his mouth. He smirked as he thought of the surprise of those who had underrated him when, in May 1108, he had been ordained a priest, appointed Bishop of London with all the men, lands and castle of Stortford, and then Henry had restored the judicial powers and privileges of St Paul's. Now he was one of the most trusted members of Henry's court. Henry knew there was nobody with such an impressive knowledge of legal matters. Henry also knew he could be relied upon to oversee the rebuilding of St Paul's Cathedral, which had burnt down some twenty-two years previously. Richard had decided this would be his legacy, and he had plans to create a churchyard, a cathedral school and to expand the lanes around the cathedral to provide the impressive environs typical in Normandy.

Richard sat back, breathed a contented sigh, and stretched his long legs before a blazing fire. He felt pride swelling in him like a warm glow. He knew how to deal with the Welsh. He thought of how quickly he had imprisoned Iorwedd ap Bleddyn, a significant leader of Powys, who had foolishly sided with Robert de Belleme in an uprising in 1102. He thought of how Iorwedd had attempted to wriggle out of his unfortunate situation with one falsehood after another, trying to use his relationship with Richard as a steward in Robert's employ. Richard had stood firm. The king had trusted him enough to leave him in charge rather than appoint another Marcher Earl who could rise in rebellion against the English Crown. Of course, he had stayed close to the imprisoned Iorwedd: even incarcerated men might be useful. He had been formulating an idea that would mean a change in fortunes for Iorwedd. If he could serve Henry in any way, regaining the Norman supremacy in Wales would please the king more than anything he had done before. Now a heaven-sent opportunity had presented itself.

Bishop Richard took a little more wine and enjoyed revisiting each step of his plan. It did not matter why Owain, son of Cadwgan, King of Powys, had abducted the beautiful Nest. It might have been for love, and Henry claimed she was irresistible; it might have been a challenge to Norman expansion in Wales, a patriotic gesture. It may have been a prank gone wrong. Whatever it was, the young fool had not only taken the wife of one of the most powerful Normans in South Wales, a woman who was also Henry's lover, but he had taken Henry's son.

The bishop shook his head, laughed out loud and slapped his knee. This situation with Owain was pure gold, and now Richard would hunt him down and bring the Welsh down with him, one by one. He thought of the vulgar Cadwgan ap Bleddyn, Owain's father. How he would make him squirm. He thought of the self-righteous, proud Gruffydd ap Cynan, considered by most Welshmen as their High King. How he would humble him. Hervey le Breton, Bishop of Bangor, had been so terrified of Gruffydd that he had fled and refused to return to Wales, so a new bishopric had to be arranged for him in Ely. Well now, perhaps it was Gruffydd's turn to be terrified, and if things went as he expected, matters could be concluded very satisfactorily.

A knock on the door, and a meek, curly-haired young servant, impeccably dressed and scrupulously clean, announced that the bishop's guests had arrived and had been taken to the hall. Richard adjusted his tunic, gave his fur-lined cloak a little shake, and strutted off briskly.

The two tall, powerfully built men were standing by the fire. In an instant, he could see that they considered themselves warriors. They were not wearing mail, but their leathers were thick, and he noted their heavy boots had been sewn with metal strips for protection. Their cloaks were long, thick, and woollen, dyed black. They turned and bowed as Bishop

Richard swept into the room, his fox-like face lighting up as if this was a meeting of rare delight.

'Lord Madog ap Rhyrid and Lord Ithel ap Rhyrid, let us not stand on formality. Please be seated.'

The bishop pulled a large carved oak chair closer to the two men. Now seated, he rearranged his cloak around him and adjusted the thick twisted gold chain around his neck that held a solid, emerald-encrusted cross. He leaned forward a little and stared unsettlingly into their faces. Both men would be considered handsome, although Madog's nose showed the remnants of an old break, and Ithel had a scar from lip to left eye, which was slightly puckered at the corner. Madog's hair was thick, dark, and unruly, but Ithel, an angular man and the taller of the two wore his chestnut locks somewhat longer than conventional in Wales but neatly cut. Madog's eyes were flinty, hard, and intense, the eyes of a man who would not hesitate to slit a throat, yet the bishop could see that both men were uncomfortable in the enforced silence, so he extended it just a little longer.

'You must be wondering why I have called you here,' he said, finally.

The two glanced at each other before Madog replied shrewdly yet a touch pompously, 'As a man who has intimate knowledge of what is happening in Wales and a representative of King Henry of England, we might speculate on your intentions, Lord Bishop, but we would not be so bold as to come to any conclusion of why we have been summoned.'

Richard smiled, turned slightly to beckon his servants forward with wine and a large platter of food for his guests, and then sat back in his chair. As the servants removed themselves to the back of the hall, he spoke again.

'You are aware, of course, of the outrageous behaviour of your cousin, which has angered King Henry.'

Ithel bristled, drew himself up, and spoke sharply. 'Our cousin Owain was betrothed to the Princess Nest when her father's lands were taken from him. Her father and other members of her family were slaughtered or scattered. My cousin is recovering some of what is rightfully his from those who have benefitted from that travesty.'

Richard's eyes narrowed and darkened. He sat a little straighter in his chair.

'King Henry did much to avenge that wrong, taking the Princess Nest into his personal care.'

'He made a whore of a princess of Wales,' spat Ithel, yet his brother grasped his arm to restrain him.

'I had brought you here to discuss matters which would significantly benefit you both, yet it seems I am mistaken in my thought that we might be able to work together,' said Richard, his voice as cold as freshly sharpened steel. He pushed himself out of his chair with a jerk.

'Wait, Lord Bishop,' said Madog, jumping to his feet, his eyes blazing a warning at his brother, whose jaw muscles were working inside his stony face. 'Let us not be hasty. My brother speaks the truth, and kinship is important in Wales. Owain is our kin and, from the Welsh perspective, is righting a wrong. From the Norman perspective, our cousin has absconded not only with the Princess Nest, with whom King Henry has a close relationship but also with King Henry's son. Is it your wish, Lord Bishop, to use our influence to restore the Princess Nest to her husband, her children, and recover King Henry's son?'

The bishop glared at Ithel and then turned to Madog, gesturing that he should sit before adjusting his cloak and returning to his chair.

'King Henry would have Nest restored to her husband, and Owain found and brought to justice.'

Madog looked at his brother sharply and spoke again.

'We might well be able to restore the Princess Nest to her husband, but we would have no harm come to our cousin. As I said, kinship is important to the Welsh.'

Richard smiled a small smile.

'Welsh kinship. It is an interesting subject, is it not? I am fascinated by Welsh history and, fortunately, I have had some time to delve into it. Now do correct me if I am wrong, but your father was Rhyrid ap Bleddyn. He was one of the sons born of your grandfather Bleddyn's first wife. When your grandfather was killed in 1075, the oldest son, your Uncle Cadwgan, not yet twenty-eight years old, was too young to reign, so the throne of Powys was held by Trahearn ap Caradog. He was slain not long after in 1081, and the sons of Bleddyn divided up Powys between themselves. Am I correct so far?'

'You have great interest in the story of our family,' said Madog tersely and Richard knew the brothers were waiting for the catch. He was enjoying himself.

'Then,' he continued, swilling his wine in his goblet, 'in 1088, your father was killed in battle, along with his brother Madog, fighting against Princess Nest's father, Rhys ap Tewdwr. We must bear in mind that Rhys was married to your father's cousin. Kinship, kinship, kinship. You see, the three sons of your grandfather, Bleddyn, were trying to wrest Deheubarth from Rhys ap Tewdwr, just as we Normans tried to do rather more successfully later.'

A servant came forward and filled the goblets of the three men.

'Fine wine, is it not? It comes from Normandy. Now where was I? Yes, Cadwgan survived the battle which killed two of his brothers, one being your father, and he now rules Powys while your Uncles Iorwedd and Maredudd look covetously at Cadwgan's lands. But I will come back to that. Please, gentlemen, do help yourself to refreshment after your long journey.'

The two men looked uncomfortable, but Ithel took an eating knife from a leather sheath at his waist and stabbed a piece of meat.

'Now Owain ap Cadwgan, the cousin you protect, is not quite as considerate of his kin. Am I not correct that Owain killed two noblemen of Powys three years ago, both sons of Trahearn ap Caradog: Meurig and Griffri? They were kin, were they not?'

The men glowered at him, saying nothing, and he continued matter-of-factly.

'But you know it is possible that those men might also claim Powys as their birthright, and it is possible that Cadwgan encouraged his son Owain to get rid of any contenders for the throne.'

Bishop Richard enjoyed the silence of the two men and the tension in the air.

'Now, your Uncle Iorwedd, just for a very short time, was very prominent in Powys. Do you remember the rebellion of the barons against King Henry in 1102? You would have been quite young, but your Uncle Iorwedd detached himself from his brothers in assisting the traitorous Robert de Belleme and negotiated for Powys, Ceredigion, half of Dyfed, Ystrad Tywi, Gower, Cydweli; in fact, much of South Wales and West Wales. For this, he was willing to bring down Belleme and his brothers. Iorwedd also captured his brother Maredudd and handed him over to the king. However, Henry decided that Iorwedd should be arraigned before a royal tribunal. He was convicted and imprisoned and remains there to this day, which is ironic because his brother Maredudd, the sacrificial lamb for the family's avarice, escaped.'

'What need have you to delve into our family, Lord Bishop?' scowled Ithel.

'Well, I am interested in history, as I say. Also, I want to truly understand the obligations of kinship. I may be mistaken, but I had thought that the backing of the English crown in flushing out Owain and Nest and in gaining any of the lands Owain and his father possess may have been of interest to you. We might come to some agreement.'

Now the two brothers looked alert. He had discovered that they were just as acquisitive as the rest of their family.

'King Henry did not honour the agreement with Iorwedd. How do we know that any agreement we might make will be honoured?' said Ithel, eyeing Richard cautiously.

Richard's blue eyes turned icy cold. 'I have not risen to my position in the church through dishonouring agreements. As I understand it, Iorwedd himself dishonoured the agreement with King Henry.'

There was another silence, and Madog leaned a little closer towards the bishop.

'If we were to flush Owain out and return Princess Nest and her children to her husband, you are saying we could keep any lands that were Owain's?'

'I would think that that would be fair. After all, he is an outlaw now.'

'And his father, Cadwgan?'

'Has been asked to present himself with his son to King Henry and has failed to do so. What I am trying to avoid here is bloodshed. Henry is of a mind to send in armed forces.'

The two men considered this.

'And if someone is harbouring Owain? How would Henry view that?'

'Harbouring an outlaw who has acted against the King's family? If that were the case, then that person might well find themselves forfeit of their lands.'

The two men digested this, and Madog's grey eyes were filled with the realisation of all this could mean. Bishop Richard leaned forward and filled the men's goblets with more wine.

'You will not be alone in this. I will instruct Llywarch ap Trahearn and Uchdryd ap Edwin to assist you. You will find them the truest and most faithful companions.'

'But Uchdryd is Cadwgan's man.'

'Uchdryd, as was his brother, Owain, has sometimes been more than helpful to King Henry.'

The brothers exchanged looks but said nothing.

After the men had left, for he had offered them no further hospitality on that dark, cold night, the bishop returned to his study, where he penned a message and sealed it, writing the recipient's name with a flourish. He then prepared another just the same. He put it aside for a few minutes and warmed himself by the fire, picking meat from his crooked teeth. Then smiling triumphantly to himself, he called for one of his servants.

'Tomorrow at first light,' he instructed him, 'you ride to Tegeingl and give this into the hand of the Lord Gronwy. Find someone else to give this one into the hand of Uchdryd ap Owain in Powys.' He sat back, puffed up with satisfaction.

A servant came in and lit more of the bright beeswax candles that stood in rows on iron trees on his walls. He breathed in the sweet perfume and smiled to himself as the wind howled and rain dashed against the building. He wondered if the two men would stay at one of the taverns in Shrewsbury, perhaps find company for the evening. No, they were eager to exploit the opportunity before them and would even now be hastening to Powys. He imagined the two men riding in darkness, wet through but urgently spurring their horses on, and it gave him great comfort.

Chapter 3: Secrets (January 1110)

Nest fell into a deep curtsey and looked up at Gruffydd, her soft cheeks glowing from the cold, her eyes full of anxiety. She seemed smaller in stature than the alluring lady Angharad had met at Shrewsbury more than eight years before, yet she had aged little. Her complexion was flawless, her lips still full and red, her figure trim. She smiled up at Angharad through long lashes, her wide-set sage eyes already pleading, vulnerable.

Owain bowed formally to Gruffydd and Angharad, then put his arm around Nest protectively. Angharad had always thought Owain arrogant and foolish, a man as petulant as a child, yet seeing him now, she understood that it was not he who had spirited Nest away but she who had conquered him. Here stood a delicate woman whose life experiences should have made her fragile, yet she had a steel core of resilience and held the heart of a russet-haired warrior who had learnt what it was to love.

'Lord King,' said Owain in an earnest tone Angharad had never heard him use before, 'I throw myself and the Princess Nest upon your mercy. If you choose to give us up into the hands of King Henry, then we will accept your decision, but, though our fortunes are low right now, that will not always be the case. If you help us, my debt to you will never be forgotten.'

Gruffydd looked around him at four sets of questioning eyes, then addressed the Princess Nest gently and politely.

'What is your wish, Princess Nest?'

'Lord King, I do not desire to return to my husband. I desire to stay with Owain. I would and have given up all I hold dear and am willing to follow him, though we have nothing.'

Angharad gave a little gasp, and her eyes widened.

'What of your children?' asked Gruffydd, still softly, holding Nest's gaze. Angharad observed her carefully as she spoke while Uchdryd watched Gruffydd intently.

Nest's head lifted a little, and Gruffydd noted the set of her determined chin. 'Lord Uchdryd provided four armed men to take the children to my husband. They will be safe with him. He will not harm them.'

'Including King Henry's son, Henry FitzHenry?'

'Yes, including my son, Henry.'

'And you would leave your children?' said Angharad, in a tone of disbelief.

'My choice is made,' she said, looking up at Owain, who returned her look with one of infinite concern, 'but I will always love my children.'

'You know that they will be searching for you, and they will come here,' warned Gruffydd.

'They will need to scour Powys first, and my father is trying to put them off the trail,' returned Owain.

'But they will come here. I can help you for only a few days. Meanwhile, I will arrange to get you to Ireland. You have kin there.'

'I have. Thank you,' said Owain sincerely.

'You will remain in this room, and we will keep those who know about your whereabouts to the minimum. Bethan and Susannah will bring you food and anything you require. I would trust them with my life. And Hywel, whom you know, of course, I will charge him with finding the means of getting you to Ireland. Just so we are all clear, I am not happy that my family, friends, and land are at risk, and I do not condone what you are doing. For the sake of your father and Lord Uchdryd, I will help you. I will not betray you.'

Owain nodded thoughtfully and muttered, 'I understand.'

'Uchdryd, it is late now, but at first light, you must get back to Powys. Are the horses on which these two rode worth anything?'

Uchdryd seemed confused by the question but answered, 'Lord Owain rode a black stallion, only a few years old with a fine temper, and the Princess Nest rode a mare from Cadwgan's stud.'

'Then, if anybody asks, you brought me two horses from Cadwgan's stud that I will use for breeding.'

Uchdryd nodded slowly, then grinned broadly.

'I will send you back with four of my men in case there is any trouble.'

'I need no one to ride with me; I can handle myself,' protested Uchdryd, a defiant set to his jaw.

'You will take four men at least to the border with Powys,' barked Gruffydd. 'If you are attacked, we will likely bear the consequences.' Uchdryd lifted his bushy grey brows and nodded agreement, somewhat reluctantly.

'Angharad, I will let you take the Princess Nest to your chamber to find her something appropriate to wear. You speak to Susannah and Bethan but under no circumstances let the children know that we have guests.'

Angharad nodded. 'I will find Susannah and Bethan now and swear them to secrecy.'

'Uchdryd, you come with me to find Hywel. Owain, make yourself at home. There is ale in that jug, fruit and nuts on the table, and it looks like you could do with some sleep.'

Owain gave a wan smile of appreciation, and as Gruffydd and Uchdryd went out of the door, he caught the king by the arm.

'From the bottom of my heart, I thank you, Lord King. Life is unpredictable, and there may be a time when I will be able to do a service for you. I will never forget this.'

Gruffydd nodded curtly, and Uchdryd struggled to keep pace with him as they headed towards the practice yard.

'Well, Uchdryd, I hope to Hell that if Henry is paying off one of my teulu for information, he is not at the llys at this time!'

'I am sorry, my lord. We had few choices, but you know, Owain has grown up a lot and one day, God willing, he will be King of Powys so ....'

Gruffydd stopped abruptly and turned to face Uchdryd cutting across the older man sharply. 'After this? I think not. I have seen King Henry with Nest, and I can tell you he married her to an old man for a good reason. He will never forgive Owain, and if Henry is against him, Owain will never be King of Powys. Now we need to talk loudly about those horses from Powys in front of everyone here and then again at dinner so that the servants can hear.'

'My lord,' said Uchdryd mildly, 'come now, you are angry with me and Owain. You know what it feels like to be in love, and you yourself married your enemy's daughter because your heart would have broken without her.'

'Your brother was not my enemy! Yes, he was allied to the Normans, but I did not sneak into his manor and take Angharad by force. It was done properly, following Welsh law.'

Cries rang out from the corner of the yard where Rhys was training the four children. Cadwallon and Rhys were fighting with wooden swords, and Cadwallon, as tall as Rhys, if much skinnier and younger, was driving Rhys back into the corner.

'You mean a forehand slash like that?' mocked Cadwallon. 'Followed by a feint, step ahead, strike, and the step back. Like that? Is that what you mean?'

Rhys was red in the face with embarrassment, even more so because the other children were calling encouragement to him.

'Strike back, Rhys, strike back!'

Gruffydd strode across the yard and took Cadwallon by the scruff of his neck.

'You, young man, will apologise to Rhys right now!'

Cadwallon struggled at first, but as his father's grip on his neck intensified, he coloured, his blue eyes flashing with pain, and spat out a half-hearted apology. His father let him go, but Gruffydd's face was thunderous.

Rhys looked abjectly miserable that Gruffydd, and even Lord Uchdryd, had witnessed his humiliation.

'Do not fear of hurting him, Rhys. He must learn the same as everyone else. A few good bruises and blows would do him good.'

'Yes, Lord King,' said Rhys.

'Cadwallon, you will do fifty circuits of the yard and then clean out the stables. We have two new horses there that need attending to as well.'

'Yes, Father,' said Cadwallon sulkily and started to lope around the perimeter, long legs easily covering the ground. When his father turned away, he glared menacingly at Rhys, his thoughts of vengeance spurring him on.

'Father and Uncle Uchdryd, would you like to see Owain and I mock fight?' asked Gwenllian.

'Show me, you young imps,' said Uchdryd, who had great affection for his great nephews and nieces. The two began to show off what they had been learning.

'By God, they are good,' said Uchdryd, 'but she is as fast as I have seen. Look, she keeps up with her brother blow for blow but seems to sense what he will do before he does it.'

With that, Owain found himself on the ground with his sister's sword at his neck.

'Yield!' she shouted triumphantly. 'Remember not to lower your guard! Now Cadwaladr, it is your turn, but because you are younger than Owain, I will keep one hand behind my back.'

Cadwaladr whirled and spun, his blade flying in all directions, but he was no match for his sister. She dodged him effortlessly, and eventually, he too had to yield.

Gwenllian was grinning from ear to ear. 'Remember what Father says,' she yelled at him, inflaming his ire, 'the weapon is part of you!'

Her brother scowled pugnaciously.

'Would you let your sister get the better of you?' said Uchdryd to the two boys. 'You need to spend more time on getting the basics right; then nobody will be able to beat you. Practice, practice, practice, boring though it is, will pay its way in the end. Make it instinct for you. You won't even have to think; your body will move itself, and your sword will become an extension of your body.'

Despite his heavy heart, Gruffydd gave Gwenllian a proud smile. The tiny dot who had nearly died at birth brought him immense joy. He loved all his children deeply and would give his life without question for any of them, but there was something about Gwenllian that made his heart sing. She shared a love for everything he did in life, understood when to be silent, sharing a quiet moment, and when to make him roar with laughter. She was generous, kind, and had fierce courage.

Gruffydd and Uchdryd moved to where Hywel was going over tactics with men at arms. He looked up and smiled broadly when he saw Uchdryd.

'Hywel, you change little,' said Uchdryd warmly, 'Gruffydd, he keeps so young and fit because he has no wife to nag him to despair!'

Hywel blushed, and Gruffydd wondered for the thousandth time why such an eligible young man had not found a woman he could settle with. Women adored him. He was handsome, kind, and formidable in battle, but although he liked women, he always said that a warrior's life made him shun the responsibility of a wife and family. He claimed he would feel fear in combat if he was always worried about a family being left behind should he be killed. Gruffydd had often assured him that as Hywel was his sworn man if anything happened, it was his duty as his lord to look after his family as his own. Despite that, Hywel would just shake his head, smile bashfully and excuse himself.

'Come to see the horses Uchdryd brought for me,' said Gruffydd. Hywel called to Aeddan to take over from him before walking alongside them, his thick hair shining in the weak winter sunlight, the colour of horse chestnut.

'We have a problem,' said Gruffydd when they were out of earshot and explained the issue. Hywel's face lined with concern.

'You need to get them to Ireland, lord.'

'I know, Hywel, but the problem is that Gerald, Nest's husband, will have ships out looking for them. He will know they will find safety there. It may be possible to avoid them, but even then, there is also the issue of ensuring we can guarantee silence from whoever takes them over the sea.'

'It needs to be a skiff,' said Hywel, looking as anxious as Gruffydd felt, 'otherwise there is a big crew involved, and a slip of the tongue would have consequences. It will be difficult, especially this time of the year, but I will make some enquiries.'

At that moment, a small, wiry, mud-splattered messenger arrived at the gate, his Welsh mountain pony white with sweat. He handed his weapons to the sentries and, seeing Uchdryd, dismounted in a bound, hurrying his way towards them, his thick leather boots splashing through the puddles of the courtyard.

'It is Davydd, one of my men,' said Uchdryd, a look of alarm crossing his face.

The small, serious man bowed and acknowledged the party and, removing his thick leather gloves, pulled a sealed parchment out of the lining of his heavy woollen cloak. Uchdryd immediately tore it open.

The men watched the changes on Uchdryd's face. He handed the letter to Gruffydd to read, and then for Hywel's benefit, he explained grimly, 'Bishop Richard of London, Viceroy of Shropshire, Henry's man in these parts, is instructing me to assist Madog and Ithel ap Rhyrid in their quest to capture Owain ap Cadwgan. Despite being Owain's cousins, that pair are as greedy and ruthless as you have ever met. They have an appetite for destruction you would barely credit. The bishop tells me they have permission to confiscate Owain's lands.'

'That will go down well with Owain,' said Gruffydd in a low voice.

Uchdryd lifted his eyebrows in agreement. 'My friends, I have no luxury of a night here; I need to get back to Powys before they sweep through Owain's followers and anyone else who gets in the way: they are not over fussed whom they kill, maim, or terrorise.'

Uchdryd turned to speak to the messenger, but Gruffydd held his arm. 'Why ask you to assist? The bishop knows your relationship to Cadwgan.'

Uchdryd shrugged his shoulders and looked uncomfortable.

'Something does not smell right here, Uchdryd, by God,' spat Gruffydd warily.

Uchdryd hesitated. 'I know no more than you, I swear it. Surely you of all men do not doubt me?'

'I do not doubt you, Uchdryd, yet I am uncertain why Henry's man calls on you of all men. What would be his purpose? He is a cunning man who, somehow, sees some advantage in it. What size are Madog and Ithel's warbands?'

Uchdryd puffed out his cheeks and shook his head a little. 'They are strong and young and hungry. I do not know the number, but combined, they would be a force to be reckoned with.'

Gruffydd pursed his lips. 'Hywel, find four men to escort Lord Uchdryd to the border. Fully armed. No packhorse, just what they can fit into their saddlebags. Fastest horses you have.'

Hywel nodded and turned on his heel.

Angharad had watched the three men as they strode to the stable and had seen the messenger arrive. It was hard to interpret what was happening, but Gruffydd looked like he was steaming as they returned to the llys. Behind her, Nest was putting on a fine green woollen dress that brought out the colour in her beautiful eyes.

'You judge me because you think I have abandoned my children,' said Nest softly, breaking a silence between them.

Angharad swung around sharply and saw hurt in the other woman's face, her eyes filled with emotion.

'It is not my place to judge you. We all live our lives as we see fit. I would not be able to do it, to leave my children.'

'I love them.'

'I do not doubt it.'

There was another small silence, and Angharad knelt to look for a shawl in one of her clothes chests. A smell of lavender wafted out when she lifted the lid. All her clothes were neatly folded with linen sheets separating different kinds of items.

'It is different for you,' Nest went on. 'I have only ever been treated as useful for alliances. You would not understand because Gruffydd chose you for love.'

'I was fortunate,' admitted Angharad carefully as she moved the clothes aside, 'but my father had intended to marry me to Hugh the Fat to strengthen a political allegiance. I do understand something of what you are talking about.' Nest looked surprised.

'Hugh the Fat was considered a beast even by the Normans,' said Nest.

'Yes,' said Angharad, quietly concentrating on the items in the chest.

Angharad handed her a delicate woollen shawl that matched her dress and a pair of kidskin slippers. She thought back to that time when she was consumed by the misery of knowing she would be the property of a vile man and that her father, whom she worshipped, was willing to make that sacrifice. She shuddered as Nest spoke again, softly, wistfully.

'We were betrothed, Owain and I, when we were but children. He would visit with his father, and even as a child, I was mesmerised by him. He was taller than the other boys, handsome, spirited, and fun. He would bring delight and laughter. It was a good allegiance, Powys and Deheubarth, and we grew fond of each other. Then the Normans killed my father, separated me from my family, and I found myself at the English court.'

She sat on the bed to put on the slippers, and Angharad sat beside her.

'Henry noticed me, and soon I was his favoured mistress. He had many. I had little choice; how could you refuse a prince? In truth, I liked the security of being somewhat protected. As his mistress, none of the other men at court would dare touch me. He seemed besotted with me, and I thought that when I fell pregnant, he would marry me. Foolish me! Now I see how naive I was, but that is what I believed. As if I could be regarded worthy of an English royal marriage, being a lowly Welsh princess with almost nothing to my name. I had few friends, I was out of my homeland struggling to fit in, my family were scattered or dead, and I pinned my hopes on Henry.'

'That is understandable,' said Angharad, gently squeezing the other woman's shoulder.

'It was not my wish to be someone's mistress. I was brought up in a Christian home, the same as you. My values were no different, but my choices were thrust upon me.'

'You do not need to tell me this.'

'I do need to tell you this because I know that you are putting your lives in danger for us, and I need you to know that you are not doing this for a worthless, wanton woman.'

'Please, Nest…'

'You are known for your piety, my lady; it would be hard for you to hear my story and not feel that my Christian virtues are lacking.'

Angharad thought for a moment, wondering how best to respond.

'I try to do what is right in the sight of the Lord, but I am also more than aware of how Norman women are treated. I hope with all my heart that my own daughters will be safe enough to find husbands whom they love and choose, and that love and respect are returned.'

She grasped Nest's hand and held it in her own. Nest looked deep into her eyes, then smiled thinly and Angharad sensed a touch of envy in her voice.

'Even though you have been married so long, your husband worships you. I saw it in Shrewsbury. I see it now. You are truly partners. Your story, how Gruffydd fell in love with his enemy's daughter when she was little more than a child, is well known and oft told to give hope to all women.'

Angharad coloured, and she felt the emotional sting of tears threatening. 'My father was not exactly an enemy, but he indeed accepted, even encouraged, Norman overlordship, whereas Gruffydd did not.' She sighed, her face with a faraway look. 'I know not everyone is as fortunate. I wish that were not so.'

Nest gave a small, twisted smile. 'Henry rewarded my pregnancy and the birth of his son by sending me in marriage to the man who was the custodian of the very lands my father had ruled: Gerald FitzWalter of Windsor, Constable of Pembroke. Here I was again, back in Wales, yet the wife of a man old enough to be my father. He is kind enough, but my children are raised in Norman fashion with Norman nursemaids. He keeps me at a distance from them in case I should speak a word of Welsh to them or teach them Welsh custom.'

'I am so sorry.'

Nest was determined to tell her story, to justify her actions and those of Owain, and it came tumbling out.

'Gerald was in Normandy, and Owain just arrived one day at Pembroke Castle. He had come to discuss some issues about the Flemings encroaching on his lands. It was so easy with him. We met again and then again. Sometimes we would arrange to chance upon each other when I was out hunting, and I had a few loyal to me who kept their silence. As time passed, it became more difficult to keep the secret. We wanted to be together. I thought perhaps we might escape, that Owain could hide me somewhere, and no one would know any different. I thought people would not know who had taken me and think that perhaps I was dead. I imagined a life where Owain would come to me, and we would be free to love each other.'

'But you know that cannot be.'

'I know now that it cannot be, but I will settle for what time we can have together, Owain and I. At least once in my life, I will know what it is to be loved, truly loved, for who I am. He does not love me because I am Princess Nest, who can encourage loyalty among the dissolute Welsh. He does not love me for who my parents were or what royal lineage I am heir to. No. He loves me for who I am and has given up everything for me.'

'But your children?' ventured Angharad again, still unable to shake the incomprehension of anyone leaving their children.

'My children will not even notice that I am not there. I have been forced to be a mother in name only.'

Angharad drew Nest into a warm embrace and felt Nest's hot tears against her neck. She had enormous pity for this lovely woman.

'All I think about when I am not with Owain is what he is doing and reliving our times together. When I am with him, I feel complete and utterly happy.'

'Nest, how was it that you and Owain managed to escape, that there was nobody hurt, no loss of life?'

Nest gave a small smile. 'That night, I put a potion into the wine and beer. I made sure everyone was happy, drinking. I even doctored the meat for the dogs. Then I made sure the doors were open. Gerald, my husband, did not drink enough that night. He had been careful, hoping for a night of passion, I suppose. When the attack came, and his guards did not respond, he flew into a panic. I persuaded him to escape by the garderobe. Showing great courage, with no thought for his wife or children, he went off into the night.'

Their conversation was interrupted by a knock on the door. Uchdryd was standing outside. Angharad ushered him in while Nest turned, wiping away the tears streaming down her cheeks.

'I must go now, my ladies,' said Uchdryd formally, glancing uncomfortably at Nest.

'Why so soon?' asked Nest fearfully, turning to face the man who had been so kind to her, despite her shame at crying.

'King Henry is setting the wheels in motion to confiscate Owain's lands and decimate his followers. He has requested Lord Madog ap Rhyrid and Lord Ithel ap Rhyrid, Owain's cousins, to hound him throughout Ceredigion and to confiscate his land, goods and retainers. What is more, Bishop Richard has asked me to help them! I find myself in something of a bind. I need to get back to take control of the mayhem that will be taking place, slow things down, and get the hounds off the scent, so to speak. There is not a moment to lose.'

Nest's face fell, and she let out a little gasp.

'Oh Lord Uchdryd, you have endangered your life for ours, and I hope you will be safe. You have protected us, and I pray God will protect you.'

'Thank you, my lady, but there is no need to worry about me! I have faced many difficulties in my life, and I am still here! Neither worry about your safety. King Gruffydd is a man of his word and resourceful, and my honourable niece always finds ways of ensuring things turn out right. She is made of stern stuff.'

He bowed to Nest and then to Angharad, who ignored the formality by embracing her much-loved uncle.

'Uncle, be careful. It is getting late, and Henry's spies are everywhere.'

Uchdryd shrugged, though he looked grim.

'I was delivering horses! Thank you for what you are doing. You are true Christians!' he said. Then, returning to the courtyard where Davydd was waiting with four of Gruffydd's mailed men, he hauled himself tiredly onto his mount and cantered out of the llys.

Chapter 4: Brotherly Love (January 1110)

'Mother, come and see,' called Cadwaladr the following morning. He had raced into the hall and dragged his mother by her hand to show her the party of riders announced by the shouts of the guards and a flurry of hoofbeats. 'Look who has come!'

A stout man on a high chestnut stallion seemed to take over the courtyard. He was clad in full mail, covered by a thick black cloak held in place with a silver boar's head. He wore a silver helmet with heavy silver on his harness. He was followed by a lithe, long-legged noble, wearing thick leather apparel and six fierce-looking companions dressed for an altercation.

The leather-clad rider smiled broadly as four lively children burst out of the llys door. He slid easily from his horse and was immediately pounced upon by Cadwallon, Owain, and Gwenllian. At the same time, the younger Cadwaladr swooped under his uncle's swirling brown cloak, yelling, 'Uncle Meilyr, Uncle Meilyr.' Angharad's joy at seeing her brother, Meilyr, to whom she had always been very close, was quashed by her fear that they might discover their visitors. The mailed rider dismounted stiffly, his piggy brown eyes already taking in everything and not disguising his dislike of the children, who made no attempt to greet him.

'Children, you have not greeted your Uncle Gronwy,' their mother reprimanded them sharply, and the children reluctantly left Meilyr's side and dutifully paid their respects.

Gronwy grunted, gave the children a piercing glare and, without any pleasantries, asked his sister, 'Gruffydd is here?'

'I am here, Gronwy,' a deep voice said behind her as Gruffydd stepped into the courtyard.

Rhys hurried forward to take the reins of Gronwy's horse, and Gronwy gave the boy a long look.

Cadwallon took Meilyr's grey gelding from him and led the other men with their sturdy Welsh horses to the trough outside the stable.

'Welcome to you both and your men. You should have sent word that you were coming as being unexpected our welcome is not fitting enough for honoured guests. What brings you here so early this cold morning?' asked Gruffydd.

'Owain ap Cadwgan,' said Gronwy without smiling, searching the reaction on Gruffydd's face.

Angharad's heart began to beat so vigorously that she felt sure that her brothers would hear it, and she bent down to the children, whispering them some instructions so that her face did not betray her.

Gruffydd was, as ever, calm under pressure. 'What does your friend need of me?'

Gronwy's slightly protuberant eyes narrowed, and he growled, 'Shelter.'

'Shelter?' asked Gruffydd, his head on one side as if confused. 'From me? But I forget my manners; come out of the cold and into the hall.'

The children were skipping alongside Meilyr as they all clamoured to tell him the small stories that coloured their everyday lives. Gronwy flashed another scowl at them.

'I beat Owain and Cadwallon in swordfight easily yesterday, Uncle Meilyr, and Uncle Uchdryd said he had never seen a child so fast, especially a girl! I heard him tell Father.'

Gronwy stopped on the steps to the llys swinging around suddenly to pay attention to the chatter.

'Uchdryd is here?' Meilyr looked up at his brother sharply. Angharad saw that look, and her heart sank. Neither brother was a fool, but Meilyr also had the children's trust, which made the Aberffraw family vulnerable if he was aligned with Gronwy.

Gruffydd did not turn around to the brothers but walked on, saying casually, 'You missed him. He left yesterday. He brought me a stallion and a mare from Cadwgan's stud. Fine beasts. I will show you later.'

Gronwy continued up the steps.

'Perhaps if you would like, we can go hunting after we have eaten as I am keen to try out the stallion, and there are plenty of deer about.'

Gronwy stopped Gruffydd with his arm and leaned in close.

'Uchdryd will have told you then that Owain and the Princess Nest are on the run together. They are romantically involved, though why anyone would risk life and land for a woman is beyond me! Henry of England is sending men to find him and return the Princess Nest to her husband. He is offering a significant reward for Owain's capture, but equally, anyone harbouring them will feel his wrath. Lands will be redistributed, so to speak. Uchdryd would have told you that, surely.'

The children were listening attentively, and Gwenllian and Owain exchanged glances.

'Go and find Cadwallon in the stable, and then all of you go to the kitchen for something to eat. It is freezing out here!' said Angharad, anxious that the children might say something else that Gronwy would swoop on. They ran to find their brother, hoping to sneak some apples to the horses.

Gruffydd led his brothers-in-law towards the hall.

'Gronwy, if Owain has had an affair with someone else's wife, that is nothing to do with me. I am not sure why that would bring you here. You are always welcome, both of you, and we are pleased to see you, but I am somewhat confused as to what all this is about.'

'Just to be plain, Lord King, I would be happy to share in any reward which might bring additional land to Gwynedd. Bishop Richard of London has written to me expressing his desire that I assist in bringing Owain to justice.'

Gruffydd's face showed his distaste. 'Gronwy, you and Owain were friends from childhood. Would you denounce that friendship for land?'

Gronwy's eyes flashed, and the broken veins on his cheeks and nose turned purple. 'Owain has put at risk a very harmonious relationship Wales has with the English throne. I would be a fool to think that Henry would not use the excuse of an insult to himself and one of the most powerful Normans in Wales, the abduction of his son no less, as an excuse to take lands he has had his eye on for his favourites for many years. Owain has given him the justification, and I want no bloodshed. So no, that friendship does not hold me back from turning him over to Henry or gaining favour for it. I administer the eastern part of Gwynedd, Lord King, and I want my people to know I am doing everything possible to keep them safe from Norman invasion.'

'I hear you, Gronwy, but I am not sure why you would come in person all the way from Tegeingl to tell me this.'

'I will not mince words because you and Cadwgan are very close, and if I were Cadwgan, I would advise Owain to find shelter with you. I intend to be the one who finds Owain ap Cadwgan.'

Gruffydd said nothing, but the harsh venom in Gronwy's words had caused his hound's hackles to rise as she growled softly, her eyes fixed on Gronwy.

'And if I were Uchdryd, that is also what I would advise Owain,' Gronwy continued, 'and Uchdryd has just been here.'

The tension was thick in the air, and the usually easy-going Meilyr looked decidedly uncomfortable. He leaned against the wall, silent, arms folded across his chest, observing the interchange.

Gruffydd knelt to hush his hound, his long fingers ruffling the hair behind her ears, then he stood up and looked at Gronwy coldly.

'I thank you for your warning, Gronwy, and your concern. I have heard nothing from Bishop Richard. Uchdryd was here fleetingly, and he and I spoke mainly about horses. The matter of Owain and Nest was in passing, and he did not seem overly perturbed. This will blow over as all things do.'

'Well, I have warned you. After all, kin is kin.'

Meilyr's intelligent eyes flicked to Angharad, whose head was swimming, and she noted a hint of sympathy in them.

Thank you, Gronwy,' said Gruffydd, making clear that the discussion was closed.

Gronwy glared at his host and, with sullen anger, swung around to his men who had followed them into the hall, ordering them to ride out to make enquiries around the island. Gruffydd raised his eyebrows, and Angharad wondered how Gronwy could expect loyalty from his men when he had no interest in whether they were tired, cold or hungry after their journey. His men's welfare was always forefront of Gruffydd's mind.

'You split up in twos and look in every barn, church, and farm you can reach. You check wherever a boat comes in or out, and you question the ferry. Let them know there is a reward for information about Owain ap Cadwgan and his companion. Let it be known that I will leave one man here for a week in case anything comes to light. If you find them, you do not harm them but bring them back here to the llys. Do you understand?'

Gronwy's men had been warming themselves at the fire which burned in the courtyard through winter in Aberffraw. They had been looking forward to some rest and refreshment but, seeing their master's mood, they jumped to their task and went to retrieve their horses.

Gruffydd gestured to a maidservant to bring food and drink and invited his guests to sit at the long oak table.

'Now let us get you fed, and then maybe you will have the energy to go hunting with me. The woods are teeming with deer and wild boar, and I am in the mind for some sport! Angharad, would you make sure your brothers' men are well fed before they leave?'

Angharad smiled assent and left the room hastily. She gave instructions to the kitchen and then made her way quickly to Gruffydd's chamber. She knocked on the door furtively.

Owain let her in. She was pleased to see that they had closed the shutter window.

'We saw them arrive,' said Owain immediately, 'but I am not too worried. Gronwy is my friend.'

'Gronwy is my brother, Owain, but I would not risk him finding out you are here. Bishop Richard has charged him to find you.'

Owain's eyes registered shock, and he sat back heavily on the bed. Nest looked at him and said quietly, 'Uchdryd was very clear about the danger when you suggested you might find safe harbour with Lord Gronwy.'

Owain nodded slowly. 'He did say that, but I did not believe it. As they say, in times of trouble, you find out who your friends really are. Does he know we are here?'

'He doesn't, but he suspects. The children blurted out that Uchdryd had been here, and now he is adding everything up. My brother is greedy for land, and his hatred of my husband and, sadly, of me is well known.'

As the implications behind her words sunk in, Owain looked glum.

'That bishop from Hell is trying to tempt those closest to me to betray me.'

Nest looked alarmed. Owain immediately pulled her in close to him and gently stroked her hair.

'Somehow,' said Angharad, 'we must get you away from here as soon as possible, but I am not sure how or to where. Gronwy's eyes are everywhere.'

'He wouldn't come in here, Gruffydd's chamber?'

There was a noise in the corridor, and Nest jumped up, alarmed. They all listened in silence, but it was only one of the maids. They waited until her footsteps had passed.

Angharad spoke urgently. 'I know Gronwy. Before he leaves, he will have checked every corner. As I said, Gruffydd and he are not on the best of terms. Nothing would make him happier than to see Gruffydd hauled in front of Henry and for Gronwy to usurp Gruffydd.'

Owain closed his eyes and shook his head.

'I am truly sorry,' he said sincerely. 'This has all become a bigger problem than we imagined.'

Nest sat beside him and nestled into him like a small bird. He put his big arm around her tiny frame and pulled her towards him tightly. Angharad felt a wave of compassion for the two, whose souls had been captured by love. There was no sign now of the brash, confident, arrogant youth who had once tried to seduce her.

'We cannot fight him.' Owain sounded exasperated. 'If it were my sword alone against him and his men, I would have no fear, but Bishop Richard is behind him, meddling as always in Welsh affairs. Putting Gronwy out of the picture would serve no good purpose.'

Angharad blanched.

'I am sorry,' confessed Owain, miserably, 'I was thinking out loud, and my thoughts were not worthy. Your brother will come to no harm. Nobody will come to harm. If Gronwy finds us, I will swear that I forced you to shelter us on pain of your children's lives.'

'There will be no need for that. Somehow it will all come right. Gruffydd will find a way,' said Angharad, more reassuringly than she felt.

'Keep still and quiet and bolt the door. Do not let anybody in and I suggest you wear the clothes you travelled in yesterday. We will need to get you out of here as soon as possible.'

'Very well,' Owain agreed, bowing his head and squeezing Nest harder into his embrace.

Angharad returned to the kitchen and gave further instructions regarding the food for the visitors. Her four oldest children were by now eating a thick lamb stew filled with vegetables, and seemed well occupied, chatting merrily amongst themselves. 'Keep in the warmth here,' she told them. 'I would rather you stay in here this morning.' Then she went in search of Hywel.

There was no sign of Hywel in the practice yard, which was unusual for this time of day, but she spoke to Aeddan, who said that Hywel had ridden out earlier that morning and had not said where he was going. Now her heart was pumping wildly, and her mind raced as she agonised over what was best to do in Hywel's absence. He was the only one who could help them. She felt desperately vulnerable. She wondered if she should somehow get word to Father Luke to see if he could hide the pair, but then she realised what she would be asking. As a religious man, he would be implicated in harbouring two people who had violated God's law, and as a man of God, she knew he would not lie.

She walked towards the stables, and as one of the guards was being relieved of his post, she stopped him.

'Have you seen Hywel this morning?'

'Not since early, my lady, but I saw him riding out before your visitors arrived.'

She thanked the man and wondered what else she could do. Perhaps, she thought, she could get Nest and Owain to the llys at Caernarvon, but someone was sure to recognise them in that place. She held the little gold cross at her neck and prayed silently, then turned back to the llys realising that Gronwy would be getting suspicious at her prolonged absence. She had one final duty. She went to her quarters, where Bethan and Susannah were with the younger children, and swiftly apprised them of the situation. Bethan coloured when she knew that Gronwy was at the llys, reminding Angharad that Bethan, of all people, realised what they were up against.

The queen returned to the hall as calmly as she could muster. The kitchen servants had worked quickly, and platters of food were already on the table. Gronwy was tearing apart roast pigeon and stuffing it into his mouth as he eyed the moist sliced pork.

'I have persuaded these two brothers of yours to join me hunting after we have eaten,' said Gruffydd, speaking in a tone she understood to convey a different message.

'But I have heard no family news,' said Angharad, forcing joviality.

'Plenty of time for that tonight,' said Gruffydd, shooting his wife a meaningful glance. 'They will not leave before tomorrow.'

'Dear God!' thought Angharad, and a cold chill shot up her spine. Of course, they would not leave before the next day. Clever, though, that Gruffydd had tempted Gronwy with the one thing her brother loved almost as much as seducing women. Gronwy was renowned for his hunting skills, and his vanity would not allow him to pass up a chance to better Gruffydd.

'You leave so early?' she said, trying to imbue as much disappointment into her voice as possible.

'Tomorrow, we go to Caernarvon and then make our way to Powys. We feel certain Owain will be coming to Gwynedd, and we can ask along the way if anyone has seen anything unusual. I imagine that Nest would be hard to miss,' explained Meilyr, staring at her curiously.

Angharad knew that she had paled, so she moved to fill their goblets, hoping to detract attention from her poorly covered deceit.

'You are welcome guests at our llys in Caernarvon tomorrow, naturally, and I will send word ahead. Will you join us on the hunt, my dear?' asked Gruffydd conversationally.

'Oh, it is much too cold out there for me,' his wife responded quickly.

'You are right to be careful, sister,' said Gronwy slyly, 'you do not look yourself. You are very pasty and seem out of sorts. Cold weather can bring on all sorts of unexpected troubles.'

'But we men are born for the thrill of the chase, cold weather or not,' said Meilyr pleasantly.

'Yes,' said Gronwy, with a touch of malice. 'There is nothing like the thrill of the chase, and even better when you are rewarded with the kill!'

Gruffydd kept the talk to hunting and how the rivers were teeming with fish. When everyone seemed full, he stood up. 'I do not want to hurry you, but we only have so much light at this time of year, and I am keen for you to help me bring home one deer at least.'

All the time, Angharad knew that Owain and Nest were close enough to hear their conversation in the hall through the walls. Owain's words had unnerved her, and she half imagined him impetuously bursting into the hall with his sword aloft. Gruffydd had remained calm, and though Gronwy drank his fill, the king had drunk very little.

Meilyr's dark golden-brown eyes were taking everything in. Angharad felt sure he knew that they were hiding the fleeing pair. She wondered if he would side with them or Gronwy should their deception come to light. Angharad and Meilyr had an extremely close relationship. She knew he respected and admired Gruffydd, but his relationship with his older brother had become stronger in recent years. It had to, for Gronwy was head of their family now, and he held power over his three brothers.

It seemed an interminably long time before the hunting party left. Gruffydd opened the invitation to join the hunt to all his own men as well but, to avoid any awkwardness with Gronwy, asked Rhys if he would mind spending time training the older children. Rhys's face was filled with disappointment, not understanding Gruffydd's desire to protect him from any hurt.

When they finally left, Angharad gave them ten minutes until the sounds of the hounds and men had died into the distance before she decided to ride out looking for Hywel. She needed to warn him that

Gronwy's men were patrolling the island. Grey clouds were billowing towards the hills, and she hoped the rain would not bring the hunters back too early.

She dressed to ride and was leaving the llys for the stables when Hywel cantered in. Before he had dismounted, Angharad had run across the courtyard to speak with him.

'Oh, thank God you are here,' she said fervently and began to tell him what had transpired, while he held his smoky gelding, listening anxiously.

'Do not worry, lady,' he said at once. 'I have found a skiff and someone who will take them to Ireland at dusk today to have the best chance of avoiding anyone scouring the sea. The skiff's owner will keep his silence. We must ensure they are warm and dry and have enough food, as the crossing will be icy and wet. The timing is good. We need to work out how to get them to the boat unseen.'

'But Gronwy's men are checking anywhere boats come in and out!'

Hywel smiled. 'I thought they would be doing that, but the boatman has taken his boat out now as if fishing and will come into the cove below the woods. We will ride down to the woods' edge, and I will tether the horses well-hidden just before dark. We can scramble down from there, and nobody will see us.'

'But someone will notice you coming back with the horses. It will seem odd.'

Hywel made a quick decision. 'I will go out with my own horse and a packhorse as if taking provisions to the hunt. They will ride two to a horse. When I return, I will say I missed them in the woods and return with half the provisions. Nobody will notice that the things they are taking with them are gone. I can draw the guard from his post by telling him you wish to see him.'

'What will I say to him?'

'Perhaps make much of warning him that he must be on the lookout for Owain and Nest and, if there is any sign of them, not to let them in. While you are keeping him occupied, Owain and Princess Nest will be able to slip outside to the woods. I will close the gate, making a show of leaving myself later, and catch up with them in the woods.'

Angharad was so relieved that there was a plan in place that she uncharacteristically threw her arms around him, thanking him. Hywel was totally taken aback. Her soft skin was touching his cheek, he smelled the faint fragrance of her hair, and he felt her warmth. He wanted to embrace her but restrained himself, standing with his arms awkwardly on hers.

She pulled back and looked up at him; he thought he had never seen her look so breathtakingly beautiful. 'Hywel, you have so often come to my aid and never a thought for your own well-being. Thank you so much! I really did not know what to do,' she admitted.

'It is nothing. You have no need to thank me.' He wanted to wrap his arms around her, pull her to him so that her small face, pressed against his chest, would hear the wild pulsing of his heart, and know how he longed for her.

'Most certainly I do need to thank you,' she continued, 'for all the times you have put yourself in awkward and dangerous situations.'

He smiled and took a step back from her with some reluctance. To him, she was the most alluring creature on Earth. Nobody could compare with her.

She returned his smile, her blue eyes shining with gratitude, and then said urgently, in a hushed voice, 'Come, we should go to Gruffydd's chamber.'

Hywel looked astounded, 'Lady, …' he stuttered.

She looked at him strangely and then said, 'Ah yes, you are worried anyone seeing us will think it strange if we both go there together.'

Hywel stared at her.

'I will go ahead separately to let them know you are coming to acquaint them with your plan. I asked them to dress in the clothes they arrived in to look like a couple of Uchdryd's men,' she said, before gliding hurriedly back across the courtyard and into the llys.

Hywel looked up at the sky and let out a small groan to himself, cursing his stupidity. Of course, Owain and Nest were hidden in Gruffydd's chamber. What idiocy had possessed him for those few seconds? Had his thoughts seemed transparent? He was sickened at the unseemliness and disloyalty of what had crossed his mind. He hoped that Angharad had not noticed the blunder. With shaking hands, he tied up his horse next to the trough and made his way inside, but now he was not thinking clearly. He had not considered who may have been watching.

***

Rhys had had just about enough of Cadwallon. The others were polite enough, but Cadwallon always seemed to be out to prove that Rhys was a fool. He noticed he did not treat others this way. Cadwallon knew that Rhys was Lord Gronwy's bastard, and, although it was never discussed, Rhys wondered if that was why Cadwallon regarded him with such disdain. He felt life was so unfair. He should have been a lord's son and acknowledged as such, but Lord Gronwy had not married his mother. When he had asked his mother why not, she had said that his father, Lord Gronwy, had to marry someone from a wealthy family because that was what lords did and that she was poor.

Everybody thought Bethan was attractive, kind, and happy, but she was lowly born. It was almost impossible to change your circumstance when you were lowly born. When Lord Gronwy had arrived that day, Rhys had seen an opportunity to ask him if he could join his teulu. He practised what he would say, 'I can fight, read and write. I am your son. Take me with you,' but how pathetic it sounded. He was sick of being humiliated by Cadwallon. Even though he would miss his mother desperately, he would be so happy to go away somewhere where he would be respected.

He was tidying up in the practice yard when he saw his mother come out of the house with a huge bag that she was struggling with.

'Mother,' he shouted, 'let me help!'

He hefted the bag easily, asking his mother where to put it. She seemed flustered.

'I just have to take it to the stables,' she said, 'I can manage. You had better get back to what you were doing.'

'I'll take it for you. I have almost finished tidying up. It's heavy. What's in here?'

'Some provisions for the hunt, I think.'

'But the hunting party left a while ago.'

Hywel was in the stables loading a packhorse and seemed surprised to see him.

'Rhys was just helping me with this,' Bethan explained. She was blushing, and it crossed her son's mind, not for the first time, that she probably liked Hywel.

As he put the bag down next to the packhorse, it opened slightly, and he saw there were furs inside.

'Thank you, Rhys, we can manage from here,' said Hywel curtly, which was unusual because he was always unfailingly polite and cheery to him.

Rhys left the stables and went back to the yard, but something seemed odd. He kept his eye on the stables. His mother was still in there with Hywel. Then the llys door opened, and he watched the queen come out of the llys and walk swiftly to the stables. His mother came out and hurried back into the kitchen, but Angharad had been in the stables with Hywel for a long time. When she did come out, she seemed flustered for her: she was usually a very calm lady.

Chapter 5: A Long Journey (January 1110)

Uchdryd was bone tired. Ancient wounds gnawed at his limbs, and he felt like he carried a heavy metal collar on his neck and shoulders. He, Davydd and Gruffydd's men had ridden easily through the freezing afternoon, keeping to less used tracks as far as they could. Uchdryd did not want people speculating about his trip to Gwynedd at the coldest time of the year. Now they rode through the night, thanks to a clear sky and a full moon, but he was cold and wet through. He just wanted to wrap himself in his cloak in some straw in a barn and sleep, but he had so much to do and far to go. Gruffydd's men turned back at the border, and he was grateful that they had not thus far run into Madog and Ithel or their men.

Feeling his age, Uchdryd followed Davydd, who rode his sturdy Welsh pony along well-marked tracks leading back to the llys which Uchdryd had built in Cymer, Merionydd. Davydd would never complain if he had to take his master to the ends of the earth and back. He thanked God for Davydd and again for their trusty Welsh mounts, which would keep going relentlessly in all conditions. Uchdryd smiled to himself as he thought how those Norman horses bred for battle looked very impressive but would not have had the stamina for this swift journey across rough country.

Davydd was looking down and from side to side, and Uchdryd knew he would be using his scouting skills to read whether they were safe, where tracks had shown something had frightened an animal, where bushes had been brushed aside by horsemen, where hooves had gathered, men dismounted, where danger lay. His sight and hearing were keener than Uchdryd's, but Uchdryd remembered when he was as skilful as the young man plodding ahead.

Branches dripped from earlier rain, and a trickle found its way under Uchdryd's cloak hood. He sighed and longed for the days when, at age fourteen as was custom then, he had entered the training of his lord Bleddyn ap Cynfyn. His mother had been Bleddyn's sister, so he grew up with his cousins Madog, Rhyrid, and, of course, Cadwgan. Ah, they had been inseparable and ambitious. Poor Bleddyn, king of Powys and co-ruler of the Kingdom of Gwynedd with his brother Rhiwallon, had been slain in his prime, like so many Welsh kings. Slain by his first cousin King Rhys ap Owain of Deheubarth, betrayed by the lords of Ystrad Tywi. He had been a kind and merciful king, though fierce in battle. What fools the Welsh were to betray their kin in search of power and land. He shivered involuntarily as he thought how many kings had given their lives to hold onto such inhospitable lands as the cold, bleak, windswept regions of much of northern Wales. He admonished himself silently for succumbing to the misery of a freezing winter's night.

Davydd stopped and raised a hand. Uchdryd fingered his sword. His horse pricked up its ears, and he gave him a gentle pat. After a moment or two, Davydd shook his head, and they moved on. Uchdryd returned to the reverie of his youth. His youngest cousins, Iorwedd and Maredudd, were tiny toddlers, and he had never really had the same relationship with them that he had enjoyed with the volatile but generous Cadwgan. When Cadwgan took over his father's land, Madog and Rhyrid had tried to fight for land of their own but found death at the sword of Rhys ap Tewdwr when they tried to take his lands in Deheubarth. This made Cadwgan and Uchdryd even closer. His thoughts turned to Owain ap Cadwgan. How ironic that after all these years, Cadwgan's son had fallen in love with Rhys ap Tewdwr's daughter, and that was why he found himself plodding now through the darkness, guided by instinct and a watery moon. Trouble always seemed to find Owain, but he was Cadwgan's son, and Uchdryd owed Cadwgan many times over.

'I am pulling in here to have a piss,' he called to Davydd, and he dismounted stiff and uncomfortable. The older he got, the more stops he needed to make. It was not so easy to relieve yourself in mail either. Davydd waited until his master had mounted again and then went into the bushes himself.

'What do you think?' asked Uchdryd. 'A few hours more?'

'Three if we keep the pace,' said Davydd.

'It is bloody cold; we will be like a pair of icicles by the time we arrive.'

The horses reverted to their easy rhythm, and Uchdryd's mind wandered to his family. He and his first wife, Nest, had been so fortunate in their sons. They all had their mother's temperament and looks. He missed Nest, whose grandfather and uncle had served kings as the head of their teulu and who had encouraged Uchdryd to aim high. His heart filled as he thought of his beautiful Nest ferch Llewelyn Fychan. When she had died, he felt his heart would break into a million pieces. Marrying Angharad ferch Rhys Sais ap Ednyfed had comforted him, but they were companions of an age, not a love match. He chuckled. His second wife would undoubtedly chastise him for his involvement in this matter with Owain ap Cadwgan, and, he reflected, as he had done many times before, that she would probably be right!

Just before dawn, they reined in to rest the horses briefly, sharing bread and cheese and taking water from a spring to wash their faces and curb their thirst. Two hours later, they reached Uchdryd's own lands, and there was his wife, glad to see him home but, as he had predicted, with plenty to say. He dismounted and walked stiffly towards her, stilling her scolding with a bear hug and bending to kiss her warm face. The home felt comfortable, food was already on the table, and a fire was burning enough to warm the whole of Powys. He thanked the Lord for such comforts. The exhaustion from the long journey was catching up with him, but before he tumbled into his bed for an hour, he sent servants to raise his warband. By the time his loyal men had gathered at his llys, Uchdryd had washed, changed into clean clothes and was once more the man of action.

'Madog and Ithel ap Rhyrid have been charged with laying waste to Owain ap Cadwgan's lands and capturing those loyal to him,' he told the men gathered around his hearth. 'Bishop Richard has asked me to 'assist' them in their search, which I am bound to do, but they are brutes and will destroy everything they see and slaughter anyone they come across.'

A cry went up at his words, and the mood was one of outrage. Bishop Richard's interference was resented, and many of these men had fought with Owain; plenty had benefitted from his generosity and that of his father. Uchdryd calmed them, insisted on the need for haste, and then ordered half of them to accompany him and the other half to go to Owain's lands. Once there, they were to instruct any of those living on Owain's land to take everything of value and to make their way to Uchdryd's manor for safety.

'Make sure they take whatever they can move with them and anything they can use as a weapon. Let us hope they do not need to fight. Bring the animals; those with oxen can take what they can on carts. They will probably lose everything left behind, and their homes and barns will be burnt, but better to save their lives at least.'

He sent a message to Cadwgan, outlining what he was doing and suggesting he lay low or, even better, take a merchant ship to Ireland from Aberdovey while he still could. Then he set off to find Madog and Ithel, taking with him his most trusted men-at-arms, Rees, Cadoc and Davydd, and the rest of the party assigned to the task. They kept a brisk pace, and when they did slow to rest the horses, Uchdryd encouraged a cheery banter amongst them.

Most of the hamlets they rode through were quiet, with only the smoke escaping through the thatch, betraying that there were occupants inside. A cold wind was blowing, and despite his bearskin cloak, Uchdryd shivered. When Cadoc, a muscle-bound giant with a mane of black hair, suggested they stop briefly for refreshment at his cousin's farm, tucked into the lea of a stone crag, Uchdryd hastily agreed. Most of the men dismounted and stretched their legs or stamped their feet outside the dwelling, accepting warm ale and hunks of bread and cheese, but Uchdryd, Rees, Davydd and Cadoc went inside to stand around the blazing fire. Rees, a short man with slightly bowed legs, broad shoulders, and huge hands, took off his helmet to rub his bald head, then held out one damp boot and then the other towards the flames. Pungent steam wafted into the air.

The home smelt of the few animals huddled at the far end of the building, but though there was little furniture or comfort, it was neat and clean. Two small boys hid behind a sack containing the fleece of the Soay sheep, which the farmer raised. Their shy mother had been spinning the soft fine wool when the visitors arrived while the father had been repairing the handle of a tool.

'Has anyone been through this way in the last days?' Uchdryd asked of Cadoc's cousin, a small, wiry man with a limp, who was as unlike his giant relative as it was possible to be.

'I have seen nobody for at least a month,' said the farmer. 'At this time of the year, there is no cause to travel in the bitter cold. Cadoc tells me you are looking for Owain ap Cadwgan. A man can hide in a thousand places in the mountains and never be found.'

Before they left, Uchdryd reached into the leather pouch he kept on a belt around his waist and pressed some silver into the farmer's hand. The farmer's wife, who had bustled around them quietly enjoying the break in the winter's monotony, gave a toothless smile as her big eyes saw the gesture.

It was less than an hour before the horsemen arrived at Madog's llys, and it was obvious that preparations were well underway from the number of horses and the people milling around a massive fire that had been lit outside. Sparks flew up into the air and then fizzled to nothing as they hit the cold earth.

'Lord Uchdryd!' called Madog, in greeting, striding across the courtyard to greet him with a spring in his step. 'You and your men are welcome.'

Madog looked to see if any more of Uchdryd's men were following, then frowned, 'But there are so few of you.'

'Others will join us, but at this time of the year, there is little appetite to leave the hearth!' responded Uchdryd.

'Even for Owain ap Cadwgan's booty? You surprise me!'

'That pup will not have much booty for us, but his lands, I understand, will be yours.'

Madog looked uneasy, his colour deepened, but he shrugged. 'And we will make sure we reward all those helping us. The bigger reward will be from King Henry for the capture of Owain himself, and I must admit I was surprised that Bishop Richard gave us your name as one who would be able to 'assist'.'

'Cadwgan is my lord, and I have given my oath to him, but I have no love for Owain and he none for me.'

Madog looked deep into Uchdryd's eyes and nodded acceptingly when the older man kept his eye. 'Well, as I said, you are welcome indeed. We ride within the hour. I am waiting for some of Ithel's warband to arrive, and then we will make our way to Owain's llys.'

'This afternoon? Madog, you are too hasty.'

'What do you mean?' Madog shot back, his manner defensive.

'The days are short, and you will have the men arriving in the dark.'

'We have no fear of that, and there will be the element of surprise.'

Uchdryd raised his bushy eyebrows, and his voice was full of scorn. 'And men will say you have no honour to attack your cousin in the dark. It is not noble, and I will have no part of it.'

Madog's mood immediately soured. Men had now surrounded Uchdryd, eager to hear what the famous warlord was saying, and some of them muttered agreement. Madog's discomfort was evident. It seemed he resented being made to look foolish by a man who commanded so much respect from every side. Here was a heaven-made opportunity to make a name for himself and garner respect, but he felt it slipping away.

Madog suppressed his pique, and when he spoke again, he adopted a tone of nonchalance though the way he rolled his shoulder and stretched his neck to one side was a tell-tale sign of an internal dilemma. He gestured toward the entrance to his llys. 'Come inside, Lord Uchdryd, you and your men. Let us eat, drink and discuss.'

The men crowded into the llys built of solid oak with a high beamed roof. The hall was dark, and a central fire roared, filling the room with smoke. This was a man's domain, with little to soften the interior. A hound slunk out of the shadows to Madog's side and was rewarded with a kick to its ribs, leaving it whining as it lurched away. Uchdryd felt the bile rise in his throat. He moved across to the dog, and though it flinched, he knelt and felt its ribs. Satisfied that no serious damage had been done, he rose to see Ithel, with his usual expression of surly suspicion, standing by the fire with a few other men, carefully observing those entering. Ithel left his companions and immediately came over to welcome Uchdryd.

'Thank you for joining our company,' he said, unsmiling but genuinely enough, then indicating the table. 'Come, there is food and ale for you and your men.'

Uchdryd thanked Madog's younger brother, and his men sat as Ithel himself poured them ale.

'Lord Uchdryd,' said Ithel finally, after the men had eaten, 'it surprised me that Bishop Richard should refer to you as 'the truest and most faithful companion'. I would have thought that as warlord for Lord Cadwgan, you would be protecting his son, not working with the Normans.'

Uchdryd snorted. 'Ah, I answered the same question to your brother. What Owain ap Cadwgan has done is not a noble act. What he has done violates common decency. He has stolen another man's wife and brought dishonour to the Welsh.'

'And you would gain from that misdemeanour.'

'Gain? Gain from my lord's son? This is not about gain for me. Honour is not a matter to be taken lightly.'

Ithel looked around the room, nodding. 'Exactly my thoughts, Lord Uchdryd. Honour is not a matter to be taken lightly.'

'But we must also act honourably. As I was telling your brother, there is no honour in ambushing your cousin at night. We must approach him in the day and offer him safe passage to King Henry or the opportunity to fight.'

'And there is no suggestion of you turning sides in such a fight, Lord Uchdryd?' said Ithel slyly in hushed confidentiality.

'You have my word that if we face Owain and his men tomorrow, I will be on your side.'

Ithel gave him a long look and nodded his head firmly. 'Then maybe what you suggest is more 'honourable', and I, for one, would prefer to see the faces of the men we fight and not give Owain the opportunity to escape in the darkness at our approach.'

Uchdryd felt a wash of relief, but he was not pleased with his cunning. He had said nothing untrue but knew his words had misled the brothers and that soon enough, they would know he had tricked them. It was not something he wanted to be associated with his name, and yet his deep bonds to Cadwgan made it an unpleasantness he must live with. Ithel stood now and, looking across to his brother, said in a voice loud enough to be heard by all.

'At first light, we should be ready.'

'At first light, as you say,' Uchdryd agreed, stifling a yawn.

Uchdryd retired early but slept lightly as the men drank and caroused while rain pelted onto the thatch roof, dripping through the hall. He heard the two brothers arguing, and though he could not hear clearly what it was about, he could guess. In the morning, tempers were frayed, and some of the warband were the worse for drink. He pulled on his leather jerkin and mail and went to the fire to warm his aching bones.

Davydd, sprightly and gleaming with health, grinned broadly as he saw his master approach. He held out a beaker of warmed ale and looked around to make sure no one was listening before he said in a low voice,

'Lord, there is going to be an outburst of fury when this lot realise that Owain's men have fled and taken all their possessions with them.'

'We will have to deal with that at the time and see how it plays out. The rest of our men will join us before then. We will be more than a match for these drunken hotheads if things turn nasty.'

'Lord, Madog is coming this way.'

Uchdryd grimaced, then turned with a ready smile lifting a huge hand in greeting.

'Madog. I hope you slept well! What are our plans?'

'To ride to Owain ap Cadwgan's llys before he gets wind of what is happening.'

'That's your plan?' said Uchdryd, snorting and affecting an air of incredulity.

'What do you mean?'

'With due respect, we must surround the estate to cut off any escape routes. The group must be divided, each with tasks according to their abilities; otherwise, it will be a laughable disorder. We need to make sure the leaders of each group of men are clear in what they are doing.'

Madog's face grew thunderous as he complained, 'Is this another delaying tactic, Lord Uchdryd?'

Uchdryd raised himself to his full height, chest out as he towered over the other man. He spoke quickly, his voice grating with cold disdain, his eyes watching Madog's intently.

'I have been leading men since you were sucking at your mother's breast, and I will not have my name associated with some half thought through attack. We gather the leading warriors now and apply some discipline to this. I can see now why Bishop Richard was keen to employ my assistance if this is how you intend to proceed.'

Madog's face spoke threat, but he suppressed his anger. After a few moments, he dipped his head but said somewhat resentfully, 'Very well, we will assemble everyone now and ensure they understand their roles.'

He strode off towards his bleary-eyed brother, who scowled towards Uchdryd and Davydd before they split up and approached various members of their warband. Uchdryd waited until everyone was out of earshot and confided, under his breath, while putting out a stray spark from the fire by grinding his boot, 'Well, that has slowed them an hour.'

Davydd watched a confrontation between the two brothers. 'They will be furious when they discover that Lord Owain's llys is empty and all his retainers gone. Madog has a violent temper. I hope it is not directed at us.'

'Oh, it will be,' said Uchdryd shrugging, 'but what will he do? He cannot kill us since he does not know my relationship with Bishop Richard. He cannot report back to Bishop Richard that he made an error in asking me to 'assist' them. No, it won't be nice to watch, but I think we will be safe enough! I just hope we have delayed them long enough that Owain's followers have been able to take most of their things with them!'

'They will take his land, though.'

'Yes, they will take the land, but if I know Owain, he will not be too long getting it back one way or another!'

Chapter 6: Manhunt (January 1110)

Rhys kicked a stone across the practice yard. He tried not to feel resentful, but he just could not help it. He bristled angrily as he thought of all the others on the hunt. He, meanwhile, had been forced to nursemaid Gruffydd's children, and Cadwallon had been his insufferable self! It was utterly unfair. Gruffydd had often commended him on his hunting skill, and he would have loved his father to see he was good at something. Perhaps Lord Gronwy would have noticed him, but instead, here he was, one of the few remaining at the llys.

He finished tidying up the practice yard and was coming past the dairy when he saw Hywel and Queen Angharad come out of the llys. They stood close together and seemed to be in deep conversation. He pulled himself back into the shadows of the dairy doorway and peered out from behind the leather curtain that protected against the rain and snow. What was going on today? What was happening between those two? His mind raced. This was the second time he had observed them together today, and the last time, he had seen his queen embrace Hywel. Well, well, well, what would King Gruffydd make of that if he knew? He liked Hywel, but the way that he had spoken to him in the stables in front of his mother had hurt him. Even Hywel had treated him like a nobody.

He watched as Angharad looked around furtively, and then the queen, who usually moved gracefully, darted back inside the llys while Hywel went over to the guard tower and called up to Heifyn on gate duty. All the other guards were in the guard house playing cards and awaiting their turn to go on sentry duty. He saw Heifyn show some reluctance as Hywel beckoned him, but he shrugged his shoulders and came down from the palisade. He and Hywel strode across the courtyard and went into the llys. This was very odd. King Gruffydd always had a man on the gate. Always.

Nothing seemed to be happening, and Rhys was about to follow Heifyn inside when the llys door opened, and he watched the queen come out of the llys with the two servants who had accompanied Lord Uchdryd. That was strange. Why had they not been in the hall sleeping with the rest of the men last night if they were still here, and why did they not go back with Uchdryd? They were both hooded, but there was something familiar about the tall one. He just could not put his finger on it. What would the queen be doing with servants she did not know? He watched as Hywel exited the stables on foot, leading his horse and a packhorse. He left them at the stable door. The queen joined him with the two servants, and then his mother appeared and seemed to curtsey to them or was she curtseying to the queen? He was not sure what to make of it.

Hywel went to the guardhouse, and Rhys could hear the men laughing. A mean thought crossed his mind that Hywel was pleasant enough with those men though he had treated him rudely. Meanwhile, the two servants walked to the gate, looked up and, seeing nobody there, the taller man easily lifted the wooden bar and swung the gate open before they went through. Hywel then came out of the guardhouse, nodded to the queen, closed the gate, replaced the bar and hurried into the stables.

Rhys ran across and took the palisade steps two at a time. Looking down, he expected to see the two men making their way down the road, but it was empty. He scanned the surrounding area and saw some movement behind a holly bush. He heard the kitchen door close, and Heifyn crossed the courtyard to his post while Hywel came out on his horse with a lead rein to a pony with a sack across its back. Why would Hywel be taking furs to the hunt? It did not make any sense. Heifyn opened the gate for the two horses to pass, secured it and then came back up to the palisade as Rhys watched Hywel follow the two men towards the woods. They came out from behind the holly bush, and then a strange thing happened: the tall man lifted the smaller one, just as you would a child, to sit on Hywel's horse and then mounted it himself while Hywel led the pack horse himself. Rhys kept his eyes on them until they disappeared deeper into the woods. Something was very odd.

'It's a cold one!' said Rhys to the guard, a stocky, cheerful man stamping his feet and rubbing his gloved hands together.

'Rhys,' exclaimed the guard, smiling broadly, 'I did not see you there. You did not go with the others?'

'No, I was training the youngsters. Most of the others have gone, and I was surprised to see Hywel still here. Where is he off to?'

'Taking bread and cheese to the hunting party.'

'Bit late in the day for that, is it not?' said Rhys looking at the faint sun dipping towards the horizon. 'They will surely be back soon.'

'Not for me to question. Queen Angharad told him to take them supplies. Lord Gronwy has a big appetite by the look of him, and I expect he would wolf down a bit of bread and cheese if it were offered. I gobbled down a bit myself while I was in the kitchen,' he winked.

'Those two men who came in with Lord Uchdryd went with him.'

'I did not see them.'

'They went out of the gate when you were in the kitchen and joined Hywel afterwards. He had them on the back of his horse, and he led the packhorse.'

'Typical of Hywel to help them out wherever they were going. I heard they brought a couple of nice horses up for breeding.'

Rhys had not elicited the kind of response he had expected, and the guard was not much interested.

'Well, I might head inside,' he said, leaving the guard to his duties. He entered the llys and settled down by the kitchen fire to warm up with a bowl of thick vegetable soup. After a short while, he felt a light touch on his arm. His mother's smiling face looked down at him, and he moved along the bench to make room for her. Her face lit up as it always did for any small gesture of consideration.

'The hunt will be coming in soon, I expect,' he said conversationally.

'Yes, I suppose it will!'

'It will be a full house here tonight.'

'Yes, it will be a madhouse, that's for sure.'

A few others joined them at the table, and there was general speculation about the weather that week bringing snow and what meat the hunt would return with. Susannah brought a bowl of soup for Bethan and refilled Rhys's bowl before sitting at the end of the bench and stretching her swollen legs out.

'Those men of Lord Uchdryd's went with Hywel to take some food for the hunt. I am not sure what was happening there,' he said to Susannah loudly for the benefit of anyone who might shed some light on it.

'I do not know who you are talking about!' his mother replied too sharply, with a quick look at Susannah.

'The men who came with Lord Uchdryd,' Rhys persisted.

She looked irritated. 'I just mind my own business, and it is best for you to do the same.'

He gave his mother a dark look, pushed his bowl to one side, twisted off the bench and stomped back outside, fuming that even his mother was now treating him like a child. He turned at the noise of men and horses and saw the hunting party was returning through the gates. They all looked weary but in good spirits. Gronwy was riding beside a pack horse with a brace of deer hanging over the saddle.

Rhys went forward to help with the horses and stood beside Gronwy's as he dismounted. Gronwy gave him another long look and asked, 'You are Rhys, Bethan's son, aren't you?'

'Yes, my lord.'

'You have grown up, I can see.'

'Yes, my lord. I am almost sixteen now.'

Rhys's heart was beating fast, and he hoped Lord Gronwy would continue talking, but King Gruffydd was calling across the courtyard.

'Well done, Lord Gronwy, you have provided a fine feast. Men, everybody come inside and let us warm our perishing bones by the fire. We will have something hot to eat and some drink to fill our bellies!'

Gronwy was enjoying the attention. His brother, Lord Meilyr, slapped him on the shoulders and led him towards the llys.

Rhys helped others remove the deer and lead the horses into the stables. He was pleased that his father had noticed and spoken to him, but his mother's sharp words in front of everyone still rankled.

Inside, though there were only half the men in the hall that there would be at other times of the year, the scene was a merry one. Gruffydd's mead and ale were flowing, and there were platters of food enough to feed even the hungriest.

Gronwy was ebullient, and Angharad felt anxious as always when she saw her brother drinking heavily.

'Gronwy does not change,' she whispered to Meilyr when they had a chance to talk to each other without being overheard.

'Gronwy is Gronwy. Since Father died, he has managed his affairs well: he is no fool and knows how to handle the issues that crop up. His temper is his downfall, however. He doesn't take after our father in that.'

'You have always been able to deal with his tempers better than I ever was.'

'I do not pay much attention these days. Look, he is a grown man now, as am I. We both have our land and our families. I admire him for turning his share of father's land into a very profitable concern.'

'He was ever ambitious.'

'Oh yes, and of course, that is why we are chasing down the heir to Powys. He hopes to get extra land from turning in Owain ap Cadwgan to

King Henry.'

'And you?'

'I also have a growing family, sister, and I need to provide land for my children. This is an opportunity. Cadwgan's whole family fight each other like dogs. We know that King Henry and Bishop Richard encourage the hostility, but if it suits King Henry that we should own some of Powys, then better Welshmen own it than more of the Marcher Lords. Do you not think?'

He lifted an eyebrow at his sister in question, but her attention was captured by one of Gronwy's men who had entered the hall to speak to his lord. An expression of exasperation, almost anger, crossed Gronwy's face. Meilyr followed his sister's gaze and watched as Gronwy stood a little unsteadily and followed the man to the door.

Angharad tensed up. Her first thought was that she had seen nothing of Hywel. What had Gronwy's man discovered?

'Angharad, what are you worried about?' asked Meilyr, watching her frightened eyes as she followed Gronwy across the room.

She quickly turned back to Meilyr, realising he could sense her anxiety.

'Meilyr, I do not know where Owain and Nest are, but if they are somewhere on Anglesey, I fear for the Princess Nest if Gronwy humiliates her,' she said, desperately trying to cover up the myriad of emotions with something plausible enough to satisfy her brother.

'Why would Gronwy humiliate her? If Owain has made his way here and is discovered, only Owain will be humiliated, surely?' questioned Meilyr with a frown.

Before she could answer, Gruffydd was at their side, 'Come Meilyr, I have had no chance to ask you about your family and how things are with you,' he said, guiding Meilyr close to the fire.

Angharad's unease was only increasing. She cursed herself for bringing up the subject of Princess Nest with her brother. She should have said nothing rather than raising it. She made her way across the hall as if to the kitchen but stood just inside the passageway between, where she could hear Gronwy outside.

'And you searched everywhere you could reach?'

'Yes, my lord.'

'And you made clear that there was a reward for information?'

'Yes, my lord.'

Gronwy grunted and dismissed the man while Angharad, feeling relief wash over her trembling body, returned to the hall. As Gronwy turned back into the warmth of the passageway, he saw Bethan entering Gruffydd's chamber. She had not lost her curves, and as she moved, the gentle sway of her backside stirred something inside him. He lurched up the corridor after her and saw the door was ajar. Bethan was changing sheets on the bed. He licked his full lips and watched her for a while through the crack of the door. He imagined her surprise if he pushed her onto the bed, her pleasure as he fondled her ample breasts and pushed her skirts up while separating her legs with his knee. He remembered the sweet honey taste of her mouth. His breathing became heavy. Something made her swing around, and she saw him there. She jumped back, almost guiltily, and he swung the door open, standing across the doorframe.

'Hello, Bethan. We have not spoken to each other in a long while.'

'No, my lord.'

Gronwy walked into the room, disappointed at her reaction. He moved around, looking at Gruffydd's things but keeping himself only an arm's length away from Bethan.

'I spoke with Rhys today.'

'You did, my lord?'

'He is a fine boy.'

'He is my lord.'

He watched her nervousness as he picked up a small silver box which he shook and replaced carelessly, then Gruffydd's seal, which he looked at intently before knocking it with the back of his hand across the tabletop. She suppressed a gasp as he leant down beside the table and picked up a comb, the teeth of which entangled a little dark hair similar to her own. She knew immediately that Nest had used the comb and wondered if Gronwy would realise it was not his sister's.

He pulled the hair out of the comb and wrapped it around his index finger, sniffing it and touching it to his lips.

'You naughty girl,' he said, 'you have been using your lady's comb.' His eyes seemed hooded, and he moved closer to the nervous woman pushing a strand of hair back under her cap with his stubby fingers.

'You have not lost your looks, Bethan!'

'Thank you, my lord!' she flushed, stiffened, and avoided eye contact, looking straight ahead.

'And you look after King Gruffydd, do you?' he asked with a leer.

'I, I, I am not sure….,' she stuttered.

'I only mean that you are making his bed. It seems late in the day for that. Do you see to all his lordship's needs?'

'I ….'

'Do you make sure his bed is warm for him, Bethan? Like you used to do for me?' She could feel his spittle on her cheek, and smell his breath.

'She is making up the room for you, Gronwy.' Angharad's voice was sharp and cold.

Bethan jumped, flustered, and coloured up.

'We were missing you in the hall, brother.'

Gronwy looked at his sister shrewdly. 'Tell Gruffydd I will come shortly. I need to give some additional instructions to my men.'

Angharad waited at the doorway, her mouth dry; she felt a surge of fear. At first, Gronwy did not move, his eyes scanning the room and flicking between Bethan and his sister. Finally, he nodded at Bethan, licked his lips, and nodded again before lumbering outside into the cold air. The two women were scouring the room for any trace that Owain and Nest had been there.

Bethan was trembling. 'He found that comb on the floor and took some hair from it. I think he thought it was mine. Mistress, I do not know what else he saw.'

Angharad blanched and thanked God that Bethan's hair was so close in colour to Nest's. She had heard his words and did not care what her brother thought had transpired between Gruffydd and Bethan, just as long as her family was safe.

'There was nothing else?'

'I do not know. His eyes were everywhere.'

The room suddenly felt claustrophobic. Gruffydd was always fastidious; now his chamber smelt of Gronwy's heavy sweat, of alcohol, of horses.

'Open the shutters,' she said too abruptly, and realising that Bethan was still shaking, she squeezed her shoulder gently.

'I am sorry. I just need him to be gone.'

Outside, Gronwy, seeing his man at arms, went over to where he stood talking to the guard on duty and pulled him aside roughly. 'Ask around again to see if there have been any unusual visitors, will you? Quietly.'

The man dipped his head and went over to the guardhouse.

Gronwy hawked and spat as he thought about his sister; the old resentment flared in him again. His fingers played with the ring of hair, toying with it between finger and thumb. He was about to go back inside when Rhys came out of the stable. His eyes fixed on him briefly, and then he looked around before calling, 'Come here, lad.'

'Yes, my lord,' replied Rhys, swiftly running to Gronwy's side.

'You know who I am?'

'Yes, Lord Gronwy.'

Gronwy sniffed, looking around again, and moved closer towards the boy.

'You know that your mother and I were close once.'

Rhys flushed. 'I do know that, Lord Gronwy.'

'Yes, of course, your mother would have told you.'

Gronwy said nothing for a while, just observing the boy's eager expression, enjoying Rhys' desperate need to be liked.

'Are you happy here?'

Rhys hesitated just a second too long. 'King Gruffydd treats me well, but...'

'But…'

Now was the time to be bold. 'I would like to be part of your teulu, Lord Gronwy.'

Gronwy looked hard at the boy and chuckled. He sniffed. 'Would you now? Can you fight?'

'Yes, Lord Gronwy! I teach the royal children how to fight as well.'

'Those brats! They have been spoilt.'

Rhys said nothing, but the look on his face was enough for his father to realise that he had struck a chord: Rhys had no love for the royal children. Gronwy stared into the distance, seeing nothing, and considered how he would play this one. Finally, he decided.

'Joining my teulu, eh? That might be possible, but what I need now is someone here in Anglesey that I can trust, someone who would be willing to help me keep things lawful.'

Rhys' eyes widened.

'Who better to trust than my own son? You are my blood, after all.'

Rhys beamed; his eyes alive with interest. This was what he had wished for. His father was acknowledging him and wanted him to do meaningful work.

Gronwy saw the effect his words were having on the boy. He had learnt from his father how to read people. 'Tell me, have there been any visitors to the llys in the last few days?'

'Well, Lord Uchdryd came, lord, and three of his men.'

'What were their names?'

'I do not know their names, lord.'

'What did they look like?'

'One was older, he came yesterday morning, and Lord Uchdryd had to return to Powys immediately, and he went with him.'

'Why?'

'I heard that Bishop Richard had called him to help find Owain ap Cadwgan and the Princess Nest.'

'You heard about that, did you?'

'Yes, Lord Gronwy.'

'But there has been no sign of them here?'

'No, Lord Gronwy.'

Gronwy considered this information and turned back to Rhys. 'What about the other two men? They did not go with Lord Uchdryd. Where are they now?'

'They went with Hywel to find you all at the hunt.'

'Is that so? Where is Hywel?' Gronwy asked suspiciously.

'I have not seen him come in yet.'

'Hmm. Can you describe these men to me?'

'One was tall, and one was short.'

'Young or old?'

'One seemed older than the other. One seemed just like a boy.'

'The colour of their hair?'

'I do not know. It is cold, so they had hoods on.'

'Thin? Fat?'

'The little one was skinny, and the other was not fat but well built.'

'Taller than me?'

'A little, maybe. They could have been father and son.'

'Why do you say that?'

The tall one lifted the short one onto a horse, just like you would a child.'

Gronwy considered this information, chewing the inside of his cheek. He spat again and played with the ring of hair between his stubby fingers. Maybe this was nothing, but if Hywel was involved, maybe it was something. Strange that Hywel had not been on the hunt even though Rhys seemed to think he had tried to catch up with them. Odd that. He needed to think this through carefully.

He moved closer to Rhys so that Rhys could smell the mead on his breath which blew in warm clouds by the torchlight on either side of the great door into the llys.

'Your grandfather, my father, helped King Gruffydd to become king, you know. Without him, Gruffydd would be nothing. My father was ruling the whole of Gwynedd. Still, my sister persuaded him to do some deal with William Rufus, the English king and the Lords of Chester and Shrewsbury, which made Gruffydd rich and powerful but diminished our family's prospects.'

This was not what Rhys had heard the bards sing of. They sang of all Gruffydd's victories and of a terrible battle where Gruffydd was betrayed by mercenaries and fled to Ireland. They sang of how the great King Magnus Barefoot had defeated the Normans at the Battle of Anglesey Sound and how Gruffydd had been restored to his kingship. He had also heard Gronwy's father referred to as Owain Fradwr, Owain the Traitor. He must have looked doubtful as Gronwy worked on him again.

'Do you not believe me, lad?' and there was a touch of irritation in his voice.

'I am sure you speak the truth, lord, but the bards sing of it differently.'

'Who pays the bards?' scoffed the older man, 'Gruffydd, of course, so they sing what he tells them to sing but believe me, our family has a right in Gwynedd. And a time will come when that right is exercised.'

That made sense. Gronwy edged closer, and Rhys wondered if he was including him when he talked about 'our family'.

'King Gruffydd does not seem to have much of a warband here,' said Gronwy with a slight sneer.

'He has given them properties and lets them spend time with their families at this time of the year.'

'Very generous,' he mocked, 'and what if he is attacked?'

'They are all close by and would come quickly, lord.'

'Is that so?' Gronwy rubbed his chin. 'Do they train regularly?'

'Every day when they are here, lord.'

'Are they good?'

'They seem very good, lord.'

'And Hywel is the leader of the warband.'

'Yes, lord.'

There was silence for a while. Gronwy belched and then put his arm around Rhys' shoulder. 'You know, I probably shouldn't tell you this, but I would have married your mother except that my sister thought she was 'below' me. She influenced my father against it; well, times have moved on, and now I am married.'

Gronwy's lies flowed with convincing plausibility. He could almost feel the effects of his persuasiveness on the receptive youth, and he leaned into him.

'Queen Angharad, Lord? But she has always treated me as part of the family.'

Gronwy gave a derisive snort. 'Yes, yes, she always seems so perfect, doesn't she? But you cannot always believe everything. I am her brother, and I have watched how she has manipulated people since she was a child.'

Rhys felt anger rising inside him. He had been thwarted from his inheritance, his proper place in the world.

'I expect King Gruffydd will have seen through her by now. Probably interested in other women, is he?'

'Oh no, lord, no sign of that; in fact, it is more likely the other way?'

Gronwy turned sharply like a cat cornering a mouse.

'What do you mean, lad?'

'Nothing, lord, it was stupid of me to say?'

'Come on; it is only us talking together man to man.'

'Well, I think she may be fond of someone else, lord.'

Gronwy was grinning now, hardly believing his luck. His wits felt sharp, and he was ready to exploit this gem, but he had to tread carefully. 'Really, who would that be?'

'I am not sure, I may be wrong, but I saw her embracing Hywel today when you were all on the hunt, lord.'

'Well, well,' said Gronwy, licking his moist lips and pulling a gold coin out of a pouch he held at his waist. 'You see, that is the sort of information worth me knowing so that if there are any family 'difficulties', I know how to handle them.'

Rhys smiled up at Gronwy. 'I understand, lord.'

'So, for now, we have an understanding, do we not?'

Rhys nodded.

'This is just between us. You look out for information which may be useful, and then, when the time is right, you will be able to join me and my teulu. You are my son, after all.'

Rhys' chest swelled with pride, and he fingered the gold coin.

'Thank you, lord,' he breathed and flushed.

When Gronwy returned inside the hall, Rhys ran across the courtyard and leapt into the air. At last, things were changing for the better!

Chapter 7: The Cost of Love (January 1110)

Hywel left the two fugitives sitting on a rock in a small cave strewn with seaweed from the last high tide. He scoured the area to ensure they were all safe, and now they just had to wait for the boat to turn into the cove. It was almost dark, and their passage to Ireland was expected soon.

Nest was sheltering and shivering under Owain's thick black cloak, and as Hywel returned, he heard Owain saying,

'I am not pressuring you to do this, you know. If you have any doubts, Hywel can arrange to take you back to your children. You know as well as I do that it will not be easy for us at first.'

Nest looked up at him determinedly, her face grey in the dusk winter light. 'I am coming with you. We stay together.'

He nodded acceptance and replied by hugging her close. No matter how much she was already missing her children, she was utterly intoxicated by her love for him.

'I'll just take the furs and food down to the beach. Nobody will be out there to see us now,' said Hywel. 'We will be safe enough.'

'I will give you a hand,' offered Owain, taking off his cloak and wrapping it about Nest before easily hefting one of the sacks Hywel had filled with furs and supplies to move it to where the waves broke on the sand. Hywel dropped the other sack next to it, and they both stared out to sea as the first stars started to appear and the moon began to rise like a vast silver orb.

'Why Hywel, of all the women in the world, did the one I love have to be someone else's wife?' Owain asked, not expecting an answer, and surprised when Hywel responded.

'At least you are together, lord, and she returns your love.'

'But at such cost. She loves her children, and when this first flush of passion is over, driven as much by being kept apart, will I be able to compete with her desire to be with them? As for me, I am an ambitious man. Will I start to resent giving up my lands, my wealth?'

'True love is worth such cost, Lord Owain.'

Owain looked at him sharply and gave a small bitter laugh.

'You speak like a man who has some experience. You have never married, have you?'

'No, lord,' Hywel replied, a faint flush rising from his neck.

Owain was silent for a while. He looked back at Nest. 'You are right, Hywel. The cost is worth it. The risk is worth it. I would give my life for her without thinking. I have had many women, but I have never felt like this before. I did not know such love existed. Yes, you speak truly. If you get such a chance, you must take it; otherwise, what is life about?'

The conversation had unsettled Hywel, and he was grateful to see a vessel nosing around the cliff's edge.

'The boat is coming, lord,' said Hywel waving his reed lamp at the skiff approaching the cove. Owain beckoned Nest forward, and as the boat neared the shore, he lifted her and waded to the vessel, putting her down inside and greeting the boat owner. Hywel collected the rest of the provisions and then divided the bread and cheese from one sack, taking it back half-filled to load onto the pack horse, tethered with his horse a little way into the wood. Should there be any questions, he wanted his story to seem plausible.

'God's speed to you both!' he called softly as the boat set out towards the tranquil open sea. As lapwings called their soulful cry from the water's edge, he watched the three figures grow smaller.

As the dark absorbed them, Hywel felt a melancholy descend upon him. With a heavy heart, he pulled himself together, retrieved the mounts, and headed back along the road, meandering along the side of the wood towards the llys. He hoped he could get back in without any questions. A deep sense of loneliness filled him as he reflected on the day and how Angharad had embraced him. Even now, he was still embarrassed by the stupidity of his reaction. How long had he ached with love for her? How long had he anguished with mental restraint, hiding his feelings?

He had seen her first when she was no more than a child, nubile and wide-eyed. Even back then, he had told himself that his hopes were not realistic, yet, when Gruffydd claimed her as his betrothed, it had hurt. It was a wound that would not heal. Now she was a rare beauty, but her real worth was not her appearance but the kindness and warmth which shone out of her like a beacon for everyone to see. He remembered how her head had rested on his shoulder as she slept in the boat on their way back from exile in Dublin. How, in the cold of the night, he had wrapped his cloak around her, and for a time, her cheek had touched his. He remembered how he had never wanted that moment to end. Yet, even then, he was torn by his sworn bond to a man who had given him every chance in life and saved him from certain death more than once. His thoughts returned to Owain and Nest. Owain, who had taken Nest, another man's wife, yet Nest had no love for her husband such as Angharad had for Gruffydd. Would she turn to Hywel for comfort and solace if anything happened to Gruffydd? Could she ever love him? He cursed himself for such thinking! It was not worthy.

He had reached the llys gate and called up for entry.

'You are late in,' said the sentry as the gates opened. Hywel swung down wearily from his horse, bringing the packhorse alongside.

'I took some provisions for the hunt, but they must have come in earlier than I thought. I followed their trail for a while but missed them somewhere.'

Across the courtyard, Hywel saw Gronwy's leading man at arms striding purposely towards him.

'What makes you so late back to the llys?' the man asked gruffly as if he were in charge there.

Hywel was irritated at his audacity, looked at him squarely and then forced a grin as he patted his packhorse.

'Not that it is any of your business, but I was bringing provisions to the hunt. I didn't find the hunt, but it was a dark wood on a moonlit night, and you might say I found other company.'

'Fair enough,' Gronwy's burly offsider accepted with a return grin and change of attitude. 'Have you seen anything suspicious out there? The Lord Owain ap Cadwgan and the Princess Nest are running from King Henry. There is a reward for those who bring them in.'

Hywel adopted a grave look. 'I have not seen anything suspicious.'

Burly grinned again, 'Too busy to notice if they walked right past you, I expect!'

Hywel grinned back and walked off into the stable as the heavy gates were closed and barred from the inside.

He could have asked one of the stableboys to sort out the horses. Still, there was something comforting about going through the familiar motions of removing the saddles and bridles, wiping the horses down to ensure they did not catch a chill, and had food and water. The stables smelled of fresh straw and were always kept scrupulously clean: cleaner than many places he had slept in. Tonight, the stalls were full because of Gronwy and Meilyr's visit, and the horses communicated with each other with grunts and whinnies, shuffling around in their allocated spaces. They were such intelligent animals and watched everything around them. He often marvelled that horses, which were used to extreme physical exercise, only needed about four hours of sleep at night.

'I wondered why you hadn't joined us for supper!' a thick voice broke through Hywel's reverie, and he turned sharply to see Lord Gronwy.

'Excuse me, Lord Gronwy. My thoughts were elsewhere.'

'Yes, I can just imagine where your thoughts were, and I am so sorry to interrupt them,' said Gronwy sarcastically.

'Lord?'

'You are your master's faithful man, are you not? Hywel, who is always so obliging, always at your master's side, always willing to serve. And yet I was confused, you see, because tonight, here we all were feasting, and there was no sign of you.'

Gronwy lurched closer, and Hywel kept himself calm. Had Gronwy guessed that he had been helping Owain and Nest? Could anyone have spotted them? He had been so careful. Surely not!

Gronwy poked a fat finger into Hywel's chest. Hywel's immediate reaction was to draw his blade, but he held himself in check. This was his queen's brother, and he had to be shrewd.

Gronwy saw how Hywel had flinched and continued relentlessly. 'Guilty, are you? I know all about you! I know what you were doing while we were on the hunt. At the time, I thought it was odd that you, Hywel, are held in such high esteem, yet you were not on the hunt. What could you have possibly been doing to prevent you from joining the hunt?'

His words were met with a shrug, and Hywel kept his voice even. 'I am sorry, Lord Gronwy, I am at a disadvantage. I do not know what you are talking about.'

Gronwy pulled a face and mimicked Hywel in a high voice. 'I am sorry, Lord Gronwy, I am at a disadvantage. What do you take me for, Hywel? A fool? Shall we ask my sister what you were doing while we were all at the hunt?'

Thoughts raced through Hywel's mind: Gronwy knew about Nest and Owain; Angharad was implicated and therefore in danger; Gronwy was unguarded, alone, and unsteady on his feet. There were no sounds of anyone in the courtyard. The stables had enough straw to cover a body in the short term.

'Ask our sister what?' a calm voice cut across the stables, and Hywel saw Meilyr silhouetted in the doorway.

Gronwy spun around unsteadily, spat, and pointed at Hywel.

'We should ask our sister what she has been doing behind her husband's back!'

Hywel opened his arms wide in confusion, his eyes huge with disbelief.

'This is the queen of Gwynedd you are talking about,' said Meilyr icily. 'Show respect to our sister.'

'A whore deserves no respect!'

Everything that Hywel had ever felt for Angharad, the never-ending agony of his unrequited love, boiled to the surface, and he sprang at Gronwy and, with a punch to his face, knocked him to the ground. In as swift a move as Meilyr had ever seen, Hywel had the sharp cold blade of his dagger against Gronwy's fleshy jowls.

'You are an animal,' he roared. 'How dare you speak such filth about my queen?'

Gronwy's breath was completely knocked out of him, but almost as swiftly, Meilyr took Hywel firmly by the arm and pulled him up.

'I must protect Lord Gronwy,' he said in an undertone, gripping Hywel's right wrist.

'And I must protect my queen,' said Hywel, eyes flashing, holding his knife firmly but shaking off Meilyr's grip.

'Ask him why he was not on the hunt and watch his face,' roared Gronwy, wiping the bloodied spittle from his mouth on the back of his hand. 'Then ask him what he was doing with two of Uchdryd's servants, riding with them into the wood. Ask him! Ask him who they were!'

He clambered to his feet but kept distance between himself and Hywel, his eyes pools of rage.

Meilyr turned again to Hywel, his eyes searching his face, but Hywel was concentrating on returning his knife to its pouch on his belt. Finally, Hywel looked up, holding the eyes of the man for whom, over the years, he had only the greatest respect. He spoke quietly, but the threat was clear.

'I will walk away now, Lord Meilyr, but let it be clear if there is any repeat of this nonsense, I will have no hesitation in finishing what was begun here. My honour is under attack, but the honour of my mistress is of greater import. As for Lord Uchdryd's servants, I offered them a seat on a horse for the beginning of their long journey home. If Lord Gronwy wants to question them, I am sure he can find them on the road back to Meirionnydd.'

Meilyr stood firm, his face grim. 'Let me deal with this but let me also be clear. From now on, no man lays a hand on my brother, Hywel, no matter our friendship over the years.'

'So be it, but my words stand.' Hywel strode out of the stable without a backward glance as Meilyr pushed his brother against the stable door, holding him there with a hand on his chest.

Meilyr waited until he was sure that Hywel was out of earshot. 'This time, you have gone too far, Gronwy. The drink has mastered your tongue. What are you trying to do here? Make enemies you can do without? You convinced me to hunt someone who was supposed to be our ally for the wrong done to Princess Nest. I was willing to be persuaded, but by God, I will not hear you accuse our sister so foully.'

Gronwy spat and glared at Meilyr.

'You are such mealy-minded shit! You have gone too far, brother and forget your place. I am the head of our family; I snap my fingers, and a hundred men are at my side. Our sister dishonours us. She lies with that scum, Hywel, mark my words, and when it suits me, this will come out. Then you will eat your fine words of honour, and that arsehole who calls himself King of Gwynedd will feel humiliation, I promise you!'

'This kind of talk will get us killed, Gronwy.'

'Really? Always so worried about your skin! They know more about Owain than they are telling us. Hywel is the key; if you had not interfered, I would have got to the bottom of it. This place stinks of whores and liars, and whores and liars stick together. I will find out, sister or no sister. I will see them left with nothing! Nothing, you hear me!'

***

The air was icy cold. Hywel could hear the laughter inside the hall, knew how warm it would be with the fire roaring and realised that he should report back to the king and queen regarding the safe sailing of Owain and Nest to Ireland. He had little desire to face anyone and less appetite to join in the frivolities.

His anger rose again as he thought of Gronwy, his foul accusations and the unjust words he had overheard as he stepped outside the stable into the cold night. He punched his fist into the dairy door. The purity of his love for his queen and his honour were the reason for his being, yet Gronwy had somehow tarnished both in his mind. He felt ashamed that he had often dreamt of holding Angharad in his arms. Hywel had never hated anyone, but now he found that he hated Lord Gronwy with all his heart. He imagined the satisfaction of drawing the dagger across Gronwy's throat and watching him gag to death. As a warrior, he had done this many times in battle but never from hatred, and he had always sent up prayers for those whose lives he had taken. In his mind, Gronwy was the incarnation of evil. He wondered if he had done enough to prevent Gronwy's foul mouth from causing hurt to Angharad and Gruffydd but knew that he must ignore Gronwy now or risk inciting outright conflict.

Hywel did not know how long he stood there in the dark, the cold biting through his cloak, but eventually, when the noise inside the hall subsided, he pulled himself together and faithfully, as always, made his way inside to give his report and warning. Gronwy and Meilyr were absent. He knew Meilyr would use his powers of persuasion to curtail his brother's intents. As Hywel entered the hall, Angharad's eyes sought his, and he gave an almost imperceptible nod. She smiled, and once again, his heart was firmly captured!

Chapter 8: Relationships (May 1110)

A May dawn was colouring the heavens with a rosy glow as Angharad opened her eyes to see her husband dressing at the end of the bed. She breathed a sigh of sheer contentment as she watched him tall, his broad shoulders strong above his narrow waist, the muscles of his body taut as when they had first met. He looked up and caught her eye, smiling.

'Go back to sleep! It is early.'

'Come back to bed; it is far too early!' she enticed him, gently propping herself on one elbow.

He came and lay beside her again, running his fingers through her thick hair.

'You are a temptress!'

She smiled up at him.

'Come under the covers.'

Her hand reached out for his, and she lifted her face to kiss his lips, her fingers running through the matted hair of his chest, then feeling the tight muscles of his stomach.

'I should go,' he muttered but reluctantly.

'You should not!'

His mouth was at her neck, and he moved the covers aside to kiss her breasts.

'What a fool I would be to leave your bed,' he whispered, and soon they were moving together, satisfying their desire.

Afterwards, they lay, deep in their own thoughts, her head on his shoulder, his firm arm around her as they listened to the early morning sounds of the household getting up to their duties, the sound of birds nesting in the roof above them, the pattering of mice somewhere in the thatch.

'I should go,' he sighed but made no move other than to brush her soft lips with his.

'Just a few more minutes. Let us just pretend that it is just us in a hunting lodge in the woods with no duties, no obligations, nobody to please but ourselves.'

He closed his eyes and sighed. 'Hmm, that would be nice.'

He gently kissed her forehead and asked, 'What are you thinking?'

'Oh, all sorts of things. I was thinking about Owain ap Cadwgan and the hunting lodge he hid in with Nest, hoping they could find heaven for a while. I feel so sorry for them. We should think ourselves fortunate. We have the children with us, and we have peace.'

'I thank the Lord for it daily and never forget that life is fragile. We might have lost everything by helping them.'

'But we did not, and it was the right thing to do.'

'Every risk we take ourselves affects not just our family but all our people.'

'I know.'

'Gronwy came so close to finishing us. I swear he was on the trail of Owain, trying to find Uchdryd's mysterious men. The way he was throwing money around for information, I felt sure something would come out of it.'

'Thank God for Hywel. He saved us.'

He nodded and looked down at her seriously as she sat straight-backed, her arms looping around her knees beneath the covers.

'How did Gronwy get wind of Uchdryd's servants? He knows much of our business before he should. I wonder if he has an informer here.'

'No, surely no one would do that. Why? You treat everyone fairly,' she protested.

'Someone who can gain something more than I can give them or am prepared to give,' he mused. 'We must keep our business to ourselves.'

'Of course. I am sure we are always discreet. I wish that sometimes we could be free of looking over our shoulders. Have you heard any more of Owain and Nest?'

'Since they came back from Ireland? Only that they are still hiding somewhere in the mountains. Nest has not returned to Gerald. Owain is causing all sorts of havoc on Norman-held lands.'

'And Uncle Uchdryd has avoided suspicion that he helped Owain?'

'Oh, there is plenty of suspicion, but he saved most of Owain's supporters. Many ended up with him and being supported by him; others found safety in Arwysth, some in Maelenydd. A few went to Dyfed, but Gerald of Windsor wanted their necks. Fortune smiled on them thankfully, and Gwalter, the high constable of Gloucester, who was in Carmarthen at the time, gave them protection. Maredudd ap Rhydderch also gave a few men haven in the Vale of Tywi.'

'So, all escaped?'

'Only those who decided to go to Arwystli met their deaths at the hands of the men of Maelenydd. Mind you, it is not surprising they were killed because only a few years ago, Owain killed Meurig and Griffri, the sons of Trahearn ap Caradog, whose lands were in Arwystli. It was because of some claim they were making against Powys.'

'So, it was vengeance. I would not wish death on anyone, but Meurig and Griffri were always talking about their claim on Gwynedd as well, through their father, weak as it was. I wondered if they had not been killed, if they might have taken up arms to try to wrest Gwynedd from you.'

'True indeed,' Gruffydd conceded gloomily. 'There are always those who would try to wrest our lands from us.'

Angharad gave a small sigh. 'Madog and Ithel would have been furious with Uncle Uchdryd.'

'They were indeed, but they could not touch him, did not dare touch him. It did not stop them causing destruction throughout Ceredigion and burning Cadwgan's stud with all the buildings. Bishop Richard gave them their reward. They now have Southern Powys, so they have done all right out of it. Gronwy is very sore at that, I hear. For all his efforts at tracking down Owain, he got nothing.'

'Gronwy is openly looking for opportunities to get more land, and he has no love for us.'

'I keep an eye on Gronwy, don't you worry. Just as he seems to know what we are doing, so I have an idea of what he is doing.'

Angharad gave a little shiver. She ran her hand over his arm, seeing the old familiar scars. 'And Cadwgan, what of him?'

'Cadwgan pays a price for his son's attacks against the Normans and Flemings. King Henry 'allowed' Cadwgan to gain Ceredigion back from Madog and Ithel on the condition of his living in his Norman wife's manor, paying a hundred pounds to the English crown, and keeping Owain under control.'

'As if Cadwgan could keep Owain under control.'

'Yes, Owain cannot be tamed. Yet, when I hear about Owain's attacks on the Normans and the Flemings, I am delighted. It makes my blood boil that King Henry dispenses with Welsh lands as if the territories were his. Those men from Flanders come in and displace the rightful Welsh owners. Henry is even trying to settle Flemings in Rhos.'

'I thought there was a cooling of relationships between King Henry and Count Robert of Flanders, so why is Henry encouraging the Flemish to settle in Welsh lands?'

'Not so much new Flemings but ones already in England. Do not forget that Mathilda of Flanders was the wife of William the Conqueror and King Henry's mother, so many of the noble families from Flanders were already coming to England in her time. They were all given lands for their efforts, but they bred, and there is always pressure on Henry to keep providing for their offspring. Then, many Flemish mercenaries provided to William from Flanders, also settled in England.'

'I heard a story that Queen Mathilda was tiny, only four foot two inches tall, and that when Willliam the Conqueror sought her hand in marriage, she sent word to him that she was too high born. Apparently, he rode to her in fury and pulled her off her horse by her plaits, and after that, they fell madly in love.'

'Well, marry her he did, and now one of Henry's problems is that he has too many Flemish in England and not enough land to keep them from causing trouble, so what better solution than to send them to Wales to control the troublesome Welsh.'

'We would all be less troublesome if everybody left us in peace.'

'Well, Cariad, we have had more peaceful years in Gwynedd than I expected, and if we are wise with our alliances, keep ourselves well-armed and well-informed, and have enough money in the treasury, maybe we can have many more such years. I am not progressing with any of those safeguards while you keep luring me to bed.' His tone was slightly mocking, but he smiled broadly as he threw back the covers and stretched.

'Rubbish, you are working on your alliances,' Angharad laughed, forming her hair into a thick, tidy plait as she slipped her long legs out of bed. She watched as her husband pulled on his supple calf hide boots and his leather jerkin over the moss-green linen tunic. He saw her studying him.

'Are you gauging whether I am still strong enough to protect you?' he asked, his head on one side and a pretend frown on his brow.

'You would protect us all to your dying breath,' she smiled, shaking her head.

He strode over to her and brushed her cheek with the back of his hand while kissing her on the top of her head. Her hair smelt of some sweet herb that reminded him of sun-filled meadows in summer. She looked up at him with the easy smile he loved so much, her eyes sparkling in the softness of her face.

'I suppose you know how much I love you,' she said huskily.

'And I suppose you know how much I love you,' he grinned, closing his eyes to kiss her lips one last time before the day began in earnest.

***

Within the hour, the routines of the day were absorbing their lives. The rattle, clanking and thudding of the men at arms practising weapon training in the yard was interspersed with cries of protest or laughter. Gruffydd and his principal advisors were dispensing justice inside the Great Hall. The kitchens were already bustling to provide fare for a feast to which local dignitaries had been invited, and the courtyard was busy with servants. Cows were being milked, butter churned, and cheese was being made. Water was being carried from the well in big wooden buckets, and some servants were building up the fire for the spits, which would be turned throughout the day with the venison and sweet mutton fed on grasses near the estuary.

Angharad went to the kitchen, where steam billowed from cauldrons already hung over the fire, and the smell of baking bread was mouth-watering. A sweet-faced girl was concentrating hard on making little pastries filled with onions or meat while her mother made the steamed puddings everyone loved so much. Confident that all was in order, Angharad made her way out to the stables, where her four older children were already mounted. She was taking them to see the progress of a new church they were building out of stone.

Clouds scudded across the sky, white and fluffy, creating shadows on the land and sea ahead. Angharad looked at her children proudly: a mother's eye would always see the best, but her children really were strong and good-looking. Gwenllian in her new russet cloak, hair flickering bright copper in the sunlight; Cadwallon in a deep blue cloak and new long black riding boots; Owain, in pale green, sitting straight and easy in the saddle; and Cadwaladr in a pale blue cloak with matching cloth hat over his unruly hair. They needed to look their best as they were representing the Royal House of Aberffraw.

'Look, Mother, daffodils,' pointed Gwenllian excitedly. Clumps of yellow blooms were growing near the edge of a small thicket where catkins blew in the breeze.

'Oh,' Angharad breathed out in delight, 'spring is truly here.'

Owain whooped and cantered across to the flowers, leaping off his horse and collecting an armful. He rode back grinning broadly and, with a considerable flourish, presented them to his mother.

'For the Queen of Gwynedd from her loving son!'

Cadwaladr rolled his eyes at Cadwallon and Gwenllian, but Gwenllian just laughed and gave him a poke in the ribs.

'First to spot a skylark,' shouted Gwenllian.

'Too easy,' said Cadwallon pointing up at the sky, 'a chaffinch!'

'A chaffinch's nest!' returned Cadwaladr. 'At least make it a bit difficult!'

'Right then, a wren's nest, with eggs!' countered Gwenllian, and the three rode to the edge of the woods, where they looked among the bushes and trees for a wren's nest.

Owain hung back with his mother, still smiling at her reaction to the flowers. He watched as his siblings competed over the finding of the nest.

'Gwenllian will know exactly where to find a wren's nest,' he confided. 'We were out here the other day and saw one, she and I.'

'But you did not beat her back to the spot?'

'No, let her enjoy her little victory, but if she knows I know and I say nothing, then another time she will keep something important to me a confidence.'

Angharad smiled at the mixture of maturity and childishness her son was demonstrating. Their horses had found a clover patch and were munching happily at the green leaves much loved by wood mice. The pinky-red rounded heads would appear in a few weeks, lasting all summer and attracting bumblebees seeking nectar. Angharad remembered how Hywel had told her that he regularly allowed his horse to graze on wild clover, believing it increased speed and energy. She smiled.

'I love this time of the year when the woods are in bud,' she mused out loud.

'Father spent a whole morning with Cadwallon and me last week, explaining the importance of woodland to Gwynedd,' said Owain, lifting his face towards the sky, eyes closed to absorb the sun's heat.

'What did you learn?'

'That woodland was more than just fuel and that, for many people, their survival depends on it. He talked about how tools and household items were crafted from wood; how important wood was for buildings, and brushwood for our fires. Then he talked about using bark for leather tanning and how local people depended on a good supply of resin and turpentine.'

'And the food we find in the woodlands.'

'Yes, nuts, berries, mushrooms, honey, acorns for feeding pigs, and the animals we hunt: deer, wild boar, hares, martens, squirrels, and so on.'

'And did he talk about the lord's responsibility for the woodland?'

'Of course. He always talks about the lord's responsibility and reminds us that we should always take care of our lands so that our lands take care of us.'

Angharad smiled. Despite always being busy, Gruffydd still found time to teach the children things important to their community's smooth running.

'We are fortunate that there is so much woodland here,' she commented before asking, 'Did your father speak of the laws of Hywel Dda concerning the king's forest?'

'Yes, he told us how the laws valued trees at different prices and that the oak was the most expensive, being worth two cows. He told us that the laws allow any man to cut wood, even from the king's forests, for church roofs, spear shafts for use for the king, funeral byres and if anyone should see an animal darting into the wood, they could follow it and kill it.'

Angharad was pleased that Owain had memorised everything so well, but she knew he had an incredible memory.

'Also,' he continued, his face serious, 'he told us that the laws say that no brother is allowed to clear woods belonging to another brother without yielding him wood equal to that cleared by him.'

'You have learnt well. Do you understand why we should know the laws of Hywel Dda?'

'Yes, of course, Mother. If we did not have laws, there would be disorder. Nobody would know what they could or could not do, and everybody's property, and even lives, would be at risk.'

'Quite right. The law is one of the most important pieces of learning handed down to us from the wisest in the land. You have remembered well. Did your father talk about how the Welsh treat the woods and forests differently compared with the Normans?'

'Yes, he explained about Bernard de Neufmarche establishing a forest in 1093 on the lands owned by Princess Nest's father Rhys ap Tewdwr, and that anyone using those woods or hunting there, other than the lord and those he permits to join him, will be severely punished.'

Angharad's mind was cast back to when she had heard of the death of Rhys ap Tewdwr. Gruffydd had gone to Rhys to warn him about the Normans encroaching on his land. Rhys had not listened or wanted to believe it, and suddenly, he was a victim of the push from the Norman Marcher Lords. His young daughter Nest was taken to the English court while his elder son, Griffith ap Rhys, had fled to Ireland.'

'Mother?' came Owain's voice, disturbing her reverie.

'Yes?'

'Is it true that Bethan's Rhys is Uncle Gronwy's son?'

'Why do you ask?'

'In temper with Cadwallon, Rhys brought it up. He said his father had as much claim on Gwynedd as ours. Is he telling the truth?'

'Well, he is Uncle Gronwy's son, but I think Bethan would prefer that it was kept quiet. He should have thought about his mother's feelings before saying that.'

'And the other bit? The bit about his claim on Gwynedd?'

'No, that is not true. Your father is the rightful king of Gwynedd, descended directly from Rhoddri Mawr and, after that, Hywel the Good who made our laws. Your grandfather, Owain ap Edwin, had a weaker claim but was also descended from the royal house of Mercia.'

He nodded, but Angharad could see him chewing at his lip.

'Rhys said that one day Uncle Gronwy would stand up for the right to the whole of Gwynedd.'

'Uncle Gronwy is an ambitious man, but your father's men are stronger, and your father works hard to be a good king. His people love him, and he tries hard to please them.'

'How? How does he please them?'

'Well, like the church we are seeing today, for example. He is building a fine new church for the people. He makes sure there is money to repair bridges or the port or to invest in things which will bring money to Gwynedd through trade. He makes fair decisions in disputes and is not unfair with taxes and renders.'

Owain nodded again, his eyes distant. 'You taught us that Gruffydd ap Llewelyn was betrayed by his people because he did not treat them all the same and was greedy.'

'Yes, that's true.'

'So that is why we travel from llys to llys in different parts of our lands, ensuring we meet the people and get to know what they are worrying about.'

Angharad was stunned at the way he seemed to understand so much. He was still a child.

'That is also true, but we try hard not to impose too much on any maerdref. Each maerdref or, if you like, administrative area, provides all the food for our family and those who travel with us while we are in the llys. That is why we try not to spend more time at one than another.'

'Yes, I know. Hywel explained that to us when we were talking about how the maerdref have mountain pastures they look after, where the cattle graze, and that it is important to protect those pastures and the herds.'

The other children were racing back now, Gwenllian in the lead on her snowy pony, her voice ringing out as she scorned her slower brothers on their darker mounts.

'Mother,' continued Owain, looking at her quizzically, 'Rhys is always asking if we have seen or heard of Owain ap Cadwgan or Princess Nest. Why is he so interested in them? What exactly have they done?'

Gwenllian drew in her pony and breathlessly thrust some violets at her mother, who smiled broadly and arranged them with the daffodils, letting her reins rest gently on her old but faithful mare, Seren.

'Are you talking about Princess Nest?' the girl asked, eyes brimming with excitement.

Angharad gave a little frown and wondered what best to say. The children heard much from listening to the chatter around the llys, so she took a breath and tried to explain as simply as possible.

'Princess Nest was betrothed to Owain ap Cadwgan but taken by the Normans to an English court when her father was killed. There she met Henry, who is now King of England. She had a child by him, Henry FitzHenry. King Henry arranged for her to be married to another Norman, Gerald of Windsor, and they too had children together. Owain had never forgotten Princess Nest, and she still loved him, so Owain decided to take her from her husband, and they chose a life together. King Henry was furious at Owain because he had taken his friend's wife and his son. Princess Nest persuaded Owain to send her children back to her husband and Henry to his father, but King Henry still wants revenge, so he has men hunting down Owain for a reward.'

'Is that why Rhys keeps asking us?' asked Owain. 'He wants the reward?'

'Maybe, but Owain is hidden somewhere in the mountains with many men following him and supporting him, so he would be hard to catch, even if Rhys had such a will.'

'I heard he fights the Normans and takes their cattle and valuable things,' said Cadwallon.

Angharad paused before replying. 'He fights the Normans and the Flemings, whom the Normans brought to Wales, because he believes that Wales should belong to the Welsh.'

'Does he have a llys in the mountains?' asked Cadwaladr.

'I would expect it is just a camp, not a llys. Maybe some caves.'

Gwenllian's eyes widened, 'And Princess Nest lives with him there, under the stars in the mountain, and helps him to make raids on the

Normans?'

'I do not think Princess Nest fights, Gwenllian. I think she just supports him in his camp.'

'Ah,' declared Gwenllian, eyes burning, 'if I were Princess Nest, I would take my sword and go with him to fight the Normans, the Flemings, and everyone else trying to steal Wales from the Welsh. We are the Britons of old and have the right to the land.'

'Sometimes you are so stupid,' scoffed Cadwallon, blue eyes narrowing. 'No girl is going to win anything in a proper fight. You only win against us because we are being kind to our sister.'

Out of the corner of his eye, he saw a movement as Gwenllian sprung catlike out of her saddle. With a thud and a cry, she and Cadwallon were wrestling on the ground. He showed no mercy for his sister now as he punched her in the ribs, but she hit him in the throat and kneed him in the crotch as he pulled at her hair. The pair were twisting, punching, and shrieking at each other when their mother's stern voice cut through their anger. It was a voice to be obeyed.

'Stop, this moment. How dare you behave in this unseemly fashion.' Her face was drained of colour, her eyes blazing with suppressed fury.

Gwenllian tore free of her brother's grip, and he sat bent double with pain but with a fistful of Gwenllian's red mane in hand.

'Gwenllian, you have behaved like an animal, and Cadwallon, I would have expected so much better from you. Both of you are banned from the practice yard until I am satisfied you know how to behave.'

'Noooo!' Gwenllian let out an agonised wail, her whole body trembling with emotion. 'Please do not do that, please do not. I am sorry, Cadwallon and I are sorry, see!'

The wretched girl flung her arms around her brother, hissing, 'Say you are sorry, say it!' in her brother's ear.

Her mother's voice was icy cold. 'Do you understand the importance of family? There is enough fighting in the world without sister and brother attacking each other. My punishment stands, and you will conduct yourselves with decorum until I am certain you understand.'

'But ....'

Her mother's warning look was enough to silence her daughter and dampen Owain and Cadwaladr's enthusiasm for the spectacle which had unfolded. She looked at her children, their cloaks filthy from the dirt, Cadwallon's face bloodstained, and Gwenllian's rosy from a bruise spreading across her cheek. Gwenllian held her head where her hair had been yanked out, and though her eyes brimmed with tears, her jaw was set determinedly so that they would not drop.

'Fetch your ponies and ride behind.'

'But I am firstborn,' protested Cadwallon, 'I should not be behind the others.

'Firstborn you may be, but your attitude and words have far to go before you will do justice to the title Heir to Aberffraw.'

The two children stomped off to get their ponies which had skittered away from the commotion and were now grazing a few feet away.

'You will see that I will fight for Wales as well as any man,' muttered Gwenllian to her brother as she mounted her pony and turned back towards the others, 'and I will not practise in the yard, but that doesn't stop us fighting each other on the beach!'

'With pleasure,' her brother returned with a low growl.

Gwenllian shook her copper hair out, wiped her face on the inside of her cloak and scratched at the dirt on the cloak's outside, then, with the most innocent of looks, trotted meekly behind her mother. One day, she decided, she would camp in the mountains, leading her troops down to fight the foreigners: she would make Wales strong. Until she was old enough to fend for herself, she would learn everything she could about fighting, war, and how to lead people. She would be learned and loved, known for being fair. She could see her mistake that morning: never disclose your weakness to the enemy.

Meanwhile, Cadwallon fumed. Pain coursed through his body from his sister's blows, and his tongue was bloody where he had bitten it as Gwenllian had launched herself on top of him. He closed his eyes as he thought of how ashamed he was that his sister had got the better of him in front of his mother and siblings. It was never going to happen again. He would practise harder and more, watch for her weakness, and put her in her place.

Chapter 9: Freedom (May 1110)

With long robes swishing expensively as he glided along, Bishop Richard wrinkled his nose against the stench. Long, gloomy, damp corridors led to his destination. The two soldiers in front, guiding the way with rush lights, looked as if they had not seen daylight for some while. They were grim-faced, stoutly built, and the bishop wondered whether guarding prisoners was a punishment for them also. Shadows jerked over the stone walls in time with the stamping of their heavy boots and the clinking of keys around their waists against their metal chain mail, shining when the light reflected on it. Bishop Richard wondered if they spent the long hours doing little, cleaning their chain mail with vinegar and sand: a thankless task!

'This one,' said one of the guards stopping abruptly.

The two men had halted at a small door of solid wood and iron, and the stockier of the two, whom Bishop Richard now saw had a scar from below his left eye to the left corner of his lip, fumbled with the bunch of keys until he found the right one. He opened the door, and a worse stench washed over them. The bishop put his hand over his nose and peered into the space ahead of him, where the figure of a man was slumped against the far wall. He asked one of the guards, a pock-faced lugubrious fellow, to accompany him inside with a rushlight and ordered the other to wait outside but to keep the door open.

'Iorwedd ap Bleddyn, it is some years since we have met.'

The prisoner peered myopically at the sprightly figure before him, keeping a dignified distance. As his eyes became accustomed to the sudden brightness, recognition came to him. All the bile he had been storing up for so many years, all his hatred rushed to the surface. He gave a toothless grin, leant his head back against the cell's cold, moist wall, and, with a voice grating from lack of use, welcomed his visitor. 'Bishop Richard. Great promiser of all things good. Forgive me if I do not get up. What tidings have you for me?' he said sourly, closing his eyes.

'That depends upon your willingness to agree to certain conditions.'

The prisoner did not even open his eyes. He gave a long sigh and then started to speak words he had imagined speaking to the bishop a thousand times when he had roamed the darkness of his cell.

'Conditions, you say. I was promised by King Henry himself that I would be lord of half of the Britons. Powys was to be mine; Ceredigion was to be mine; Ystrad Tywi was to be mine, and Gower and Cydwelli. What a King I should have been! All I had to do, King Henry and you said, was to break up the alliance between Powys and Robert Belleme. And I did. I betrayed my brothers Cadwgan and Maredudd for King Henry and for you.'

'Wait! You took your brothers' lands and all the chattels Belleme had hidden in Powys. Have you forgotten?'

The prisoner gave a hollow chuckle. 'Yes, I remember now. King Henry gave me my brothers' lands. A foreign king gave me my brothers' own lands, but what he promised me, all of what was promised that hot summer, I was never given. By the autumn, by the end of that September, I had given Henry the biggest prize of all, Belleme. But how did Henry thank me? He gave me what was already in the hands of my family: Powys and Ceredigion, and I shared what was already theirs with my brothers. You see, you are mistaken. I did not take their lands.'

'That was your choice.'

Iorwedd's eyes opened quickly, and he blinked hard. 'My choice but not a choice that satisfied Henry, so he asked me to hand over my brother Maredudd to him as a hostage. He asked that we all work towards stability and peace, and I had little choice in the matter. But where was the promised Southern part of Dyfed? Where was the promised Ystrad Tywi? Where were the promised Gower and Cydweli? Not in my hands. No, a

Norman, the knight Sear was given Pembroke, and Ystrad Tywi was given to Hywel ap Goronwy.'

'Neither of whom has those lands now!'

Iorwedd snorted. 'Yes, I remember. Another promise that King Henry reneged on. Knight Sear was removed in favour of Gerald of Windsor so that Princess Nest, Henry's lover, could sleep in Welsh lands with her new Norman husband. And Hywel ap Gronwy, what of him?'

'Welsh treachery. He was a scoundrel who burnt the houses and crops of Norman subjects in Ystrad Tywi. Hywel ap Goronwy's close friend and foster father to one of his sons, Gwgan ap Meurig, was so lured by Norman gold that he invited Hywel to his home in Carmarthen, removed Hywel's sword and spear while he slept and sent word to the Normans who surrounded the village at dawn. Hywel escaped only to be caught by his 'friend' and given over to the Normans, who beheaded him. Another Welsh king betrayed by his own!'

'You say he was a scoundrel who burnt the houses and crops of Norman subjects in Ystrad Tywi? Bishop, they were the lands of *his* subjects, the very lands he was 'given' by King Henry.'

'Well, those lands are now Richard Fitz Baldwin's, who brought his tenants to take over the lands and rebuild the castle of Rhyd y Gors in Carmarthen. The lands are faring better than under Hywel.'

'So you say!'

Bishop Richard snorted contemptuously, 'Hywel ap Goronwy died over five years ago, helped to his death by his Welsh enemies, do not forget. Do you think going over all this old ground is helping your cause?'

Iorwedd had waited so long for a chance to rail against his plight, and he would not stop now.

'Helping my cause? Am I to make another pact with the Devil and betray my kin again? Is that it? For what? Do you think I forget that your king gave me a fine invitation to his court, an invitation I could not refuse, an invitation which suggested he was to anoint me with such blessings? Yet the fine invitation was as sincere as Gwgan ap Meurig's. Yes, if it pleases you, I acknowledge the Welsh can be deceitful too, but it is easier to forgive your own! Now I find myself here, eating slops, shackles if I complain, never seeing the light, pissing and defecating into a bucket that spills over filthy and foul.'

'You did not keep to your bargain.'

'I did not?' Iorwedd spat. 'I did not? What lies. Henry made promises and reneged on them. Henry's objective was not peace but to set brother against brother, thus eliminating the power of Powys so that he could march in and take everything.'

'If that is what King Henry wanted, he would have done so long before now.'

'Then why does he leave me festering here? Seven years I am told I have been here! Even Maredudd has long since returned to Powys from his incarceration, and I, who have done nothing to seriously offend my neighbour king, still lie with mice for bedmates and cockroaches for companions.'

The bishop was close to gagging from the stink. He wanted to be in the fresh air away from this man with his list of woes, the sores on his arms and legs, the cracked lips and threadbare rags.

'I am not here to argue with you, Iorwedd. Are you interested in liberty or not?'

Iorwedd looked suspiciously at the bishop whose calm, icy eyes penetrated the gloom and, using the wall behind him, he raised himself shakily to his full height. He was skeletal, a shadow of the warrior he once was, but there was a flicker of hope now in the deep dark pits of his eyes. He sometimes thought of the caress of the silk he had worn, the waft of tender roast meat, the smell of fine soft leather boots, the rush of excitement as he galloped his proud bay to hawk, the sound of the sharp steel in his hand cutting through the air. He could hardly believe that his life had ever been thus. 'Despite everything, despite my distrust, I am too weak to wave you away. Yes, Bishop Richard, I want my freedom.'

'I will make arrangements, and we will discuss this further, but understand you are our man now, Iorwedd, and you report to us,' said the bishop abruptly, his robes swirling around as he retreated down the corridor. He heard the guard slam the cell door, bolts sliding home to shut in the filth and stench and the prisoner pawn.

Inside the darkness, Iorwedd walked slowly around his cell, using his right hand to guide him along the damp walls he knew so intimately. How he dreamt of the green fertile fields of Powys, the craggy snow-topped mountains, a lover's touch. He shuddered. What lover would kiss his toothless mouth, not feel revulsion at his wasted flesh? His bile rose again as he thought of King Henry and how that Norman swine had turned him from one of the foremost warriors in Wales into little more than a maggot. He was wracked with coughing and had to stop his progress around his domain.

Footsteps were coming along the corridor, and Iorwedd turned his head to one side, wondering if they would stop at his door. They marched on past. He sighed, and something made him remember William Pantulf, the two-faced Norman bastard from Hell. Pantulf had convinced Iorwedd to back Henry, to fight Henry's battle. Let him rot in Hell!

He sat back on the filthy floor and remembered how proud he, Iorwedd, the wheeler of swords, had been, ravaging Shropshire for Henry, knowing that he would be the true lord of the lands Robert Belleme, Earl of Shrewsbury, and his brother Arnulf, claimed to be theirs: Powys, Ceredigion, and half of Dyfed. Well, pride comes before a fall, they say. How generous he had been with his brothers sharing the lands. Yet, how he had lusted over Ystrad Tywi, Cydweli, and Gower, the lands Henry promised to him but gave to Hywel ap Goronwy. How stupid he had been then as Bishop Richard had started to screw him down. He had given his own brother as hostage for peace, something he regretted every day. Poor Maredudd had gone smiling, trusting Iorwedd, thinking he would be treated with honour.

Iorwedd gave a hollow laugh as he remembered how suddenly, in 1103, he was arraigned before the royal tribunal in Shrewsbury, not a tribunal of Welsh princes, no, rather by a foreign prince exacting loyalty and money from an impotent neighbour. A Norman, scoffing at a weak, gullible neighbour. Now what was he, Iorwedd, Prince of Powys, going to do to smell the sea air and see a land so beautiful it hurt? To rid himself of the lice which bedded in his tattered rags, his hair, and the filthy crevices of his skinny body, he was going to sell his soul once again.

As Bishop Richard walked into the fresh air, he stopped and looked up at the sky. It looked dark and ominous. He knew he should hurry, or he would be drenched. The boy who held his horse ran over, and he gave him a coin before pulling himself into the saddle. He had not enjoyed being in the filthy prison, which had assaulted his senses, but he was pleased with his work. He had listened to Iorwedd's rambles and assured himself he was not entirely mad after his long years in that place. He would suffice for the job he had in mind.

Still running through his plan, the bishop started down the hill at a smart trot when suddenly the earth shuddered. His horse skittered sideways, and birds flew into the air, startled. Dogs began howling, and huts fell in a heap before him as other wooden dwellings crashed to the ground.

In his cell, Iorwedd felt the shaking, and his chains rattled. A chill ran through him as he wondered if the building would tumble on top of him, but the movement subsided. He held himself against the wall and experienced a wave of nausea. What was the meaning of it? Had the Welsh dragons been unleashed under the earth? He knew that whenever the dragons fought, it was a sign of bloodshed to come. Whose blood would spill?

All over Shrewsbury, people ran into the streets crying and screaming, terrified by the shaking and the darkened sky. An earthquake had hit Shropshire.

***

Owain pulled aside the leather curtain hanging over the doorway of the tiny dwelling that smelled of rot and watched the cold relentless rain sleeting across their camp. He leaned against the doorframe, bare-chested, and spat out into the cold. On a pile of woollen blankets in the corner of the hut, slumped against the damp wall, was Princess Nest, hollow-eyed, pale, and shivering, despite the fur cloak wrapped around her skinny frame. She leaned over suddenly and vomited bile into a bucket by the makeshift bed. Owain grimaced as he listened to her retch and retch. Finally, she leant back, eyes closed, shaking uncontrollably. He felt exasperated and trapped. He knew she needed him to show his love for her, but he felt only the distraction from what he needed to do. He had left behind him the gentle lovemaking, laughter, and intimate conversations in the comfort of the Irish Court: here, he had men who looked to him for their survival. Here, he had a country to win back; for that, his mind had to be clear.

He let the leather flap drop and moved across the gloomy room to the small fire, prodding it with a stick and throwing a log on top of the coals spitting as the rain leaked through the thatch. He picked up a blanket from a pile in the corner and warmed it by the fire before gently tucking it over Nest's tunic inside the fur cloak. He sat heavily on the rugs beside his lover, but she averted her eyes.

'I am sorry,' she whispered. 'I have not been right since we sailed from Ireland. I am not usually so sick when I am carrying a child.'

'You cannot stay here, Nest. You won't survive.'

'Give me a few days only, and I am sure I will be myself.'

'Nest, my love, it makes it hard for me to lead my men and fight as I must, while I worry if someone may betray us and come to you when I am gone.'

She closed her eyes and felt tears pricking the lids, threatening to spill over. She knew she had to pull herself together despite feeling so wretched. She pushed up with her skinny arms and steeled herself.

'Owain, I am not going back to Ireland without you.'

'Gruffydd and Angharad, then.'

'No, Owain, I stay here with you until you win back your land, and we have a proper home.'

They were interrupted by the sound of voices outside, alerting them to a visitor. Owain jumped up and grabbed his sword from the sheath resting against the door frame. He pulled the leather curtain back and ducked his head outside.

'Ieuan, come inside man,' he called welcomingly. 'You look drenched.'

Nest pulled the fur cloak more tightly around her as a stocky, pale-faced man with thin brown hair plastered around his face came in out of the cold. His clothes were dripping and filthy with the mud he had ridden hard through to come with the news. He bowed his head to the woman in the corner and looked awkwardly at Owain.

'Sit down,' said Owain, indicating a couple of stools near the fire. He went to a roughly assembled table, carved a couple of thick slices of beef, put a chunk of bread on a platter and thrust it towards the tired rider.

'Thanks to the Flemings.' Owain indicated the meat with a smile of bravado. 'One of the cows they let me borrow did not make it!'

He gave the man a little time to eat and poured him some ale. Then he said phlegmatically, 'Well, spit it out. You did not ride hard through all this rain to bring me good news.'

Nest looked alarmed, and Owain raised his hand to her to be patient.

'Iorwedd ap Bleddyn, your uncle, has been released from prison by Bishop Richard, who has made him ruler of Powys.'

Owain leaned back on his stool, stretched, and scratched his head as he kept a rein on his emotions. This he had not expected, and he felt sick to the stomach.

'My uncle Iorwedd,' he sighed, 'was my idol once. He could make a sword dance, kill an enemy swifter than he could blink, but the Normans played with his nerve. He betrayed my father and my uncle Maredudd, you know.'

'I remember it,' Ieuan nodded.

'All three of them were siding with Belleme in his revolt, and they would have been victors but for the slippery-tongued uncle who persuaded them to change sides. And then? Then Maredudd was given as hostage by Iorwedd, and if it had not been for some neat sidestepping by my father, it would have been my father in prison in Shrewsbury, not Iorwedd. So, why have they let the old dog out?'

'To hurt you. The Normans are saying you are everywhere: Ceredigion, Meirionnydd, Cyfeliog, Dyfed, and wherever you are, there is fear and destruction.'

Owain grinned broadly, 'Oh, for once, the Normans speak the truth!'

'They want Iorwedd to get rid of you, but on the day they let him out, an earthquake hit Shrewsbury, and the people of Powys are saying it is a sign.'

Owain lifted his brow. 'An omen.'

'The Welsh on the border say it is the red dragon moving.'

'A red dragon moving. It needs to move in these times,' commented Owain remembering the legend of the two dragons, one red and one white, who would fight under the earth. 'So, they let him out of prison just to chase me? No, I do not think that would be the only reason.'

'He had to pay three hundred pounds to King Henry, which he can give in oxen or horses or whatever amounts to that much, and he had to give up the sons of different lords. Your father's son, Henry, by his Norman wife, was one of them sent to the English Court as a hostage.'

'Henry is welcome to the little shit!'

'But your father Cadwgan has paid a hundred pounds to get him back.'

Owain laughed mirthlessly, 'That is a waste of a hundred pounds. Henry would have paid my father a hundred pounds to fetch him if he had left him there a week. The little turd is as manipulative as his namesake, the king. You see, this is where we Welsh have it all wrong. We are paying Henry to allow us back onto our own lands. We are giving him the authority he doesn't have, and the more authority you give, the more likely he will continue to behave as if this is his land to dispense with as he will.'

Ieuan puffed his cheeks and blew out, his brown bloodshot eyes soulful, 'Flemings are farming the land that was mine by right. Henry sent them there, and they drove my family out.'

Owain spat into the fire. 'Well, we will give them a taste of their own medicine because that sort of story gives me a fury which will not abate.'

Ieuan grinned. His eyes shone as they reflected the firelight.

'Madog and Ithel have been causing trouble for Henry as well,' he said as Owain cut him another generous portion of Flemish beef.

'Well, that doesn't surprise me. As they say, if you lie with dogs, you get fleas.'

'They have been raiding the Normans in Wales and into England as well. Their warband increases with young men who have no land because of the Normans and are out for vengeance and booty.'

'As we are!'

'Bishop Richard has requested Madog to turn his followers over to the English crown, but he refuses, of course.'

'He has more balls than my uncle then.'

'Well, I do not know about that. Your uncle is determined to bring law to Powys. He is pulling together his old warband and has been told by Henry that he must seek out all the troublemakers.'

'And my father?'

'Your father, Cadwgan, pays money to Henry and is told to keep you out of trouble.'

Owain sighed. 'My father is old. If he joined me, we could eliminate the lot of them, Normans, Flemings, all the foreigners who take our land. Sadly, his heart is not in the fight: he thinks only of drinking and whoring, and I hear he is too old even for that now.'

When Ieuan had left Owain to join the rest of the band in the makeshift hut they had crafted to provide shelter, Owain moved across to Nest and took her face gently in his hand.

'My love, you heard what Ieuan had to say. My Uncle Iorwedd is no fool. He knows the mountains better than I do, and he can find us, especially if you are with me. You will not mean to, but you will slow me down.'

She looked searchingly into his face. 'What then?'

He cradled her head against his chest and swallowed, 'I see only one solution.'

Chapter 10: Fighting (May 1110)

The sounds of the practice yard were torturing Cadwallon and Gwenllian. They tried to focus on their Latin while their mother calmly embroidered a silver lion on the collar of a fine grey tunic.

'Mother,' said Cadwallon finally, when he could stand it no more, 'you have made Latin a punishment for us, but I thought you wanted us to love learning.'

Gwenllian looked earnestly at the parchment before her, but her lips twitched with merriment at the mischief in his voice.

Their mother lifted her long lashes and looked at Cadwallon coolly from beneath them. Gwenllian noticed a softening around her mouth. 'I cannot make you love Latin; that is up to you. I cannot teach you wisdom, that is up to you, but I will ensure you are not wasting your time.'

Gwenllian watched Cadwallon's calculating blue eyes above his high cheekbones, knowing he would not leave it there. He cleared his throat and assumed an air of what he considered was reasonableness.

'Mother, my duty as your firstborn is to protect you, my family, my teulu, and my subjects. While Owain and Cadwaladr are out there gaining valuable skills, I am here, slaving over a language that is not even my own.'

'But it is the language which will allow you to gain knowledge, and knowledge, my son, is the way to wisdom.'

Cadwallon gave a heavy sigh of exasperation but could not see how to win this war of wits.

'Mother,' tried Gwenllian, 'we really are sorry. You can see how sorry we are; after all, it was my fault. Will you let Cadwallon go back to the practice yard? Just punish me.'

'Well, Gwenllian,' said Angharad slowly, 'that is very generous of you. I will not allow Cadwallon to return to his training yet, but I will let him leave the room to watch what the others are doing. As for you, Gwenllian, you will stay here with me for a while.'

'Thank you, Mother,' said Cadwallon, leaving as hastily as he could, 'thank you, Gwenllian.'

'Thank you, Mother,' said Gwenllian, somewhat subdued as her tactic had not worked quite as she expected. She bit her lip.

'Gwenllian, put down your pen and listen to me for a moment,' said Angharad carefully. 'You are ten now and have already started your courses.'

The girl flushed deeply and looked down.

'Do not be embarrassed. It is a wonderful thing, which means that you are on your way to being a woman and one day a mother.'

Gwenllian looked up at her mother uncertainly.

'It does mean, though, that you must be more ladylike. What happened the other day made me realise I have not encouraged you enough to be womanly and love womanly ways.'

'But Mother, all I want is to fight for Wales, to be a warrior princess.'

'Cariad, that is just a dream of yours. It cannot really happen. You know that as our first-born daughter, your duty is to marry well, to form an advantageous alliance for Gwynedd.'

'But Mother, I still can. I can still make a good marriage, but to someone who loves me because I am good at fighting.'

'Gwenllian, it must stop. You are still thinking like a little girl rather than a girl who is turning into a woman.'

'Fighting is the one thing I am good at. It is all I think about!' the girl pleaded.

Her mother eased a little closer to her, and her voice was sympathetic but firm. She saw that Gwenllian's eyes were beginning to well up and that her daughter was trying hard to fight the urge to cry.

'It is not the one thing you are good at. Your languages are excellent; you are well-organised and kind. Your singing voice is beautiful, and you play the harp well.'

'I will work even harder at them if you just let me still practise with the boys. Please, Mother, please.'

'Gwenllian, this is not to be discussed further. I have told you my wish, and that should be enough.'

'But, Mother, you did not do what your father wanted,' Gwenllian challenged.

'What do you mean by that, young lady?'

'You persuaded my grandfather, Owain ap Edwin, to agree to give Father and you power in Gwynedd so that Father became King, whereas perhaps it should have been Uncle Gronwy. You tricked Uncle Gronwy out of his inheritance.'

Angharad's eyes opened wide, and she clasped her daughter's wrist. She had hoped this would be the last she heard about such a lie.

'What are you talking about? Where did you get such a stupid idea?'

'Rhys told Cadwallon when he was angry with him one day, and I heard.'

'Gwenllian, that is not true. Your father has always had the superior claim to Gwynedd. He is descended right back from Rhoddri Mawr. His father died young, and until your father came of age, when he could claim his kingdom, other people ruled, but only in his place. There has never been any serious question over that.'

'But your father, Owain, was also descended from royalty,' the girl protested.

'My father was also descended from royalty, but his claim was not strong unless there were no other better contenders for the throne, such as your father. When I persuaded your grandfather to help your father, it was when the Normans were so powerful. Your grandfather had allowed and helped them to establish themselves in Gwynedd. They respected him, and when he spoke on behalf of your father and Cadwgan ap Bleddyn about how a peace might be managed, they listened to his advice. His advice was that your father would rule well, was the rightful king, and if the lands were well managed, it would be less costly for the Normans. There was never a question of Gronwy being King of Gwynedd. Do you understand?'

Gwenllian nodded. 'But why would Rhys say that if it was not true? He told Cadwallon that Uncle Gronwy told him that.'

'I am not sure why Uncle Gronwy or Rhys would say such a thing, but there is much jealousy in this world. What we have is very precious. We are fortunate as a family: we have eight healthy children, and we all love each other. We are fortunate as a royal house: our lands are fertile, our people are happy, and we prosper. Such things make others look at what we have and feel we do not deserve it. They do not see how hard we work to ensure that our family is strong and that our kingdom is safe and thrives. They do not see how we lost some of the dearest people we knew in the battle for Anglesey against the Normans. They do not see how hard it was for us in exile in Ireland. They do not know the burdens on our heads every day, wondering if someone might try to usurp the throne and kill our family.'

'I understand that, Mother,' said Gwenllian humbly, but Angharad had more to say.

'Your father works endlessly to make sure that he appeases the nobles if they are dissatisfied, that he strengthens the bonds that tie them to him, that he nurtures those who till the land, who fire the forges, who run the mills, who fish the rivers and seas. He reaches out to other princes and lords in other countries, promising to assist them in a time of desperation, and in return, they promise the same to him. It is no easy task, Gwenllian, and one day, when you are perhaps the wife of a great king, you might begin to understand what work your father and I put in to ensure that you could be that queen, a true descendent of your glorious ancestors.'

Gwenllian was feeling very ashamed by now and had never heard her mother speak with such passion.

'I am sorry, Mother. I did not think it through. I know you and Father like Rhys, and I saw no reason for him to say such a thing unless he believed it.'

'You spoke what you thought was true, but we must make sure that nobody else falls under the same misapprehension.'

'I won't say anything to anybody about what Rhys said, Mother. I promise. I only said it then because I was angry.'

'Well, you must learn to control your anger.'

'Yes, Mother.'

'You know that I only want the best for you, Gwenllian. Your father and I love you so much, and we do not want you to be disappointed in life.'

'I beg of you again, Mother, if you love me, let me continue to practise with the others in the practice yard.'

'Gwenllian, I have spoken, and you must obey me on this. Now leave me; continuing lessons is not good when you cannot concentrate. Find Bethan and send her to me.'

'Mother, please do not get Rhys into trouble because of me.'

'Gwenllian, we will not discuss this further.'

Gwenllian tidied her things, and, giving her mother a little bow, she went to find Bethan in the kitchen, as requested, and sent her to her mother. Then, running into the stables, which she found empty, she threw herself down on a pile of straw and sobbed uncontrollably.

***

When Rhys had finished tidying the practice yard, he saw his mother was waiting for him. He gave her a wide grin as he strode across to her, but her face was stony.

'What's the matter, Mother?'

Bethan looked around cautiously before she caught him by the arm and looked up into his eyes.

'What lies have you been spinning to the royal children?'

Rhys looked incredulous.

'What do you mean?'

'What you said about your father. You said that the queen tricked him out of his rightful inheritance. You said that he had the better claim to Gwynedd.'

'I only told them what my father told me: the truth.'

'The truth? You stupid boy. Such a thing is not true. Gruffydd ap Cynan is King of Gwynedd because he has the stronger claim and the stronger army and support. And he is a good king: a loyal king. He has been good to me and good to you.'

Rhys sniffed sneeringly and looked away.

'You would say that!'

'I would say that? What do you mean?'

'You hate Lord Gronwy because he wouldn't marry you, and the queen persuaded his father not to let him. She made sure he could not marry you!'

'Queen Angharad did nothing of the sort. Without her, I would have been homeless and may not even have been able to bring you into the world. She has made sure you have been treated as an honoured member of this household. You have been taught to read and write; you have been clothed and fed; and you have been taught to fight with the finest warriors in the land. How could you have said such a thing?'

He snorted. 'I wanted them to know because they look down on me,' he spat. 'Cadwallon humiliates me in front of everyone because I am a bastard. Well, one day, my father will wipe that mocking smile off his face. That's for sure.'

The blow across his cheek was not powerful, but it shocked him. His mother had never hit him before. He put his hand up to his face and stared at her.

'Do not ever speak like that again, Rhys.'

'Why, because you are frightened that my father might march in here one day and send them all into exile? You do not want to hear it? Well, when that day comes, I will be with my father because he wants me to be part of his teulu.'

Bethan stood, mouth open, shocked to the core, not believing this was Rhys speaking. In a small voice, she said, 'Your father lies, Rhys.'

At that, he turned, stomping away from her, and she felt her heart fall to her stomach.

***

Gwenllian had stopped sobbing. She lay watching the dust specks in a shaft of light coming through the open door and thought about how unfair life was for a girl, especially one raised in a royal family. In her mind, she was the ultimate victim and was wallowing in her despair when she heard the firm heavy tread of someone coming into the stables. She quickly stood up, brushing off the straw as a stable broom was hurled across the floor. It was Rhys swearing and furious. She cleared her throat to let him know she was there, and he turned quickly, taking in her red eyes and blotchy face. He had always had time for Gwenllian; in all the years he had known her, he had never seen her crying.

'Are you all right, Princess Gwenllian?' he heard himself say, though why should he care?

'Yes,' she said, her voice tremulous.

He stared at her quizzically, and she felt some explanation was warranted, 'I have argued with my mother.'

He made a slight sound in his throat. 'That is funny!'

Gwenllian looked at him defiantly and snapped in a cracked voice. 'It was not funny at all.'

He shook his head, 'No, I meant it was odd because I have just argued with mine.'

Gwenllian gave a weak smile. 'Sorry.'

'It was not your fault.'

Gwenllian bit her lip and winced.

'I think it was my fault.'

He gave her a searching stare.

A flush began spreading over the girl's cheeks. 'I heard what you said about Uncle Gronwy being robbed of his true position by my parents, and in my temper with my mother, I let it slip.'

He looked at her, saying nothing, his anger burning inside.

'It is not true,' she said lamely.

'So, your mother says,' he sneered venomously, his guts churning.

'No, it really is not true,' she protested, 'we have learnt about the line of descent from Rhoddri Mawr from the bards, and it really is not true, though our grandfather, yours and mine, was descended from Saxon and Welsh royalty.'

He looked at her in surprise. He had always thought she would discount their family connection, but she had said, 'Our grandfather, *yours* and mine'.

'I do not know much about that, and things can be written which are not true; I only know what my father told me to my face. I shouldn't have said anything, but I did, in my temper.'

She gave a hint of a smile, 'As did I!'

'So, what was the argument about, though I can guess?'

'My mother won't let me practise in the yard anymore.'

'That's a shame. You are very good.'

A smile touched the corner of her mouth. 'I know, but she won't have it. She says it is not 'womanly', and now that I am older, I shouldn't do that sort of thing.'

He looked around thoughtfully. Here was an opportunity presenting itself. If he got closer to Gwenllian and won her trust, she might be willing to disclose little bits of information valuable to his father. The last time Gronwy's man had met him secretly, he had almost nothing to report, and he worried his father would think little of him.

'What about Boudicca?' he said, 'She was a great queen and warrior.'

Gwenllian laughed. 'Can I tell you a secret?'

'Yes, of course,' he said, assuming his most earnest voice.

'I have always wanted to be like her. I know I am good at fighting. Just like she tormented the Romans, I want to torment the Normans. I can do it; I know I can, but not if I am not allowed in the practice yard.'

'I can help you,' he said slyly, seeing his chance.

'How?'

His eyes narrowed, and he ran his tongue over his top teeth as his idea blossomed. 'We can practise together somewhere where we won't be seen. I know a cove on the beach which nobody ever goes to.'

'But how can I get there without anybody knowing?'

'Can you not say that you are getting up early to pray or something?'

'I could,' she ventured hesitantly. 'Nobody goes to the chapel in the morning, so if it was very early, I think I could get away with it. But Rhys, I do not want you to get into trouble. If anyone found out, my parents would come down hard on us both.'

Rhys shrugged and looked into the distance.

'I'll take the chance,' he said. 'Getting out of the place is going to be the hardest part.'

'That's easy,' said Gwenllian, inspired now. 'There's a secret tunnel in the chapel for escape. I know where the panel is. It is small and a bit cramped, but Father had it built years ago. We were sworn to secrecy and not to let anyone outside the family know, but you are family.'

Rhys gawped at her. Gwenllian had just delivered something priceless into his hands. If his father knew about the tunnel, he could bring his men directly into the llys if it came to a fight.

'Tomorrow morning at dawn, by the dairy,' he said suddenly.

'Rhys, thank you so much for listening to me and believing in me,' she said sincerely, looking into his eyes, and then she almost skipped out of the stables into the bright sunshine.

He felt a surge of guilt. Gwenllian had always been kind to him. Then he thought about the fight with his mother. He knew he needed to toughen up.

Chapter 11: More Secrets (June 1110)

Gruffydd read and reread the message holding it close to the candlelight before handing it to his wife. She took it, frowning as she read the contents.

'They have some nerve, do they not?' he growled.

'They need our help, and it is not as if Owain asks to come and stay here himself. It is only Nest he wants to send.'

'Only Nest, when Gerald, her husband, would, with Henry's backing, march right into Gwynedd to retrieve her and slit our throats into the bargain. I will not do it.'

'Oh, Gruffydd, this would seem small of you. This is not the person you are, and we never know when we might need mercy to have one of our own families sheltered. If there was any fear of reprisals from King Henry, we could immediately send her back to her husband to avoid conflict. Surely Nest would have to agree to that.'

Gruffydd considered this, threw his head back, and closed his eyes. He tapped his little finger against the oak table where his seal and writing materials were arranged.

'Other than it makes me seem 'small' if I do not, and allowing for some possible future favour for our family, why would I help them yet again?'

'Because one day Owain ap Cadwgan will be a leader in Powys; because he is fighting against those who would take Wales from the Welsh just as you did at his age; and because you have said yourself, if he can get his warband back together he is a force to be reckoned with. Did you not tell me that young men who feel dispossessed and angry are flocking to him? Besides, would you not want someone to help me if I was in trouble?'

Gruffydd stood up, walked to the window, and ran his hand through his hair. 'You are my wife, Angharad. Nest is not Owain's wife. She is Gerald's wife.'

'She could come in the guise of educating Gwenllian,' Angharad persisted.

Gruffydd turned and looked at her in exasperation. 'Everybody knows you educate, Gwenllian. You educate all the children.'

'But everyone knows that Gwenllian is wild...'

'Gwenllian is not wild!' said Gruffydd firmly, 'Gwenllian is an intelligent, beautiful, generous, kind, high-spirited girl who happens to be one of the most promising in swordcraft that I have ever seen male or female.'

'You are one-eyed about her, Gruffydd. She can do no wrong, but her behaviour is not becoming of a woman from a royal house, and she will soon be a woman.'

'I am not one-eyed. The child is exceptional.'

'You must put a stop to this fighting nonsense. It gives her ideas that will make her unacceptable to any future husband.'

'The girl is ten.'

'And at ten, it is not uncommon for a girl to be betrothed. Perhaps to an up-and-coming Welsh noble living not too far from here.'

'You were not betrothed at ten! Anyway, who are you suggesting she becomes betrothed to? There is nobody out there good enough for her. She is not an ordinary girl.'

'Gruffydd, for goodness' sake. It is no wonder Gwenllian is as she is and has that streak of stubbornness. You must look at her more objectively.'

'Streak of stubbornness? Angharad, nobody is more stubborn than you when you get an idea in your head.'

Angharad was about to say something, but, with admirable restraint, she held her tongue. Gruffydd held her face in his hands, looked down at her, and spoke softly again.

'I do not want to talk about this anymore, or we will end up quarrelling. Let the girl be a child, Angharad. She is full of dreams and joy. Do not stop her fighting with her brothers. It will do no harm.'

He looked out the window at the sky and saw a huge star moving across the sky from the northeast.

'Look,' he said, 'there is that star with a tail crossing the heavens. Here we are arguing, and up there is something so beautiful passing silently over our heads.'

She came to the window and snuggled against him.

'It has been in the sky for a couple of weeks now. Do you think it is a sign of something?' she asked.

'A good sign, I hope! For something so beautiful, I hope it is a good sign.'

'This and then last month, we had the moon extinguished little by little in one night, then grown again before dawn.'

'And that was the night all the fruit trees were eaten by frost.' Gruffydd remembered, and his brow furrowed.

'There was a star that came before the birth of Christ,' Angharad mused.

'The church keeps telling us that Christ will come again. We sorely need him.'

They stood and watched the star for a while, and then as Gruffydd turned away, Angharad said, 'Maybe if Gwenllian had Nest here to learn from, it might be good for her, and if she shows signs of calming down, behaving in a more ladylike fashion, then there may be no harm in letting her continue with the swordcraft if she is still interested.'

'Are you trying to bargain with me, Angharad?' he asked irritably.

'I would know better than to bargain with you, my king,' she smiled coyly, not allowing him to be cross, 'but it does seem that allowing Princess Nest to stay here until Owain has sorted himself out could be advantageous.'

'Cariad, you are like a dog with a bone. Let me think about it overnight. The messenger needs food and rest, and I would talk with him further before I make my decision.'

Angharad raised herself on tiptoes to kiss her husband's cheek, and he slipped an arm around her tiny waist, pulling her close.

'Do not be too hard on Gwenllian,' he whispered into her ear. 'We nearly lost her once. She is a precious joy we have been given.'

'As are all our children, Gruffydd, every one of them, but I will think about what you said and make sure I do not treat her differently.'

'Meaning?'

'Meaning that I will not be over harsh with her.'

***

Something stirred in the room, and Cadwallon's blue eyes flashed open. In the half-light before dawn, he could see his willowy sister collecting her cloak and boots, taking the small cross she carried with her to church, and tip-toeing her way out of the room they shared with their siblings. The llys was still, yet, and he turned over under the coarse linen blanket and went back to sleep.

Soon after dawn, the young prince made his way to the kitchen and sat at a bench near the blazing fire, long legs crossed at the ankles. The savoury smells already emanating from the activity around him made his mouth water. He began to eat some fresh hot bread and cheese with milk warm from the dairy as he watched the young girls swaying and swishing in their various duties. Marged, a wholesome dark-haired beauty with a mischievous smile, slipped him a piece of sizzling bacon, and he coloured as she brushed across him to place it on the platter.

Golden and regal, his mother sailed into the kitchen to give orders to the bustling servants. Seeing him, she smiled, sitting sideways on the bench opposite so that the fabric from her pale blue robe tumbled to brush the reed flooring. She leant across, tousling his hair with her hand, and he could smell a soft floral perfume. He frowned that she still treated him like a child in front of everyone, but he knew better than to pull away.

'I think Cadwallon, you can return to the practice yard today.'

He looked up astonished, and his face broke into a grin.

'I think you have learnt your lesson, and your father is steadfast on the importance of constant practice.'

He swallowed. 'Thank you, Mother.'

'I do want to see less arrogance and more humility, however. One day you will be king of Gwynedd, and the mark of a great king is not only his ability to fight but also his wisdom. You must treat others as you would wish to be treated, as befits not only a good king but a good Christian.'

Cadwallon adopted the look of humility he knew his mother was fond of but hoped the lecture would not last too long.

'One day, you will need to lead a teulu willing to follow you to their death. To gain that sort of support, you need to show that you work harder than any of them, care about them and their families, and have sound judgment. Many Welsh kings have been betrayed because they grew too arrogant, selfish, and greedy.'

'I understand, Mother, and I will do my best. Can I go to the practice yard now?'

Angharad sighed. No matter how often she brought this up, it did not seem to sink in. 'You can, but your father wants you to sit with him later this morning.'

'Again?'

'Cadwallon!'

'Yesterday, I had to sit with him and the advisors when they went through the Cyfraith Hywel,' he complained.

'It is important to go through King Hywel the Good's laws to see what needs to be amended and added to,' his mother reminded him.

'It was really boring, Mother!'

'But essential if we are to administer the law fairly. Cadwallon. Your father had nobody to teach him these things. You are fortunate that you have such an opportunity to learn.'

Cadwallon looked up resignedly. 'Very well, Mother. What is it today?'

Angharad sighed. Her son, with his high cheekbones, long-lashed dark blue eyes, wavy golden hair and lithe body, looked every inch a prince, but he was more interested in fighting, hunting and horseplay than in the serious matters a future king must absorb. He was intelligent but learnt his lessons grudgingly, applying the minimum of effort. She worried he could be arrogant and vengeful sometimes, but she hoped he would learn to temper these traits in time.

'Your father is looking at the expenses for Gwynedd over the last months, looking at what expenditure there must be and deciding what will be spent in improving Gwynedd.'

Cadwallon's eyes lit up. 'Ah, so he may talk about the stud and getting new horses.'

'He may.'

'That sounds more interesting. Thank you, Mother!'

Angharad got up gracefully and smiled at him.

'You are fortunate to have a father who wishes to give his time to teach you, Cadwallon. Remember that. Is Gwenllian up yet this morning?'

'Yes, but I think she has gone to church. She was carrying her cross.'

A look of delight passed over Angharad's face. 'Really? Then that is very good. If you should see her, send her to me.'

***

In the little cove, Rhys had set up a dummy for Gwenllian to practise on, fashioned from a branch of a small tree padded with straw and covered with an old brychan. The sword was of heavy wood, and the crosspiece and hilt were made of leather. It was not quite as heavy as a real sword, but it would get her used to wielding something that needed muscle behind it to give it true direction. It was harder on the sand than in the practice yard, but she did not complain. He had her go through all the drills repeatedly, but she instinctively knew them already. Her body flowed as he called out the moves; thrust, backhand, sidecut, overhand. She was quick and decisive, dancing almost with a natural rhythm. It was the same with the shield training, she moved as if with intuition, knowing where she must block an overhead cut, or a sidecut, and she had learnt all the manoeuvres, stances, and parries so that they were second nature. At the end of the session, he would fight against her. Even though he was taller and far stronger, she would weave and duck from his blows, and there were many occasions where she could have caused him actual harm. It was a week now that they had been at the beach for dawn, and he could see the improvement already.

'We had better get back,' he said, 'you have done well. Remember to own the ground. That is what your father always says. Soon there will be little I can teach you.'

'No, I do not think that is true,' she replied modestly, 'every time I practise, I learn something I did not know before.'

She was flattered, though, by the attention Rhys was giving her. She watched him move effortlessly to pick up and hide away the tools they had been using, carefully wrapping them in sackcloth and stashing them away under a bush. He was not handsome like her father, brothers, or Hywel were, but he was kind, friendly, and easy with her. She felt he was more of a friend to her than her brothers half the time.

'Is your mother still unwilling for you to come to the practice yard anymore?' He stood back, looking at the hiding place, and, dissatisfied, moved to it again. She liked that he cared for things, and he was more like Owain than the arrogant, insolent Cadwallon or her stirring little brother, Cadwaladr.

'No,' she lamented, 'although she has hinted that she may allow me to sometimes if I learn my 'womanly' skills well.'

'Oh,' said Rhys, readjusting the sackcloth holding the makeshift dummy under the bush and carefully covering her sword and shield. 'I am not sure what 'womanly' skills are really.'

'Oh, you know, being mild and gentle, learning how to be demure and stay in the background while paying attention to everything that is going on, being humble, that sort of thing.'

'Oh, I see,' he said, falling into step beside her as they walked towards the path that would take them up to the clifftop. The bushes were lively with birdsong, and there was a fresh salty breeze.

'Can you keep a secret?' Gwenllian asked him on impulse.

'You know that I can.'

'She has a lady to come to teach me how to be more 'ladylike', and you will never guess who it is.'

'Who?' asked Rhys, his heart beating fast.

'It is Princess Nest, but I am not to tell anyone. You were always asking us about Princess Nest; well, she must have left her true love, Owain ap Cadwgan, because now she will be living with us.'

Rhys' mouth dropped open. 'Are you sure?'

'Yes, Mother told me.'

'When does she arrive?'

'Soon, I believe. They are sending Hywel and a few men to fetch her. She is not very well, I think.'

He felt an almost childish rush of excitement. Now he could see it all playing out perfectly. In three days, Gronwy's man would meet him at the usual spot in this cove before dawn. He must make sure to put off Gwenllian that day. He would send a message through him to his father and tell him about the secret tunnel. His father would be able to come in with his men, attack the llys, and send Princess Nest back to her husband. There would be a reward in that for him. He flushed with the thrill of it.

***

'What was all this praying about?' Cadwallon wondered, frowning thoughtfully as he watched his lithe sister slink out of the room for the sixth morning in a row. Even though he was back in the practice yard, he was still irritable about his punishment, and he blamed her. It was not like her to be so pious, and, in fact, she was barely able to keep still for a moment when they attended a service, swinging her feet or looking around. He slipped out from beneath the rugs rubbing his long legs. Hywel said the throbbing pains he felt in his calves at night were growing pains. He knew that he had shot up in recent months. Each morning the pains passed, and he hoped they would not return. His mother had suggested he needed to rest and study for as much of the day as possible, rather than running, weapon training, or horse riding. He was certainly not going to take her advice. He pulled on his brown calf leather boots and green woollen tunic and, throwing his warm brown wool cloak over his shoulders, he made his way across the llys to the courtyard outside.

Gwenllian, her copper hair escaping from her hood, her cloak flapping in the wind, was disappearing into the chapel, but with Rhys. That was strange. On instinct, he kept to the shadows to avoid being seen. He followed them inside the limewashed church wincing at the sound of the door squeaking, but to his surprise, there was no sign of anyone inside. Then with a sinking feeling, he realised where they must have gone. He pushed the wooden panel, which led to a small, dank passageway shored up with oak posts and beams. He had been here before many times, but this was not for anyone outside the family to know about, particularly Rhys, whose comments about his father had made Cadwallon very angry.

Taking a taper, which he lit from one of the candles burning on the altar, Cadwallon entered the damp cobwebbed tunnel closing the door quietly behind him. He could hear voices echoing at the end of the tunnel and see the distant movement of a taper used to guide the way. He jumped and nearly cried out as a rat ran across in front of him but pulled himself together quickly, reminding himself that he should never allow himself to be taken by surprise. If a rat caught him off guard, how easy it would be for an enemy with a knife.

Where were they going? As he eventually emerged into the misty morning through a well-concealed exit surrounded by thick scrub, he saw the pair picking their way down the overgrown path leading to a little cove. Below, the steady sound of waves tumbling onto the shore was interspersed by disturbed seabirds wheeling and crying. A lapwing screeched its shrill call and flew away from him, distracting him from its nest. He moved to the top of the cliff, hearing faint voices drift through the damp early morning. Rhys and his sister were utterly unaware that they were being observed. He waited, almost expecting a boat to glide into the cove to spirit them away, but instead, he shook his head as Rhys started to put Gwenllian through her paces. He was furious. He had never liked Rhys much and had been waiting for an opportunity to get at his sister, so he would use this to his advantage. He was not sure how, but he would.

Cadwallon wandered back to the llys ensuring he had covered his tracks, making his way out of the church and across the sun-filled courtyard to the kitchen, which was bustling as usual. He was surly and angry. Even the curvy charms of the flirtatious Marged could not snap his mood. He was toying with his food and deciding what to do when Hywel came in.

'Ah, Cadwallon, I am glad I find you here. Your father would like you to accompany me today.'

Cadwallon looked up. 'Where to?'

'We are going to collect the new lady coming to teach Gwenllian.'

'Really?' said Cadwallon, instantly brightening. He loved being with Hywel, especially when it was instead of being inside studying.

'Half an hour be ready and saddled up,' Hywel said with a grin. He also had a fondness for Cadwallon, who yet had some growing up to do but had much of his father about him. Cadwallon, with his restless spirit and physical prowess, would be a man's man, but he knew that his father feared he lacked the gravitas to make a good king. Hywel felt Gruffydd was hard on his firstborn and that he should let him have his youth while he could. Responsibilities would come later.

Within the hour, Cadwallon, Hywel, Aeddan and Meirion had crossed on the ferry and were on the cart road towards Caernarvon. Cadwallon gazed at three vast mountains of the Eryri, which loomed above them, stunning beneath the most transparent blue sky. His father had told him that on a clear day, he had once seen Ireland, Scotland, the Isle of Man, and England from the highest peak. Cadwallon had always been fascinated by these mountains; there were many stories he had heard about them. It was believed that King Arthur killed the giant Rhitta Gawr on the slopes of the highest mountain and that the mountain became the giant's tomb. When Arthur himself died, he was laid to rest below a cairn of stones at Cwm Tregalan while his great warriors were laid in a cave on a nearby mountain, Y Lliwedd. One day, it was said, Arthur would rise with his warriors and recover the kingdom of the Britons. Cadwallon let his mind wander, daydreaming about fighting alongside King Arthur. If Christ had risen from the dead, then why not King Arthur?

A short time later, they turned off into the woods that skirted the well-used road they had travelled. As they climbed, they were glad of the cool shade afforded by the pine trees as it was becoming a warm day. Occasionally, they would stop beside the tumbling clear water of the mountain streams. The horses, bred for steep climbing such as this, were sure-footed on the narrow paths and across the rocks. Hywel put a little distance between himself and Aeddan and Meirion, who had been with Gruffydd since his early days before even he had met Angharad.

'Cadwallon, you know who we will be meeting today?'

'Yes, I do.'

'It will not just be Princess Nest, Owain ap Cadwgan himself will be bringing her. He will have some of his band with him.'

'Oh, I see.'

'Your father wants you to meet Owain. Later, when you are king in your own right, Owain might be King of Powys. It is good that you should have allies you can trust. Owain is putting great faith in your father to look after Princess Nest, and your father is putting trust in Owain by sending you along to meet him.'

Cadwallon turned wide eyes to Hywel. 'Because if he wanted to hurt my father, he could kill me?'

'But he will not. He owes your father his life. It is important that when he thinks of you, he remembers that debt. He will remember who met him this day. Your father trusts him, so there is nothing to be concerned about.'

'But you cannot trust everyone,' said Cadwallon doubtfully, and Hywel picked up that there was something the lad was trying to say.

'No, not everyone,' said Hywel. 'Some people will belie a trust for money, or revenge or to make themselves feel important.'

'Like my Uncle Gronwy, for instance?'

'Why do you say that?' asked Hywel so sharply that Cadwallon's face registered only shock at his tone.

Cadwallon flushed and said simply, 'Because my Uncle Gronwy believes he should be King of all Gwynedd.'

'Who told you that?'

'Rhys told me one day in his temper. He said that my parents had tricked Uncle Gronwy from being the rightful king of Gwynedd.'

Hywel's gentle face turned thunderous. 'So, Lord Gronwy told Rhys that! I can only imagine what is going on in that boy's head. He is such a decent boy, and Lord Gronwy has meddled with his thinking.'

Cadwallon's irritation rose at Hywel's sympathy for Rhys, who had landed Cadwallon in trouble on more than one occasion as he seemed to enjoy watching the heir to the throne of Gwynedd humbled. He said nothing for a while and remained surly, but then he saw a way of dealing Rhys a blow he could not deflect, as well as getting back at his sister. He let his spite take hold of him.

'Rhys is not so decent as you may think.'

'What do you mean?'

'You know how my sister and I were banned from sword training.'

'Yes.'

'Well, every morning, they go down to that little cove where you took me to see seals once, and they practise there on the sand.'

'But how do they get there without going past the sentry? He would have questioned it and told me surely.'

Now Cadwallon flushed deep crimson seeing his mistake.

'No,' said Hywel, 'not the chapel?'

'I, I was not sure you knew.'

'Outside of the family, I am the only one who knows about the passage until now. I will need to deal with this when we get back. I pray it is not too late. Cadwallon, you should have gone to your parents or come to me at once.'

Cadwallon started to feel very uneasy. He was even angrier with his sister than he had been before. The young prince started to piece together what Hywel had inferred. A dark cloud of uncertainty had spread over his secure world.

They came to a spot where they could look down at a large blue lake nestled between the mountains and where a cairn stood. Hywel threw his leg over the pommel and slid to the ground.

'We wait here. Aeddan, can you scout ahead and give us the signal?' he gestured to the others to dismount and checked the sun to judge the time.

Aeddan's blue eyes sparkled, crow's feet set deep in his tanned face as he gave an animated grin.

'No peace for the wicked!' he joked and, with a twitch of the reins, led his horse on through ferns, following the curve of the mountain until he was out of sight.

Meirion took food out of their saddlebags. He was a tall, heavy-set man but moved easily, throwing his cloak down and dropping to his knees to lay out the provisions. They sat on the ground to eat bread, cheese, dried meat, and oatcakes. The horses cropped at the sweet grass and leaves lying around. Somewhere an eagle sounded, and Meirion looked up with his large sad eyes, sallow face set firm on the cloudless empty sky.

'He called four times,' he muttered, catching Hywel's eye, 'there are four of them.'

The sound of a horse trotting towards them alerted them to Aeddan's return. He slipped off his horse smoothly.

'Owain ap Cadwgan, Princess Nest, and two of Owain's men. One of them is the tall blonde one that always looks miserable, and the other is the weasel pock-faced one who cannot keep his eyes still.' He knelt at the stream and cupped his hand to drink the water.

'I know them,' nodded Hywel with a grin. 'All right lads, back on your horses, Cadwallon beside me; keep your horse still and greet them when they come.'

Above them, an eagle soared across the sky, and Aeddan laughed, 'My call has found me a mate!'

Meirion did not look up from packing away the food but, with his dry humour, commented, 'Took its time!'

Cadwallon looked up and saw the majestic bird cross the sky effortlessly. His heart was beating with anticipation. Owain ap Cadwgan was a name to be feared, and Princess Nest was renowned for her beauty. Weasel Face came around the corner first and raised a hand as he spotted them. Cadwallon stilled his horse with a pat on its neck as it skittered sideways on seeing the other horses approach. The prince drew himself up to his full height in the saddle, shoulders back, head raised as he had been taught.

'Welcome to Gwynedd,' said the young prince and Weasel Face, seeing that no swords were drawn, the calmness of the men offering no threat, bowed his head.

'Prince Cadwallon,' he said, taking a guess, hitting the mark, and then twisting in his saddle, gave a low whistle before waving his companions on.

Cadwallon was awed by the presence of the man who came into sight. His chiselled face framed by a shock of red hair seemed hard, as hard as his tall frame, lean but muscled, his cloak flapping in the mountain breeze. He guided his horse with one hand and, with the other, led a slight, pale-faced woman with red-rimmed eyes and thin, lanky hair beneath her fur cloak as she drew her pony alongside him. Princess Nest was not the great beauty Cadwallon had been expecting.

'Princess Nest, Owain Prince of Powys, you are both welcome in Gwynedd,' said Cadwallon.

'Both of us?' retorted Owain, eyebrow raised. Cadwallon glanced sideways at Hywel to see if he had made a mistake. Hywel gave him an imperceptible nod.

'While you stay in Gwynedd, you are under my father's protection,' he continued, fumbling, trying to sound as regal as possible. 'My father invites only those who are welcome.'

'Well said, Prince Cadwallon, you are a fine ambassador for your father. Tell him his kindness will not be forgotten and that although it disappoints me not to be able to partake in one of his celebrated feasts at this time, I am certain there will be another time, a more peaceful time, when I can enjoy his generosity.'

'I will tell him, sire, and I wish you well in whatever strife you face. May God and the right of the Welsh be with you.'

Owain smiled broadly at that, and then his face clouded, 'Just a few moments, and I will let you return to your llys. May your journey be safe.'

Cadwallon nodded acknowledgement and watched as he dismounted, lifted the frail woman off her horse, and guided her along the path out of earshot. They spoke, and he kissed her, and then the young prince saw her body shuddering with sobs as she held onto him, not wanting to let him go. He took her face in his large hand and wiped the tears flowing down her cheeks before whispering in her ear and holding his other hand over her belly. Cadwallon was captivated with what was unfolding in front of him, but Hywel, perhaps to give them some privacy, cleared his throat and gave a small jerk of his head, beckoning Cadwallon to come forward to speak to Weasel Face and the lanky blonde horseman.

'I hear that things have been difficult in Powys since Iorwedd is back on the scene,' Hywel volunteered.

Weasel Face cast a look at his companion and spat. He looked grim, his face narrow and thin, and his long yellow teeth showed when he spoke.

'He and Cadwgan are under Bishop Richard's thumb and do his bidding. Iorwedd's warband has taken the land, which was my lord's and lately Madog's, and now they hound us out of our own place while the Normans make themselves comfortable.'

'Cadwgan does not give Prince Owain any support?'

'Cadwgan hides behind Iorwedd. My lord received a letter from Iorwedd telling him that if he found my lord on his land or Cadwgan's land, he would be forced to hunt, imprison, or kill him according to the demands of King Henry. The very land that was my lord's by right. This message was also relayed to Madog, we understand.'

Hywel whistled low. 'He would kill his nephew. Cadwgan would kill his son?'

'So the letter said, because to support my lord means that they themselves would lose their land and would be killed or imprisoned until death.'

'And Lord Uchdryd?'

Weasel Face shrugged, 'He was ever Cadwgan's loyal man.'

'I thought Madog was Bishop Richard's man along with his brother Ithel?'

'Ithel, Bishop Richard has imprisoned with the help of Iorwedd. Meanwhile, Madog has raided into Cheshire, adding Saxons to his band. King Henry calls for him to surrender them to him, but Madog refuses to betray his men, so the bishop turns against him. Many men now come to join Madog and more to my lord, so our strength is growing.'

'They choose to live in the mountains,' remarked Hywel.

'These young men have no property thanks to the Normans and Flemings who have stolen their birthright, so now they raid with us. We are taking enough booty and captives for the Irish slave markets, and they get their share.'

Cadwallon listened and said nothing but could not imagine that his father would ever desert him as Cadwgan ap Bleddyn seemed to be abandoning his son. He thought of his father's strong arm around his shoulders, his broad grin when Cadwallon did well, and how he would cut the finest meat from his platter and pass it to his heir. He felt great pity for Owain ap Cadwgan. Something brought his thoughts to his uncle. Yes, he could well imagine his Uncle Gronwy exiling him, or worse, if he had been born to him. Then he remembered Rhys, and a shiver ran up his spine.

Princess Nest was back on her pony now; her eyes cast down. Her lover pulled her towards him and gave her one last demure kiss. She held the reins of her pony with white-knuckled fingers. Owain was gruff.

'I commend the Princess Nest into your care.' He swung easily into his saddle, half turned, and called, 'Merddyn! Gethin!' It was a voice that demanded obedience. On his signal, Weasel Face and his blonde companion joined their master, who kicked his horse on abruptly without looking back. They rode swiftly away.

Chapter 12: Lies (June 1110)

When Gwenllian was summoned to her father, she had thought she was to meet the Princess Nest. Susannah helped her put on her pretty cornflower blue tunic, dressed her hair with small matching flowers, and she slipped on some fine blue slippers. She looked at herself in the polished bronze mirror and saw Susannah's ruddy face smiling proudly at her. Feeling pleased with herself, she sauntered to Gruffydd's chamber and respectfully knocked at the door.

'Enter.' Her father's voice sounded harsh.

She went inside, her bright smile lighting up her face but was surprised to see not the Princess Nest but Hywel sitting alongside her father at the oak table, which held his great seal, with her mother standing beside him. They all looked grave, and her mother's stare had an icy chill. Gwenllian's nervous eyes darted from one to the other, and she anticipated what was coming.

Gruffydd's mood was a dark one.

'Gwenllian, would you like to tell me what you have been doing each morning at dawn?'

She knew immediately that to lie now would be worse. Her face burned with humiliation. She began to tremble, her knees shaking as she stood looking at her three accusers.

'Father, I have been training sword and shield with Rhys.'

'Where?'

'At the cove with the seals.'

'And how did you get there?'

Three pairs of eyes, cold and unsympathetic, were fixed on her. Her knee was jerking violently, and her mouth was dry. As she tried to speak normally, her throat seemed to be closing, and her breath coming too fast. Her heart beat loudly in her ears.

'Through the tunnel, Father,' she whispered.

'With Rhys.'

'Yes, Father.' She tried to control her breathing, and the sick feeling in her stomach only increased when her father snarled.

'That was something only known to the family and Hywel. Now Rhys knows.' Her father was restraining his temper, but his glare did not waver.

'He is family.'

Gruffydd's scowl became more severe, and he looked at Hywel, who had the expression of someone whose horse had just died.

'When you are told to keep a confidence within the family, we meant just your brothers and sisters. If there is a fault on that count, then it is ours for not making that clear. Are there any other confidences which you have let slip to Rhys?'

'No,' she protested initially, then a look of guilt passed over her face, and she stammered, 'Oh, I told him about Princess Nest.'

There was a gasp from her mother, who sat down heavily on the stool beside the table, the back of her hand against her mouth. All three exchanged glances.

'You will not discuss with Rhys what has taken place here. You will tell him you cannot meet him tomorrow or any other....'

His daughter cut in quickly, her voice cracking from nerves, 'I was not going to meet him tomorrow, anyway, because he said he had to meet someone else. I thought maybe he was meeting a young lady.'

Her father's voice had a keen edge, 'Then, in that case, you say nothing until we have decided what to do. You will remain in your mother's chamber for the rest of this evening and tomorrow until we fetch you. Your dishonesty we will discuss at another time. Now we have graver matters to address.'

Her eyes flicked to her mother for comfort, but far from providing any, Angharad glided across the room with her eyebrows drawn together in anger, took her daughter firmly by her arm, and guided her out the door.

Gruffydd slammed his fist onto the wooden table, closed his eyes, and pinched the bridge of his nose. He sighed deeply.

'She is only ten years old,' said Hywel kindly.

'And disobedient and deceitful,' Gruffydd replied grimly, pursing his lips.

'It is not in her nature, and she has acted out of character, but what she loved doing the most had been taken from her. She tried to find a way around it, thought she had found a friend she could trust, but he took advantage of her innocence.'

'We will need to come down hard on her for this,' Gruffydd continued.

'So, what do we do now?'

'What choices do we have, Hywel?' Gruffydd muttered, leaning back in his chair with his hands behind his head, 'That information may already be making its way to Gronwy, who is just waiting for his chance to take us down.'

'Perhaps it has not, lord,' said Hywel calmly. 'If fortune is with us, it is Gronwy's man whom Rhys is meeting tomorrow morning, not a young lady at all. With everything happening so quickly, it is possible Rhys will not have been able to alert Gronwy to anything yet.'

Gruffydd sighed again, looking doubtful. 'That he knows of the tunnel makes us vulnerable. Good God, nobody knows of it outside immediate family, yourself, and a handful of those who worked on it and have been sworn to secrecy. Now anyone could come in and slaughter us all while we sleep.'

'We could block the tunnel from the bottom section and take it in one or two different directions.'

Gruffydd played with the idea. 'We would need to make an alternative entry, block the existing one maybe a third of the way down the passage so that anyone aware of it would think it is still there.'

'We could make a new entrance below this room. It runs below here anyway.'

'And then there is the issue of keeping the damn thing secret. When the original tunnel was completed, the llys was empty and abandoned. It is a lot of work just to save the life of someone who has betrayed us, and while it is being completed, we would be forever looking over our shoulders.'

'But it is Bethan's son, and he is your kin,' Hywel countered mildly.

'Hywel, I brought the boy up like my own son. Do you not think this sickens me to the stomach?' He bunched his fists on the table. 'It is not only my own family but all of you who live here at the llys and all our subjects in Gwynedd who could be put in danger by this idiotic, ungrateful boy.'

Hywel looked glum and opened his mouth to say something but looked away.

'Spit it out, man. Say what you have to say.'

Hywel looked back at Gruffydd and spoke quietly. 'You are known for your fairness and justice. To take the life of kin is against God and would not be well received. Our Welsh laws revile killing kin; our culture abhors it.'

Gruffydd snorted, 'Hywel, do not tell me what I already know. I do not need you being sanctimonious with me.'

Hywel looked shamefaced, 'I am sorry, it was not my place.'

Gruffydd thought for a while and stood up, clapping a hand down on

Hywel's shoulder. 'No, Hywel, you are right, and it is your place to remind me that we have laws to keep us safe, but, by God, I wouldn't be the first to break them. It is common. Look at our history. How many thrones have changed hands because kin have killed kin?'

'It is common, but you stand apart because that is not who you are. I will do what you tell me to do; I am your man, but if there is another way, no matter how inconvenient, we should take it.'

'In truth, I would gladly have you dissuade me from that course. Do what you must. Save what you can out of this mess.'

***

Rhys leaned over the parchment, tongue out at the side of his mouth, eyes concentrating to keep his letters well-formed and lines straight. Making sure his map was accurate, his quill scratched across the surface as he imagined his father reading his news. He pictured himself waiting for his father on the shore and then marching with him to the tunnel entrance as he brought his troops in. He saw himself watching as they searched the llys, the family bound in the cold courtyard. It was an image he had conjured up a hundred times in the last few days, but now that he was on the cusp of success, his enthusiasm seemed to be waning.

He kept thinking of Gwenllian, red hair flying in the wind, smiling up at him, talking of 'our grandfather'. He kept reliving the shocked expression on his mother's face before she hit him. He tried to make himself feel that same exuberant joy he had felt when the power first lay in his hands to redress all the wrongs and injustices he had felt at the hand of Gruffydd ap Cynan's family, but somehow it had dissipated. He thought of Cadwallon, that insolent, arrogant little turd, but hadn't his parents humbled him publicly for his rudeness. He thought of the other children and tried to remember their slights against him, but he could not. Then he thought of the queen and how she had manipulated her father so that Rhys' own father, her brother, could not rule all of Gwynedd.

Something seemed strange about it, however. If she hated her brother so much, why had the queen not abandoned Rhys and his mother? Why had she brought them here to Anglesey? Why had she educated him? Was it perhaps because she felt guilty? Was there any other time she had been shown to be sly or manipulative? What about with Hywel? Was she betraying Gruffydd with Hywel? He tried to use that to justify what he was about to do, but it felt hollow. What of Gruffydd? He racked his brains and could not think of anything with which to condemn him except for not allowing Rhys to go on the hunt. Was that enough to send the family into exile? He wished his mind was not so confused and tried to push his guilty thoughts away. He took the sand and dried the ink before rolling up the parchment and hiding it in the straw.

A full moon was rising over the chapel as he walked across the courtyard to the hall. Young Owain and Cadwaladr were sitting cross-legged, playing a board game on the rushes, and as he came in, they smiled up at him.

'Do you want to take on the winner?' Owain asked him, 'I will have won here soon!'

Cadwaladr punched his brother on the arm and frowned intently at the board.

Rhys grinned. 'Nah, have you seen my mother?'

'She was here a minute ago. Maybe she has gone into the kitchen.'

'Thanks.'

He looked around the hall again in case he had missed his mother, but only the usual men were drinking and laughing, the bards singing and playing their instruments. The king and queen were not there. Nor Hywel, whom he knew had been to collect Princess Nest today. He made his way towards the kitchen, and when he saw his mother leaning over, putting oatcakes on the edge of the fire, he felt a pang of guilt. Bethan felt someone looking at her and turned round; her face instantly filled with her warm smile, and then a shadow passed over it.

He went forward and took her in his arms as she got up, giving her a big squeeze and receiving a bigger one in return.

'I am sorry,' he said, feeling awful that he had avoided and not spoken to her in days.

'I am sorry too. You know you are my world, and I have never hit you before. It hurt my heart more than it pained you,' she admitted with a sad smile.

He looked at her shamefaced and sat beside her, relating the trivialities that had made up his day. Eventually, he knew he could hold back no longer.

'Mother, I have decided to go to live with my father, be part of his teulu. That is where I truly belong.'

His mother blanched. 'No, Rhys,' she gasped.

'It is what is best. After all, I am half of his.'

Bethan was silent for a long time, holding back tears. Finally, she said, 'I cannot stop you, but you are making a mistake. He is not the man you think he is.'

'Let us not quarrel, Mother. It is time for me to learn to be a man, where nobody knows me, and I can be who I want to be. Here, they will always think of me as a child who does not quite fit in. I am not family, and I am not just a servant either. I can take my skills, and if my father acknowledges me, what honour that will bring. Later, if you want to, perhaps you can come back to live with my grandparents, and we will be close to one another.'

'Please do not do this, Rhys. You are breaking my heart.'

'Mother, I am grown up now and want to be more than just the one that trains the royal children in swordcraft.'

'Please, Rhys, be wise. You are more well-liked and respected here than you realise. There you would have to start from the beginning.'

'That is exactly what I want. I will prove myself.'

He gave her another hug to stop her pleading, and they sat down together, drinking warm honeyed milk while the oatcakes cooked. Bethan gave a brittle smile, ruffled his hair, and kissed him, biting back tears. He was her life, but if there was a chance that Gronwy would acknowledge her son, then she should not rob him of it.

It was very late when Rhys collected his few things into a cloth bag and settled for a few hours of sleep.

***

Hywel stayed up that night observing and waiting quietly though he was dog-tired. Just before dawn, Rhys came into the courtyard. Hywel moved back into the shadows and watched as he saw the youngster furtively enter the chapel. He knew where he was going. He took his horse from the stable and asked the sentry to open the gate.

Rhys emerged from the tunnel clasping the parchment under his cloak and made his way to the cove along the usual route. He shivered from the chill in the air and was almost breathless, anticipating what he was about to do. As he reached the cliff top, he peered down anxiously and saw Gronwy's man waiting for him on the beach below. He scrambled down the slope, his stomach tense and his heart beating faster. The sea was as calm as a mill pond this morning, and the sunrise a rosy pink, lighting the cliffs in hues as stunning as a rainbow.

As Rhys strode across the sand, the man lifted a hand. His face was worn by weather and conflict, his hair shaved close and rough stubble covered his chin.

'You are early,' said Rhys, giving him a nod and looking down to pull the parchment out from under his cloak.

'Or you are late,' retorted the man gruffly and then gave a grunt and gurgle.

Rhys looked up with a start as the man slid to the sand, his throat a red gash, blood pumping out of the wound, and his eyes bulging as he hit the ground.

Hywel stood behind him, wiping the blade he carried inside his cloak.

Rhys froze.

'Why?' Hywel asked, simply looking sorrowfully at Rhys.

Rhys stared open-mouthed.

'This is Gronwy's man; I recognise him. Why were you giving him information, Rhys?'

'I was not; I did not tell him anything.'

'Why?' Hywel asked again reasonably.

Suddenly Rhys' temper was up. He felt trapped, and he spoke without thinking.

'Because the queen tricked her brother out of his right to be king of Gwynedd.'

Hywel laughed and looked out at the grey sea, 'That is not true, Rhys. Gruffydd ap Cynan was ever the rightful heir to the throne of Gwynedd. The queen would never deceive anyone in that way.'

'You would say that,' said Rhys, the old anger rising to fever pitch, 'when you are lovers.'

It happened so quickly that Rhys did not have time to fear his death. Hywel knelt on the sand beside him and gently closed his eyes. He muttered a prayer as he looked out on the storm, which would come soon enough, washing the blood away. He picked up the parchment, which rolled around in the breeze at his feet, and unrolled it. Rhys' boyish script scrawled over the page with blots of ink and crossings out.

'To Lord Gronwy, my dear father, there is nothing of interest to report. All is quiet here. King Gruffydd is trying to boost Gwynedd's trade with Ireland. There is talk of him buying new horses, bigger ones still, to sire the Welsh mares. This llys is sleepy, and nothing ever happens or will happen with King Gruffydd cautious and determined on peace, so I have decided to come to you, to learn from you, and support you. I will come more slowly than your messenger on horseback, so you have time to think about me coming. I have my mother's blessing. Your loving son, Rhys.'

Hywel dropped the parchment onto the sticky blood-stained sand, put his head in his hands and wept.

Chapter 13: Hopes (August-September 1110)

Nest's belly had begun to swell noticeably in the months she had spent at Aberffraw. The sickness had stopped, and her face had started to look fuller and brighter. She had been made to feel very welcome, although she was referred to as Angharad's cousin Lady Nest ferch Ednowain. Nobody seemed to question it, and Owain had told her that if she had to lie, try to make it as near the truth as possible.

She sat now with Angharad and the young irrepressible Gwenllian, whose temperament had improved remarkably in the time Nest had been there: she was much more considered and calm, much less excitable. As she looked down at her embroidery, Gwenllian asked, 'Lady Nest can you tell me about the camp where you stayed when you were hiding in the mountains.'

Nest glanced sideways at Angharad, who gave a slight nod. She was used to the girl's endless questions.

'It was in the mountains. Owain's men had built some little shelters around an old shepherd's hut.'

'Was it hard to find?'

'Impossible if you did not know the way. It was surrounded by forest, close to a small spring, and sheltered by a rock wall.'

'How did you find food?'

'The men would go hunting or fishing in the streams. Sometimes if the men had been raiding, there would be a cow or sheep.'

'It sounds like a dream,' said Gwenllian. 'Did you sit around the fire at night and watch for shooting stars?'

'The men would huddle around the fire for warmth, drink and joke, but I stayed in the hut mostly.'

'Did you not want to hear their stories of how they had fought the Normans and the Flemish?'

'No. The hut was cold, damp, and dark, and I wanted to be in a safe, dry, comfortable place where I did not need to fear if people were chasing or threatening us.'

'If it were me, I would stay by the fire every night listening to the stories, looking at the night sky, and only going to bed in the morning!'

Nest gave a small laugh. 'Gwenllian, I hope you never have to experience what I experienced. I promise you it is not wonderful. You cannot sleep because every sound might be an enemy.'

'But you were with Lord Owain, and he loved you so much that he gave up his lands to be with you.'

'Yes,' said Nest sadly. 'He gave up so much to be with me; now he wants his lands back.'

'When he gets them back, will he come to fetch you?'

'Gwenllian, enough now,' said her mother warningly. 'Show me your embroidery, and then go to practise with the harp.'

'Yes, Mother.' Gwenllian agreed meekly. She was still wary of upsetting her mother even months after the incident with the tunnel.

After the girl had left the two women together, Nest said, 'She has such a love of life!'

'She is difficult to handle! She says all the right things and behaves impeccably, and then I find she has been practising her sword drills with a broom handle, vaulting onto her pony, jumping off the beams in the barn.'

'Angharad, let her have her childhood. In a few years, she will be married and be responsible for running a household or llys.'

'Yes, that is what Gruffydd says. I have her sit with me when I have appeals or complaints to deal with or speak with my advisors, and she takes it all in. One minute I feel she has turned the corner, and the next, I find she has been climbing some cliff to look at birds' eggs! Why? Because she was in a dispute with her brothers about whether they were blue or green. The girl is incorrigible. Who would want to marry such a girl?'

'I used to fight with my brothers when I was her age. Griffith, my brother, and I would get up to all sorts of mischief. We would scamper over the stable's roof, throw rotten apples at the guards, and then duck down, giggling. We would spend more time up a tree than learning to read or write. He would get soundly smacked, and I would be sent to practise the harp! When you sent Gwenllian to do just that, it reminded me.'

Angharad smiled. 'Do you hear from your brother?'

Nest beamed. 'We were with him in Ireland, Owain and I. He has turned out to be quite handsome and just as enthusiastic about everything as ever. He wants to come back to Wales and win back our lands. He would like to try to free our brother Howell from his imprisonment at the hands of Arnulf de Montgomery.'

'Could Lafracoth help? She is still married to Arnulf.'

'She and her husband are estranged, and she hates him. He would not take her advice.'

'So, Griffith hopes to win back your father's throne.'

'He has support, but I do not think he knows how difficult it is. He it was who encouraged Owain to come back and fight, not that he needed much encouragement.'

Angharad sensed an undercurrent and carefully averted her eyes as she saw a few silent tears fall down Nest's cheeks. Nest pulled herself together.

'I told Owain to ask his uncle or father to intercede with Henry, but they would not do it. Imagine? They refused.'

'They are frightened,' suggested Angharad gently.

'They are cowards now. Just old men who have no power,' Nest murmured resentfully.

'And what will you do when the child is born?'

Nest shrugged. 'I do not know. In the beginning, I heard from Owain every few days, but I have not heard from him in weeks. Perhaps he has forgotten me?'

Angharad got up and knelt beside her friend, looking up into her sad face. Her rich, warm voice resonated with sympathy, 'No, Nest, he will not have forgotten you, but it is dangerous for him to send messengers.'

Nest bitterly shook her head, 'His warband was much more alluring than I. The thrill of planning a raid, descending on an unsuspecting community, burning, plundering, taking slaves, sending them to Ireland. There became less and less time for us to be together and intimate; anyway, a sick, pregnant lover is a burden. Perhaps our love is cursed because I ran from Gerald. It weighs on me heavily. I could die in childbirth, and if Owain does not love me, then I die a sinner for nothing.'

Angharad put a hand up and stroked Nest's hair as you would a child. 'I will pray for you, Nest, that everything will work out well.'

Nest closed her eyes and whispered, 'I have been praying that since the Easter that my Father was killed, my brother fled to exile, and I lost my family.'

***

Rhoddri, Gruffydd's bard, positioned his musicians and called for quiet. The Great Hall at Caernarfon stilled as Rhoddri's deep tenor voice sang of Gruffydd and Cadwgan's battles against the Normans.

Cadwgan looked pleased. 'They still sing of us, then, Gruffydd?'

Uchdryd looked up sharply, sensing that his lord's melancholy was only a few goblets of mead away. 'They will always sing of you both! You united the Welsh princes. You brought them victory.'

'I have heard they sing of my son, now. They sing of how he ravaged the Welsh princess who was sleeping with the enemy, won her heart and whisked her away to the mountains of Eryri, then came down like a lion and tormented the Normans.'

Gruffydd caught Uchdryd's eye and said nothing.

'He should be lord of the lands I worked so hard to get, but instead, Henry has me like a bull on a ring. If I give succour to my own son....' He made the sign of a knife across his throat with his finger.

Gruffydd shook his head and spoke gently to his old ally. 'This is not what we fought for, Cadwgan. How has it got to this?'

Cadwgan pulled at his beard, eyes red-rimmed, lids drooping. 'You tell me! Ask my brother! When they tricked him into appearing before the court in Shrewsbury seven years ago, he was as fine a fighter as you would see. A man in his prime. When they released him from his gaol, he was toothless, hardly able to walk. They had tortured him for fun. And they dangled him in front of me and promised me that if I help my son, they will do the same to me; no matter how many men I have, they will hunt me down.'

Later, when Cadwgan had passed out in his chair, head back, mouth open, Uchdryd and Gruffydd sat near the fire watching the antics of the jesters without seeing.

'Powys and Ceredigion are a mess,' Uchdryd said sadly. 'There is no leadership. When Cadwgan was in his prime, he kept all the youngsters in line: they looked up to him, and he gave them the promise of hope. Henry has taken the balls of the powerful old men and exiled the powerful young ones. The youth of Wales is dispirited at the lack of land and power. Now they have nobody to look up to, so they turn to the likes of Madog and Owain. There is some disturbance every week; properties are burnt or ransacked, booty taken, slaves sent to Ireland, and sometimes it is not only the Normans and Flemish who are the victims. Sometimes they target the Welsh they perceive as being loyal to the Normans.'

'We are fortunate here. We have not had any dissidence.'

'Because you are your own man and rule as a Welsh king should! Now Madog has joined his bitterest enemy and brought along with him the Saxons whom he was protecting from Henry, the ones who were raiding into England.'

'They are still together.'

'You had heard? Well, it was a surprise to me. Owain and Madog are together, and every day more ynfydon, more hotheads, join the throng.'

'And Iorwedd?'

'Iorwedd was always easy to manipulate, and his warband does Henry's bidding. They are an extension of the Norman machine. Iorwedd has cleaned himself up but is Henry's toothless dog.'

'With Ceredigion and Powys in chaos, this will not serve Henry well.'

'Henry's intention has ever been to undermine the Welsh. He would have us fighting amongst ourselves. We are good at that without his help, but what he has done is not only hurt Wales but also him. His own Norman nobles live in fear. His communities of Flemings live in terror. Soon, I think, I will move back to Gwynedd. I will leave the properties I have to my sons. I am getting old. My head still thinks I am twenty, but my bones ache, and every blow I have taken comes back to haunt me at night.'

A dance was taking place at the far end of the room, and Uchdryd, who had always appreciated beauty, was drawn to the attractive group who had formed a ring. Angharad, golden-haired and luminous, held Hywel's hand on one side, and Cadwallon, as tall as his mother now, took her hand on the other. Next to Cadwallon was the sparkling, copper-haired Gwenllian, who held the hand of her more serious but fine-featured brother, Owain.

'Ah, look at that,' said Uchdryd mischievously. 'Do not the beautiful Angharad and the handsome Hywel look a comfortable pair.'

Gruffydd turned from the fire entranced as Hywel watched Angharad's every move. She smiled and laughed as they danced around in their circle. He was still as he stared at them. Uchdryd turned to see why he had had no response, and observing Gruffydd's face, his old, lined eyes widened.

'My lord,' he leant across and spoke reprovingly, 'it is not unusual for a man to be in awe of his queen.'

Gruffydd's lips became thin, and he seemed transfixed as they twisted and turned with the dance.

'Hywel is like our brother,' he said finally, but his words had no conviction.

'Gwenllian is as beautiful as her mother,' said Uchdryd, changing the conversation and cursing himself for his stupidity in sowing a seed of doubt where there should be none. Gruffydd was a man in his prime and a fine-looking specimen, but Uchdryd wondered whether his years bore down on him when he looked at his youthful wife. That could happen to men of his age, he knew. There was a pause as Gruffydd seemed to drag himself away from his reverie.

'Gwenllian,' he said, still watching his wife, his voice distant and then snapping back to attention, he added, 'Gwenllian is beautiful but wild, Uchdryd! I have encouraged her love of fighting, and that is what she lives for.'

'Let her fight, Gruffydd. God knows in these uncertain times it may be a skill which will save her life.'

'Yes,' repeated Gruffydd, watching Hywel and Angharad laugh breathlessly as the dance ended, 'you may be right.'

Uchdryd followed Gruffydd's eyes and cursed himself again that, with a momentary quip, he had dallied with the one thing Gruffydd felt sure of. Gruffydd was a man whose depths it was impossible to fathom. He was a good, honest man, but like most good men, he had his insecurities. Uchdryd sensed his mood and, try as he might to lighten it, he knew what he had said was niggling at his friend like a sore.

When most of the party had retired, Gruffydd watched how Hywel sat, deep in thought, gazing into the fire. He left the hall without disturbing him or the revellers for whom sleep would be much longer coming. He knocked gently and entered his wife's chamber. She turned and gave him a smile that never failed to warm him. She looked at him with her head on one side and, taking the pins out of her hair, let it cascade over her breasts. The room smelt of beeswax and lavender. He watched her slide into the bed, pulling the sheets and furs up around her chin, her big eyes watching him. He undressed slowly. He felt older than he should. He felt stale and tired. He slipped into the bed beside his wife, her head finding his shoulder, her hand caressing his chest, moving slowly down his body. He hesitated, and Angharad wondered if he had understood her desire for him. Her hand moved again, and he was engulfed with the need to take her quickly, powerfully. She responded with equal passion, and afterwards, as they lay wrapped in a familiar embrace, the same thought tormented him. It was a baseless thought, but he could not shake it off.

He was unsure how long they had slept, but an urgent tapping on the door woke them. Angharad raised herself reluctantly, slipped out of the sheets and heard Susannah's voice.

'Mistress, Lady Nest's time has come earlier than we thought.'

The queen sprang forward, pulled a robe over her, and went quietly through the door, leaving her husband remembering an ache which seemed more painful in the darkness of the early hours.

In the morning, when the light flowed through the shutters, and he could hear activity in the rest of the llys, he roused himself. He was still alone in the bed. He felt the place where his wife had been sleeping, and it was cold. He lay still, thinking and thinking, but his thoughts were troubling. He thought of the hotheads in Powys and Ceredigion and what this would mean for the future. He thought of the songs that were being sung of their bravery. He thought of Cadwgan, Iorwedd, and Uchdryd: old men he had looked up to. How time had slipped by. He thought of Angharad and Hywel and their joy as they danced. Where had his happiness gone?

Angharad crept in and, seeing him, teased him, 'You are lying there still. Do you not have the whole of Gwynedd to attend to and guests to be feted?'

Before he could say anything, she had sat beside him, kissing his face, and his common sense told him that her natural, easy manner was one of a loving, not duplicitous, wife.

'Nest has had a fine baby boy, and she is doing well. It was an easy birth, and the babe is suckling.'

'I am glad,' he said and squeezed her hand. 'Do you think she would let Cadwgan see his grandchild? He loves his son despite everything and has little to look forward to now.'

'He knows she is here despite us hiding her away?'

'He asked me. I told him. He had guessed that she did not have many options for a place to hide and had heard from someone that she was not with Owain now.'

'I can ask her,' Angharad said thoughtfully as she got up and went to the wash bowl.

'There is something else,' he ventured; his mouth dry.

She turned and looked at him guilelessly. 'Yes?'

'You must give me an honest answer.'

'Of course,' and her eyes smiled at him, her head on one side.

He paused, and for all the warrior he was, he realised he did not want to hear the answer to the question that troubled him. He thought quickly.

'Would you be much displeased if I asked you to allow Gwenllian back in the practice yard?'

Her face clouded over. 'I am not happy about the idea, but even Nest says I should let the girl enjoy her childhood.'

'As Uchdryd said to me. He also pointed out that it might save her life one day.'

Angharad paused and fingered the ivory comb she held.

'Gruffydd, those who wield weapons are always in danger. Maybe her love of fighting could take her life one day. She could be scarred or hurt or…'

'She practises safely with the boys. She is sensible, more sensible than they are, truly. Nothing will scar her though bruises she might well have, yet she climbs trees like a squirrel and rides horses like fury. She could do herself more harm doing that.'

Angharad was resigned that this was a battle she could not win. 'Then let her do it.'

'Would you like to tell her?'

'No, you are her father, and it is your wish. If nobody wants to marry this wild child, then I will remind you that we should have dissuaded her from loving the sword too much.'

'It will not come to that; you will see.'

'I hope not.'

When Gruffydd had left her chamber, Angharad's mind returned to Nest suckling Owain's child. She could not condone Nest leaving her husband and children to flee with her lover, Owain. Nevertheless, she did feel enormous sympathy for Nest. She mused that King Henry had outlawed Owain from a land which was not Henry's. How unfair that was. Also, how many married women had Henry seduced? Had he not tried to seduce Angharad at Shrewsbury Castle right under Gruffydd's nose soon after Gwenllian was born? This was not dispensing justice: this was using people's lives to play politics, and Bishop Richard and King Henry cooked up reasons to extort money from the likes of Cadwgan and Iorwedd, to take lands for crimes that did not justify the punishment and to set kin against kin.

As she walked the corridors of the motte and bailey castle, which Hugh the Fat, Earl of Chester, had built and which her husband had captured and now used, she thanked the Lord once again that she walked here now as Gruffydd's wife and not, as her father had once planned, as the wife of Earl Hugh.

When she reached Nest's chamber, she tapped gently and found mother and babe awake. With a nod, she dismissed the young woman attending to Nest.

'He is so much like Owain,' Nest reflected when the servant had left the room. The same determined chin and his eyes are mischievous, just like his father's.

'How will you let Owain know he has a son?'

'One of Owain's men, a bowyer, comes to Caernarvon to sell his bows. He camps and fishes for a few days on the River Seiont, close to the castle. He comes on the full moon and the half-moon. I send my messages with him to Owain, and sometimes he returns with a message from him. I am going to ask him again to plead with Henry for a pardon. Henry pardons others who have done far worse.'

'Nest, he is unlikely to pardon Owain while you are still together.'

'Well, we are not together, as you see.'

Angharad wondered if Nest had given up hope of being with her lover, the father of her child. She had hinted before at Owain's waning interest in her. By pleading with him to ask for pardon, did she realise that this would probably mean they could not be together? Then, Angharad mused that perhaps Nest was being selfless and freeing her lover of guilt from a generosity of spirit. Nest was facing an uncertain future; a woman, alone with a child, with little to her name.

'Nest, you know that Owain's father, Cadwgan ap Bleddyn, is here at the castle.'

'Yes, I do,' she replied meekly.

'Gruffydd asks a boon. Would you be willing for me to show Cadwgan his grandson?'

'Would the father who has denied his son want to see his grandson?' Nest asked a trifle scathingly.

'Nest, Nest,' came the gentle reproof. 'Cadwgan is the plaything of King Henry and has been forced to renounce Owain publicly but loves him all the same. While he has vowed not to help him, he has not done anything to harm him either.'

'Nor should a father hurt his son.' She looked at Angharad levelly.

'Even so.'

'So many of us are playthings of Henry,' Nest responded sadly. She looked down at the little mite, now sleeping, and kissed him on the forehead.

'What harm can it do? If it reminds Cadwgan that he is also a father, then take him.'

***

Angharad brought the babe to Cadwgan in Gruffydd's chamber. Uchdryd was beside him, beaming as he saw how touched the old man was.

Gently, Cadwgan held out his arms and looked down at the tiny child.

'He has the look of Owain,' he said firmly, 'and Owain ever had the look of me.'

'Nest asks if you would like to name the child. Owain had told her that when the child was born, he was going to send to you for your blessing and ask you to give the babe a name.'

Cadwgan's old eyes lit up and watered. The baby opened his mouth in a soundless roar.

'Llewelyn.' he said stoutly. 'Llewelyn, because this little one is like a lion. Tell her thank you for making an old man happy.'

Outside were children's voices and the shrill sound of Gwenllian dancing around her brothers with her wooden sword. Uchdryd looked down into the practice yard.

'There's the future,' he said. Angharad joined him and saw her husband demonstrating some point to an animated Cadwallon with Gwenllian eagerly pushing in at his shoulder. Her brother turned and glowered icily. Owain stood, going through the move slowly as his father had demonstrated, trying to understand the merits of how he had been shown. Meanwhile, little Cadwaladr was chasing a magpie with his sword, incurring his father's rebuke.

Cadwgan came to the window with the tiny bundle. 'They grow too soon. I did not spend enough time with mine. I was too busy trying to create an empire, and now it is in ashes at my feet, and my son is in hiding.'

'Go to Henry,' said Uchdryd. 'Go with Iorwedd and plead for him. You have the money; buy his pardon.'

Cadwgan shook his head. 'Henry would have us in prison as soon as look at us.'

'Lord Cadwgan,' said Angharad very calmly. 'When we were in Ireland together in exile, I thought I had little hope of persuading my father to help us, but he did. Surely there is something Henry wants which could buy you a pardon.'

At that moment, the baby seemed to look up at Cadwgan, his eyes deep pools. Cadwgan took his big paw and stroked the little face tenderly.

'I will speak with Iorwedd,' he said, gently handing the little one back to Angharad, his big fingers trembling. 'Yes, I will speak with Iorwedd.'

Chapter 14: Blood is Thicker (November 1110)

Princess Nest shone like a star. She had bloomed in her late pregnancy, and now that her little one was a few weeks old, she had regained her figure, her skin was glowing, and her hair was glossy. Gwenllian was captivated by her. She would imitate how Nest moved silently and gracefully, lithely swaying her hips. She copied the way that Nest wore her tresses. She began to speak more slowly, as Nest did, inclining her head to one side and then flashing a doe-eyed sidewards look in conversation. Just as she found it easy to mimic swordplay, she found it easy to imitate the alluring woman who was her mentor.

'Please, tell me again about your childhood and the English Court and King Henry,' Gwenllian pleaded, her gestures Nest-like. 'I hate embroidery, and the llys is boring with nothing happening. I wish we could be fighting our enemies or something. Listening to your stories is the only way I can bear it.'

Princess Nest laughed her small, white-toothed laugh and tilted her head to one side.

'Gwenllian, you should never wish for war.'

The girl sighed and then coaxed Nest to recount her story.

'I have told you so often now that you could tell my story yourself.'

The young princess flashed her eyes and begged sweetly so that Nest gave a little sigh and started relating her story.

'I was not much more than your age when I was sent to the English Court. You know, of course, what happened to my father Rhys ap Tewdwr, King of Deheubarth, and my half-brothers.'

Gwenllian's colour rose, realising the stupidity of her earlier remark about war to someone who had experienced the unthinkable. She nodded solemnly and vowed not to speak out so frivolously again.

'It was terrible, but it can happen when you are royal. That is why your parents are so careful to try to avoid conflict. It is why your father is trying to teach you all diplomacy and how royalty should negotiate their way out of trouble.'

Gwenllian's eyes were wide, and she thought of her father. She had to admit that he always treated everyone respectfully, whether they were visiting royals, lords, or even ordinary people. Always! Yet, she knew her father was one of the greatest warriors Wales had ever known. Nobody would ever beat him when she saw him practise fighting: he was as quick-witted as quick-footed, his moves unexpected, his swordcraft artistry, his arrows accurate.

Nest watched her intently and continued, 'William Rufus was on the throne when I was sent to England.'

'He was William the Conqueror's second son, I know. What was he like?'

Nest gazed into the distance momentarily and then said, 'Excessive!'

Gwenllian looked bemused.

'Everything he did, he did to the extreme. For example, he was obsessed with hunting and would hunt for days. When he ate, he would gorge himself so that later, towards the end of his life, he had a pot belly. He would drink until he would vomit, hold wild gatherings where people would drink so much, they became ill or did ridiculous things.'

'What like?'

Nest shook her head and tutted, 'So many things.'

'Please, just tell me one.'

'Once, one of the knights had been drinking heavily and decided to frighten everyone by pretending to be a bear. He wrapped himself in a bearskin, which still had the bear's head and teeth attached, and crawled around on the floor, growling menacingly. He did not realise that his tunic had ridden up, exposing his private parts to the world. The more the other knights laughed, the more he growled and capered, but while he was doing that, the king's wolfhound had come up to investigate this strange creature and took a bite out of the poor man's behind so that he could not sit for a week.'

Gwenllian's eyes sparkled with delight.

'Please, tell me about where you lived.'

'I lived at the Royal Residence in Westminster. It was on the banks of the River Thames. That site had been used by Saxon royalty right back to King Canute. King Edward the Confessor had built a huge royal palace alongside his great abbey, and King William Rufus then built a great hall where all the feasting took place.'

'Is it as big as our llys?' asked Gwenllian.

'It was the biggest hall in Europe, perhaps ten times the size of your llys, with stone walls six feet thick, huge archways and windows, and walkways.'

'And you would feast there?'

'Yes, we would feast there. Huge feasts with no expense spared. There would be fire-eaters, musicians, jugglers, and mountains of food of every description.'

'You would feast every day?'

'Oh no. Most days, the royal household would eat in a smaller hall, but if William Rufus or Henry, his brother, wanted to impress anyone, they would have a feast of enormous magnitude.'

Gwenllian was quiet for a moment.

'Such a display of grandeur, and yet we all laugh at William the

Conqueror and William Rufus because they could not even read.'

Nest cocked her head again and considered this.

'They did not need to read because they had advisors who would do all the reading or writing for them.'

'Father says you must learn to read in many languages so nobody can fool or trick you. Even kings can be tricked.'

'But also because the world of the written word is a gift to the educated. You can learn so much about the world.'

'Father says that we can read of the glories of others and learn from them and their mistakes.'

'Yes,' agreed Nest wistfully, 'we should learn from the mistakes of others, but more often than not, we do not.'

'But can King Henry read and write?'

'Yes, he can. He was to have been a bishop, so he was well educated.'

'Well-educated for a Norman king, but not well educated for a Welsh king,' remarked Gwenllian stoutly.

'Perhaps not,' replied Nest, 'the Welsh value education highly. Henry values education, too, and has surrounded himself with some of the brightest thinkers in Europe. He has a talent for finding people who may not be wealthy but are clever and ambitious. He uses their ingenuity to roll out better ways of managing his kingdom and then rewards them well.'

'Mother says that when Father collects his advisors together, he usually finds good solutions before any of them.'

'He still allows them the opportunity to give their wisdom, though,' said Nest, 'which is what King Henry does as well.'

'So, are there many wonderful people at the English court?'

'Lots of interesting people. Some are royal themselves, like Prince David of Scotland, who is more Norman now than the Normans. He is the

English queen Mathilda's brother. His father, King Malcolm, was killed at the River Aln along with his elder brother, Edward, during an invasion of Northumberland. That was in the same year as my father was killed. Then there are princes of the Roman Empire. Also, there are people of wealth and talent who bring fascinating ideas and fashions to the court.'

'Is there wonderful music and dancing?'

'Of course. King Henry is a great patron of arts and music.'

'Like my father. Father has brought us new bards from Ireland to work with the best of our bards. My mother says there is no court in Europe with such a rich collection of music and storytelling.'

'What your mother says is true,' said Nest gently, with a hint of a smile that Gwenllian did not miss, 'but our Welsh courts are tiny compared to the English court. You cannot imagine how vast and vibrant, rich, and sumptuous everything seems at Henry's court.'

Gwenllian flushed and momentarily looked away, hurt that Nest had seemed to belittle her father's court and heritage. Nest had not meant to upset the young princess, but she did not want her to be as naive as she had been when being thrust into a different world. She tried to soften the impact her words had had.

'The wealth we have in Wales is not as great as the Normans have, so they can employ many more artists and artisans, for example, to rebuild their cathedrals and fill them with wonderful light and art.'

Gwenllian had always been told she had been brought up in great privilege and felt a pang of resentment against Nest, who seemed to be in such awe of the Normans, yet despite them being so wonderful, here was Nest gladly accepting the hospitality of her parents because she had fled from her foreign-born husband. She had put Nest on a grand pedestal, but her mentor now teetered on the edge as the young princess' hatred of the Normans swelled. However, Gwenllian was astute enough to realise she had been given an advantage in learning from Nest. Her father had repeatedly reminded his children that knowing as much as possible about your enemy meant that you were halfway to defeating them.

She composed herself, subdued her feelings, and asked, 'What cathedrals did they build with their great wealth?'

Nest did not miss the sting in the question but continued levelly.

'They are like enormous grand castles with great soaring towers. The naves are long, and as you walk along them, there are more and more things to see: massive columns, wonderful wooden carvings, and beautiful paintings. The sound of the huge choirs singing as you move through the inside is breathtaking, overwhelming.'

Gwenllian, despite herself, was impressed and fascinated but continued loyally, 'I would love to see them, but I think the cathedrals we have in Wales are beautiful too, and I love the little lime-washed churches we have all over Gwynedd. They feel happy places where God can find us.'

'They are happy places and truly for God's glory.'

'But those enormous cathedrals must inspire the glory of God even more. The wealthy Normans must be God-fearing if they put their money into such things.'

'The Normans see those buildings as opportunities to remind people of their power and wealth.'

'So, if they have such wealth, why do they steal land from our bishops? Why do they need to take what is ours?' Gwenllian challenged the older woman and was confused at the conflicting direction of her response.

'Because they are greedy.' Nest looked out of the window into the distance and added, sadly, 'Nothing is ever enough.'

They sat silently for a while, Gwenllian allowing her thoughts to roam as she stitched. She thought about greed and how stupid it seemed that avarice drove the Normans to build towering cathedrals to preach against it.

Nest bent over Gwenllian's embroidery and smiled at her.

'You are doing this beautifully; your work is excellent.'

'Thank you, but I would rather be practising my knife throwing or swordcraft.'

Nest clicked her tongue.

'Gwenllian, it is good to be able to do both.'

Gwenllian still felt a sense of pique which emboldened her to ask Nest a more personal question.

'Please tell me more about King Henry. Is he handsome?'

Nest looked up and brought Henry to mind. 'He is not handsome so much as attractive. He has clever eyes and a nice smile. He is exciting to be with because he is always interesting. While he is with you, he makes you feel special.'

'People say he is very arrogant.'

'Oh yes, he is very arrogant. He was very sure of himself. Very aware of his power.'

Gwenllian was itching to ask Nest if she loved the king but knew that it would be a step too far. Instead, she asked, 'Were you pleased to be married to Gerald de Windsor?'

'He brought me back to Wales. He had been the constable of Windsor Castle and the Keeper of the Forests of Berkshire, which was quite an honour, but it was as Constable of Pembroke Castle that he brought me home.'

'You preferred to be in Wales than at the English court?'

'Yes. It was a fascinating time to be at the English court with so much change, and for me, so much that was different, but I longed to be back with my people.'

'And when you went to Ireland, how was the court there?'

'Oh,' chuckled Nest, 'very wild. Very raucous, loud, and rough, but everyone was kind to me.'

'My mother told me that she and my father escaped to Ireland when Anglesey was invaded; she was very welcome.'

'Yes, the Irish are strong allies of the Welsh and have many family ties. I was reunited with my brother Griffith there, and that was very special because we had been parted for so long. The Irish had kept him safe and taught him much.'

'Will your brother ever come back to Wales?'

'Oh yes. He will come. He will come to regain his inheritance.'

Now Gwenllian felt her curiosity growing even more.

'Will he come with fighting troops from Ireland?'

'Perhaps.'

'Will he camp in the mountains and raid like my father did until he wore the enemy down?'

'Perhaps. I hope he will not need to camp in the mountains.'

'But the mountains are the heart of our country, where our souls are. No money could buy those mountains,' enthused Gwenllian.

'Not so wonderful when it is cold and bleak, and you do not know where your next meal will come from.'

'But that would be so exciting: living on your wits, needing to catch your food and make fires, and sleeping under the stars.'

There was a knock on the door, and Nest's maid, Ceridwen, entered with little Llewelyn. Nest nodded to her, her face lighting up to see her baby and smelling the little one's milky innocence. She turned back to Gwenllian.

'Gwenllian, you have much to learn,' said Nest kindly. 'Do not wish for other than you have. You have done beautiful work today, and you should take it to your mother.'

Gwenllian got up, bristling at what she felt was another slight, yet she thanked Nest respectfully. She gave a little bow and, taking her embroidery carefully rolled and wrapped in a piece of linen, sought out her mother.

Nest watched the girl go cradling her baby in her arms. The conversation with Gwenllian had unsettled her, and she felt restless. She longed for Owain to see the little boy, so much like his father. She gazed into the fireplace where small bright flames of gold licked the edges of the oak log.

Ceridwen, a mousy girl with the palest blue eyes, sat in the corner of the room, altering a shift of Nest's to fit her more snuggly after her pregnancy weight had gone.

'Ceridwen, please would you take Llewellyn while I write a message?' asked her mistress, kissing the baby on his forehead before passing him over. The girl's face dimpled as she held out her arms.

Nest went to the window but took nothing of the activity outside as she contemplated what she would write. After a while, the words clear in her head, she sat at the small table and, taking up quill and ink, penned her note on a sheet of parchment.

"My Love, it is a long time since I have heard from you, and I pray for your safety every day. Little Llewellyn is thriving. He is hungry and healthy and kicks his little legs incessantly. He looks like you. His red hair is thick, and his eyelashes are long.

If we are ever to be together again as the little family we are, then surely you will need to be pardoned by King Henry. I would be satisfied spending just a night with you now and then rather than live without the hope of ever being in your arms again. Now that your fame is rising and men flock to you, Henry may want to keep you onside. If he kills you, he gives life to the cause you stand for. If he exiles you, he will be unsure what foreign help you may enlist against him. If you still love me and desire to know your son, then reconcile with your father. Ask him to plead with Henry for a royal pardon and tell him that you would be willing to leave the Normans and Flemings in peace in return for your lands and title."

***

Gronwy harboured such a hatred of his sister and Gruffydd ap Cynan that it was the first thing he thought of when he woke in the morning and the last thing on his mind before he slept. His loathing had fermented into a plan which he was sure would lead to their downfall.

He realised that if Gruffydd had a weakness, it was not in his troops, who fought with the precision and confidence of elite warriors and were unquestioningly loyal to their king. No, if Gruffydd had a weakness, it was his love for his whore of a wife. He thought of how Gruffydd was always so solicitous to her, always praising her virtues, watching her like a lovesick hound while the head of his warband was rutting with her behind his back. What an idiot to let that happen under his nose. If Gronwy's wife, Genilles, tried something like that, he vowed, he would shame her in front of everyone and then send her packing.

Genilles, however, was a timid sickly little thing who shrank from his touch. She had almost died having his son, Owen, and though he wanted the son, he had hoped that she might just fade away, leaving him to make a better match. Genilles had not faded away. Genilles had given him a lively young daughter as well. Nowadays, she was always hiding in dark corners or spending hours on her knees praying, her pale lips whispering her pleas repeatedly. Even God had no time for Genilles because she prayed with more urgency every day, which confirmed to Gronwy that God had abandoned her. Genilles would not look him in the eye, and when he came to her bed, she would bite her lip, her pale skinny body shivering as if she had a fever. She had no passion, and the thought of her seducing anyone made him laugh out loud.

So, Gronwy had put his energies into devising a strategy to bring down the King of Gwynedd. The best thing about the plan was that there would

196

be almost no bloodshed at first, just dismantling the foundations of a marriage, a family, and even men's respect for their king. It would be ruthless destruction, and he was glad of it. Thinking of that power thrilled him, driving him to satisfy his lust between his women's thighs so often that he would be distracted even when adjudicating in court or hunting.

Gronwy had been contemplating whom to use for his plan, considering the men who were part of his band. If Gronwy knew anything, he knew that some men just lived to enjoy other men's pain. Often, they were masters of avoiding trouble themselves but had an innate ability to cause it for others. They would be close to whatever disaster was unfolding but not close enough that fingers might be pointed at them. They would smell a weakness or fault in someone, work on it, and then, once they had alerted everyone else to that person's shortcomings, would somehow seek advantage from the situation. Hova and Gogan were such men.

Hova and Gogan were the kind of troublemakers who always caused dissension in Gronwy's men. They were involved whenever there were outbreaks of violence but always on the sidelines. They were insidious stirrers to whom the mud never seemed to stick. To remove them would mean that there would be fewer issues arising amongst Gronwy's men and, therefore, less escalation to him. Positioning them so they would end up at the royal court in Aberffraw would also mean he would eventually get reliable information about what was happening there. Rhys, his bastard son, had seemingly vanished into thin air with the man he had sent to channel any information Rhys had. If Gruffydd had uncovered his spies, nothing had been said about it.

He called the two troublemakers, and they stood cautiously before him. Gogan was slightly shorter than his companion, wiry but strong. His hard eyes darted around the room, searching for clues about why he had been summoned. Hova's sparse greasy hair fell lankly to each side of his pale face, and his thin lips twitched.

Gronwy came to the point quickly. He did not like them and did not want to spend undue time in their company.

'I have chosen you because I need men with a certain intelligence.'

They looked surprised but pleased.

'I want men who can live rough for a while, fight like the devil, fit seamlessly into any group, and begin to influence them, help them to come around to a certain way of thinking.'

The men looked confused, unclear about the task or why they had been chosen, but they were smart enough not to ask questions. Let the task unfold and see what opportunity arose from it.

'You have heard of Owain ap Cadwgan and Madog ap Rhyrid?' he asked them now.

They confirmed they had.

'I want one of you in each of their camps.'

Their eyes widened.

'As spies, my lord?' asked Gogan.

Gronwy smiled. They were on the right track.

'Initially, yes, but what I have in mind is to right some wrongs in the royal court of Gwynedd.'

***

For the hundredth time, Owain ap Cadwgan wrapped the tiny wisp of hair around his finger and smiled. Then he reread the message from Nest and the old longing for her rose in him. He picked up his sword and resumed running a whetstone down the length of it to take out the nick caused by the last lunge and cut of an unfortunate Norman. Perhaps Nest was right, he thought, what harm could come from asking his father and uncle again to intercede with King Henry for a pardon. There would be more peace in Powys and Ceredigion if Henry gave him a pardon: he believed the old men had lost control of their lands and their allies, and the invaders were afeared.

The woman beneath the furs stirred, and as the thoughts of Nest aroused Owain's lust, he joined her. As they coupled, he allowed his imagination to wander elsewhere.

He awoke with daylight filtering into the hut. He felt the warmth of the young woman, saw the mop of hair tangled across her face, and let his hand drift across her breasts, fingers playing with her nipples. She was drowsy but responded, and he parted her thighs.

His passion spent, Owain felt no inclination to linger beneath the covers. He got up, wandered to the fire to revive it with some dry kindling, and tugged on his clothes before twitching aside the leather hanging that provided limited protection from the bleak drizzle outside. The disappointment and resentment he had harboured for so long started rising again.

Owain stood in the shadows for a while, seeing that Madog had arrived and was sitting on his haunches, warming himself with a small group of his men, mostly surly and silent. Owain observed Madog's stern face and downturned mouth and wondered what had happened to the young, high-spirited cousin who had always shown such enthusiasm for life. Then it crossed his mind that people might wonder the same about him. Not liking his train of thought, he wandered outside to the campfire. He had reservations about the conversation he knew he had to have.

His cousin nodded to him, and Owain indicated with a jerk of his head that they should talk. Madog signalled to his men, and they moved away.

'You have something to say?' asked Madog, picking meat out of his teeth with a splinter of wood.

'I have a son,' said Owain.

'By Princess Nest?' Madog asked.

'By Nest.'

'Congratulations. You could make a fine army from all your sons, and their mothers would fight each other like cats.'

'This son will be a prince,' retorted Owain, 'descended from two fine lines, and one day he will take my place.'

Madog narrowed his eyes, looked at Owain sceptically and spat into the fire.

'Prince of the mountain camp?' he commented acidly.

Owain was unamused but kept his temper. 'I am beginning to think we can do better for ourselves.'

'I am all ears,' Madog replied, though he was eyeing Owain suspiciously.

'Cousin, we can do this in two ways. We can take our men, attack, and burn every Norman stronghold, every Flemish dwelling in our lands, or we can appeal to my father and uncle once again to intercede with King Henry.'

Madog raised his eyebrows but let Owain continue.

'The first is a more enjoyable experience, but it comes with a high chance of death for us both and many of the less accomplished of our warbands. The second cost us our pride, yet my father and our uncle are old men and have not held up well under the ravages of time. The way I look at it, if we get a pardon, we get our lands back, and then we pressure them to retire to a monastery so that we rule our lands peaceably.'

'I was lord of your lands while you were in exile. Are you suggesting I retire to a monastery as well?'

'I said, 'we' Madog. There is enough land for us both, and we will gain more by dispensing our enemies quietly once we have our pardon. In honesty, King Henry wants to be rid of them as much as we do, so he sent them to Welsh lands.'

Madog looked askance at Owain. 'My uncles have done nothing to safeguard my neck. Why not take them out? Create a vacuum. Step in. Rally our forces and take on Henry.'

Owain shook his head and cast his eyes skyward. 'Madog, your hasty ambition will be the death of us all. No matter what they have written, I will not lay a hand on my father or uncle. They are kin.'

'You had no such scruples when you killed Meurig and Griffri ap Trahearn.'

'There is a difference between killing a second cousin and killing an uncle or a father, Madog. I intend to be King of Powys in time, I make that clear now, but I want to be king in an accepted way. I want to be respected.'

'Owain ap Cadwgan has a child out of wedlock, and he wants to be respected and revered,' scoffed Madog.

'You can look at me however you wish, but mine is not a half-thought-out ambition. This, what I do now, is stabbing at the enemy, weakening the enemy, reminding the enemy he is in our land, but all the time, Madog, I think of what it takes to be a king who goes down in history.'

Madog rolled his eyes, but Owain continued, 'We are not strong enough now to take on a mighty army. Our men fight like savages and are a threat to the unprepared, but against a disciplined army, we would be carrion for the crows. No, we must take our time and win victories where we can. A pardon would be such a victory which would allow us to establish ourselves.'

'You make it sound like you chose this path rather than being banished because your prick ruled your head!'

'Is that what you think?' spat Owain scornfully. 'Then you are a fool. Princess Nest was promised to me, and I took back what was mine. I would do it again. I would do it a thousand times. She stands as an emblem of the violation of the Welsh by the enemy. Do you even understand that? This was a stand against years of subjugation and infiltration of our lands.'

'You are full of bullshit! You can talk eloquently about your high ideals, but when it comes to it, you are driven by the same passions as I, Owain. You feel the thrill when you cut a man's throat or take his wife while he watches. You crave wealth and power. However, it may come. You lust after recognition as I do.'

Owain glowered at his cousin but let him continue.

'You make many assumptions about the future. King, you or I may be, my friend, and do not forget that while we had the same grandfather, my father was the older brother, not your father. You will not go down in history as the most just, admired, and revered. No, Owain, our blood is the same, but I am more willing to face up to who I am than you are. Would I have killed you to gain Powys? Yes, in a heartbeat! So, Owain ap Cadwgan, you need to kill me or make it worth my while to be your ally.'

'And shall I kill you, Madog ap Rhyrid, would-be King of Powys?' Owain forced a laugh, 'Not while you are helpful to me. I am not such a fool as you think! But I promise you this, touch me, and I have sworn oaths from twenty men that you will die before the sun sets. So, with or without you, I will ride to speak with my father.'

'Try if you will, and if you pull it off, then I am for an easier life but cross me, Owain, and I promise you any plans of yours to safeguard your back I have also made for myself.'

'We understand each other then?'

'I think we do, Owain ap Cadwgan.'

Owain got up, stretched, yawned, and easy-limbed sauntered over to the woodpile, picked up a substantial log in one hand, and tossed it into the fire so that smouldering embers covered Madog's boots and legs. Madog scowled, the insult not lost on him. Owain nonchalantly went off to do what he felt he did best, making his men feel valued and important. This was a lesson he had mastered over the last year. He had seen but not valued it at his father's court; he had learnt it by watching King Murtagh in Ireland. Owain could now appreciate how King Gruffydd in Gwynedd had made concern for his men central to his kingship. He had also listened, fascinated, by Nest's stories of the English court and the manipulative Henry's total mastery of his nobles.

Madog leaned against a tree trunk raging silently. He scanned around the camp catching a sour look on Merddyn's weasel face as their eyes met, and he vowed to watch his back while he was around.

***

The hooded man slipped off his horse and hammered authoritatively on the heavy door, which formed a small entry in the vast wooden and iron gate at the front of the llys. It was late, but a sentry or two was always on duty.

'What do you want?' a gruff voice answered the interruption to what had otherwise been a quiet night. A small wooden flap was opened, and the sentry peered out into the moonless night dark as pitch.

'I come with a message from Bishop Richard for Cadwgan ap Bleddyn,' said the hooded messenger.

'Oh, wait there.' There was a sound of muffled discussion and boots crossing the courtyard.

After what seemed like an age, the sentry returned and opened the gate enough to let the messenger and his horse into the courtyard. The hooded man dismounted and followed the sentry to the entrance to the llys. There was the squeak of hinges as a thick door opened, and a veritable giant of a man, armed and wearing leathers, peered under the lintel at the men standing in the shadows. He lifted a torch to see better.

'You can bring your horse in and leave all weapons with me,' the giant grunted.

'Thank you,' said the messenger mildly and unstrapped his sword.

'Knife,' demanded the giant firmly, and the man took the knife from his belt.

The giant came close in and checked the visitor's body roughly to ensure he was not carrying any other weapons, then led him into the great hall, instructing him to wait while he spoke to his lord.

Cadwgan was sitting with a few of his men and looked up at the hooded man standing at the edge of the hall. He stopped what he was saying to his companions to take in what his guard was relaying, stared fixedly for a moment, then stood up hastily and said, 'You are from Bishop Richard. Come with me.' He turned to the men at the table, 'Excuse me, my friends, I will deal with this and return.'

He almost stumbled as he stepped off the dais, and the messenger moved quickly to take his arm.

'I am all right,' Cadwgan muttered, and when they were far enough from the others, he said, 'You have taken a hell of a risk coming here.'

The messenger said nothing, his eyes darting around the hall. They moved to Cadwgan's chamber, and when the door was firmly closed, the visitor threw back his hood, and his father embraced him with tears in his eyes. They held each other long and fast.

'My son, my son,' Cadwgan repeated repeatedly, squeezing Owain in his clasp each time he said it.

'Father,' said Owain, 'I was beginning to think we would not see each other again.'

His father smelled like an old man now. The room reeked of aged hounds, damp, and mead.

Cadwgan pushed him away while still holding him and looked at him long and hard through bleary eyes. He shook his head with disbelief.

'You look older,' he said finally, 'but hard living suits you. You are strong! Look at you! You remind me of me in my youth!'

Owain laughed, 'You look older, but soft living does not suit you! You remind me of why I should curb hard drinking and whoring!'

His father let out a bellow and embraced his son again.

They sat by the firelight, and Cadwgan said, 'I met my grandson by Princess Nest.'

Owain smiled wistfully, 'I know. You have met him, and I have not.'

'He is a fine lad. Strong. He will make you proud as you have made me proud.'

'That is not what you said in your letter, Father,' said Owain mockingly.

Cadwgan blew contemptuously, 'If you did not see through that, then you would not be here.'

'I saw that if I travel in your lands or Iorwedd's lands, you will be forced to kill me or lose your lands and life.'

'Whose words do you think those were?'

'Well, I am still hiding in the mountains no matter whose words they were.'

Cadwgan scoffed again, 'Not hiding much! You are the talk of the place. This one has seen you here, that one has seen you there, and wherever they have seen you, there is a trail of destruction.'

'We have destroyed only the property of those who do not belong in these lands or are Norman supporters.'

'And where does that put me with my Norman wife, paying through the nose for your indiscretions?' the old man blustered.

'It is lucky you are my father because, unlike what you have done for your son, I would protect you with my life!'

Cadwgan jumped up unsteadily, 'And you think I would not?' he growled.

'Well, you have taught me to read and that I can do, and it seems quite plain that you have denounced me.'

'Owain, Owain! Was I not in Ireland with you? Have I not pleaded with Henry on numerous occasions?'

'The letter, Father?'

'Means nothing. Henry forced Iorwedd to make a big show about his control of matters.'

'How is Uncle Iorwedd?'

'You think I have aged, my God; you should see Iorwedd. He is gaunt and toothless; his stomach and bowels rule his life, he twitches and cannot sleep. His life was a living hell in that prison. If Bishop Richard told him to eat his own turds, he would do it.'

They sat silently for a while, Owain contemplating the fate of an uncle he had once seen as a superior being, a warrior of renown.

'Son, you must not let them capture you. Once they have you, you are forgotten and will lay festering, shackled, and starved.'

'I do not intend that they do.'

'Know this, whatever your intentions, Henry will not forgive you while you are with Nest.'

'I am not with Nest.'

'But she has not returned to her husband?'

'The husband who was forced upon her, the old man.'

'The old man to whom she swore an oath in holy matrimony.'

'A Norman wedding, not befitting a Welsh princess. Another example of those bastards pillaging what is ours and watering down our culture with theirs or that of their Flemish friends.'

'That's true,' Cadwgan conceded, 'but I can tell you, those bastards, and most of them are, are here to stay, so you would be a wise man to stop your pillaging. If you ever were to go to Henry's court, you would almost die of shock. They live in a different world. We seem like cavemen compared to them. Their army is like a military machine. We are the ancient Britons facing the might of Rome all over again.'

'Did you not teach me that the Ancient Britons won many victories over the Roman might? Did you not teach me that Wales should be united? Did you not teach me the importance of our heritage, culture, and royal line? And then you write me a letter?'

'Finish with that letter, Owain. Do you think I enjoyed writing it? Do you think it made me feel like a man? Like a good father? Enough! If you can win back Henry's favour, your life would be easier, as would mine, because all these grand ideas will come to nothing when the Norman force faces us.'

Owain scoffed, 'Grand ideas? You sound like Madog. He tried to take me to task over my grand ideas, but Father, these ideas were yours.'

Cadwgan sat back in his chair and closed his eyes.

'Do not make me feel more of a failure than I already feel.'

'Then help me.'

Cadwgan's eyes snapped open. 'How?'

'You go to Henry, then. Ask him for a pardon for Madog and me.'

Cadwgan shook his head. 'I have tried already.'

'Try again. Tell him I have hundreds of men deprived of homes and land, angry and want vengeance, and more are joining me daily. Tell him that those men have learnt how to fight, how to take slaves, how to watch and attack when least expected. If he restores my lands and Madog's lands, we will control those men and keep the peace.'

Cadwgan winced and sighed. 'I have already spoken to Iorwedd. He was against going back to Henry. Mind you, now; he realises he cannot keep control. Maybe he might be more open to a journey to court. I will give it a try.'

'Thank you, Father.'

'And Nest? Your son?'

Owain shook his head and stared into the distance, 'I just do not know. Unless Gerald of Windsor dies, then we cannot easily be together.'

'She should have poisoned the bastard when she put the sleeping draught in the wine, not just send him to the latrine!'

Owain threw his head back and laughed, 'You heard about that, did you?'

'Heard about it? The whole of Wales has heard about it.'

Owain smiled. 'Shame he did not drown in there!'

The two men talked until the fire died down. Cadwgan poked at it, but it gave just a sad little flicker.

'I left it too late,' he said, giving the ashes another prod to no avail.

'Time for me to go, I think.'

Cadwgan pursed his lips and raised his eyebrows, then sighed. Putting his arm on his son's meaty shoulder, he embraced him. A tear glistened on the old man's cheeks. 'I will send Uchdryd to Bishop Richard in the morning. Uchdryd has a way of charming even his adversaries, and the bishop seems to trust him. Let's see where that gets us. If the signs are good, I ride to Henry's court and convince Iorwedd to join me somehow.'

As he pulled the hood over his burnished curls, Owain gave his father a look of genuine gratitude. 'Thank you, Father,' he said simply and vanished soundlessly into the corridor.

Chapter 15: Temptations (Late 1110)

Bishop Richard had arrived in Windsor the evening before to catch King Henry early in the day before crowds of those seeking an audience would gather at the royal chamber door. Henry's work time was the morning, and he covered a prodigious amount. By lunchtime, anyone still clamouring for an audience would be dismissed until the following day. The King would lunch and sleep, and then it was time for other pursuits. Henry had always had an insatiable appetite for pleasure.

King Henry spent more time in Windsor these days, so Richard often attended the Great Councils in the castle, where all the leading magnates of the day considered state affairs and made new laws. Archbishops, bishops, and even abbots would sit alongside the mighty earls and barons, their voices just as important.

The bishop ran a cool hand over his finely wrinkled face, brushed a crumb off his upper lip, drew his cloak closer, and stepped out of his lodging into the early morning chill. Men and women, many stooped as they carried enormous loads, were heading towards the centre of the village, and he remembered it was market day. Already vendors were setting up their stalls which provided for the increasing populace driven by the activities at the castle. They all made time to bow to him as he passed, and he nodded magnanimously.

'Lord Bishop, try my honey!' a plump motherly woman called out, but he just smiled and hastened on. Bishop Richard rarely bought from the traders himself, but it was interesting to see the fine quality and range of the goods on offer. His clear, steady eyes scanned the stalls meticulously. There were the usual food goods: milk, butter, cheese, eggs, bacon, fish, apples and flagons of cider or ale. He also noticed some fine leather goods and briefly inspected an intricately stitched calf leather pouch. The bishop had many such, but when the ebony-haired, round-faced merchant offered it as a gift, he thanked him and slid it deep into his robe pockets. He was used to merchants hoping they might buy their way into his prayers; a bishop's prayers were potent in the commoner's mind.

Avoiding the sparks coming from a fire, the bishop observed a heavy, bull-necked, thick-muscled blacksmith wielding a massive hammer on a smoking hot sword blade. The rhythmic clang of metal on metal starkly contrasted with the bronze church bells ringing nearby. There was plenty of call for weapons, with men flocking to fight in Normandy or make their way to earn a place in heaven through their efforts in the holy land.

Next to the blacksmith, a curly-haired stallholder with a thick bushy beard was laying out a selection of knives, but the man's leading trade that day would be to sharpen blades with the coarse and finer whetstones he had lined up behind him. Another stand caught the bishop's eye; the owner, a narrow-faced, freckled man with few teeth, had piled high fine-coloured fabric that looked like it had come from Flanders. While flax was grown in Flanders to weave into linen, the fine woollen cloth with its strong, long fibres came from English wool which was easily spun. Much of the king's revenue came from a tax on the wool leaving English ports, and now the English merchants had brought it back to dress those who could afford such luxury.

Bishop Richard liked Windsor. There was something special about the place where even the sky seemed a deeper blue and the grass a richer green. The solid wooden castle looked down at the sweeping Thames River, and the old Saxon hunting grounds were rich with prey. Richard had never enjoyed hunting, and he smiled as he thought of how King Henry had incurred the wrath of so many noblemen prevented from hunting in their estates because Henry had commandeered them.

In truth, Bishop Richard had little time for the aristocracy with vast tracts of lands handed down from their ancestors. No, he preferred the company of men from humble origins such as his own, clever men like Geoffrey Ridel, who, like Richard, had been born modestly but, because of his brains and acumen, now administered much of Henry's law in

England. Geoffrey was only in his mid-thirties, but his power was immense. Then there was Roger of Salisbury, who was originally a priest but now was in charge of increasing the royal treasury. He wondered whether there was any truth in the story that before Henry became king, he had heard Roger giving a sermon and was so impressed by his speed and skill that when Rufus died, Roger suddenly found himself Chancellor! Yes, Henry had an eye for men with intelligence and efficiency.

Henry had just had new domestic quarters furnished for himself in the castle, and Richard was keen to see them: no expense would have been spared. He sidestepped two little boys who ran out into the street chasing a piglet, disturbing dozens of pigeons who flew up into the air. The bishop made his way up the gently sloping road admiring the building ahead. It was not only marvellously constructed and secure, but it was also an intimidating reminder of Norman domination. Soldiers stretched on the soaring walls, their mail and weapons glinting in the morning sunlight. Richard looked around to see if there was anyone he cared to meet with, anyone who may have something worth listening to. It paid to know what was happening and sniff out any intrigue.

One of the first to arrive, Bishop Richard was swept into the chamber where Henry, still an athletic figure, greeted him warmly. As always, the king was richly attired in a long purple silk tunic embroidered with silver thread with exquisite matching silk slippers. Like his brother, William Rufus before him, Henry enjoyed luxuriant fabrics and colours, but unlike his brother, Henry did not take everything to excess. Whereas Rufus would enjoy wearing extremes of fashion, Henry's clothes were always tasteful. Rufus would often start drinking again as soon as he woke, while Henry ate and drank sparingly in the mornings to keep his brain sharp.

Formalities completed, Henry indicated that the bishop should explain his business.

'Owain ap Cadwgan, sire,' Richard began, licking his top lip.

Henry's forehead furrowed, and his dark eyes became smoky, 'Well?' he asked impatiently.

'I understand he is seeking a pardon.'

Henry snorted dismissively. 'He thinks he will get a pardon from me?'

'It may be worth considering,' the wily bishop ventured cautiously.

Henry looked at the bishop shrewdly. 'This I have to hear.'

The bishop noted the king's brows drawn together over narrowing eyes, and his face had a heightened colour. He steadied himself and met the cold, piercing eyes.

'Well, sire, Owain ap Cadwgan is attracting support like flies to a dung heap. He is shrewd, capable of leadership and seemingly handy with a sword.'

'So?' Henry responded icily, straightening in his seat.

'Sire,' the bishop suggested carefully, 'perhaps it would be useful to be able to engage Owain and his ruffians in pursuit of your ends in Normandy, but before that, to get him to restore peace in his homeland.'

'Cadwgan and Iorwedd are not keeping their people in check?' Henry's manner was increasingly brusque.

'Sire, they are old now, and we have made them toothless beasts, but Owain and his cousin Madog still have energy. They are disruptive on the loose, but if we harness their endeavours, they could serve our purposes.'

Henry tapped his ringed fingers as he thought for a moment.

'It might be useful to take Owain to Normandy if he is as capable as you suggest. By severing his commitment to Wales, we could keep the nobles happy and rid ourselves of a thorn in our side.'

'Indeed, sire.'

'And Princess Nest?' Henry feigned a casual disinterest.

'I understand from my network that Owain ap Cadwgan and Nest are not together. He is in a mountain hideout, and I am unsure of the princess's whereabouts. She was with Owain in Ireland and maybe there yet.'

'Princess Nest is used to a certain standard of living, so I cannot imagine her camping in the mountains with that Welsh heathen. From what I hear, I suspect that the Irish court would not suit her much better.'

'I can make discreet enquiries, sire.'

Henry shrugged. 'It is unimportant to me, but her son may like to know where his mother is, and her husband is keen to have her back.'

The bishop inclined his head. 'And so, sire, you are open to a pardon for Owain ap Cadwgan?'

'I will take your advice.' Henry nodded somewhat grudgingly.

The king stretched his back and glanced towards the door. Bishop Richard was smart enough to know not to prolong the conversation. He bowed low, took a few backward steps and, with a swish of expensive fabric, headed for the door.

'I appreciate everything you do, Bishop Richard,' called Henry after him. 'You use your wits and work tirelessly, and your loyalty is appreciated.'

The bishop coloured with pleasure at the compliments. As he swiftly walked past the mass of petitioners outside the door, his clasped hands behind his back, his eyes alert, he smiled. He would inform Uchdryd that the king was indeed open to the pardon.

***

Owain bristled as he hunched against the rain. He was riding high in the mountain with a small group of retainers, having narrowly extricated them and himself from an ill-planned skirmish of Madog's. Dark clouds had obscured the peaks which towered around them, and the paths were slippery and treacherous.

'Curse them all!' Owain muttered under his breath. He hated being in this position. He wanted to be at his own home, his comfortable llys, in his land, with a warm fire, good food, servants, Nest, and with his son but bloody Madog, that brainless cousin of his, had stirred up trouble again. He had turned his back for one evening, and Madog had slipped off with Owain's best men to cause damage and destruction despite Owain's express request to lie low while he negotiated the opportunity of a pardon.

A rage was growing inside him as he rode toward his camp. Madog's relentless attacks on Norman supporters when Owain needed Powys to seem trouble-free had put his cause at risk. He cursed for the hundredth time that he had been stupid enough to team up with his mad cousin. The man was fearless and could fight, but he did not plan carefully: he had no real strategy other than that driven by his raw ambition. Owain also knew that the future in Madog's eyes was one where Madog ruled, and Owain was left kicking his heels in Ireland or on the slopes of Eryri.

Closing his eyes, exasperated, he thought of how close Madog had come to ruining everything. 'Perhaps it will be all right,' he counselled himself. He reminded himself that no actual harm had been done since he had asked his father to intervene with Henry. If he kept his nose clean, maybe this could still work out. Yes, they had caused a disturbance today, but nobody had been killed, and the injured were few. Cadwgan could probably gloss over any reports of events to Henry by blaming Madog and attesting to his son's desire to rule his lands peaceably.

'Careful here!' Owain's scout called from ahead, 'The mud is deep. Keep to the side.'

Owain directed his mount away from the path and returned to his reverie. The main thing was to get control of his lands and perhaps keep Nest hidden while he thought of a way to dispose of Gerald of Windsor without the blame falling on him. A sudden sickness would deal with Gerald, perhaps, and he was sure he could find someone willing to assist for a fee. God, he missed Nest. His mind wandered to her lying naked, her milky full breasts, rounded hips, and long legs. He felt desire course through him despite the driving rain.

The icy wind was blowing in their faces. They leaned into it as they made their way along the mountain paths, their horses contending with thick roots, slippery rocks, and sometimes stumbling on holes covered with sodden leaves. Snowflakes began to float around them, and within minutes the snow was so thick that the way in front of them was impossible to see.

Owain swore. There was no way they could reach their hideout today, and a heavy fall of snow would make the going almost impossible once it had settled. Behind him, the men were already complaining. It had been a hard few days. He felt time heavy on him and wondered how he could keep the men confined at camp long enough for his father to succeed in getting the Norman king's pardon. There was nothing worse than men idling without purpose. He knew they would drink and fight, pent up with frustration, wanting to wreak vengeance for the lands they had lost. It was hard enough to keep them satisfied in camp for a day or two, but his pardon could take weeks. How in hell would he keep them occupied, warm and fed?

There was a shout from behind. He jerked around in the saddle to see his men making way for two newcomers on horseback.

He nodded to them, recognising them as the pair he had sent to get supplies from one of the hamlets at the foot of the mountain. They left their pack horses at the back of the party as they pushed their horses forward to reach him.

'Gwilym! Ivor! What is it?' he asked, his hand on his sword hilt.

'Bloody Flemings,' Gwilym responded enthusiastically, his broad, flat-nosed face gripped with excitement. 'Wealthy bloody Flemings. Not far from here on the main road. A bishop accompanied by a small, richly dressed group.'

Owain turned his head to one side.

'It's William de Brabant,' said Ivor, small, hard-faced, and greedy. 'I have seen him before.'

Owain was silent for a moment turning his head away to gaze into the distance. Tempting as this opportunity was, it would not pave the way to the life he craved if his father could get a reprieve for him.

'Let him go. We need to find ourselves shelter of some sort before we freeze to death, and there are a couple of wounded men to attend to.'

'Scratches, my lord, we can fight,' Afan protested. He was one of the wounded whose head was swathed in a blood-soaked rag where he had lost most of his ear. The two other wounded: a lugubrious bearded man and a feisty, bald Powysian, joined in, assuring Owain they were ready for another fight. The bearded one had a bandaged left hand, and the bald one's calf had taken a slash but was saved from significant injury by the thick leather boot casing his leg. The boot had once belonged to a wealthy Fleming but now flapped open, revealing bloodied skin beneath. The three wounded men sat more upright in their saddles, purporting fitness. The whole of the weary, dishevelled band was suddenly engaged. They all knew that opportunities to access the kind of booty a Flemish bishop would carry with him did not come about often.

'Lord, he carries on his person alone more wealth than we have seen in months,' urged Gwilym, the stout, swarthy red-faced veteran of many of Owain's forays against the invaders. His partner, younger, pockmarked but muscle-bound, nodded vigorously.

'You heard me,' growled Owain, 'we leave him to go.'

A grumble went through the group. 'Enough!' Owain yelled, competing against a snow flurry. His resolve was weakening, and they all sensed it. He turned his horse towards the mountain and nudged him to move. Even the horse seemed reluctant to plod into the unfriendly bleak world ahead.

'They are just ambling along as if they own the place, arrogant bastards,' Ivor yelled persuasively, jerking his head in the direction of the road far below. There was a chorus of encouragement from the band.

Owain struggled like a starving man with his hand reaching a plate of roast meat. He knew to his very core that to attack the bishop was madness. One stupid mistake from his men, and he would have sent his father to the English court for nothing.

'Lord, they need to be taught a lesson,' came a call from one of his henchmen, his nose dripping in the cold.

The wind blasted snow into Owain's face, and his horse shuddered. He wiped his hand across his eyes. He tried to manage temptation by imagining Nest but affection, even lust, was replaced by a feeling gripping him, that feeling that he always got, the craving for the confrontation, the desperate ache he felt when he thought of how foreigners were on his land. He nudged his horse on, trying again to suppress the ache for vengeance, but he started to argue with his better self: if they were careful, how would anyone know it was him and his men anyway? It was enough, more than enough, to tip the balance of his decision.

He stopped, twisted, and lifted a hand, rising in his stirrups to address his band as a great gust blew snowflakes around them. His deep voice carried across the sound of the wind to the eager men.

'Listen to me, all of you.' He paused, and they watched him unblinking. 'Not one injury, not one wound to any of them! Why in hell's name should the Flemings sleep warm tonight when we, the outlawed owners of the land they are on, are cold and hungry?'

There were wild whoops of agreement.

'Back, boys. Let's give these bastards a night they will not forget in a hurry.'

Gwilym and Ivor elbowed each other, grinning widely.

'Keep hoods up and do not talk,' Owain ordered. 'We make this easy on ourselves. Do you understand? No violence or any action that can lead back to us. We catch up with them, take their valuables, and vanish into thin air.'

With the snow beginning to blanket the mountainside, the group swiftly descended the mountain track. Reaching the wider road, muddy from cartwheels and cattle on their way toward the English market, they stopped in a secluded thicket to confirm their plans. The horses seemed jittery with excitement, and the men were anxious to get on with it. Owain waited until he had everyone's attention before speaking again.

'Not one of you is to harm the bishop and his party, you understand. Threaten but keep your weapons still. After we have taken their valuables and horses, we split up in twos and find shelter where we can: we have enough friends in this country. We come back here to this spot first light tomorrow. Afterwards, we return to the heights and keep ourselves quiet for a few weeks until we get news from my father. If I get my lands back, there will be homes for all of you! No slinking into the mountains! No sleeping in the snow!'

Everyone roared assent, and there was an air of joyous expectation. All the men knew of the wealthy William de Brabant, a bishop who had been the figurehead for the arrival of hordes from Flanders and England. Those men from Flanders had been promised rich Welsh lands and an exemption of tithes by the English crown. They had brutally evicted the Welsh landowners whose ancestors had farmed the land for hundreds of years. Even the most fertile land in Llanstadwell and St Ishmael's, which had belonged to the Bishop of St David's, was seized with no respect for fellow ecclesiastics. Owain nodded at Ivor and Gwilym.

'Onwards.'

Owain moved his weight forward, spurring on his horse which responded with a burst of acceleration down the road. The small party surged after him, mud flicking up, cloaks sailing out behind them. About a mile in front, a cart had stopped around a corner where a sacred spring gushed out of rocks below a steep wooded incline.

William de Brabant's retainers were gathering around the spring, and one man was holding a silver chalice, presumably for the bishop's refreshment. The noise of hooves pounding towards them had been masked by the water and the tree-lined curve of the road, so the element of surprise was with the Welshmen. The bishop sat at the front of the cart next to a tall, lean blonde driver carrying a long whip. The pair turned to look as the riders slid to a halt and quickly surrounded the unprepared retinue.

Bishop William was a tall man, big as were many of the men of Brabant, where easy living on rich soils reflected in the populace. His fair skin was reddened with heavy drinking, and his broad frame carried excess weight achieved from a diet that knew no hardship. Under his thick cloak of otter skin, which was keeping him dry, the bishop's alb, a creamy long tunic, heavily embroidered at the bottom and sleeve ends with gold thread, was immaculate. As he turned on his seat, his cloak gaped open, showing his shoulders and upper arms covered by a maniple of linen embroidered with crosses. Around his waist, he wore a silk cincture heavily ornamented with gold chain and precious jewels, and on the fourth finger of his right hand, he wore a thick gold circlet with a splendid ruby, which melded into insignificance under the majesty of his heavy gold pectoral cross. In his left hand, he carried an ivory crozier. He was as exquisitely adorned as if conducting a service at a fine cathedral.

The display of wealth and the pristine garb was so at odds with the Welshmen's filthy, tattered appearance that Owain swelled with the rage of the usurped for the usurper. The men of the bishop's retinue were terrified as the fierce horsemen surrounded them, but the bishop held his pectoral calmly and regarded the ragged band of men coolly.

'Get down,' ordered Owain, pointing his sword at William de Brabant, who merely raised his eyebrows above piercing blue eyes. The bishop showed no sign of moving, ignoring the threat and calling for his companions to walk on. The bishop's retinue looked at each other and started to shuffle, but Owain moved in front of them, looming above the pair on the cart while the other Welshmen began to circle the foreigners, gradually closing in.

'Be gone!' de Brabant ordered Owain contemptuously.

Six of Owain's men held longbows of yew at the ready, hemp bowstrings drawn back, arrows nocked. The retainers who had had no time to draw their weapons knew that if they so much as moved, they were dead men, and Owain could smell their fear. One Flemish man standing next to the cart tried to lift his spear, but in the blink of an eye, Owain was brandishing his sword, and the man let out a wordless cry of anguish, letting his spear drop.

'Get down,' growled Owain again, and now his anger was tinged with embarrassment that this interloper was refusing to budge from the cart. He did not want anyone to be injured because that would hurt his cause and his chance to be reunited with Nest and meet his child, but he was a prince and could not be humiliated in front of his men. Inside his tunic, he could feel a leather pouch on a thong which held the wisp of hair from his child's head. It reminded him of what he had to lose, and he bit his cheek to control himself.

The bishop looked at the men surrounding his party and glared defiantly at Owain.

'Only God and the King have the right to command me,' he retorted arrogantly, his heavily accented voice further inflaming Owain's ire.

'And which king are you referring to?' asked Owain savagely, his resentment boiling over. 'One of our Welsh kings or that fornicating, ignorant son of a bastard who claims lands that he has no right to?'

The bishop pushed the pectoral in his hand towards Owain. The Welshmen looked nervous now as everyone knew that the pectoral had a special magic, but Owain had little fear of a cross. He edged closer towards the bishop and then slashed the chain with a deft move of his sword so that the pectoral tumbled into the dirt. There was a collective gasp from the Flemish.

Two things happened simultaneously. With a backhand flourish, the driver swung his whip toward Owain, who cut the whip in half as the bishop raised his crozier. It was an instant reaction from Owain. He swept the crozier aside with the side of his sword, but the bishop held it firm. At that exact moment, the horses pulling the cart skittered sideways, and the unbalanced bishop fell onto the heavy wooden wheel, hitting his head hard. Blood gushed out from his temple, down his face, and splattered his fine linen alb as he lay in the dirt, his eyes staring fixedly.

Owain closed his eyes briefly, raised his face to heaven and ordered, 'Kill them all!'

The arrows flew true to their targets, and swords and knives cut throats mercilessly.

Gwilym moved his horse up beside Owain's and surveyed the slaughter.

'Well, the pickings are for the taking, I suppose. Shall I strip the bishop?'

'Strip him. Take everything, including the horses.'

'Lord Owain,' called one of the men as he knelt beside a cowering young boy, 'the Irish will give good money for a healthy, strong boy. Shall we take him?'

'No, kill them all I said. Are you stupid? If this gets out, we will have heavy prices on our heads. If nobody is alive, then nobody can prove our part in this. Scatter boys and meet where we agreed.'

The clean-up was quickly done, and then the horsemen left. Bodies were left strewn where they had fallen, but all valuables and weapons had been removed. Some bodies lay barefooted as the band of men had spotted better leather than they wore themselves.

In the trees above the road, a fair, skinny youth stood in the shadow of ash where he had been relieving himself. His white face was a mask of terror, and for a long while, he stood unmoving. He had seen everything. He had heard everything.

'Oh, God! Oh God!' the youth muttered, his knees shaking.

Eventually, he made his way down to the carnage and checked each of the bodies, pulling them to the side of the road as if leaving them in a tidy pile would give them some comfort. He had known and respected these men his whole life: his mentors, friends, and older brother. With tears coursing down his cheeks, he took the cloaks left on the dead, covering them individually. William of Brabant's rich cloak had been taken, so he placed his own poor cloak over the bishop, closing the man's eyes as he did so while uttering prayers for the bishop and his comrades. He broke off some low branches and piled them over the bodies. Then, believing he could do no more, he started to lope along, sobbing and moaning, taking the opposite direction to the horsemen, hoping to find help before nightfall.

***

'But why were they even on your land in the first place?' asked Gruffydd as he passed Uchdryd the mead.

Gruffydd's teulu had gathered around the fire, riveted by Uchdryd's story. Outside, the llys snow, which had been falling all day, now silenced Aberffraw, and the bitter chill had driven everyone to seek what warmth they could. Only the occasional call of an owl or a fox navigating beneath the clear star-filled sky disturbed the peace.

'Owain ap Cadwgan went to see his father and asked him to intervene with Henry on behalf of himself and Madog. His father agreed and sent me to test the waters with Bishop Richard. The bishop was surprisingly accommodating and agreed with our approach although suggested we could make a better petition to King Henry with Iorwedd on our side.'

'The bishop is up to something,' warned Gruffydd seriously, his fist tapping his mouth as he listened.

'True,' Uchdryd agreed. 'Well, Cadwgan set off to his brother Iorwedd, persuaded him eventually, and the three of us, a small number of our warband, and Iorwedd's most trusted men, headed off to Henry's court. Well, that is not exactly a few hours' journey.'

'It would have taken you a week,' Hywel guessed, and Gruffydd gave him a withering look as if he had said something stupid. Hywel felt hurt. These days Gruffydd was cold towards him, and he wondered whether Gruffydd blamed him for killing Rhys. Hywel knew they should talk it out, but when he tried to raise the subject, Gruffydd made excuses preventing them from being alone.

222

'A week, give or take,' said Uchdryd, smiling at Hywel kindly. Uchdryd missed nothing. 'We were not killing ourselves. Meanwhile, in Owain's absence, Madog had taken it into his head to attack Norman supporters in Iorwedd's country but had taken Owain's men with him. They are a mad lot and eager for a fight. Owain heard of it and set off to try to stop his cousin and retrieve his men, but he reached Iorwedd's land just as the fun was over. The warband left behind by Iorwedd had driven Madog back and, overwhelmed by numbers, Madog and Owain's men were driven away.'

'And that is when they made for Meirionnydd hoping to find safe harbour in Cyfeliog with you?' suggested Gruffydd, moving slightly as a thin stream of winter sunlight lit up his face, momentarily blinding him.

'That's right, but I was not there, you see. I was crossing England on my foolish errand, sleeping in flea-ridden inns with poor food, paying tolls to cross rivers, and trying to avoid gangs who would rob us blind. Anyway, I had instructed my sons not to get entangled with Madog or Owain. When they heard that both men were on their way to Cyfeliog, my sons and their band entreated Madog and Owain to leave peaceably.'

'Did they?' asked Aeddan while Uchdryd took a deep drink.

'Madog took umbrage and lost control of his men who started attacking ours, so when it was clear how it would end, my sons and their men set on them with purpose and drove them off. They said, mind you, that the opposition by Owain and Madog and their band was fierce, and my boys surprised themselves that they managed to overcome them.'

'Well done to them. They had a good teacher.' Gruffydd nodded, leaning forward to stoke the fire so that hundreds of tiny sparks erupted above it. Hywel's heavy boot was ready to stamp out a stray ember that had landed on the reed flooring.

Uchdryd's face beamed, and he sat back, rolling his broad shoulders. 'Of course, we knew nothing of this as we made our way across the English countryside, sampling English ale such as it is, and some of our group exploring temptations, but that is another story. In Meirionnydd, Madog and Owain quarrelled badly and separated.'

'It was bound to happen with those two,' said Aeddan, 'it is a wonder they did not kill each other!'

'I am with you on that,' agreed Uchdryd. 'Owain was livid that Madog had not been able to control his men and, knowing that he owed much to me, Owain had not wanted to cause me distress.'

'Yet he has caused you problems all the same,' pointed out Gruffydd sceptically.

'Madog was wild, apparently, like a cornered cur, dragging up old wounds and spitting that he had been robbed of his short-lived kingship. By then, his men had lost their appetite to fight against their own. He had been humiliated by Owain in front of them.'

'It was an unusual alliance, Madog and Owain. Both have their eyes on the crown in Powys,' commented Hywel.

'True, but there is no question who the people of Powys would prefer,' said Uchdryd.

The men of the teulu nodded and voiced agreement.

'Madog made his way to Powys and Owain to Cardigan. Now if he had been wise, Owain would have just let things rest until he heard back from his father. Still, no, succumbing to the lure of easy pickings and the pressure from his warband when he heard that Bishop William de Brabant was also on the way to London and close by, he thought he would take a little revenge for all the Welsh farmers whom the bishop had forced off their holdings.'

There were mutterings from the teulu in support of Owain. Even though they had respect for the clergy, William de Brabant had himself violated God's laws as far as they could see.

'I have heard that Owain had only intended to steal from the bishop, but somehow something went wrong, and Owain ordered that all the party be killed.'

A collective gasp emanated from the teulu. The theft was one thing: the murder of a bishop and his retinue was another.

'Good Lord, preserve us,' said Gruffydd, shocked and shaking his head.

'Unfortunately for Owain, one young man was hiding and saw and heard everything, including his men calling him 'Lord Owain'. After Owain and his men had left, that young man found his way to a Flemish community, and they relayed word to de Brabant's brother, who rode immediately, with a small group of men, all the way to the English court to seek justice.'

The men murmured and sighed, all in agreement at Owain's stupidity.

'The Flemings arrived just as Henry had almost agreed to pardon Owain,' Uchdryd continued shaking his head. 'Suddenly, a Fleming barged in shouting that Owain ap Cadwgan had murdered his brother Bishop William de Brabant and all his retinue. Not only that, but it turned out that when Owain realised that there were armed men everywhere looking for him as the murderer of the bishop, he decided that since all was certainly lost for his pardon, he would turn his band to Dyfed and exact vengeance on the enemy. He razed a town to the ground, took captives and set off to Dublin in the ships he had brought with him from Ireland, which had waited for instruction from him in Cardigan.'

'He has brought about his downfall,' Gruffydd remarked tersely.

'He has,' agreed Uchdryd, 'and he almost brought about ours. King Henry was outraged at the barbarous treatment of a man of the cloth and railed at Cadwgan, accusing him of violating his agreement with him not to allow Owain onto Cadwgan's lands, let alone succour him.'

'And what said Cadwgan?' asked Gruffydd.

Uchdryd opened his eyes wide and held open his big hands, shrugging his shoulders. 'That this was done completely without his knowledge. Henry flew into a passion the like of which I have never seen, pronouncing that since Cadwgan was unable to control his son, his lands would be given to one who could. Cadwgan was given twenty days to order his affairs and move out of Wales.'

'And that is how Gilbert Strongbow now finds himself Lord in Ceredigion and immediately erects two castles, one upon the mouth of the River Ystwyth and another upon the Teifi River near Dyfed at Dyngeraint,' Gruffydd surmised.

The teulu immediately began to lament amongst themselves.

'Now, if I am correct, Gilbert did not get on well with William Rufus, yet Henry rewards and supports him,' continued Gruffydd thoughtfully.

'Yes, you are right. Henry was waiting for an opportunity to give Gilbert lands, and Owain conveniently presented him with such an opening. Now we will have trouble.' Uchdryd sat back in his chair and stretched his arms above his head.

'And Madog?' asked Hywel.

'Off like a hare to Ireland as well, leaving Gilbert easily able to make it look like he has brought about peace. Madog's and Owain's men have largely disbanded, and many good fighters are amongst them. If they are of interest, you might quietly let it be known you would welcome them.'

Hywel glanced at Gruffydd but found no response there. As the leader of the warband, Hywel needed to keep the respect of the men: he must be seen to lead. He decided he would say his piece.

'Trouble is brewing, and I do not like the Normans having it so easy, gaining land that is not theirs. We need to make it difficult for them.'

This brought firm assent from the teulu.

'Where will they be marching next?' Hywel persisted. 'They are meddling to set kin against kin in Powys, to weaken the power so they can infiltrate more easily. When Owain fled with Nest, Bishop Richard tried to do the same here in North Wales. Gronwy ap Owain was ready to take advantage of any opportunity that arose. I say we welcome those men who find themselves homeless, and we may be glad of their swords in times to come.'

An angry murmur of agreement ran around the group.

'You worry too much about Gronwy,' said Gruffydd disparagingly, but a quick glance around the room pulled him up. Hywel was well-liked and respected by his men, and they did not appreciate the tone their king was using. Gruffydd felt a pang of envy. His relationship with his teulu was a matter of pride, and this slight wavering from the complete respect he was used to, felt like a chink in his armour. He knew he needed to curb the powerful emotion which seemed to be engulfing his day-to-day actions and relationships. When he spoke again, he forced a warmth he did not feel.

'I do agree with you, Hywel. Those men need to find leadership, and where better than here? With some well-planned raiding and disruption, we may even make the castle building a bit trickier for our friend Gilbert.'

The broad grins on the faces of the men confirmed their king had hit the mark, but somewhere deep inside, he wondered whether he was taking the slippery road to Hell just to please a warband impatient for action.

'Our policy, outwardly, should be peaceful relations with the Normans, but why should they have it so easy? They have no respect for traditional owners of our lands,' Gruffydd continued.

'Henry is also very occupied now with this so-called 'Exchequer' he has brought in,' reflected Uchdryd.

'What is that?' Aeddan asked the question almost all of them had on their lips.

'This system was introduced by one of Henry's 'new men', Roger of Salisbury. Henry is a wily fox. He takes men from humble origins and promotes them into positions of authority that otherwise would have gone to the aristocracy,' Uchdryd explained.

'Keeping the aristocracy in check,' added Gruffydd.

'Exactly,' Uchdryd agreed. 'You know, when you think about it, King Henry's father created eighteen earls who caused him endless problems, but Henry has got rid of most of them. Now only seven earls hold power, but that's another story.'

Gruffydd lifted one eyebrow. The teulu grinned and chuckled. Uchdryd always had another story.

'I digress again,' said Uchdryd amiably. 'Old age makes a brain wander'.

'Not yours, Lord Uchdryd,' said Gruffydd. 'Your brain is sharper than anyone's.'

Uchdryd looked pleased with the accolade and, flushing slightly, continued. 'Anyway, young Roger, keen as possible, saw that the crown's income was not properly accounted for. Henry had to raise a huge dowry for his daughter Matilda and the administration fell to Roger.'

'That is a job I would not want!' commented Aeddan.

'Nor I!' agreed Uchdryd, 'But imagine this. Roger constructed an enormous counting table, ten feet by five feet, covered with a chequered cloth decorated with vertical and horizontal squares. Each column represented money; you see pennies, shillings, and multiples of pounds. The top row was covered with counters representing what was to be collected by the crown, while the row below was for what was yet owing to the crown and had not been paid. Then, tallies of payments were recorded on a stick notched on each side, showing how much had been paid and the stick was split down the middle. So simple but so effective. Old Henry has no forgery now when the sheriffs come in twice a year to pay over the king's revenue.'

'So that system is being rolled out nationwide?' asked Gruffydd.

'Yes, so there is much administration keeping Henry tied up. Then there is this marriage of Matilda. That is also keeping him busy.'

'And the difficulties with Louis of France,' added Gruffydd.

Uchdryd could see a few blank faces and explained. 'Louis of France is supporting the rights of Robert Curthose's son, Henry's nephew, William Clito. Henry tried to kidnap Clito, but it went awry.'

'Embarrassing.' Gruffydd winced.

Uchdryd nodded. 'Then there are the twenty-odd illegitimate children to marry off to create useful connections and networks. Fair play to Henry, though; he gives himself tirelessly to bedding all his courtier's wives and daughters to produce more bastards to secure the English throne.'

This brought hilarity to the table. The teulu always enjoyed Uchdryd's contagious good humour. Only Hywel, who remembered King Henry's overtures to Angharad when they had met, did not laugh.

Gruffydd noted the expression and wondered sourly again if it were possible that Hywel was too friendly with his wife. Was he picking up the vestiges of shame? He would ensure that Hywel was away from the llys for a time creating difficulties for Gilbert, the eager new Lord of Ceredigion.

'So, a good time to make things uncomfortable for our foreign friends in Powys then,' Uchdryd guffawed but, seeing Gruffydd and Hywel's serious faces, he added reassuringly, 'Your support will not be forgotten. Powys has a long memory.'

The teulu hit the table with their palms. Excitement over the prospect of raiding was apparent.

***

Nest was sitting near the fire in her room. She turned as there was a tentative knock.

Angharad entered, and as soon as Nest saw the expression on her face, her worst fears were confirmed.

'It is true then?' she asked, remaining controlled and dignified, willing her beautiful face not to betray her.

'Gruffydd says that Owain and his men led the attack on Bishop de Brabant.'

Nest looked back towards the fire, closing her eyes and breathing deeply.

'And his father, Cadwgan?'

'He has been given only days to leave Wales. His lands have been given to Gilbert Strongbow.'

Nest let out a little gasp.

'Owain has provided King Henry with a fine excuse to reward Gilbert with lands at no cost to himself, and now Gilbert will chip away to carve himself a rich holding.'

'I am sorry.'

Nest looked across at the little cradle where Llewellyn was sleeping contentedly.

'You have been kinder than anyone could expect, but now I think it is time I returned to my husband.'

Angharad gripped the other woman's arm, 'Surely not, Nest.'

'I have kept hope alive for so long, but Owain's love for me and our son was not enduring enough for his restless soul. No, I must think differently now. I will return to Gerald and convince him that with all I have gleaned from my time away from him, I see it is important to keep the Welsh on my side. He fears a Welsh uprising. Then when my brother, Griffith, leaves Ireland to seek the restoration of his inheritance, I will insist that he stays with us. I will concentrate my thoughts on helping the Welsh. My brother can learn about the enemy from within.'

'Nest, is it wise what you are proposing?'

'My lovely friend, if I might call you that, I have had so much time to think. I had some months of real love, reciprocated love, and now that is over. From here, I will be mistress of my domain, outwardly a compliant wife, but I will work for the ends of my true family. In Ireland, I felt deep sisterly love for my brother. He is a man of honour, but his passion runs high for his homeland and the return of his family's inheritance.'

Angharad nodded. 'It was so with Gruffydd when he was in Ireland.'

'The Irish have been true friends to Owain and my brother Griffith.'

'As they were to us,' admitted Angharad. 'You would not return to Ireland, to Owain?'

'I would not run after him now. He has made it clear where I stand. If I had not been born Welsh, I could live in Ireland, but no, I will clear paths for my brother and fight my silent war against the invaders. After all, I was a princess born.'

Angharad grasped her hand.

'Will Gerald take you back so easily?' She was sure that in her place, Gruffydd would not.

Nest spoke softly. 'Oh, he will take me back. His pride will have been hurt, and I will comply with the story that I was taken against my will, that Owain did it as a sign to the Normans that they cannot take all that is Welsh so easily.'

Angharad frowned wonderingly as Nest went on.

'Gerald has always loved me even though I have only been fond of him. Is it not always the way that those you love least will love you most and those you love most will love you least.'

'Nest, I am certain Owain did love you, and he also gave up a lot to be with you.'

'A fleeting love!' said Nest with a hint of bitterness. Angharad squeezed Nest's arm.

'You will be missed here by all of us. Gwenllian will be heartbroken to lose you. You have become such a beacon in her life.'

Nest felt her tears rising and blinked them away, but when she spoke, there was a break in her voice, 'I am sorry she has only seen a weaker version of who I am. I would have had her see that women can be strong.'

'Nest, you are a strong woman. You have endured so much. Where you walk, only admiration and respect follow.'

Nest's eyes opened wide at this, and she blushed. 'You are too kind. Thank you! I am not a good example of a virtuous woman. Not a woman such as yourself, untarnished and god-fearing.'

'You are a good woman, Nest, and you judge yourself harshly. You have survived where others would have been destroyed.'

'Thank you for that.'

'What of Llewelyn? Will Gerald accept him?'

'He will accept him as he did King Henry's son, but I will make sure that Llewelyn is given a Welsh upbringing. His first language will be Welsh, he will be immersed in Welsh poetry and song, and I will have him educated so he knows our rich heritage and the stories of our Welsh saints.'

'When he is old enough, we will welcome him here for him to learn his battle skills,' said Angharad, leaning over the cradle and stroking the tousled head of the sleeping baby. She wondered what would happen to this little boy before he reached his fourteenth birthday when noble boys were sent to other families to learn the skills they would take into manhood.

Nest smiled sweetly, 'That would be an honour, and there is no family I would trust more!'

Only once Angharad had left her did Nest's shoulders sag, and her poise slipped away. Tears coursed under her long lashes, and her body heaved with sobs. Once again, life had dealt her a brutal blow.

Chapter 16: Vengeance (Spring 1111)

It was a lazy afternoon, and Owain lay along the branch of an oak tree. He was lithe yet broad-shouldered and pleased with his strength and agility. Diligent in everything he did, he would run along the sands as soon as the cock crowed, forcing his body to more incredible speed until he could almost feel his muscles hardening. He brushed away heavy, rich brown hair from his face in an action reminiscent of his father's. His intelligent hazel eyes gazed up at a pigeon cooing securely from a branch far enough above to allow quick escape.

Below Owain, in a v-shaped split in the trunk, his sister, Gwenllian, copper hair tumbling in curls down past her waist, crouched, examining a ladybird as it explored the length of her slim arm. They were both hidden from view by the luxuriant drooping green foliage. Cadwaladr, below them, leant back against the tree's rough trunk. He was serious-faced for once under his chestnut mop, carving a small dog out of a piece of wood.

'Damn!' Cadwaladr cursed when his knife slipped. He had grown tall but was still gangly, with his long legs stretched before him. The older he got, the more he favoured his father in looks but not temperament. Cadwaladr, unlike the siblings lolling in the tree above him, had little concentration for tasks which required too much effort. He had a massive sense of fun and was much beloved by his friends, but he tended to test boundaries and had a propensity to get away with it. His cherubic green-eyed look and boundless curls endeared him to all, but his carelessness and flippancy meant he was often not taken seriously.

A little distance away, their small sisters were making potions as they squeezed the 'juice' of leaves and flower petals into a dish filled with water while Susannah and Bethan, who were watching them, gossiped in the stillness of the afternoon. Annest, bossy and red-haired ruled her younger sisters and instructed them on what to find and where. Rainaillt and Marged, so alike they might have been twins, frowned up at her from their round ruddy faces, then ran off together hand in hand, their golden hair streaming behind them. Baby Susanna, who rarely cried and whose dark blue eyes always beamed with pleasure, sat on her well-padded bottom, and sucked her ginger hair.

Owain turned his attention to his father, every inch the warrior king, striding across the courtyard towards the stables, his arm along Cadwallon's shoulder. His golden-haired brother was looking up at their father proudly, and Owain felt a twinge of envy. Whatever his father told Cadwallon would be forgotten as soon as he was racing his horse across the sands or drinking ale with his sycophantic friends as they played games of chance or as he tumbled away from prying eyes with red-faced girls from the llys.

Owain ap Gruffydd knew his place. He was the second born and would always be loyal to his brother even though he thought himself a much better future king. Cadwallon was too impetuous, lacked attention, and could not see the consequences of his actions. One day, Owain was sure, Cadwallon's arrogance and short temper would lead him into serious trouble. Owain flicked an ant out of his thick brown hair and gazed soulfully after his brother and father. His father found it awkward that he, Owain, often showed up his older brother, and that was why he had stopped teaching them together: it was embarrassing for Cadwallon when Owain was quicker at understanding than he was, a better swordsman than he and Owain knew that his father found it easier to talk to him than his firstborn. Still, that altered nothing. Being born a second son was something which would never change.

'What are you thinking? You are very quiet!' Gwenllian broke his train of thought, her twinkling blue-violet eyes penetrating as if she could read his mind.

'I am thinking about Rhys and wondering how he is going at Gronwy's llys,' he lied quickly.

Gwenllian grimaced. 'I think Gronwy's llys would be a horrible place to be. Can you imagine? Gronwy does not believe in fun!'

'He believes in drinking himself into a stupor. You could get away with anything while he slept it off!'

Gwenllian laughed, the filtered light dancing across her face as a slight breeze blew. Her father did not ever get drunk. Never. He had encouraged them to have a little alcohol from the time they were small so that they were used to it and would avoid stupidity when they were older.

'Always control it, not it you,' her father would tell them all. 'You must always keep your mind clear because you never know what important decision you must make or what attack you must defeat.'

'I cannot understand why people drink so much that they vomit and go around with sore heads all day,' Gwenllian mused out loud, 'To do it once, I understand, but to do it all the time is idiocy.'

Her brother agreed.

The ladybird Gwenllian had been observing flew off, and she looked down to see how Cadwaladr had progressed with his carving.

'The carving looks good,' she said encouragingly.

'The knife is not sharp enough, and my fingers are getting blisters,' Cadwaladr complained.

'Do you want me to do some?' she asked.

Cadwaladr looked up and rolled his eyes.

'How is your great huge tapestry coming along?'

Gwenllian sighed dramatically. 'I hate it to the bottom of my soul. If I must stitch one more flower, bird, or hound, I will think about drowning myself!'

They all laughed. Gwenllian broke a straight twig off a branch and started parrying and thrusting with it.

'Do you want to use my knife,' Owain asked Cadwaladr. 'I sharpened it this morning.'

'I'll try it. Throw it down. Thank you!'

Owain threw the knife accurately, so the blade landed between Cadwaladr's legs.

'Hey, careful,' he yelled up at Owain, scowling ferociously but, admiring the sharp blade, started to work on the carving again.

There was a shriek as Marged spilt potion onto Annest's dress and then ran. As Annest tried to grab at her sister, Marged swerved in and out of trees keeping just out of her reach. Susanna squealed with delight, and Rainaillt egged her young sister to run faster. Bethan stood up, hands on hips, calling, 'Come on! Settle down. No real harm done.'

'Have you heard anything of Princess Nest?' Owain asked.

'Only that her brother, Griffith, is supposed to come from Ireland to join her.'

'Where?'

'In Pembroke. He will be staying with Nest and Gerald of Windsor as well.'

'With Gerald of Windsor?' Owain repeated incredulously.

'Yes. I am not sure how that will work out. Griffith hates the Normans. I heard Father say Griffith hopes to reclaim his lands with support from Ireland. Father said that he would expect support from Gwynedd too.'

Owain sat upright.

'That would mean war for sure.'

'Yes,' said Gwenllian excitedly. 'King Henry would not allow that would he?'

'How is it that you hear these things?' Owain asked, peeved.

'I am a girl. I am overlooked. I just fade into the background with my harp and keep my ears and eyes open.'

'What else have you heard?'

Gwenllian considered. 'Mother heard from someone in Ireland that Madog hated it there and has returned to Wales. He did not like their customs, but I heard Mother say that he thinks, with Owain out of the way over there, he has a chance to get his band together and maybe even try to regain his lands.'

'King Iorwedd would not be happy about Madog being back.'

'Oh, I heard something about that too,' Gwenllian crowed, and her elder brother tried to contain his exasperation. 'Iorwedd got word that Madog was back and issued a proclamation that he forbade any of his countrymen from aiding Madog in any way and that they would be penalised harshly if they did. Oh yes, Madog was considered an 'enemy' and should be brought to him as a prisoner.'

'Not a friendly way to treat your nephew!' remarked Owain sarcastically.

'Well, what would you do?' asked Gwenllian.

Owain considered. 'I would not want to be banished like Cadwgan ap Bleddyn, so I would send him money to stay out of my lands and keep to the hills and mountains. I would encourage him to attack the foreign settlers but not from my lands.'

'Maybe that is what he has done, and he is just issuing the proclamation to please Henry,' suggested Gwenllian.

'No, the proclamation humiliates Madog and puts him in danger of people seeking a reward for his head. People say that Iorwedd has always been nervous of Madog but terrified of Henry.'

'I heard Father say that Iorwedd was a bag of wind.'

The two boys laughed.

'Anyway, Father also said that Madog has sworn revenge on Iorwedd.'

'He should not have done that. Now Madog will need to carry out his threat, or he will lose the respect of his band. He should have silently decided to get revenge but not proclaim it. Then if the winds change, he can still ally with Iorwedd,' reasoned Owain.

Gwenllian tossed her hair over her shoulders. 'I like the idea of proclaiming revenge. Then everyone in his band would see Madog as strong and want to support him.'

'Hmm,' said Owain, unwilling to argue with his deliberately antagonistic sister. 'Anything else we should know about?'

'Nothing of much interest. You know that Hywel, the warband, and Owain ap Cadwgan's men who came here are attacking the Flemish villages and castles Gilbert Strongbow is constructing. That is supposed to be a secret.'

'Everybody here thinks they are protecting our borders against stray hothead bands,' said Owain.

'Well, we are not going to say anything, are we?'

'Of course not!' said Owain. 'Cadwaladr?'

'Of course not! I do not understand any of it. If it is all happening in Wales, why does King Henry even come into it?'

Owain sighed. 'Because all the Welsh kings accept him as an overlord.'

'Why?' asked Cadwaladr. 'I have never understood it. What does he do for us?'

'Not annihilate us,' said Owain.

'How could he do that? He has not been successful before?'

'Because if he decides to attack with all his might, we could win some battles, but we would lose most of our fertile lands.'

'Why? We are great fighters,' argued Cadwaladr.

'Because we are not united. The Welsh kings betray each other, making us weak,' explained Owain.

'Father had fought them before and won,' Gwenllian corrected him stoutly.

'He did before we were born, but then the Irish Norse, who were supposed to be on the Welsh side, changed sides to the Norman side and defeated Father in battle. They burnt Anglesey to the ground.'

Gwenllian was silent for a while, contemplating how awful it would have been to be in Anglesey then. She knew people who had fought at that time still carried disabling wounds. Some older friends had no fathers at all because they had fought and died at that time. She knew her father helped those families.

'Father has fought in Ireland, though,' she persisted, 'many times since then and was lauded for his prowess in battle.'

'I am not disputing how good Father is; I am saying that sometimes you must be wary of the bigger power. The Normans are dripping with riches and have thousands and thousands of men. They are like the Romans. Nobody took on the Romans too often and won.'

'Boadicea did. She led her troops against them and won.'

'Yes, she won the battle but not the war.'

'One day, one day, I am going to fight them. Lead men out against them. Defeat them. When the Welsh see a woman fighting for their lands, they will feel ashamed and unite.'

Below her, Cadwaladr laughed outright at the idea.

'What is so funny?' Gwenllian retaliated.

'One day, one day,' mimicked Cadwaladr in a high falsetto, 'you will marry someone with a great big llys and do all the boring things that Mother does.'

Gwenllian threw her stick down and knocked the knife out of his hand, so it fell to the ground. He was up in a flash, scooped up the knife, and pointed it at her.

'You do that again, Sister, and you will see where this will land!'

'Be quiet, both of you,' said Owain, and Gwenllian made a face at him.

The younger girls were now all singing and clapping as Susannah and Bethan taught them the words of an old Welsh children's counting song. Gwenllian remembered being taught the same song; it seemed so long ago.

'So,' she asked Owain. 'Are you going to allow the enemy to build all over your lands when you are of age?'

Owain's face darkened. 'Cadwallon and I have discussed this, and we will not. Believe me; we will not. We will be nowhere and everywhere. We will harass and drive them out of Wales by making their lives hell. To their faces, we will be obliging and charming, pay them what they ask, and then raid their strongholds in the darkness of the night until we have collected back a hundred times the value of what we paid them.'

'I will gladly do the same,' said Cadwaladr grinning.

'And I,' swore Gwenllian. 'You may doubt me, but I know I was born to fight.'

'Gwenllian are you talking about fighting yet?' said Cadwallon, who had stealthily crept up behind them.

Gwenllian jumped. 'You startled me. Why are you creeping up on us?'

'Aeddan has been teaching me to creep, using shadows and noises in nature like the wind or creaking trees to hide the sounds and movements I make so that one day I can slit the throat of sentries before they know I am even there!' he proclaimed, hoisting himself quickly up onto the lowest branch and giving Gwenllian a nudge to move along.

'I'd like to learn that too. Will you teach me?' asked Gwenllian.

'Why would a girl need to learn that?' scoffed Cadwallon.

'Cadwallon, I have had enough of being told what I cannot do because I am a girl. Leave it be, or else I will show you exactly what a girl can do!' Gwenllian shot back at him.

'We were just talking about how we will give the Normans no rest when we are of age,' Owain jumped in quickly before things got out of hand.

'I hate them!' said Cadwallon vehemently. 'I keep asking Father if I can go raiding with Hywel to learn from him, but he refuses me. Instead, he has just given me an hour lecture about how the Normans are trying to undermine our laws and religion and how we must deal with it.'

'How must we deal with it?' asked Owain, immediately interested.

'I stopped listening. It was so tedious.'

'Cadwallon,' Owain reproved him. 'You need to understand these things. One day you will be a king.'

'Shut your mouth. Listen to yourself. Do you know how to enjoy yourself at all? What I want to learn is how to conquer our enemies. I want to see how people fight. I want to understand what you must do with your troops to outwit the enemy, but I am not even allowed to go along on a simple raid,' said Cadwallon moodily, but he knew from their faces that his words had struck a chord with his siblings.

'Let's make a blood pact, we four,' said Gwenllian. 'Pass the sharp knife, Cadwaladr. Let's swear that we four will do everything possible to drive the Normans from Wales.'

The three brothers looked at her uncertainly.

'Come on,' she insisted, slashing her palm with the proffered blade.

'I'll swear to that gladly,' agreed Cadwallon, prompted by his sister's fearless display and pulling out his dagger.

'And I,' added Owain earnestly, his knife already cutting into the flesh of his hand.

'And I,' echoed Cadwaladr stretching up to his siblings and easily cutting his palm with his little knife so blood dripped down his arm.

The four children held out their hands; their palms slit enough to draw blood, then smearing their blood together, they made their oath. Gwenllian's eyes blazed with intensity, and her cheeks flushed with triumph.

'To Gwynedd and all of Wales!' she said passionately, and her brothers echoed her words.

***

Dyddgu combed her hair with fury while her maid, Gwir, now old and arthritic, pulled the best robe out of the oak box at the end of the bed. Gwir was white-haired, with a soft round motherly face creased with laughter lines. Her grey eyes twinkled as she watched her mistress pulling and tugging at her thick black hair, but she knew it was best to say nothing. Even as a small child in this very llys in Cedewain, if Dyddgu had become upset, it was advisable to keep a reasonable distance or be hit by whatever happened to be within reach. The only way of snapping her out of the mood was humour because, in fairness to Dyddgu, she turned from anger to hilarity in the blink of an eye. And back again!

'We could lose everything because of this stupidity,' Dyddgu spat venomously. 'I brought this llys to our marriage. Everything in this llys, just about, is from my family. Now my stupid husband will leave me and his six children homeless. Who does he think he is?'

'Lord Llywarch ap Trahearn, Lord of Cedewain, when I last heard him introduce himself, mistress,' said Gwir.

Dyddgu turned and pulled her face at the old woman but then allowed Gwir's arthritic fingers to pull her hair into plaits. Still smouldering, she closed her eyes as Gwir gently worked her hair but allowed herself to be soothed. She thought of her brown-haired stocky husband whose easy

243

nature pacified her intense moods but whose passion for her and his family had never ceased.

'I will put a little lavender oil to smooth your hair,' Gwir muttered as she rubbed the oil between her palms.

Dyddgu pondered how Llywarch pined for the lands he grew up in, which had passed to his older brother, Owyn ap Trahearn, on his father's death. She pictured the sparsely wooded mountains of Arwystli, the moorland stretching across the landscape and the fertile soil of the Caerws Basin, so small compared to the rich lands of Gwynedd or Powys. The earth was good because of the River Severn, the longest river in Wales, rising in the high ground and snaking its way through the lush valleys joined by its tributaries: the Cerist and the Clywedog. It was a poor cantref compared with others, yet the Romans had settled there, and Robert of Rhuddlan and Roger of Montgomery craved it. Even now, Powys and Gwynedd hovered over it like the red kites that climbed in circles with the early sun. Yes, Llywarch yearned for that land.

'Stay still, now, if you want your hair to last the night,' reprimanded Gwir.

'You need to hurry,'

'I am going as fast as I can,' grumbled the old woman.

Dyddgu retreated into her thoughts again. She mused that their family would never have the power of Gwynedd or Powys, but they were not insignificant. Their name was good, and Llywarch's father had ruled Powys and Gwynedd for a while. Her husband had been just a young man when his father, Trahearn, had been killed at Mynydd Carn. Gruffydd ap Cynan, the husband of Angharad ferch Owain, had only been a boy waiting in Ireland until he was of age to contest his right to Gwynedd when his cousin of the same name had slaughtered Trahearn ap Caradog. So long ago but not forgotten. It had been a brutal battle, and from it, Llywarch had learned to keep the peace, yet the ache of his loss was always inside him. She groaned and made her hands into fists. With their six children filling the house, why would her husband now risk everything? He had seen what had happened to his father.

'He should not even have agreed to see Madog ap Rhyrid,' she complained to Gwir. 'That man is evil. What man swears vengeance against his kin? And why would my Llywarch, a peace-loving man until now, need to have anything to do with a man of Powys who has burned and maimed his way into Norman hatred? Llywarch even forced us to call our baby son, Robert, a Norman name just to keep our overlords happy, and now he takes this risk!'

'You know why, mistress,' said Gwir gently. 'Since Owain ap Cadwgan killed Llywarch's brothers, he has grieved for Meurig and Griffri and their fatherless toddlers. He and his brothers, who were close in years, grew closer when their father was killed in battle. You know that for years he has walked about the llys at night. Why would he do that except that he is tormented and has not avenged them?'

'That's not true. He rode out with Madog to search for Owain and Nest to bring him to justice.'

'But that came to nothing, mistress.'

'It was at least a hunt sanctioned by Bishop Richard. This foolishness is aimed at Iorwedd ap Bleddyn, who is hand in hand with the Normans. If they lay a hand on him, we will be hunted down.'

Gwir took the robe off the bed and shook it gently so that the lavender, keeping it fresh, fell into the reeds on the floor. Her mistress lifted her arms, and the maid gently pulled it over her head, making sure not to disarrange her mistress's hair.

There was a knock, and Dyddgu's daughter, Gladwys, the spitting image of her mother, popped her head around the door. She looked up wide-eyed and smiled immediately to see how fine Dyddgu looked wearing her red robe embroidered with tiny golden flowers around the neck and sleeve.

'Lord Madog and his men are here, Mammy.'

'I will be there right now. Is your father meeting them in the courtyard?'

'Yes, he is there with the boys.'

'I will come to the main door. Is Elen washed and dressed?'

'Yes, Mammy.'

'Bring her to the front door then. And Gladwys?'

The little girl glanced over her shoulder, 'Yes, Mammy.'

'You will sing for them when they first sit, and then you will play the harp while they eat.'

'Yes, Mammy.'

When the girl had run off to find her sister, Dyddgu rose quickly from her seat, turned to face Gwir, her brown eyes unguarded and put her head on one side for approval. The old lady nodded proudly at her mistress' fine curvy figure, which had only been enhanced by childbearing. She remembered when Dyddgu had been a skinny little thing like Gladwys, but now she was a woman that a man would want to draw to him. She smiled that her mistress still needed her reassurance. Dyddgu brushed her tunic down with her hands again, stood straight, took a deep breath, and reached the door.

The sky was tinged with ominous shades of purple above the looming indigo mountain range. Madog was already off his horse being led away, and although Llywarch was introducing his sons, Madog showed little interest. Dyddgu was watching from inside, hurt and offended, yet she received Madog warmly enough when he strutted into her home, hardly acknowledging her.

'Lord, you are welcome,' Dyddgu said, bowing low.

As her husband welcomed Madog's men, Dyddgu turned to lead their guest into the hall, but she felt as if there was a cold draught on her back. She shivered. The man was tall, lean, and broad-shouldered but unkempt, and she wondered when he had last washed himself. His eyes quickly took in the modest but comfortable hall, the few precious things which graced the long oak table, and something about his obvious assessment of their family angered Dyddgu. She flashed a look of fire at her husband, but when she turned to Madog, her face was impassive.

Llywarch entered with his arms around his smallest boys as if that could appease the slight they had received. The boys looked up at him with pride and love. Madog's men trailed behind, their faces anticipating a good feed as they smelled the roasting meat and vegetable broth. Some looked haggard, their faces wan, their eyes red-rimmed, and all were unshaven. Dyddgu saw many scarred but powerful arms used to stretch the strings of their longbows until the cords of their muscles had been pulled taut.

Llywarch gestured to the long table and invited the visitors to take their seats. He nodded to his sons to take their places at a lower table with their sisters. Even though Cadafael was the eldest and much beloved of his parents, he was a simpleton, so the second son, Meredydd, guided his younger brothers, Madoc and Iorwerth, to their places. He caught the eye of the servant to bring them a platter of food to share. Cadafael, round-faced with thick brown hair, smiled blissfully when the food arrived, quickly filling his mouth with the meat so that grease spilt down his chin.

Meredydd glanced at the top table, wishing he could hear more clearly what was being said there, but Madoc and Iorwerth were too young to care about such things and just laughed with their older brother. Meredydd had dark hair hanging loosely at his shoulders, and a short temper, and his almost black eyes flashed a warning look at his brothers as their noise threatened the little he could hear of their guests' conversation.

'Sshhh,' he hissed at his brothers. Madoc and Iorwerth were also dark-haired, but while Meredydd's narrow face always had an intense expression, they were prone to laughter, their moods much lighter in keeping with their age. As he stared at the top table, he winced when he caught an expression of disgust cross Madog ap Rhyrid's face as his eyes settled on Cadafael rocking as he cleaned his platter with rye bread before cramming it into his mouth so that his cheeks bulged and juice dripped onto his tunic. Meredydd moved himself to block Cadafael from the visitor's view.

Gladwys sang as sweetly as an angel, and the song, in honour of all great Welsh warriors, seemed well received.

Dyddgu observed Madog ap Rhyrid as he leaned back in his chair in the place of honour, watching her daughter. She could tell he appreciated her beauty, which made up somewhat for his disdain of Llywarch, their home, the meal they had provided at short notice, and his disgust when he watched Cadafael, whose heart was as big as a bull's. She was furious at him for undervaluing them when he was unkempt, ungracious, and a landless beast. Madog's thick, dark hair was matted in places from sleeping rough, yet he had the air of someone who thought very highly of himself. He might have been a handsome man, Dyddgu decided, but for his broken nose and downturned mouth, he turned his cold dark stony eyes on the raven-haired beauty as he felt her gaze on him. She shivered. This man knew no restraint: she sensed a kind of madness in him. She managed a smile, but it did not reach her eyes.

Her singing over, Gladwys weaved her way through the crowded tables to her siblings.

'You sang beautifully, Gladwys,' whispered her sister Elen, her voice full of warmth. Gladwys blushed, pleased.

Elen was younger than Gladwys and took after her father; her face was broad and plain with thin lips and small watery blue eyes, whereas Gladwys had her mother's large round eyes, heart-shaped face and full lips. Both girls had their father's easy temperament. Among their siblings, they were peacemakers.

Gladwys took a crust of bread and crumbly cheese, eating hastily.

'I am to go back to play the harp while they eat,' she declared with a quick look at the guests.

'They are eating now,' commented Elen.

'I know, but smelling the food has made me very hungry. I will finish this quickly, then go.'

Meredydd leaned over to her. 'You did well. I do not like him, though,' he said, jerking his head towards the top table.

'He does not smile much and is very dirty,' blurted Elen too loudly.

'Be quiet!' Meredydd reprimanded her curtly, 'Keep your voice down. Just because he has not got manners does not mean we should be rude as well.'

'But you said you did not like him,' protested Elen with a tad of irritation.

'Not so loudly that the world could hear,' said Meredydd giving them a disapproving scowl. 'Anyway, keep quiet; I am trying to hear what they discuss. He must be here for a reason.'

Elen pursed her lips, chastised, and Meredydd strained his ears to catch the drift of the conversation among the adults. Gladwys popped the last bit of cheese into her mouth before making her way to the harp, her long black hair swaying over her shoulders. She looked to her mother, who nodded for her to commence playing, and she confirmed she would with the warmest smile.

Gladwys' hands plucked the strings with confidence and ease. Her mastery of the harp was sheer magic to Dyddgu, who loved music and dancing but was not inclined to sing or play herself. The mother's heart swelled with pride, and she glanced at Madog to see his reaction, but he was staring at a damp-stained section of the wall while her husband questioned him. She wished now she had insisted on replacing the thatch and the wall, but Baby Robert had been her priority over maintenance this season. She looked from the damp wall to Madog and then to her husband. It was Llywarch's fault. This was all too hasty, and she had a bad feeling about Madog.

'You are certain Iorwedd ap Bleddyn is at Caereinion?' her husband asked his guest, his voice barely audible above the noise in the hall.

Madog turned his eyes back to Llywarch, and she saw the challenge in them.

'I would not be here if uncertain,' he retorted arrogantly.

'And you know where he is staying tonight?'

'I know every stone in that place. It was mine, after all, until King Henry took my brother hostage in place of Iorwedd and 'gave' him my lands.' He did not attempt to disguise the acid in his voice.

Dyddgu listened with rising fury. She wanted to say that Caereinon was no more Madog's land than it had been Cadwgan ap Bleddyn's or whomever King Henry was toying with at that moment, but she kept her mouth firmly shut, her lips thin and tight.

'And he is not well protected?'

'Are you nervous, Llywarch? I can do this alone. I come here only because you said you sought vengeance for your brothers.'

Llywarch coloured in embarrassment, clenching his jaw. His wife fumed silently at Madog's audacity. Whatever faults her husband might have, he did not lack courage. Of course, he felt fear. He was not as experienced at fighting as Madog but would give a good account of himself despite his reservations. Once committed, he would be dependable. To be fearful at the prospect of fighting was to show courage. Not to feel any fear, to be like Madog, was insane.

Spurred by humiliation in front of his teulu, Llywarch tried to regain some control, and his words came out with an edge of hostility, 'This needs to be properly planned. How do you propose we proceed?'

His reference to planning touched a nerve, and Madog swung around, his eyes burning, and growled, 'We call him out to face us, and if he refuses, then we burn him out.'

Llywarch could see that some of his men were uncomfortable burning an enemy alive and hoped it did not come to that. There was no honour in it.

'I will collect my men when we have eaten,' Llywarch promised. Although she had known it would come to this, Dyddgu felt the blood draining from her face.

Madog picked at his teeth. 'No, we will leave at midnight. Let him wake from his nightmares into a nightmare. Let his Hell begin on Earth. Tonight, he will pay for betraying his family.'

'But more so for his nephew's actions when Owain ap Cadwgan killed my brothers.' Llywarch corrected him, justifying his complicity and reminding Madog that his brothers' deaths deserved respect.

'How often,' reflected Dyddgu, 'had her husband told her he detested all the descendants of Bleddyn ap Cynan? Now here he was, conspiring with Madog, the worst of them, as he set about the murder of his uncle.'

Llywarch felt his wife's disdain drifting over to him, and he looked up to see the hostility in her face that was masking her fear. He could not hold her eye.

***

Though less than an hour by day, the journey took them much longer than Llywarch had thought through the dark at a walking pace. It was a still, cold night, but a wan moon shone, guiding them along unfamiliar paths. Most men were jittery when they heard any movement in the undergrowth. Llywarch felt his hand reach for the sword at his side each time something scuttled across the path or bounded into the woodland. He knew he was breathing hard despite riding slowly alongside Madog, who seemed unusually calm.

'Not long now,' Madog turned to him, a smile in his voice as if they were about to receive a rare treat.

'And when we get there, we surround the house, then you and I shout for admittance,' fretted Llywarch, reconfirming the hasty plan.

'No, we shout for him to come out. Do you think we are going to walk into a death trap?'

'No, of course.'

'Do not worry; you do not need to get your hands dirty if you prefer not to,' Madog muttered acidly.

'That is not what I meant,' Llywarch bridled.

There was an awkward silence between them. Llywarch's doubts about the sanity of this venture gnawed at him. He wished he had not got involved with Madog. Dyddgu had been right. After all, the man wanted to kill his kin, which was fundamentally against all they had been taught since childhood. He flinched as he heard someone stumbling behind him and cursed his nervousness. Madog was so unpredictable that it had unsettled him.

Madog's men had no uniformity about them. Some walked with Norman kite-shaped wooden shields they had picked up as plunder; others held the round Welsh leather-covered shields Llywarch's men hefted. They had various weapons: spears, swords, knives, and two men, as thick and robust as old tree trunks, bore huge razor-sharp wood axes. The archers carried giant yew bows with plenty of arrows in leather holders slung over their backs. Good archers were revered; all knew it took mighty strength and an excellent eye to hit a target.

Some of Madog's men had donned armour, presumably taken from their former adversaries, while others had only leather jerkins. A few wore helmets. Llywarch's men were uniformly attired in simple brown tunics, leather jerkins, and woollen cloaks. They all wore thick brown boots made from leather from Llywarch's beasts. His men's shields were pristine, hardly touched except for when they practised with blunt weapons. Their spears were shiny and sharp, the wood sleek and smooth, undamaged by other blades. Llywarch wore his chain mail, rubbed with sand until it shone, his shield emblazoned with his standard. Whilst his coffers were not full, Llywarch ensured that he and his men were well-equipped.

As they dropped into the small settlement where Iorwedd was staying that night, Madog called a halt and swung easily out of his saddle, glaring at the latecomers and anyone who spoke. He tied his mount to a tree as casually as if he was visiting friends while Llywarch's fingers trembled, his mind consumed as to whether Iorwedd had been forewarned. They could be walking into a trap. Their progress had seemed noisy to him as men marched and stumbled, horses thudding on the earth, and the jingling of harnesses travelled on the breeze. Now Madog seemed careless in alerting those inside the house.

'You go forward in groups of three as we discussed and wait for my signal. If Iorwedd comes out, you leave him to me.' Madog's voice clearly reached the stragglers, and there was no question that he would not be obeyed.

'Do not attack anyone unless they threaten you,' added Llywarch in a hoarse-carrying whisper.

Madog looked at him scornfully and said loudly enough so that all could hear, 'Of course not. We will invite them to join us for a small ale!'

There were some chuckles and comments, but Madog shook his head and strode to the front of the house. Llywarch, humiliated, closed his eyes and clenched his teeth as he tried to control his turning guts.

Men shuffled and grinned at each other as they gathered behind Madog. For some, this was their first raid, and their eyes gleamed at the prospect. It was nothing new for others, but their hearts beat fast in anticipation. They moved forward. To the right of the house was a lively stream that sounded loud in the night air. Llywarch wondered if it would drown out their noise, but then barking came from inside the walls. A shutter opened, and somebody swore an oath causing all the dogs to howl in a frenzy. There was a muffled cry and a cow called into the night somewhere.

Llywarch waiting for movement from within, stood alongside Madog. By now, the broad-shouldered archers had strung their bows, and the rest of the men were fingering their weapons.

'Come out, Iorwedd. We know you are there. Come out, or we burn you out,' yelled Madog.

A horse whinnied. Two shutters banged open where the house sat above the courtyard wall illuminated by moonlight, and bowmen on either side took down two of Madog's men, one in the shoulder and the other in his chest. Some of their fellows ran to assist them, but a second shower of arrows fell, injuring another man and sending two more back out of range.

Madog, unmoved, his eyes harder than granite, indicated for men bearing torches to stand behind the archers who had wrapped half their arrow tips with cloth dipped in oil. At a nod, the archers set their cloth-tipped arrows alight from the torches, and it was then that the order was given, 'Fire the roof.'

Burning arrows flew through the night to the thatch. At first, it seemed like nothing was happening, and then suddenly, the fire took hold, and flames began to leap across the building. There were cries inside for water, but the job had been well done. One of Madog's archers fired through an open shutter, and there were cries from within. There was the sound of pottery shattering and another noise as if a table had been thrown on its side. A door opened, and two women flew out of the house, one clutching a tiny baby, as they made for the stream. Llywarch paled to see the screaming baby was not much older than his youngest boy, Baby Robert.

Madog's face glowed with wildness as the fire grew more intense, and Llywarch felt ashamed: he could feel no joy in this revenge. To outnumber someone and attack them this way was shameful: there was no honour. He thought of the other women and children who might be inside.

There was a commotion as the dogs were let loose. One great dark-haired beast sprung, snarling and ripping at an intruder's face tearing off his ear before he was overcome by spears piercing his body. Another, snarling, shaggy-haired, white in the moonlight, sank his teeth into a spearman's calf, leaving him groaning in a pool of blood before attacking another spearman's arm. Behind the dogs came three of Iorwedd's servants wielding their spears and pushing two of Madog's younger men toward the burning wall.

Llywarch's attention turned to a woman who fled screaming from inside, chased into the woods by a stocky red-haired man wielding a heavy sword. Luck was on her side as he heard the calls from his companions against the burning wall and abandoned the chase. The redhead turned, charging at Iorwedd's men. One of them, bareheaded, his hair a wild tangle, heard his steps and turned quickly, lunging at him with a spear, but the redhead dodged nimbly, thrusting his sword forward to run through his assailant, splattering blood across his face. Iorwedd's other two servants were distracted by what was happening behind them. This allowed Madog's spearmen to surge away from the burning wall, bringing the two men down before quickly cutting their throats and kicking them for good measure.

Suddenly Llywarch saw spooked cows and horses thundering towards them, driven onwards by a young boy deliberately trying to confuse the attackers. In their panic, rearing steeds knocked two of Llywarch's men to the ground and trampled them, eliciting screams of pain. Bared, yellow teeth snapped and bit, hooves flashed, and twisting horns pierced flesh. One of Madog's men, a red-faced swarthy man, lifted his arm to hurl his spear at the farmhand, but Llywarch caught his wrist, overpowered him, and struck him to the ground.

'He is just a boy!' he screamed, thinking of his eldest son. The boy escaped into the woods, away from the beasts and demons.

Four more men ran from the burning house, deliberately targeting Madog and Llywarch. Llywarch reacted quickly, jabbing his sword past one spearman's shield, and taking him in the ribs before twisting his blade out of the flesh and slashing the top of the spear, being aimed at his chest by another. He used his weight to push the spearman to the ground and stabbed the sword into the man's chest. When he looked at the squat spearman's face, he resembled one of his young grooms. This house was so close to his property that he might have been the groom's cousin or brother. He pulled out his sword and saw it was slick with blood even in the half-light from the fire.

Two of the four men had attacked Madog. Still, as the first swung his sword wildly at him, Madog had stepped contemptuously away, slicing the second man across the neck with a sleek downward movement before turning around quickly and ruthlessly thrusting the bloody metal between the first man's ribs.

There was a shout. Iorwedd now appeared at the doorway, sword in hand and yelling, 'Is this what you would do to your uncle, Madog?' And then, seeing Llywarch, shook his head. 'I see you, Llywarch. I know you.'

Llywarch's face was ashen, he was shaking inside, cold and clammy, but Madog seemed in high spirits.

'What took you so long?' Madog mocked.

Iorwedd came at Madog with a rush. Madog was quick and decisive, but the older man was skilled. As Madog lunged forward, his sword already red with blood, Iorwedd's answering blow was surprisingly swift, putting Madog off balance. There was the dull clash of sword against sword. Iorwedd drove Madog back towards the uneven ground, where Madog stumbled backwards, falling. Iorwedd might have ended his nephew's life there and then, but he hesitated, and at that moment, three of Madog's spearmen sent spears on their fateful journey. Iorwedd fell to his knees. Madog leapt up, hacking down on his uncle's neck. There was a guttural gurgling sound, and as he lay dying, Iorwedd's eyes turned to Llywarch as if they could penetrate his soul. Iorwedd's last thoughts were of two dragons fighting under the earth.

Madog ripped a bloodied gold chain from his uncle's throat and pulled a heavy jewelled ring from his finger.

'Take what you want,' he shouted to his men, and soon the body was naked. One man had ripped off Iorwedd's boots and dragged them on, while another had pulled the dead man's tunic over his head.

'Throw him onto the fire,' Madog ordered, his voice heavy with satisfaction. Two men lifted the emaciated frame of the King of Powys and tossed him into the doorway, where the falling lintel covered him with flame and thick acrid smoke.

Llywarch, drenched with a cold sweat, looked around at the dead sprawled across the ground. He felt sickened by it. If he had every wondered what Hell was like, he was now sure that it was like this.

Chapter 17: Jealousy (Summer 1111)

Angharad was riding with Cadwallon and two of her men at arms, Iwan and Heifen, when they spotted Hywel and his band of men in the distance.

'Look, Mother, it is Hywel,' cried Cadwallon, excited. 'Can I ride to him?'

Almost before his mother had nodded assent, he was off, leaving the two men-at-arms grinning. His mother watched her lanky son gallop at breakneck speed, golden hair steaming and green cloak flying out behind him. He was a fine young man, athletic and strong, but he had much of the child yet.

Angharad shook her head, a half-smile playing at the corner of her mouth. 'He has more interest in what they have been up to than the rebuilding at St Teilo's church or St Teilo.'

Heifen, an open-faced, plump man with wispy black hair, grinned. 'My lady, he is happy to see them back. They all get on well, and they will have stories to tell. He will begin to appreciate the saints in time, but at his age, a warrior's life is more interesting.'

'I hope so,' Angharad sighed and then, as always, started counting the men who had returned.

'They are all there?' she asked, shading her eyes with her hand.

'They are my lady,' said Iwan, whose eyes were as keen as any in the llys. He was a thin, grey-eyed, wiry, and muscular man known for his bow prowess.

Angharad felt a surge of happiness as she began to canter towards the dust-covered men. She had missed Hywel and was pleased to see him safely back. She drew her horse, Seren, alongside her friend. Despite their appearance of being tired and dishevelled, they were all enjoying Cadwallon's enthusiasm.

The queen motioned for Hywel to move out of earshot as they led the party on the last bit of road leading to the llys.

'It went well?'

Hywel's earnest face grinned broadly, and he jerked his head at the six heavily loaded packhorses. 'Indeed so, my lady. We have booty here, cattle, and a team of oxen in the mountain pastures. We also gained a few extra steeds.'

Angharad was torn between feeling pleased about the booty and the boost it would provide to the men of the teulu, while on the other hand, she felt the guilt of a good Christian for endorsing what was essentially theft.

Hywel immediately sensed her discomfort.

'My lady, it has only been taken from those that possessed lands not belonging to them. The Flemings drove out our Welsh farmers who had little enough as it was.'

Angharad nodded somewhat begrudgingly.

'We have certainly set back the castle building by a few weeks, if not months, depending on the weather.' Hywel smiled.

'I am glad of it. They will still threaten us if they can, I know.'

'Well, I believe they will think twice.'

'And they do not know who you are?'

"They may guess, but they cannot be sure. We were cautious.'

'And Madog's and Owain's men?'

'Some have returned to Madog now that he has returned from Ireland; others I have sent to the mountains with the cattle, and they will join us here in Aberffraw in a couple of days.'

'You trust them?'

'I must. I chose the ones who would be the most reliable and who want a future in Gwynedd. Men who either want to settle down or already have a family to provide for. You can usually rely on them.'

Angharad thought but did not say that nobody was as trustworthy and reliable than Hywel, yet he had no ties.

'You look tired,' she said, concerned, and he was touched.

'Nothing a good night's sleep in the warm and dry will not cure,' he reassured her.

'And a few good hot meals.'

'Oh, we have had some fine hare stews and a few roast pigs of Flemish descent that would have graced the finest table.'

By now, they were riding up the incline to the llys, and the gates opened to warm greetings from the men on guard.

Angharad leant over to Hywel, laughing.

'You see, you have been missed, or maybe they are just hoping you have brought them some fine hare stew and roast Flemish pork.'

Hywel gave her a broad grin before dropping from his horse, easy-limbed despite the arduous journey. He immediately presented himself at Angharad's side to assist her down from Seren.

Across the courtyard, Gruffydd had been crouching down with Owain and Cadwaladr drawing in the dirt to describe one of the battles he had fought in Ireland when he had taken the teulu to help his old ally, King Murtagh. He adored spending time with his boys like this, something he had been unable to do with his father. He loved how they would question him; he could see they were thriving and growing fast, bodily and mentally.

'This is something that I learnt early from King Murtagh in Ireland,' he explained, 'and it has won me battles. You must always bring your enemy to a place where you have the advantage. It is not as simple as high ground, low ground, treed land, or open field. You must look for advantages in the geography of the area. There may be a swamp or soft ground that the enemy is unaware of. There may be a place where they would need to narrow their forces to advance, meaning they can be overwhelmed more easily.'

'And if they need to come to you and their journey is difficult, they may be more tired,' said Cadwaladr.

'Or short on food, so they are hungry,' added Owain.

Gruffydd smiled and nodded. 'Exactly. Timing is also important. Time of day is not only about whether men are hungry or tired: it can be the sun's position, whether it is in their eyes or….'

He was mid-sentence when the gates swung open. He looked up, and when he saw Angharad riding in with Hywel, the two of them laughing, his stomach seemed to churn. He stood abruptly and absently broke the little stick he had used to draw out the battlefield. Owain and Cadwaladr leapt up and, seeing what had stopped their father's lesson, excused themselves and raced across the courtyard to where Hywel was assisting Angharad, hardly waiting for their mother to dismount before they started firing questions at him. Hywel put an arm around both their shoulders as one of the stableboys came to take his horse away and unload his pack.

Gruffydd tried to curb the unreasonable jealousy he felt. How long was it since Angharad had laughed like that with him? He ground his foot resentfully on the battle plan in the dirt as he saw the affection with which his sons held Hywel. He knew he should have gone across to greet the head of his warband, but instead, he turned on his heel, took the steps up to the entrance of the llys two at a time, and found the sanctuary of his chamber, slamming the door behind him.

Both Hywel and Angharad could not avoid noticing Gruffydd's strange reaction and exchanged a look, saying nothing.

Hywel drew his men's attention.

'I know you men will want to get cleaned up, have a swim perhaps, something to eat, maybe catch some sleep, but before you do that, I want to thank you all. It has been a pleasure to be with you, and not one of you has complained about the conditions or the difficulty of what we took on. You can be very proud of yourselves.'

The comments were well received, and the men's chests swelled with pride.

'There are also new men among us, and I want you all to make them welcome. They have fought next to us, and now they will see they are one of us. Ensure they know where to sleep, eat, wash, train and find friendship.'

The men dismissed, the young princes were even more desperately keen for news of the men's adventures, and they fell in step with him as Hywel walked them towards one of the long sturdy benches next to the kitchen. Crossing the courtyard, he saw the partly erased map on the ground and stopped to examine it.

'Our father told us about one of the battles he fought with King Murtagh,' volunteered Owain.

'I was there with him at this one,' Hywel said wistfully.

Were you?' said Cadwaladr eagerly, an expression of delight flashing across his face.

'I was. Your father fought like a lion. I have never seen a braver fighter. He was unstoppable. He saved my life there.'

'He did?' Owain's eyes were wide.

'What happened?' asked Cadwaladr, mesmerised.

'I got separated from the teulu somehow.' He looked about and picked up part of the broken stick to redraw and illustrate his tale. 'I had three Irishmen from Leinster attacking me here, and I was pushed back against a tree here. I took a blow to the head and could not see straight. Your father was over here, saw me struggling and came like a whirlwind, sword sweeping everyone out of his way. He took each of them down and ensured I was fit before returning to the fray. It was an incredible victory.'

'Is it anger that gives him such strength?' asked Owain, thinking of how he seemed to fight better when he was furious.

'No. Your father is very calm and methodical. He has trained for thousands of hours, knows the moves without thinking, and anticipates the foe but is fast, very fast, but whereas anger can fire the urge to fight, it also leads to errors. He moves through a battlefield as if nothing can fluster him.'

The boys beamed with pride as Cadwallon came over to join them. Inside his chamber, Gruffydd, in silent fury, looked out at the scene of Hywel with his three boys surrounding him and threw a bowl of apples across the room.

The door knocked, and he snarled his acceptance of entry.

Angharad seemed to glide through the door, and something caught in his throat at how beautiful she was. Her hair was covered by a translucent silk veil highlighting her unusually blue eyes. Her skin was flawless, and only small smile lines at the edge of her eyes betrayed her age. Despite having borne him eight children in quick succession, her body was still slim, taut, and lithe under the blue linen tunic which outlined her shape. In the torrent of emotion he was experiencing, Gruffydd reached out, pulling her to him, but uncharacteristically, she resisted, pushing her hand against his chest.

'No, Gruffydd,' she protested gently but firmly.

The hurt and jealousy inside him erupted with ire. He grasped her wrist holding it hard.

'You push me away?' he spat.

'Gruffydd, you are hurting me.'

He dropped her wrist and, paling angrily, turned away; his voice was hoarse.

'Get out,' he said abruptly.

He heard her intake of breath as she tried to comprehend his raw emotional outburst, then she said quietly, 'Gruffydd, I meant only that first you need to welcome back the men. They will be expecting it. It is the proper thing to do.'

'Here we go again,' he sneered sarcastically. 'My queen is advising me how best to behave as if I am a child.'

'Gruffydd,' her voice was little more than a breath.

'Get out!' he bellowed.

He heard the door closing and slammed his fist against the wall.

***

Bishop Richard believed that people who paid more attention to history could better navigate their future. That was one of the reasons he loved living in Shrewsbury: it had a wealth of history.

The bishop had woken early to the sound of the church bells ringing in the morning, quiet, dispelling demons and calling the faithful to prayer. He had prayed as he always did, feeling comfort in knowing that God had seen fit to give him the right to guide others. As he walked along the Severn River, he watched a heron at the edge of the sedge, legs firm on the sandy bottom, hardly moving a feather, and then, with a quick dip of its beak into the waters, scoring a sizable fish which disappeared into its long beak. The fishermen along the river would not begrudge the heron his breakfast. The river teemed with flounder, trout, carp, pike and salmon.

The waters rippled, and bullrushes danced gently. The Welsh called this river, which rose in its high mountains, the queen of rivers. The Romans called it Sabrina. Sabrina, the love child of Locrinus, drowned with her mother by Locrinus' jealous wife, Gwendolen. How vengeful love could make one, he thought. How vengeful a family could be.

The river looped around the east, south, and west of the town, and to the north, the bishop could see the red sandstone castle towering above him. The motte and bailey were built into the scarp of the eastern hill, which guarded the town from the Welsh border only miles away. The Ancient Britons, the Silures, had called this place Pengwerne before the Saxons had driven them out. Then it became the Royal Court of the King of Powys, but King Offa of the Mercians was too strong for Powys. Afterwards came the Vikings, who brutally attacked the lands, and Saxon King Ethelred, who was then at Shrewsbury, agreed to pay them 30,000 pounds for peace.

Bishop Richard looked up at the magnificent castle again. King Henry craved that castle built by Roger de Montgomery to show his power and wealth. Yet Roger's son, Robert de Belleme, one of the most brutal and feared of the Montgomery family, had rebelled against Henry in favour of Henry's brother Robert, considered by many nobles to be the rightful king on King William Rufus' death. Robert de Belleme had enlisted the help of the Kings of Powys. Henry had come down hard and besieged Shrewsbury with 60,000 soldiers promising to hang anyone within the castle. Belleme saw he had been outwitted and surrendered, handing his keys to Henry, who granted the town a charter. Yet while Belleme and his brother Arnulf had been banished, Belleme was even now causing trouble over in Normandy.

Now the bishop had reached the part of the river where Shrewsbury Abbey looked across at the mighty castle. This was where Roger de Montgomery had converted the old wooden church of St Peter into a beautiful Benedictine monastery. At the end of a life of brutality matched only by his wife Mabel, Roger became a monk at this abbey and died four days later. He had given generously to the abbey so that, whatever sins he had committed, they would pray for his soul and those of his heirs. Money was a wonderful thing!

Roger's son Robert was causing Henry angst as he rebelled against Henry's attempt to take William Clito prisoner. Robert Curthose's son, Clito, was seen as the rightful King of Normandy, and, of course, Henry had none of it. King Henry spat and fumed that he should have imprisoned Robert de Belleme when he had the chance, but instead, Robert was inflaming the wrath of the barons on the Normandy border. No wonder

Henry was tired of the Welsh issues plaguing him while he wanted his focus elsewhere. He would need to be soothed, and Bishop Richard was sure he could manage it.

The fresh air and bracing walk had cleared the bishop's head, and he felt ready to greet the king, who had brought his court to Shrewsbury. Having the king in Shrewsbury consolidated the bishop's power in the town and surrounding area: his chest swelled as he thought of his standing. Reaching the castle, he was admitted with the usual pomp, well known by Henry's guards, and he waited outside the king's chamber on a padded seat next to a window which overlooked the river.

He was deep in his thoughts when the doors swung open and was surprised to see Princess Nest exit. He got up quickly and bowed to her.

'Princess Nest, seeing you here in Shrewsbury is an unexpected pleasure.'

Princess Nest's brilliant eyes widened as she turned to see who approached her. Still, she quickly regained her composure, stopping politely to acknowledge the bishop, who noticed, despite her efforts, that she seemed uncomfortable. Bishop Richard's success relied partly on his well-honed skills of observation.

'I have come to see my son and, of course, his father,' she said, inclining her head yet keeping a civilised distance.

The bishop saw Nest as an opportunity, a valuable source of inside information on Welsh politics. What better start than the mistress of Owain ap Cadwgan? A few fine wines usually loosened the tongue.

On impulse, flashing a broad smile, he said, 'You are a visitor to Shrewsbury. I would be honoured to have you and any members of your party join me for dinner at my humble abode.'

A momentary look of alarm flashed across her face. 'Thank you for your kindness, but unfortunately, I have a short time here as my husband expects my speedy return,' she replied graciously.

'Of course, of course,' he said, but he felt the sting of rejection.

'And your husband is well? And your children?'

His gaze lingered on her as she flushed with embarrassment, lowering her eyes, clearly understanding the barb.

'They are all well, thank you.'

The princess seemed to rebuff the bishop's further attempts at conversing. She excused herself politely enough, and he observed her glide serenely down the room's length, head held high. He noticed others watching her and acknowledged that she was indeed a beautiful creature, if a dangerous one. Women could make fools of men; he had seen it often, and it made him wary of them. Beautiful women were the most perilous of all. Frowning, he wondered what Queen Mathilda would say about Nest's early audience with her husband. Still, Queen Mathilda had accepted King Henry's proclivities, delivered two children, and vanished into the background, concentrating her efforts on God.

Still feeling the slight, the bishop heard himself announced and was somewhat mollified by the ease of access he received. Henry valued him, he knew, yet kings, like beautiful women, had to be handled with finesse.

King Henry, dressed in a jewelled ivory tunic, was as pleased with himself as a cat that had got the cream. The bishop had the sense not to mention Nest but to register that he might use the unexpected lightening of the king's mood to his advantage.

The king did not waste time despite his levity.

'This business with Madog killing his uncle,' he came straight to the point. 'What is your advice?'

'Llywerch ap Trahearn was involved in it, which might be useful to us. I will meet with him, discuss your displeasure and so forth. Perhaps…...'

'We should arrest Madog,' the king interjected.

The bishop took a breath and considered his words. 'We should be seen to wish that but not to pursue it too hard. We may need him yet.'

'So, what do you suggest?' The king gave a curious smile. Bishop Richard always had a game plan.

'Perhaps, sire, we give Madog his lands: Caereinion, Traean, Deuddwr, and Aberriw.'

'The lands which were given to Iorwedd?'

'Lands were given to Madog and his brother, Ithel, initially for helping to flush out Owain ap Cadwgan, and then given to Iorwedd to tame Madog and Owain ap Cadwgan.'

'I follow you.'

'Then I suggest having removed Madog's discontent about his lands, we bring Cadwgan back as an overlord, if you like, to bring order and perhaps pardon his son. We let them deal with Madog, and he with them. Animosity, kin strife, greed will do our job for us.'

'Never underestimate the Welsh!'

'They should never underestimate us! So far, things are working to our advantage.'

'Yet the Flemings are complaining, Hugh Earl of Chester is complaining, and Gilbert Strongbow is complaining. They all carp that the Welsh are running wild, out of control.'

'The complaints will be short-lived if there is the lure of more land becoming available.'

'Then run it as you wish,' the king sighed. 'I have enough to deal with in Normandy to last a lifetime. By the way, Princess Nest has asked that I consider returning some of the lands once part of the kingdom of Deheubarth to her brother, Griffith. He is of age and wants to return from Ireland. She is happy to give him the benefit of her Norman upbringing and to have him living with her and Gerald of Windsor.'

The bishop nodded and looked out of the window biting his lip as he considered. The sun broke out from behind a cloud, and Henry's jewels sparkled expensively.

'Perhaps something small to satisfy him. He too may be useful to us.'

'As may Owain ap Cadwgan. Better for him to owe us allegiance than be a thorn in our side.'

'Exactly!'

As he left, bowing respectfully, the bishop wondered about Griffith ap Rhys and determined he would only be a minor player, having no following as Madog and Owain had. He also questioned the allegiance of Princess Nest.

***

'Are you sure?' asked Meilyr, gravely looking at his brother, Gronwy.

'I sent two men, one to join Madog and one to join Owain ap Cadwgan.'

'How did they find them?' asked Rhydir.

'They followed the word. Men were flocking to Madog and Owain because of the Flemings swarming into their lands. My two men were easily welcomed.'

'But you cannot rely on what is being said in the camps of Madog or Owain?'

'Perhaps not, but you can rely on what is being said in the llys of Gruffydd ap Cynan himself,' said Gronwy, a smug tone creeping into his voice.

'So, you have placed some of our men into Gruffydd's llys?'

'I knew that Owain and Madog would need to escape back to Ireland or be imprisoned eventually,' Gronwy crowed, 'I knew that Gruffydd would want to boost his warband. I was not surprised when I heard that

Gruffydd's teulu was looking for men with nowhere to go once Owain and Madog fled. Then it was easy. My men who had been with Madog and Owain went to Anglesey as men from Pembroke who had been displaced by the Flemings but did not want to live the itinerant life of men on the run.'

'And they were accepted with no questions?' Rhydir asked, admiring his brother's canny foresight.

Gronwy grinned broadly. 'They were indeed. Things will become a little difficult for our sister from now on.'

'So, they have been raiding across their borders with Gruffydd's men?' asked Meilyr.

'They have and will swear to it.'

'So, you will take this to King Henry,' Meilyr probed his brother.

'No, not yet. Sometimes it is better to keep the information until the time is ripe.'

'And when would that be?'

'Bishop Richard is getting frustrated with Powys. Let Gruffydd's assaults continue to stir the ant's nest. Meanwhile, we should harass Cheshire while Hugh of Chester is in Normandy.'

'To what purpose?' asked Rhydir, who preferred a quiet life.

'Twofold. Let us fill our coffers while we can, increase the number in our teulu and strength. Once Hugh of Chester returns, he will be complaining to the king, but it will not be our heads that roll but Gruffydd both for his raiding to the South and for not keeping control of Gwynedd. You wait. It will be just as Cadwgan paid the price for not controlling Powys. And that, my brothers, is when we strike.'

'We take the whole of Gwynedd?' Rhydir asked disbelievingly.

'We do a deal with Bishop Richard, and, yes, we take over the whole of Gwynedd.'

'But Gruffydd is kin through Angharad,' protested Meilyr.

'Our whoring sister!'

'That is not true; I cannot believe it!' protested Meilyr again.

'You have ever been too soft. She sullies the good name of our family.'

'This is information you got from your bastard son who would say anything to ingratiate himself with you.' Meilyr argued heatedly.

'A bastard who has gone missing. Gruffydd has murdered my son. My men have confirmed that there is no sign of Rhys, and people there believe he was coming to see me.'

'Anything could have happened to him on the way,' reasoned Rhydir.

'Unlikely. He handled himself well. No, something is not right there. He was to meet one of my men, and that man also vanished without a trace. Also probably murdered. Anyway, our new men will start to spill secrets in Gruffydd's teulu that they hoped to contain at Aberffraw. I wonder how Gruffydd will handle that?'

'Gronwy, I do not like all this,' Meilyr frowned.

'Then clear off to Anglesey!' Gronwy retorted, 'You are either with me or against me. Make your mind up!'

Chapter 18: Waiting (Summer 1111)

The Irish court was celebrating, and it was something to behold. There was music, dancers, magicians, jugglers and, of course, there were the bards. Ireland had many bardic families, but among the most famous were the Ua Cuill, Ua Sleibin and Mag Raith, whose accomplishments in this hereditary art were revered. Then there was the food including venison, partridge, heron, plover, curlew, marrow cakes, jellies, broths, fritters, pies, and, since the fashion of pilgrimage to Jerusalem, now the wealthy were beginning to adopt the exotic spices found there.

The reason for this revelling was the containment of an attack by Domnall Ua Lochlainn, who had marched his troops south. Domnall was one of King Murtagh's greatest adversaries. More importantly, Murtagh's prowess at the Synod of Rath Bresail had consolidated his position as chief secular leader in Ireland. This was no small feat. Lafracoth, Murtagh's dazzling daughter, had returned to the Irish court, and although there were rumours about her husband, Arnulf de Montgomery, nobody spoke openly about why the pair were separated. Some had seen bruises on Lafracoth's lovely face when Arnulf had been in Ireland, others had heard raised voices and screams, but Lafracoth had said nothing. She had returned with Murtagh's grandchildren, Alice and Philip, and wherever Lafracoth was, there was merriment and frivolity.

However, the Welshman, Owain ap Cadwgan, was not joyful. He had fought tirelessly for Murtagh against Domnall, recompense for his security in Ireland, but the feasting for Murtagh's success seemed to make his position ever more depressing. While Murtagh had sped back to Dublin from routing Domnall, Owain and his men had followed and bettered the few small parties who had escaped from the fray.

Owain was tired, sore, and dirty and wanted to be home in Powys. He threw a half-gnawed bone to the hounds milling beneath the mighty oak table that stretched almost the length of the hall. Finding himself a place in the shadows, he turned from the rousing songs, the roars of laughter at bawdy jests or jokes at the expense of others, he ignored the arguments breaking out amongst weary men or jealous women, and he filled his goblet with rich Normandy wine again and again.

It was later, after Owain had been drinking steadily all evening, feeling increasingly sorry for himself, when Lafracoth felt his eyes on her and, jostling through the crowd, came to join him. Over the years, they had got to know each other well, and Owain appreciated that she had been an excellent friend to Nest, making her feel most welcome.

'Your father has much to celebrate,' he said gloomily. 'Religion in Ireland is being run by Norman England these days. He seems to spend as much time changing church law to align with the Normans as he does fighting his enemies.'

'Owain ap Cadwgan,' she half teased him, thinking that his sultry misery enhanced his tall russet-haired good looks, 'you would be wise to note how the church is gaining power all over Europe. If you want to be King of Powys, you need the church. Come and sulk outside where at least we can see the stars, and you are away from the music and dancing that seems to offend you tonight!'

They moved into the chill evening air, and Lafracoth wrapped her arms across her chest to keep warm as she gazed up at a sky luminous with stars and a sickle moon.

'Since you married Arnulf de Belleme, you have become Norman in your thinking.'

Lafracoth laughed her ringing laugh, which echoed in the darkness of the courtyard.

'Are you still trying to start a quarrel about the Irish church? I presented to the Synod of Cashel and my father well before I married Arnulf.'

'Ah yes, the Synod of Cashel, where you and your father argued against the marriage of priests. Now he has wooed the Synod of Rath Bresail, where the Irish Church has been reformed and is divided into diocese and parishes: easier to manage, but, if I am right, King Murtagh is in line with the Norman view again.'

'Yes, but do not forget that fifty bishops, three hundred priests and three thousand laymen had the chance to argue for or against the new constitution, the influence of the Papacy, and the abuses in the church that currently exist. It was all done fairly, Owain.'

'Argue against Murtagh. The High King? Surely not!'

'Keep your scorn to yourself. Everybody had an opportunity, I tell you. My father is a forward thinker. He has revised the justice system.'

'Yes, indeed, your father is great, as are all your ancestors. The book he commissioned, 'The War of the Irish with the Foreigners', is almost complete, setting your great great grandfather, Brian Boru, as almost godlike.'

Lafracoth was beginning to get a little piqued. 'It is important to keep our family history clear in the minds of the Irish, Owain. Any idiot would realise that!'

Owain snorted. 'And whose idea was it to describe your family line as the Franks of Ireland defeating the Vikings, just as the Normans are the conquering Franks of Normandy and England? You have a good look at what they have done to Wales before you align yourselves with Norman philosophies.'

'You are so besotted with the Vikings then? Do you rather support the Vikings than the Franks? Do not forget the Franks were Vikings once!'

'Not so besotted, no. I understand that writing that book makes it seem that your family is the worthiest in Ireland, yet why vilify the Vikings? It is as if, singlehandedly, Brian Boru overcame the barbarian, ferocious Vikings who plundered the churches and enslaved the Irish. How superb your family line is that they have defeated such a foe.'

'How great indeed!' retorted Lafracoth flippantly.

'While in truth, it is the Viking towns of Dublin, Wexford, Waterford, Limerick and Cork that provide the wealth from taxes, the ships and the men for military ventures that enable your father to donate sustenance to the church, be a benevolent ruler caring for the poor and the sick, and give funding for learning,' While he thought his train of thought was sound, somehow the cold air and his tiredness had exacerbated Owain's intoxication. He found himself needing to annunciate very carefully.

'Yes, indeed and support those who would find sanctuary in his court,' Lafracoth reminded him.

Owain had the grace to look uncomfortable as she continued, 'So, you take our hospitality and our protection, but then your rail against our alliance with the Normans and even bleat against my father's efforts to protect the generations to come by positioning himself well in the public eye.'

'I was just saying,' he protested lamely.

'Owain, I know you well enough and if power drives you. There will be a time when you will ally yourself with the Normans just as your father did marrying his Norman wife. If you side with them, the pressure will be on to reform the Welsh church just as we have done here.'

'Never!' he slurred stoutly.

Lafracoth wrinkled her nose in disagreement as if she had caught a whiff of something unpleasant. 'Never is a long time. What my father has done is not so bad. He has spoken for the end of simony, the church's freedom from secular taxation, the right of sanctuary and the celibacy of the clergy. He agrees that certain kin should not marry and that within marriage, there is still the option for divorce.'

'Divorce,' said Owain squinting at Lafracoth through one eye, 'you do not agree then that marriage is forever.'

'I like the freedom of the old Irish Brehon law. I like that a woman can divorce a man if he is absent abroad on military campaigns.'

'Convenient for you then.'

Lafracoth ignored his scorn. 'I prefer that if a man behaves like a criminal or is insane or has an incurable disease, his wife can divorce him.'

'And that a man can divorce his wife if the wife is childless?'

'These things are fair, and I would like to see those things retained.'

'But your marriage was by Norman law like Nest's, so divorce is impossible.'

Her face clouded. 'No, not without special permission.'

He banged his fist on the door lintel. 'You are a victim then of Norman church laws just as I am a victim of their avarice.'

She looked away.

Even though Owain realised he was under the weather, he knew he had behaved boorishly, and Lafracoth's father had been generous in his support of him.

'Forgive me, Lafracoth,' he said, seeing he had gone too far, uncharacteristically humble and giving her an extravagant bow, 'I am tired from the campaign against Domnall, frustrated by not being in my own home, ruling in my way, and disappointed that what I tried to do led to my father being exiled.'

Lafracoth was silent momentarily, then reached out to hold his arm. 'Do not give up hope, Owain. If my father had given up hope every time things went wrong with his plans, he would not have achieved anything. You are driven by a wish to see Wales united against all odds just as my father is to see the same for Ireland, so make allies instead of enemies.'

'That is not so easy, no, not so easy.' His voice drifted away, and she felt sorry that a notable warrior was so deflated. She liked him better for it rather than the ebullient braggart and womanising Welshman he often was.

'Not easy at all,' she admitted, 'but you have harnessed men willing to follow you before now. It is the same. My father was just a small fish, but he saw that Ireland could be an important power just like Norway, France, or England, and part of that was making others believe it was so. He has used his family to make important alliances with those countries. He has supported the Welsh and made peaceful allegiances with Scotland. All of this will unify Ireland, and unifying Ireland means increasing power for our country.'

'I have not even got land to rule over. I am no better than the leader of a band of hotheads.' Owain was surprised to find he was feeling hot and wiped the sweat off his brow.

'Owain, Owain. King Henry is drowning in politics in Normandy. Arnulf's brother, Robert, is leading a rebellion against him. King Louis of France hates Henry, and he is a powerful enemy to have. Give it a month, and then sue again for terms with him. Play the game. Seem to be friendly to the Normans but get yourself allies who want to work towards a stronger united Wales.'

'My father played the game, and now Henry is dictating what happens in Powys, exiling him from his land. Since his marriage to his Norman wife, my father is almost considered one of them.'

'Your father is a proud Welshman, Owain.'

Owain shrugged. 'When they released my uncle from prison, the Normans took my half-brother Henri, brat of the Norman wife, and demanded a ridiculous amount for his release. The stupid thing is that my family paid it for the little shit!'

'So, you learn from his mistakes. You take note of your enemy's weaknesses; you make life easy for them, and, away from their sight, you increase your power.'

'And according to you, use the power of the church!'

'As Gruffydd ap Cynan has done in Gwynedd! He gives wealth to the church and earns allegiance. He allows Norman influence where it does not matter so much and retains Welsh custom where it does.'

Owain frowned. He was starting to feel nauseous but determined to make his point.

'Do you know the Welsh church has already lost most of its assets to the Normans? They came and took the huge estates of Llandaff and St David's. Walked in and just took them! Yes, and only by, by, by endless appeals to the pope and yes to the archbishop were some of them regained.'

'I am sorry,' sympathised Lafracoth sincerely.

'Can you believe that St Peter's in Gloucester owns many of those lands now and that fat arse William FitzOsbern gave the tithes of some of those lands to monasteries in Normandy? He gave tithes from Welsh lands! Wales is full of Norman-run monasteries protected by stone fortresses on their doorstep. Be careful!'

He was breathing deeply now, trying hard to fend off the inevitable.

'Let's go back inside; it is getting cold,' suggested Lafracoth feeling that, much as she had some empathy for Owain, she had had enough of being lectured.

Owain shook his head and wished he had not.

'Are you well?' asked Lafracoth seeing the colour had drained from his face.

He slumped against the wall and put his hands up.

'I do not feel my best.'

Lafracoth turned as she heard heavy boots running across the courtyard. A messenger had come in on a ship from Wales.

'I have a message for Owain ap Cadwgan.'

Owain held out his hand and, taking the parchment, walked unsteadily to one of the tapers burning on the wall. He fumbled for a while, looked at what was written there for what seemed like an eternity, put a hand up to the wall to steady himself and, to the astonishment of the messenger, he vomited copiously.

***

Owain had arrived at the ship's deck as the first rays of dawn light were illuminating the surface of the River Liffey so that it glimmered like molten silver. It was peaceful. In the distance, mist hovered over grasses crisply frosted by the cold night air. Grey silhouettes had begun appearing from the shadows, and now, less than an hour later, Dublin Wharf, first built by the Vikings, was as chaotic as ever. Boats were coming to the waterfront to find a mooring; others were preparing to sail out down the river, and at the port side, the cargo was being loaded or unloaded with frenetic energy.

The Welshman took a deep breath surveying the scene. Seagulls wheeled, dived, and squawked as they competed for whatever scraps were tossed aside. Ox carts heaved their load, people sweated as they hauled ropes, hefted barrels or sacks, screamed abuse or encouragement, and stray dogs fought. Two old warriors, thin and white-haired, sat yarning while they watched and told stories of when they had sailed to the islands with swords in their hands. Here, beside the wharf, their lives felt richer as they relived their past in the constant motion of the present. Two boys fought over a carved seal discarded by one of the sailors. One grabbed it and started running, but the other tripped him up and leapt on him. They would both have bruises and bloodied noses. Owain ap Cadwgan smiled as he watched and wondered how many bloodied noses he had had as a child and how many more he had given.

Further down the wharf, a ship-building yard was a hive of activity, with the smell of wood being chopped and shaved rising on the breeze. Two new ships were being built. Owain's attention turned to a group of men who were skilfully creating the keel and stems of the boat while others were overlapping planks, holding them in place with iron rivets. Inside the planking, four men held the ship's shape with ribbing.

'Get out of the way,' yelled a brute of a man as a group of young ruffians ran too close to the enormous fire where he would craft iron rivets.

Owain knew the rivets would be essential for fixing the wood in place. He marvelled at the process of coming together to create a ship. Initially, the forests were scoured for suitable trees, and then their trunks split to suit where they would be needed in the vessel. He knew that oak was favored, but oak was slow growing and, here in Ireland, had been over felled. When they could not use their preferred wood, they would use beech, alder, ash, and birch.

The Welshman amused himself, thinking of a conversation he had had with Lafracoth about how Brehon Law had classified trees into four groups: Nobles were trees like oak, yew, and wild apple; commoners were trees like alder, willow, and birch; lower orders were trees such as elder, blackthorn, and juniper; and then there was a category called Slaves. Slaves were bushes such as bracken, furze, and brambles. How Nest would laugh when he told her that. He imagined her honeyed peal of laughter and her head thrown back, showing her long white throat, her huge eyes crinkled with mirth as she looked into his. Then she would rest her head against his shoulder, and he would kiss her hair's thick, fragrant mass. He would let his hands slide down over her breasts to her waist, and grasping her neat buttocks would pull her closer. The Welshman sighed. Not long now.

Owain's lighter mood was because he was going home. He had received the message from his father that King Henry had pardoned him and restored him to his lands if he behaved quietly and loyally. Owain had decided he would indeed purport to be quiet and loyal. He smiled in contentment, thinking of Nest, his little son, and his lands and all he would do with them. He wondered what he would feel when he held the child for the first time and whether the little mite would sense that he was the father. Somehow or other, he would arrange to rid Nest of Gerald so they could marry. She would be a fine queen of Powys one day, and then Llewellyn would be his heir. He would walk openly with her at his side, drawing every man's eye in envy. Together, they would sweep through Wales, unite it, and the Normans could watch. He had had plenty of time to think how it could be done. He would make alliances between his children and all the Welsh families of note and then with the Irish and the Norse. He would play his own game, just as Lafracoth had advised, but first, he would keep the Normans quiet while building his strength.

A crewman excused himself as he passed with a sealskin bag which Owain knew held fleeces and blankets, keeping them dry. Such bags would be stored in compartments between the rowing benches on either side of the boat or in storage lockers at the stern and the bow. Being at sea in all weathers was hard, but the men who earned their living that way loved it.

Owain's musings turned to his father and the poignancy of their last meeting. He wanted to see the old man again, drunk though he would probably be. He had suffered for Owain's actions, and now Owain tried to prove he was a good son.

Looking down, Owain was surprised to see Griffith ap Rhys bounding up the gangplank with a firm athletic step. Seeing the Welshman, he hailed him good-naturedly. Griffith ap Rhys was Nest's younger brother exiled in Ireland more than eighteen years before when his father, Rhys ap Tewdwr, King of Deheubarth, had been murdered by the Normans. Like his sister, he had dark good looks enhanced by large, intelligent sage-coloured eyes and a perfect aquiline nose. He should have been King of Deheubarth when he came of age at twenty-eight years, which the Welsh considered was when you could qualify for kingship, yet the Normans were well ensconced in Deheubarth's rich fertile lands.

Griffith was so Irish now that his birthright had almost been forgotten, though not by him. Every day he vowed to take back the lands that belonged to him. Every day he had toiled with all manner of weapons, fighting bravely for King Murtagh, learning from him how to rule and keep one's enemies subdued but, most importantly, he absorbed battle tactics like a sponge. He was pleasant to everyone, energetic, enthusiastic, and, with his broad shoulders and tall, athletic body, looked every inch of a king in the making.

On Owain's first trip to Ireland during the war with the Normans in Anglesey, he met the young Griffith who, despite losing his family, had already made himself famous at the Dublin Court. Owain had not considered him much back then, but on each trip back to Ireland, he got to know him better. He had become close to him when he had been in Dublin with Nest and closer still while they fought Murtagh's enemies, and he had admired Griffith's courage.

There was something about Griffith that made everybody like him. He never complained about the hardships of life on campaign. He never openly agonised about losing his parents and brothers or being plucked away from his homeland and royal heritage. If he had a weakness, it was his love of women, but Owain knew now, only too well, that even men who boasted that they had no time for love could fall at that hurdle.

'I am coming with you,' Griffith yelled, his white-toothed smile gleaming with the sheer excitement of the adventure.

'You are?' Owain showed his surprise.

'I am, although we will part ways when we get to Wales.'

'Where will you go? You are welcome to join me and my teulu.' Owain grinned with genuine warmth at Griffith, clasping his arm in friendship. Griffith appreciated the real concern for his welfare, but something occurred to him, and he felt uncomfortable. He cleared his throat, paused for a moment, collecting himself, then answered, 'Thank you, Owain, really thank you, but no, I will not be able to join you even though it would have been an honour.'

Owain turned his head to one side, questioningly raising his eyebrows.

Griffith shrugged and moved out of the way of two oarsmen carrying a wooden chest. He focused his attention on them as he spoke. 'I am going to be educated on the enemy from within.'

Owain looked confused,

'You are going to the court of King Henry?'

Griffith gave a little awkward laugh, 'Good God, no. I will stay with Nest and Gerald of Windsor in Pembroke.'

Owain's face dropped, and he stared blankly. Griffith saw it and immediately clapped a firm hand on the shoulder of the older man.

'Oh, I am sorry. I was unsure; at least, I hoped you already knew. I wish it were not so, Owain. I honestly wish that I was not bringing you, of all people, such news. My sister has returned to that vile bastard, Gerald of Windsor.'

Owain's cheeks grew pale. He tried to compose himself, but his throat seemed to close as he spoke. He gripped the side of the ship.

'She took my son with her?'

Griffith nodded and gave a sympathetic smile acknowledging his friend's disappointment. Owain turned away sharply. There was a pause, and then Griffith tried to soften the blow. 'What else was she to do?'

Owain's words were hardly audible.

'Wait for me. She could have waited for me.'

Owain felt his hopes plunging. The oarsmen were already making their way to their places to take the ship down the Liffey, out to the open sea where the sails would do the work of crossing the Irish Sea. The ropes were being unleashed from the wharf while long poles were used to push the ship away from the side. The boat was drifting into the river now away from the clamour of the noisy port, away from Ireland, and Owain felt as if he, too, was drifting. Adrift and lost.

***

Bethan had heard nothing from Rhys, and she missed him. She loved her place at the llys but was half considering moving back to her parents if that meant she was closer to her son. She was surprised if he had joined Gronwy in his llys in Tegeingl, that Rhys had not sent word to her.

'What is the matter, Bethan?' Susannah asked her one day when they were minding the small girls in the orchard, and she was lost in thought.

'It is strange that I have heard nothing from Rhys.'

'Not strange at all,' said Susannah. 'He is a hot-blooded young man with other things to occupy his mind.'

'Yes, perhaps so, but we were so close.'

'I expect that is how all mothers feel,' Susannah ventured. 'One day, they are feeding babies, and the next day their babes have left them behind.'

'I suppose so,' said Bethan.

'Do not forget that you also left your parents behind when you came to Gwynedd with the queen. He has done it the other way around.'

'That's true.'

'And do you send word to them?'

'No, not really.'

'There we are then.' Susannah gave a self-satisfied nod. She craned to check on three of the girls hiding behind a pear tree and, satisfied they were safe, her attention was taken by the rhythmic plod of hooves as Hywel and a few of his men rode past the orchard.

Bethan looked up as she heard them, and Susannah caught her look.

'He is a fine man,' said Susannah wickedly, 'and no wife. What a waste.'

Bethan coloured and teased the curls on Rainaillt's hair as the little girl sat beside her, making an ant's house out of leaves.

'Hywel and I used to be close; just talk, you understand, but since Rhys left, he does not look at me even.'

'Why is that?'

'I think he feels Rhys has let the family down, returning to his father and all.'

They sat silently momentarily as Susannah tried to make sense of it.

'A man might look at it that way, I suppose,' she offered finally.

'And Rhys left without saying goodbye to anyone. Hywel would not have liked that. He was good to Rhys, and it was a slight on him, King Gruffydd, and his family. He would not have liked that.'

'That was not like Rhys, mind you. He was always a lovely young man, always quick to help me if anything needed carrying or if one of the children was hurt.' Susannah defended her friend's son.

'Once Lord Gronwy got into his head, though, he was different. He should have said goodbye and thanked the family, but he just slipped away.'

'But Hywel would understand that it had nothing to do with you.'

'As you say, men look at things differently.'

'They do.'

'I was half thinking of returning to Tegeingl, to my parents perhaps.'

'Oh, Bethan, you would end up a lonely woman. If Rhys wants you to chase him, then he will send word. This is your home, here. He has probably found himself a nice young sweetheart and is not looking back.'

'Yes, perhaps you are right,' admitted Bethan, although her heart ached for her son.

Chapter 19: Rumours (Summer 1111)

Gruffydd threw down his sword and looked at the sweating men around him in the practice yard.

'Be still!' he bellowed, and everybody stopped their drills, looking at him with surprise.

'It is stiflingly hot to be slogging it out here,' he growled, 'but I need you fit. There is too much going on outside Gwynedd that I do not like, too many rumours. We must be sharp and physically better than any other band of warriors.' He pointed at a small group of a half dozen spearmen. 'You stay here until I send six men to exchange with you.' Then turning back to the remainder, he instructed, 'Take off everything except your shifts and follow me. That includes you boys.'

The last comment was directed at his three eldest sons, but Gwenllian had also been sparring, and now, her smooth, fresh face shining from the exertion, she ran up to him and asked, 'Father, what about me?'

'Some things a woman cannot do. Stay here and practise.'

'But Father, what are you going to do?'

'We are going for a run along the beach.'

'I can run.'

'Not in your shift, you are not.'

'I'll run as I am.'

'As you please,' he agreed testily.

She bent down to take off her boots. Hywel approached Gruffydd and whispered, 'Lord, perhaps it is better to send the princess back to her mother, up to the llys.'

'Are you volunteering to escort her? That would suit you, I imagine!'

Hywel was silent, but his hurt at the barb was evident. Gruffydd turned away and strode off, calling for his daughter to hurry up.

'Come on, men, quick about it!' shouted Hywel perfunctorily. He was the leader of the warband, and although Gruffydd was the king, it would have been polite to discuss any change in training with him. He wanted to keep a few men fully armed wherever they went, but he knew the suggestion would undermine Gruffydd, so he kept silent.

Gruffydd led the men out of the llys at a quick pace, down the hill, along the riverbank and towards the beach.

Each step of the way, Gwenllian, stony-faced and fully dressed, kept up with them.

Gruffydd started to feel the muscles in his legs rebelling against the speed in the soft sand but pressed on. Behind him, the men had begun to string out according to their ability, and Hywel jogged along at the back, encouraging the slowest. Even this irritated Gruffydd, who silently cursed the stitch in his side.

Cadwallon jogged up beside Gruffydd, his stride long and easy, but Owain and Cadwaladr stayed alongside Hywel. This run was nothing for them, and they enjoyed Hywel's company, although he was grim-faced. Owain, always sensitive, was aware that something had happened between Hywel and his father, although he was unclear what it was all about.

They ran for about a mile until there was a rocky outcrop, and Gruffydd signalled for them to take a break. Everyone was panting hard; some doubled over, some dropping on the sand. Gwenllian was flushed, breathing deeply, but she stood. Owain dived into the sea to cool down and emerged out of the water, his hands sweeping the soaking mat of hair out of his eyes. His father noticed how much like his mother Owain was when his hair was sleeked back flat against his head. Things were not right between Angharad and himself since Hywel had returned, and it chafed at him day and night.

'See out there?' Gruffydd raised his voice to include everyone as he pointed to a rock where the surf crashed, and two seals lolled in the sunshine.

'We are going to swim out there, get up onto the rock, and then swim back, but we do it in pairs. The winners get to walk back to the llys; the losers must run.'

The men grinned, loving the novelty of plunging into the cooling waves which lunged and pulled at the sand. Gruffydd drew a starting line in the sand with a driftwood stick.

'Anyone not able to swim?'

A couple put their hands up.

'You run two lengths of the beach, and every morning from now on, you come down here until you know how to swim. We live on the coast, and you never know when it may save your lives.'

He turned to Gwenllian, who was panting and shone with perspiration, speaking softly and quietly.

'You do not go into the water,'

'Why not?' There was a hint of defiance in her voice.

'Do you want these warriors to see every inch of your body when your clothes are wet?'

Gwenllian blushed scarlet.

'You have proved your point. You ran well, but if you wish to be a leader of people one day, you must also fight your impulsiveness.'

'Yes, Father.' She sat heavily on a rock, looking at her feet.

Then he pointed to Hywel.

'You and I go first.'

The two men strode into the water and dived into the waves. Hywel was slightly shorter than Gruffydd, and both men rippled with muscle. Both wore a look of grim determination. The men cheered as they fought the surf and each other stroke by stroke. Gruffydd was hurting, but he would not give up, and Hywel, still feeling the sting of Gruffydd's words, was flying through the water, driven by sheer anger. Seeing intruders approaching them, the two seals flopped into the waves and vanished into the deep.

The two men got to the rock, clambered up inelegantly, and then dived back into the water for the home stretch. There was yelling and cheering as the pair hit the shallows neck and neck before Gruffydd, using the last reserves of his strength, threw himself onto the line half a second before Hywel.

The men roared at the narrowness of the victory but with admiration at the physical effort they had just witnessed. Hywel bowed, acknowledging Gruffydd's accomplishment, but he was seething. Gruffydd dipped his head, but whereas he would usually have clapped Hywel on the shoulders and congratulated him on a great race, he stood apart as if engrossed in the competitions between the rest of the men.

The group had divided themselves into twos, and everyone yelled and cheered as the other contestants drove themselves through the sea.

'Can we boys go as a three?' asked Cadwallon. 'And the two losers will jog back?'

'You can,' agreed Gruffydd, and the tanned boys plunged into the sea, holding nothing back. Cadwallon's stroke was fierce, his arms and legs splashing furiously. Cadwaladr went out too quickly and then lost breath. Owain, with his smooth, sleek stroke, won seemingly effortlessly.

Finally, Gruffydd called for the losers to start their jog back and the winners to walk, although a few winners were up for the challenge of a further run. Gwenllian, holding her boots and lifting her tunic slightly, strode sulkily in the shallows. She knew her father was right but hated to be left out of anything.

Her father let the men walk ahead, and he walked beside her while his three sons jogged with the losers.

'I am proud of you, Gwenllian; you have an amazing spirit,' he said softly.

'Thank you, Father.' She looked down, her face thunderous.

'What is the problem here?'

'Father, I am always reminded about what I cannot do because I am a girl.'

'Who is almost a woman who will soon be married herself.'

Gwenllian stopped and looked at her father. 'You have chosen for me?' she asked, her voice quaking.

'Not yet, but your mother and I have discussed it, and there are some families who would be good matches for you.'

'Families, Father, not then princes who would be good matches?'

'It may not necessarily be a prince.'

'But Father, you spoke just before of my being a leader of people. How then could that be unless I marry a Welsh prince?'

'You may marry a foreign prince or noble.'

'And leave Wales, Father? I would rather die.'

He was tired and aching and did not want to have this intense conversation with his daughter.

'Gwenllian,' he said firmly. 'I am not going to fight about this with you. I will talk to the men walking ahead and suggest you run ahead to your brothers.'

Gwenllian nodded obediently and took off through the sand. Her mind was so absorbed that she hardly felt the ground below her or took in what she was passing. Her father's words had unsettled her.

The winners strolled along the sand. Among them were two men who were new to the Aberffraw community. One named Gogan was short, well-muscled with a thin face and close-cropped mousy hair. He seemed to spend most of his time with his friend, Hova, beside him. Hova seemed to defer to Gogan, who had pockmarked skin, pale sly eyes, and a habit of licking his lips whenever he spoke. Most of the rest of the group were Gruffydd's men, and they laughed and joked as they made their way back towards the llys.

'What was that all about then?' Gogan asked Aeddan, who was one of Gruffydd's longest-serving warriors.

'The run and the swim?' asked Aeddan, his blue eyes twinkling. He had enjoyed himself as his tall, firm, muscled frame had loped easily across the sand and glided through the surf.

'A bit unusual!' said Hova.

'A bit of fun,' said Aeddan smiling cheerfully. 'It is good to test our strength differently.'

'A bit strange for the king to be doing that sort of thing,' said Gogan slyly.

'Not really. He always ensures he practises with us unless he is away on the judicial circuit or travelling around Gwynedd. He practises harder than anyone.'

'But is Hywel not supposed to be the leader of the warband? A bit of a slap in the face to him to suggest you warriors are not good enough, as if Hywel had not been doing his job.'

'Not at all,' said Aeddan pleasantly. 'Hywel and the king are almost like brothers; they share the responsibilities.'

'That's not all they share from what I have heard,' said Hova.

Aeddan stopped, and his pleasant expression turned to stone, 'I am not sure what you are suggesting, but we are all close here. No man talks and whispers behind another man's back. He is plain about it if he has something to say, and all differences are aired.'

'That's what we were seeing out there, then, between the king and Hywel?' said Gogan innocently. 'They were just airing differences?'

Some men were now turning to glare at the newcomers, but Meirion came across and stood beside Aeddan, facing the two men. He put a hand on Gogan's shoulder. Meirion was tall, strong, intimidating, solemn, and usually quiet.

'I think you are not understanding,' he said with menace. 'When you accept the hospitality given you in this llys, you do not stir up trouble. Maybe that was how it worked in Madog's camp, but by God, it is not how it works here.'

'Sorry, sorry,' Gogan raised his hands and backed away. 'I was only commenting on what I saw, is all.'

'Well, you see it differently from us,' said Aeddan, 'so shut your mouth, or I'll shut it for you.'

'What's going on here, Aeddan?' Gruffydd's gruff voice sounded behind them.

Aeddan looked up, startled to see Gruffydd had joined them and wondered how much he had heard.

'Just a misunderstanding, sire,' he said, not taking his eyes off the two men. 'Everything is cleared up now.'

All the men were standing around, ready to support their comrades. Gruffydd quickly diffused the tension, 'At this pace you will miss your meal, and the others will have eaten the lot.'

The men laughed, some with nervous relief.

'Go on, all of you.' Then turning to the two newcomers, he said, 'Gogan and Hova, is that right?'

The two men bowed their heads respectfully and muttered agreement.

'And whose camp did you come from? Madog's or Owain's?'

'Both, sire,' they chorused as if rehearsed.

'I was with Owain ap Cadwgan, and Hova was with Madog, but we have known each other for some time.'

'And what part of the country do you come from?'

'Near Pembroke, sire.'

'Where exactly?'

'Llangwm,' Gogan said too confidently.

'I think I have been there. Tell me, what is the name of the river there?'

'River, sire? We just call it the river,' said Gogan,

'I remember now. Is it not the Cleddau?'

'Ah yes, sire, I think you are correct,' Gogan agreed hastily.

'Legend tells us that King Arthur passed that way along the river Cleddau when he was chasing the magical Irish boar with its seven piglets. Nothing like a chase, following a trail!'

They looked at him blankly.

'It was a costly chase, but Arthur was victorious. The boar was driven into the sea.'

Gruffydd watched their eyes darting sheepishly, trying to understand the message shrouded in the legend, but Gruffydd's face betrayed nothing.

'And there is a wonderful waterfall there?' he continued.

'Yes indeed, sire.' They both agreed.

Gruffydd arched an eyebrow. 'It is strange that your accents sound not those of men of Pembroke but rather those of East Gwynedd.'

The two men exchanged a look.

'Our mothers were from East Gwynedd, sire,' Hova volunteered, licking his lips.

'Both of them?' Gruffydd looked sharply into Gogan's eyes.

'Yes, sire.'

'Where in East Gwynedd were they from?'

'We do not know, sire.'

'You have never been there?'

'Never, sire.' Their words tumbled out.

'And you have been fighting with Madog ap Rhyrid and Owain ap Cadwgan?'

'Yes, sire.' Gogan nodded vigorously.

'Where did you last fight?'

'Dyfed, sire.' Gogan looked at Hova quickly.

'Dyfed, I see. Well, I am sure the men will look after you. 'Aeddan, a word.'

The two newcomers walked hastily away, a little too hastily, noted Gruffydd.

Aeddan held back, and the king waited until the others were out of hearing.

'There is something not right about those two.'

'Sire?'

'They say they are from Llangwm, but they have never been there in their lives. They have no idea of the landscape there and less of the legends.'

Aeddan looked shocked.

'They are from East Gwynedd. Did you hear their accents?'

'I am sorry, sire, I did not realise. I did not think!'

'Keep a close eye on them, Aeddan; I think Gronwy has sent them.'

'We should get rid of them, sire. They fought well, mind you.'

'Let us leave it for a few days and see what they are about but keep them under observation.'

***

Gwenllian was hiding in the stables, sobbing. Her future, which seemed so full of promise only yesterday, now seemed wretchedly cold and bleak. She felt too young to marry, and if she was to marry, she could not bear to think of herself in charge of the day-to-day duties of a household. She thought of all the likely eligible young men she knew, and none lived a life where she could fight for Wales. Her dreams were falling apart.

She heard voices and shuffled further back into the straw pile.

'I think he knows we are not from Pembroke,' one man said.

'You were quick with your answers, though, Hova! I thought what you said about our mothers was clever.'

'I did not think we would ever be asked about the place we came from. Lord Gronwy said their questions would be about us being with Madog or Owain.'

'I think Lord Gronwy is right, however. There is something afoot between Hywel and Lord Gruffydd; that's what all that challenge on the beach was about.'

'You cannot blame Hywel, in any case. She is a beauty, all right; there is not a man who would not want to get between her legs. Good for him if he has.'

'Gronwy says it is certain; his bastard son caught them together.'

'She does not look the type, but then she is Lord Gronwy's sister; by God, he has been with every woman east of the Dee and west of the Clywyd!'

'I cannot believe this lot cannot see what is happening. Are they blind?'

'Gronwy said we were to make sure everyone knew. He wants her publicly shamed. He thinks Gruffydd will kill Hywel or vice versa when it comes out. Then we can get out of here.'

'I think Gruffydd knows by how he looks at Hywel, and did you see he did not even greet Hywel when he returned from the raiding.'

'There is a coldness between the king and queen as well. I noticed that she hardly speaks to him.'

'Makes our work easier.'

'So, we just spread the word tonight when we are eating. We just point out what is in front of their noses.'

The two men removed themselves from the stables leaving Gwenllian trembling with shock. She retched and put a hand over her mouth, breathing deeply. She started to piece things together in her mind. She had noticed that her mother and father were not as warm to each other as usual. She thought of Hywel and how often her mother would seek him out, and she retched again. Hywel was like family; it was impossible that he could be doing this to her father.

'Gwenllian?' she heard Bethan calling and shrunk further into her refuge. She kept silent and started trying to reason everything out when she heard nothing more. She knew that Gronwy was a liar. Her mind spun. Her uncle had to be lying. Then again, they had said that Rhys had 'caught them together.' Is that why he left without saying goodbye? Her legs shook violently as she thought about her mother, her beautiful, devoted, loyal mother who believed in doing good, and her upright, honest father. She thought about Hywel and his loyalty to the family. She knew, she just knew, that it could not be true. She was so distressed that she burst into tears again. All her concerns about marriage were buried beneath the disaster unfolding, and she had no idea how to stop it.

***

The Aberffraw llys was entertaining on a grand scale. Gruffydd had invited Wilfrid, Bishop of St David's, to stay with them as he made his way to meet with other Welsh bishops in Bangor. He was a well-respected proud Welshman who had supported the Welsh when they had revolted against the Normans in Dyfed but had lost lands because of it, taken by Gerald, Princess Nest's husband. He had even been imprisoned by Arnulf of Montgomery and excommunicated by Anselm, Bishop of Canterbury. Despite all this, he remained Bishop of St David's and had made his peace with Anselm, whom he respected as a god-fearing man despite their views on how the church should be run.

Angharad, gracious and self-composed, dressed in a fetching robe of palest blue linen, glided between the guests: richly dressed noblemen; merchants, whose wealth had only increased as Gwynedd thrived; men of the cloth; and the men of the teulu and their wives. She had introduced her children to the bishop, but there had been no sign of Gwenllian, who had been supposed to play a tune on the harp in his honour when he entered the hall. When she was able to attract Bethan's attention, she sent her to find the girl and to tell her that her mother was very displeased at her lack of respect.

The bards, accoutred in long colourful robes, had warmed up proceedings by reciting poems of great battles and Welsh courage, and now vast platters of meat, fish, bread, and steaming vegetables were being brought in.

The bishop, the senior men of the teulu, the queen, and Cadwallon were placed on a slightly raised dais along with the important noblemen and women. In contrast, the other men and women were on trestle tables and benches stretching across the hall. There was no fire as the weather was so hot, and doors at either end of the hall had been opened to let in the sea breeze.

Gwenllian entered, her face blotched, her eyes as red as her fine robe. She bowed to her parents, seeing her mother's knitted brows and her father's obvious disapproval, knowing that all the cold water she had splashed onto her face had done little to conceal her distress. At the end of the dais, near the entrance where she stood, Hywel was seated next to Aeddan and Meirion. He caught Gwenllian's eye and gave her a sympathetic smile before she scurried over to three rows of trestle tables that had been pushed together. The kindness she saw in Hywel's face made it seem impossible that he would deceive her father, betraying all of them.

'Gwenllian!' Cadwaladr called. She glanced across, saw Owain and Cadwaladr at the furthest end of the table nearest the dais, and started to excuse herself as she pushed through the seated crowd. It was tough to get through as the llys had invited extra guests from local families and the church, leaving little room between the tables. As she squeezed through, she could feel her parents' eyes on her. Despite hiding her grief behind her long hair hastily adorned with flowers, she felt conspicuous on the journey to her brothers, which seemed to be taking an eternity. Finally, she sat down next to Owain.

'What is wrong?' he asked immediately, noticing her swollen eyes and wan face.

'Nothing,' she said.

Her father stood up, the light glinting off the shining embroidered threads of his tunic. Clapping his hands, everyone immediately quietened, submitting to the natural authority of the golden-haired king.

'Tonight is an exceptional occasion for us as we have the much-revered Bishop of St David's here.' Gruffydd started his deep voice, rich and commanding attention. The bishop was pleased but made a small gesture with his hands indicating that Gruffydd was too kind. 'On behalf of us all, Bishop Wilfrid, I want to welcome you and let you know what an honour it is to have you here. You are a bishop and someone who has risked his life to stand up for the Welsh. You have inspired us all in dark times.'

Everyone cheered, and there was the stamping of feet. The bishop raised his hand and nodded, smiling in gratitude for the genuine affection being demonstrated within the hall.

'Bishop Wilfrid, in your honour, our bards, Rhoddri and his fellows, will perform a song they have composed for you.'

Gruffydd nodded, smiling at Rhoddri and his men, who were standing on a small, raised platform at the opposite end of the trestle tables from Gwenllian. Everybody turned towards them as the music of lyre, pibcorn, and crwth penetrated the hall.

Cadwaladr shifted to get a better view while Owain leaned over to his sister.

'You are not still angry about being unable to swim with the men?'

'Of course not,' she spat back at him and immediately felt sorry. 'I do not know what to do, Owain.'

'About what?'

'We have traitors here,' she whispered.

'Who?' he shot back.

'Those two at the other end of the table, Gogan and Hova, say they used to be Madog's men from Pembroke.'

'Are you sure?'

'Yes, I heard them talking. Uncle Gronwy sent them, and they are telling lies about Mother.'

'What lies?' he asked loudly, and Gwenllian looked around to see if anyone had heard, but they were all caught up in the performance.

'It does not matter. I cannot say.'

He caught her arm. 'You tell me, Gwenllian, or I'll ask them myself.'

'Please do not, Owain, please. We'll talk later.'

'We'll talk now,' her brother growled softly.

She looked up, catching a cool look her mother was giving to her father, and her imagination started to race. She blurted out, 'But it could be true, I am not sure, maybe it is true.'

'What?'

'That Mother does not love Father anymore.'

'What are you talking about? You are talking nonsense.'

'They are saying that Hywel and Mother are lovers.'

'What?' Owain was aghast. He looked at Hywel at the far end of the top table opposite the two men from Pembroke and saw how they were looking at him and talking from the sides of their mouths. Hywel was oblivious, gazing into his goblet while the enthusiasm for the singing accelerated all around him. Rhoddri the bard, in his purple robe, was mesmerising his audience, yet the men from Pembroke were watching Hywel like hawks watching prey.

'I heard them. They said Rhys had caught them together, Mother and Hywel.' Gwenllian whispered.

'Rhys?'

'And Rhys had told Uncle Gronwy.'

'Who is a liar,' said Owain stoutly.

Owain looked at the two men with utter hatred. Suddenly, he scrambled onto the table, running down the length of it scattering platters and goblets as he went. He was so fast that the two men were astonished when he leapt at them. With all his strength, he raised his foot and kicked Hova in the face, breaking teeth and bloodying his nose. Hova reeled backwards, but the benches were so tightly packed that he slumped against the alarmed people so that his fall was broken.

Almost simultaneously, Owain grabbed Gogan by his hair, banging his head against the wooden table. Gogan shuddered and was momentarily stunned, but Hova recovered himself, scrambling up onto the bench, despite many arms reaching to pull him away from the young prince. The confusion in the crowded space worked to Hova's advantage as nobody could hold him, though they tore wildly at his tunic and legs. The music had stopped, and everyone turned in disbelief to witness the commotion.

'Bastard!' Hova's voice was full of menace. He swept his knife forward, aiming for the boy's heart, but Owain ducked smartly, and the blade caught him instead on the arm. Owain swung around, slamming his fist into Hova's injured face. Hova staggered backwards, but at that moment of distraction, Gogan was fast. He pulled at Owain's boot so the prince lost balance, falling hard, allowing a snarling Gogan to crouch over him, his knees pinning Owain's shoulders down, one hand pressing down on his throat. Owain's eyes widened. He tried to push himself up from underneath the robust and bulky adversary, but his vision was beginning to blur. He could not breathe. The prince struggled with one more colossal effort, pushing against Gogan's arms as he saw the knife high and poised to sink into his neck. Death had come for him, and he had hardly lived.

Gruffydd saw what was happening, launching himself out of his chair, which tumbled behind him. He roared, and Cadwallon cried with shock. They both knew the distance was too far. They could not reach Owain in time. Angharad was clasping the table, white-knuckled, shouting her son's name, and wailing in agony as she saw the knife. The bishop rose to his feet, an expression of complete horror crossing his face as he started to pray, holding his cross out as if it could avert the inevitable. Gwenllian and Cadwaladr were racing down the top of the table towards their brother, screeching as they went, knowing they were too late.

Suddenly, from nowhere, Hywel was there. He had lunged across from the top table, flattening Gogan, wrenching his arm until a snap was heard and Gogan's knife tumbled. Immediately, Aeddan and Meirion were next to Hywel, and they wrestled with the two men amongst tumbling platters while those close at hand were beating the two spies with whatever they could grab. They did not know what this was about, but Owain was their prince. Nobody was going to hurt him while they had breath. Eventually, amongst great commotion, Aeddan and Meirion dragged the two battered men outside, leaving the hall full of awed murmuring.

Hywel knelt over Owain, who was gasping for breath, and, gently placing an arm under his head, lifted him to a sitting position. After giving him a few moments, he supported a protesting Owain off the table into the hallway where there was more air. Owain grimaced: he was in no mood for Hywel's kindness. He was furious and pushing him off, but the older man had him in a firm grip. Before they left the hall, Hywel turned, caught Angharad's eye nodding confirmation that her son was in no danger, then repeated the gesture to Gruffydd, who was already calming down the proceedings but whose eyes were brimming with gratitude.

It was a while before the prince calmed down. Finally, Hywel asked, 'Would you like to tell me what that was about?'

'They are Gronwy's men.'

'How do you know?'

'Gwenllian heard them talking.'

'And?'

'They are dishonouring Mother.'

Hywel took a deep breath, swallowed hard and looked away. He felt his anger rising, but no hint of it was betrayed in his voice.

'In what way?'

'They say ....'

'They say?'

'They say you and she are lovers.' Owain was watching for Hywel's reaction.

Hywel blew out his breath and closed his eyes. His face was a picture of misery.

'Is it true then?' asked Owain, his mouth dry.

The betrayal that Hywel felt was written all over his face. His words came flatly.

'It is not true, though I love your mother and father more than I could ever explain.'

'I knew it would not be true.'

'Your mother is the finest woman I have ever known. She loves your father with a depth of passion other men could only dream of.'

'I am sorry. I really did not believe what they said. I should not have questioned you.'

Even then, when his heart was breaking, Hywel felt compassion for the young man in front of him. A young man he had watched grow up with such pride. He was such a mixture of his mother and father.

'Of course, you did not believe it, but you should have come to me, not made a scene in front of the bishop, no less.'

Owain gave a wan smile.

'What will happen to them, Hova and Gogan?'

'That is for your father to decide, but right now, you need to walk back into the hall, with me, as a man in the right. Wait a few moments while I tell Aeddan and Meirion to tie those treacherous bastards up in the guardhouse.'

Owain went over to the well and washed his face and arm in a pail of water while he was waiting. He could hear singing in the hall and knew it was his sister's voice as she played the harp. He smiled. Despite everything, there she was, coolly playing the harp.

'Let's look at that wound,' said Hywel, returning from the guardhouse.

'It's not too bad,' said Owain.

Hywel inspected it under a rushlight. 'Come, we will clean it up. We'll get some moss and honey onto it.'

Owain put a hand to stop Hywel. 'You saved my life in there. I do not know how to thank you, but I am indebted to you.'

'Nonsense! You are the son of my lord, and I must protect you.'

When Owain and Hywel returned to the hall, Aeddan and Meirion had already spread the news that the two men were Gronwy's spies. Owain found everyone clapping him on the shoulder or congratulating him. Gwenllian was back in her place at the trestle, and he whispered in her ear, answering the question which was written on her face.

'It is not true,' he said tightly.

Gwenllian looked back towards her parents. Gruffydd and Angharad were talking to the bishop as if nothing had happened. Rhoddri, the bard, was preparing his men to sing again. Hywel, however, was staring into his goblet as if his world was coming to an end.

***

'Sire,' Hywel started with a sigh.

'Forget the formalities, Hywel,' said Gruffydd brusquely, 'you saved Owain's life.'

Hywel said nothing but just nodded. He had not slept the previous night and had drunk so much uncharacteristically that he had woken with a pounding head and a sour stomach.

'I know what they were saying.'

Hywel raised his red-rimmed eyes to Gruffydd and saw uncertainty instead of trust. He made up his mind.

'It is untrue, and anyone who thinks it might be dishonours their queen.'

Gruffydd's eyes flashed with a relief he could not disguise. He spoke now, but the words were not what Hywel needed to hear.

'This is Gronwy's way of hurting us. Undermining us.'

Hywel nodded sadly. 'He is rotten to the core.'

'I will not forget this. He has gone too far.'

'By paying attention to his nonsense, we play into his hands. Some will choose to believe him if we retaliate.'

'You think we should do nothing? The man needs to be put in his place.'

'If you do, then you play with fire. Any conflict with Gronwy hurts Gwynedd,' Hywel counselled.

'So how do we contain the rumours.'

'Take away the fuel, and the fire goes out. I will leave.'

Gruffydd's face registered the words with shock. He jumped up from his seat and held Hywel by the shoulder, looking into his eyes with intensity.

'No, man, do not be stupid. Your place is here, with us. You are like family.'

Hywel's words were devoid of all emotion. 'I love her.'

Gruffydd's face drained of colour as Hywel continued, 'I have loved her since before you knew to love her. I will always love her. You have been more than a king to me. I would gladly give my life to you; you have risked your life for me. I would not hesitate to give my life for any of your family, but I have tried and tried and cannot stop loving her.'

Gruffydd stared in utter disbelief at the man he had known for so long.

'Does she know?'

Hywel laughed bitterly. 'I am like a brother to her, and that is as it should be. There is only one man she will ever love. She sees nothing else. You are her world.'

Gruffydd turned away, then not to show his friend the tears welling in his eyes. He spoke thickly.

'I have been a bastard to you both.'

Hywel said nothing.

Gruffydd breathed heavily, 'I have let my jealousy go too far. It eroded any common sense I had. It has come between our friendship.'

Hywel shrugged. 'Gruffydd, we will always be friends, but I cannot stay here.'

Gruffydd turned sharply, 'Hywel, you belong here. How would I manage without you?'

'Aeddan will make a worthy leader of the warband.' Gruffydd could feel Hywel's stubbornness but still cajoled him.

'Please do not do this. Take time to think, at least. Our feelings are all so raw.'

Hywel gave a small laugh. 'I have been thinking ever since that morning in Tegeingl so long ago when you made a pledge with a girl who had stolen my heart. I have had a long time to think.'

So many emotions coursed through Gruffydd's head right then. He felt pity for his lovesick friend but also genuine anguish that the man he had thought of as his dearest friend for so long would abandon him. All his jealousy had dissipated, leaving only the most profound sense of loss.

'But where will you go?'

'I have my property on the other side of the island which needs attention, and because you have always been generous, I have the money to make it a thriving place. I will go there, work on my land, and clear my head. Later, who knows? I have been a warrior all my life. I love leading men, so eventually, I will join someone's warband. Maybe I will go back to Ireland. They are good people there. It is not Wales, but I like the place.'

'Take a few months but come back then. All this will have blown over.'

Hywel shook his head. 'How could I return after what has been spoken?' he asked flatly.

'I am sorry,' said Gruffydd sincerely. He knew he had failed Hywel. He cast his eyes up to the ceiling. He wished he had controlled his temper but could not go back in time. 'God, I do not know how I will do without you; you have been my brother for so long.'

Then he threw his arms around the other man's shoulders, pulling him towards him as if he could mend the hurt. He tried one more time to dissuade his friend from leaving.

'Hywel, do not go. I would not be king now if I had not had you by my side all these years. Honestly, man, you know every thought that goes through my head.'

Hywel squeezed his king's arms and said very quietly,

'I do. That is why I am going.'

***

'I still do not understand why you are leaving us,' said Angharad the day before Hywel was to leave.

She had sought him out after the Sunday service in their little chapel. This was when the members of the llys would join in prayer and afterwards spill out into the courtyard, chatting amongst each other. Hywel had been much in demand, and she guessed that everybody was trying to persuade him to stay and failing, giving him their good wishes.

Hywel looked into her cornflower blue eyes, knowing they would forever be imprinted on his memory.

'It is time, my lady.'

'But you belong here.'

'You have all been kind to me, but recently, I have been restless.'

'Is this because of Gruffydd? You were at odds with each other for a while, I think. Was there a disagreement?'

Hywel said nothing looking across the courtyard where Gruffydd was sitting on a bench next to Bethan with his youngest two on his knees while his next youngest children were taking turns in being thrown into the air by Cadwallon, Cadwaladr, Owain and Gwenllian. Angharad followed his gaze to Gruffydd. She was sure something had happened between them, but neither would discuss it.

Gruffydd had come to her, humble and apologetic, a few nights before, begging her forgiveness for how he had treated her. He had blamed his worries, the spies, the death of Iorwedd and a thousand other things. She was relieved that they were now open and honest after what seemed like months when they had not spoken from their hearts to each other. They had reconciled; then, in the small hours of the morning, Gruffydd told her that Hywel was leaving, and she felt his warm tears against her hair.

'Because he is heartbroken that you are going,' Angharad persisted, 'as are the children, as am I.'

He turned sharply at the word 'heartbroken.' She had said it so easily, but he doubted that she felt what he did, that any of them thought as he did.

'I will miss you all,' he confessed. 'You have been my family, but this is the right time to go.'

'You have not explained why, Hywel.'

'I cannot explain it,' he said simply.

'Gruffydd can be difficult at times, I know. Sometimes he seems troubled, though I wonder if he himself knows why. If he has offended you in any way, I know he will not have meant to. He worries about all the undercurrents we hear about and fears that hard times are coming.'

'If they do, he is the leader who can bring Gwynedd through.'

'A leader without his right-hand man at his side.'

'My lady, Aeddan will be a better warband leader than I have been.'

'Aeddan will be good, I have no doubt, but he is not you.'

Hywel gave a weak smile, his cheeks colouring.

'And you are determined?' Angharad asked him, her voice warm and soft like honey.

He steeled himself. 'I am. I will take the boat to Ireland tomorrow. King Murtagh knows I am coming, and almost immediately, I am taking a warband north.'

'Oh Hywel,' she said sadly, her eyes now brimming with tears, 'I am afraid I will disgrace myself by weeping in a moment.'

He longed to take her in his arms, to feel her close to him, her heart pounding against his. He could smell the sweet scent of her hair, her perfumed robe, and he wanted to take his finger so gently and wipe the tears from her eyes.

'There is no need to weep, my lady,' he said softly. She quickly wiped her eyes, took a breath, and then straightened herself.

'Will you promise me something, Hywel?'

'Anything, my lady.'

'If I should ever really need you if something serious happens, can I send a message to you, and will you think about coming back? I would not call you back unless I had a real need.'

'Yes,' he said without thinking, 'I promise it.'

'That makes me feel as if you are not completely gone, after all,' she smiled, and Hywel's heart lurched.

Chapter 20: Ap Bleddyn (Autumn 1111)

When a marriage into the Royal House of Mathrafal had been suggested some fourteen years before, and that she would marry a son of Bleddyn ap Cynfyn, Hunydd, the daughter of Eunydd ap Morien of Dyffryn Clwyd had been elated. Bleddyn ap Cynfyn was not only a king of Powys but a co-ruler of Gwynedd. Hunydd's father had been in Bleddyn's warband, holding an important position, so his daughter was well acquainted with the family. When she realised, however, that she was marrying Bleddyn's gentle youngest son, Maredudd, and he would not be ruling any of his father's best lands, she felt that she had been given a poor husband.

The Vale of Clwyd was not rich land. It extended from the Irish Sea, south about thirty miles, and on its eastern side was bounded by the steep slopes of the Clwydian Range while to the west were low hills. The River Clwyd meandered along the vale from its birthplace, overlooked by the massive peaks of Eryri until it cut deep into the earth, churning rocks and tree trunks as it pursued its course, swollen by the rivers Clywedog, Elwy and Wheeler. Much of the land near the river was marshland but with some land suitable for crops. The farmers tried to enrich the earth with cartloads of seaweed or sand to grow oats and barley. On the slopes, cows would graze; this is where the real wealth lay, although, compared to rich Anglesey or Powys, it was poor pickings. This is where Hunydd had been raised.

Hunydd was groomed for marriage from an early age. She was not a beautiful girl, but she quickly learned how to make the best of what she had. Her eyes were small, but she made them expressive; her face was oval but plain, yet she would laugh whenever the opportunity arose, flashing neat white teeth. She was not tall but would walk gracefully; her head held high with an alluring sway to her hips. She knew how to get what she wanted, see an opportunity when it presented itself, and tease and torment men without giving too much of herself. Dyffryn Clwyd was a backwater, but she wanted status. In her dreams, nothing was impossible.

Eunydd ap Morien was a plain man who knew the extent of his power. When Eunydd called his daughter and told her that Maredudd was a good, honourable man, she had waited to hear what land he would rule. She was not impressed by the answer. Her father, a round-cheeked, affable man, had thought that he had done well, but his heart sank when he saw her thinly veiled disappointment. Even he had not realised the extent of her hopes. Hunydd, however, decided that there was more than one way to get where she wanted.

Maredudd ap Bleddyn was not handsome, like his older brothers Iorwedd and Cadwgan. He was tall, thin, and fair, but his hair was thin, his shoulders rounded. His eyes were small but kind, and his face was gaunt. Hunydd knew she could have had her pick of many more handsome men, but they were not brothers of the kings of Powys. She left Dyffryn Clwyd, with its little farmsteads dotted on the edge of marshland or woods, and moved to Powys. Now she dreamed of being the most important lady in the land, and to be that lady, she needed to work on Maredudd.

Her first plan was to make Maredudd love her utterly. Her second was that he got used to deferring to her. Within days she had managed the first, and within weeks she had ordered the second aim so well that the lovesick Maredudd would check everything with her. Maredudd was someone whose joy came from pleasing others, so it was easy to fall entirely in love with Hunydd and let her take charge.

Next, Hunydd worked on the man himself. Maredudd had not had pride in himself, but again, within months, he cut a fine figure of a man and even started speaking with impressive authority. She watched her brothers-in-law to ascertain their strengths and weaknesses. Cadwgan ap Bleddyn's failing was his love of drink and women. He was not a careful man, speaking too hastily and letting his temper drive wrong decisions at times, yet he was a great warrior and a man people loved and knew for his incredible generosity. Iorwedd ap Bleddyn was a great fighter, a man's man, but his weakness was that he craved wealth, and, in seeing the chance to make himself rich, he would sometimes cut corners.

Hunydd could not mould Maredudd to be a born leader of warriors, outgoing and charismatic like Cadwgan, or such an esteemed warrior as Iorwedd. Still, she could make him steady and reliable where they were not. If something happened to Cadwgan and Iorwedd, she would ensure that Maredudd was respected by those who counted in Powys and beyond so that he would step in to rule Powys until their sons were of age. She believed that much could happen to change their fortunes in a volatile place such as Powys, but she also thought that you made your luck.

By the time their first son, Gruffydd, had been born, Hunydd had manoeuvred and manipulated her brothers-in-law, increased Maredudd's land holdings, and their financial affairs were well managed. She worked her way up the social order in Powys, befriending and making sure Maredudd did favours for families that sometimes his brothers had overlooked.

Then came the time when the Welsh had fought against the Normans led by Cadwgan ap Bleddyn and Gruffydd ap Cynan. Hunydd had overseen the politics and advised her husband to ready his men and, most importantly, himself. She made sure her husband was strong, well-prepared, and visible. Maredudd, eager to please the woman he loved, found that although he would never be the warrior his brother Cadwgan was, he could turn himself into a valuable asset. He supported his brother through all the battles, and his brother was more than generous, but still Hunydd was not satisfied. Now Hunydd had three growing boys, Gruffydd, Madoc and Howell, who would one day need to inherit something golden.

Hunydd watched with great interest as William Rufus, the Norman King of England, was killed by an arrow while out hunting, and his brother Henry snatched the English throne from under the nose of his elder brother Robert Curthose, Duke of Normandy. While Henry settled himself into position, there was peace with Wales. When Robert de Belleme, the powerful head of the Montgomery family, started to court the royal family of Powys, Hunydd encouraged Maredudd to be seen as an essential figure in Powysian affairs. When Cadwgan and Iorwedd joined with Belleme to fight against Henry in favour of his brother, Hunydd ensured Maredudd was with them.

The Montgomery family's wealth, particularly Belleme, intoxicated her, but she learnt a costly lesson. Iorwedd negotiated with King Henry's envoy, William Pantulf, a lord of Wem in Shropshire, and vast sums were paid for Cadwgan and Iorwedd to abandon the Montgomerys to support Henry. Hunydd took a risk and persuaded Maredudd to stay with Belleme. Iorwedd willingly handed his brother over to Henry, and Hunydd's error of judgment cost her husband five years in a Norman prison. Never did Maredudd chastise her for persuading him in his choice: nor did he love her less devotedly.

When Maredudd was first taken from her, she realised how much she had come to love the man, and she was fired with revenge against Iorwedd. She stayed calm, however, and outwardly became the desperately sorrowful and bereft mother of three who understood that Iorwedd had little choice against such a powerful force as King Henry.

Hunydd worked on Iorwedd until there was no doubt in his mind that he needed to compensate Maredudd for the wrong done to him. Even though Maredudd was incarcerated, Hunydd thrived. When Iorwedd himself was imprisoned by Henry, Hunydd rejoiced but outwardly appeared to sympathise that the Norman king had tricked Iorwedd. She presented to the world as the perfect wife, mother, and sister-in-law but did not forget what her brothers-in-law had done. Iorwedd had done the deed, but Cadwgan had remained silent.

For five long years, Hunydd plotted and planned to get her husband out of prison. She petitioned Bishop Richard regularly; she cajoled Cadwgan to provide money to bribe gaolers, but of all people, it was Cadwgan's son, Owain, who succumbed to Hunydd's entreaties. Hating King Henry because he had made a concubine out of Nest, the Welsh Princess he had been meant to marry, Owain was more than happy to take a risk to free his uncle.

Owain felt sympathy for Maredudd, who had never dismissed him as a hothead like his Uncle Iorwedd had done. Furthermore, any blow against the Normans was a good one. Late one evening, Maredudd was surprised to receive a russet-haired priest in his cell and even more surprised when the priest produced a guard's uniform from under his robes. Maredudd marched the priest out of the prison, leaving a Norman guard senseless and naked in his cell. Maredudd would never forget, and neither, more importantly, would Hunydd.

Time passed, and Hunydd watched the twists and turns of fate for Cadwgan, Iorwedd, Madog and Owain in the dance with the Norman king. Then she heard something anathema to any Welsh Christian; Madog had killed his Uncle Iorwedd. Such an act against kin was unthinkable. To force kin to exile or to rob them of their lands was frowned upon yet happened often enough, but murder was utterly unacceptable, and someone had to right the wrong.

The House of Mathrafal was in chaos, with Cadwgan and Owain exiled and Madog's brother, Ithel, imprisoned. Hunydd sat Maredudd down in one corner of their chamber and explained why he should go to Bishop Richard and receive authority to spearhead the House of Mathrafal in returning Powys to order. She also told him that he should seek out Madog, hiding in the woods, and force him to compensate for hurting his kin. Maredudd was reluctant. He did not want to show his head only to be shot down by the Normans, having escaped from incarceration and having kept a very low profile thus far. He was also reluctant to revenge his brother's death by taking up the hunt for Madog alone. He procrastinated a little too long, and by the time he was persuaded to act, Cadwgan ap Bleddyn was once more leading Powys.

Hunydd was not happy. Maredudd was reminded of his costly indecision day after day. That it was unlikely Bishop Richard would have installed him as the Powysian king over Cadwgan was not a matter for discussion. Hunydd was implacable. Maredudd wanted to please his increasingly demanding wife and secure his children's future, but he struggled to think what he could do. He was a good man, a pleaser, and he agonised.

***

Cadwgan knew he had to put things in order quickly. He grieved for his brother and dreamt of killing Madog with his bare hands, but he was wily enough to know that this was precisely what Bishop Richard wanted. Had he not thought he could destroy Powys by setting kin against kin? Had that not ever been the cheap way to gain domination over Powysian lands? No, let Madog stretch too far with his band of disenchanted men from other parts of Wales and his Saxon hotheads who railed against injustice. He felt that Madog could wait until Cadwgan's son Owain returned. When things in Powys were as he wished, there would be time to seek retribution.

Then there was Llywarch, the traitorous snake whose brothers had demanded more than their share, had threatened his family, had attacked his son and paid the price for such ambition. Owain would deal with him as well. But there would be no killings. There had been enough killing. They would be brought to justice according to the law.

He looked around at the men of his teulu. They were good men. Strong men. Their faces showed the respect they felt for him. Some of these men had been with him through many battles. He could see their faces in his mind's eye, sweat-stained, bloody but smiling with victory. He remembered his success bringing down Montgomery Castle as he rested his gaze on his Pen Cerdd, his Chief Bard, and thought of what a fine poem the bard had written to commemorate that routing of the foe. Among the men were his physician, a man of great talent and learning, his head of hounds and falconer, and others who looked after the administration. They all brought their views to the table, and he would listen to them all. They were a family, tight-knit and loyal to each other. He got himself back to the matters at hand.

'If there is any trouble in the places you go to, find those responsible and bring them in. A few days under arrest should calm their tempers.'

'And if there is stealing?' asked Bryn, one of his elders, a short, neat man of middle age whose beady eyes and red cheeks gave him the look of a robin.

'If they have stolen from us, then bring them in; if they have robbed from the Flemings, then give them a warning; if they have taken from the Normans, then congratulate them!'

The teulu roared with approval, even his physician, Madin, an angular, elegant man known to smile rarely and laugh less than that.

Cadwgan beamed and put a hand up.

'Just give them a stern warning.'

'And if we should come across Madog's men?'

'Drive them out of Powys. I do not care where they go, but I want them out of my lands.'

'What about you, lord? You are sending us to different parts of Powys, but that leaves you and the elders with a handful of men when you attend the various courts.' Madin looked troubled.

'I think we will be safe enough. Madog knows that Owain is returning, and the cost of harming any of us is too high to risk. He will be concentrating on hurting the Flemings now. I have no interest in pursuing him or revenging my brother's death, with hostility towards my nephew. Kin is kin. Madog was ever impulsive and fiery-tempered, but even he must be able to see he has gone too far. He has earned no love from the people by it.'

'May God protect you, lord, for you are a fair man,' said Madin piously. There was a groundswell of agreement from around the table.

The group disbanded, and Uchdryd waited until they had all gone before he approached Cadwgan. Uchdryd was getting on in years but still held himself tall, his shoulders back with the strength of a younger man. Cadwgan envied Uchdryd, whose children had caused him no problems, who was admired, respected, and sought out for his advice and good humour.

'Lord, it is better you keep one group of younger men to protect you while you go from court to court.'

'No, Uchdryd, that is when they will create some mischief elsewhere in Powys, knowing that my strength is where I am presiding over the courts. I would prefer my men to be everywhere, and our strength seems widespread. Besides, what kind of life is it to be hiding behind other men's shields?'

'Lord, you and I have seen enough shields that it should not matter which shield we are behind. Our glory days may be behind us, but we have earned a safe time now.'

Cadwgan chuckled. 'You are probably right. Let us see how things go this month, and perhaps I will travel everywhere with the whole host! Without a doubt, though, I think we have done a good job of ensuring Powys is safe in such a short time. The people know who is in charge here. They know we will enforce Welsh law. Renders are being paid. The grass is green, the cattle are fat, and the horses in our studs are thriving and multiplying. Will you come with me to Trallwng tomorrow and I will show you the castle I am building there? I am thinking of moving there permanently.'

'It would be a pleasure, lord, but I need to return to my lands in Tegeingl.'

'Not back to Meirionnydd then?'

'My heart is still in the land I was born, and I must visit it though my wife is in Meirionnydd. I thank you daily and will never forget those lands you granted me: Cymer, the most beautiful place in Meirionnydd, Cyfeliog and Penllyn.'

Cadwgan chuckled.

'You earned them. You are thinking of building a castle at Cymer?'

'Indeed I am. Something to keep my old bones warm and my family safe.'

'There is nothing more important than family. I am looking forward to seeing Owain. He has learnt a lot, my troublesome son, I think. I hope his reckless days are behind him.'

'Sometimes that turbulence when they are young leads to great things later in life when they have the sense to match their energy.'

'I hope so. Powys needs strong leadership. I have two sons from my Norman wife, Henri and Gruffydd, but they would never rule in Wales. Then I have four others, Madog, Einion, Morgan and Maredudd, but they are not natural leaders like Owain.'

'Are you thinking of departing us so soon with all this consideration of your successor?'

Cadwgan grinned broadly, 'I am sixty, you know. A man cannot live forever.'

'Think of all the drinking you would miss if you did not get to God's promised three scores and ten!'

'That is very true, and honestly, I am feeling strong. I feel as if I have more energy now, I am back in the saddle, and I have ideas for this land that will see it prosper for generations. Mind you, three score and ten is nothing short of a miracle in our lives. It might have been well enough for all the Israelites wandering happily in the promised land with no Normans ready to stab them in the back or waspish wives giving them no peace!'

'Well, there is plenty of living to do and castles to build.'

'Yes, indeed. This one in Trallwng is in a good position and will withstand attack or siege.'

'Not too far from Shrewsbury and Bishop Richard. Eighteen miles?' teased Uchdryd.

'It is a shame about Bishop Richard being near, but Shrewsbury town is easy enough to get to for trade. Then there is the Severn River close enough, maybe three miles from where I have built the foundations.'

'And the lake there is beautiful on the eye.'

'It soothes the soul to see it. Mind you, everything I see from the castle soothes the soul. There is a stillness there, a beauty which speaks to my heart of our heritage.'

He contemplated the land there, and though much of Wales was beautiful, his castle would be built in an extraordinary spot. 'This is the last home I will build, and it will be the finest,' he added cheerfully.

***

Uchdryd stayed that night and set out at dawn. Cadwgan came out to farewell him and saw that the sky was clear, cloudless. It would be a good day to travel. He had little liking for travel through the wet these days. As he turned, a fox appeared by the stables door and stood motionless, watching him with large amber eyes and long pupils. He was in fine shape, his coat glossy auburn-red, his pointed ears alert, and a bushy tail with a clean white tip, but silver hairs across its shoulders suggested he was an old fox. Cadwgan mused that his hair had once been that same colour but now was mostly silver. He looked down and saw the prints in the mud: five toes on the front feet and four toes on the back. He had often wondered why. He did not mind foxes. They kept the vermin down. The fox threw back his head, giving a plaintive howl before disappearing behind the building.

It was almost midday by the time the party was approaching Trallwng. The wheat was being harvested, and small groups of men and women rested in the shade of whatever trees they could find, laughing and joking as they enjoyed the break for something to eat and drink. They recognised Cadwgan on his big black stallion, one of the best from the Powys stud, and nodded in respect. He waved back, stopped, and chatted to some when they were near enough to their path. He went down on one big knee to talk to a group of small children, allowing them to take turns sitting on his fine stallion. Everybody admired the stallion as he explained that the line had come from Arab stock through Spain. Now Powys' stud was known far and wide. Women held their babies out to him and, for a robust and big man who still looked like a warrior, he was surprisingly gentle, taking

319

them in his arms and laughing when they stared into his broad weather-beaten face.

'He is a strong little one,' he would say, 'he will be fighting for Powys soon!' If it were a little girl, he would say she was a beauty and wonder how many hearts she would break. The parents were delighted, and often some coins were given to the children, which would be hoarded until they were desperately needed.

Ordinary people liked Cadwgan ap Bleddyn. The bards had much material boasting of his prowess in battle, but, for all that, he was not too proud to take the time to speak to them. They knew him as a generous man and fair at the courts of judicature. He knew the law. But everyone knew that he had a weakness for wine and women. Some also said that he gave too much authority to the Normans, but he had always protected the people of Powys, and they fared better than those in other parts of Wales. They were pleased to see him back and the restoration of order that had lapsed during his brother's rule.

Cadwgan's castle was perched high on a rocky mound as they came around the corner. He swivelled in his saddle to speak to the others in his party.

'They have made good progress, look! There will be some work inside, but they have finished all the exterior anyway. I am looking forward to showing you.'

The youngest of the party, Bryn's beady eyes opened wide as he took in the stonework above them. 'Lord, it looks magnificent. You will enjoy living there, I think.'

'The view is outstanding,' explained Cadwgan, glowing with pride. 'From there, I can see the valleys as far as Montgomery and Shrewsbury. I can see the Severn with all her twists and turns and look to the mountains. I can gaze at the mountaintops of Plinlimmon, Arenig, Cader Idris, Moelygolfa, and Aranmowddy. Think of that! The beauty of Wales all around me.'

There were mutterings of awe and surprise as they all gazed towards the castle. It was indeed something special. The sun was in their eyes as they looked up, so they did not see the men with longbows, and the first they knew of the attack was the thwack as the arrows hit. The first arrow took Cadwgan in his back. His horse was startled and jittered sideways while a second arrow caught him in the chest, and he fell onto his horse's neck. Behind him, the men who would have served justice to others were falling one by one.

Madog rode out from behind a tree and caught his uncle's horse. He lifted his uncle's head by the hair and wondered at the weight of it. The old man's eyes were wide open yet lifeless, and blood had gushed out of his mouth. He dropped his uncle's head and rode around inspecting the other bodies.

'We'll have the horses, lads and take what you want. Leave Cadwgan and his horse to me.'

When the workers in the field saw Madog ride by on Cadwgan's horse and the men behind him leading other horses, they ran from the area towards Trallwng. What they saw there was butchery. Fingers had been hacked off to take rings grown too tight to pull off over time, and the bodies had been left exposed, eyes wide open with flies already crawling over them. Fear gripped them. They wept for a man who had seemed a giant but was only a man.

***

When the mud-splattered messenger rode up to Maredudd's gate calling for the master of the house, Hunydd told her husband to make himself scarce and that she would check with the guard whom it was before letting him in. She trusted no one after what had happened to Iorwedd.

The grey-faced messenger was in Cadwgan's colours, and his message was chilling. She sent him to the kitchen to get food and rest. As the rain poured down, leaving deep puddles outside, she lit candles and took Maredudd to her chamber where they would not be overheard.

'Maredudd,' she started, having little consideration for his grief at losing a brother he had loved, 'this is no time for snivelling. You remember what happened last time, with Iorwedd. This time you go to King Henry immediately.'

'But Hunydd, Owain ap Cadwgan will surely be on his way back from Ireland having received a pardon and…'

'And therefore, you can rule on his behalf until he arrives, and you can rule that which was Iorwedd's portion. Besides, it will be no time before Owain and Madog kill each other, so there needs to be stability.'

'Hunydd, Hunydd,' he started, but she interjected.

'Do not 'Hunydd' me! You wash, dress, get your guard together, head for London, and do not move from there until you have seen King Henry.'

'But my brother is not yet in his grave.'

'Neither was Henry's, and he managed to overcome the shame of leaving his brother's body on the forest floor when an arrow shot King William Rufus. Henry rushed off to Winchester to command the treasury! Is anyone concerned about that now, with all his power and riches? No! Besides, you were a good brother to Cadwgan while he lived, which is more important than attending to a spiritless corpse. Maredudd, you take yourself to London now. I will take the boys and make sure Cadwgan's remains are properly attended to. It is good for the boys to be seen as your representatives.'

Maredudd cringed at his wife's lack of sensitivity. He could not imagine a world without his brother Cadwgan, his idol. Cadwgan had loomed large in his life with his wild ways and a huge heart. He had made him feel safe. He could hear his boys messing around in innocent horseplay in the next room, not knowing yet what had happened. It seemed wrong that life continued as always while his mighty brother lay cold.

Following his wife's instructions, however, gave Maredudd purpose in his loss, and as he stripped and scrubbed himself with slow care, he considered how he would put his case to King Henry. First, though, he knew he must write to Owain to tell him the bad news and explain what he was doing. He did not want Cadwgan's son to think he was trying to usurp him.

Less than an hour later, Maredudd and his small grim-faced guard were heading to London in the pouring rain. The journey was fraught with difficulty: the roads and paths were treacherously muddy, and in places, trees had fallen across the way so that they needed to hack their way through the undergrowth; inns were overburdened and full of undesirables, and the weather turned from pouring rain to snow. On the last day of their journey, the snow had stopped at night but was bitterly cold. They had no joy in the glistening landscape or the crystallised icicles and ponds.

By the time Maredudd and his men had reached London, he was tired, every joint ached, and he had had much time on the road to grieve and reflect. His men, sensing his mood, had been quiet and solicitous. They liked and were loyal to their master, knowing he was always eager to help them in strife. They also knew that the real power in their llys was Hunydd and, in the five years of Maredudd's imprisonment, she had been a hard taskmaster, yet they realised their master would walk through fire for her.

Maredudd was worried that Henry would imprison him again, as he had Iorwedd, but primarily he was concerned that Henry would think him not man enough for the task, so he would have to face Hunydd's disappointment. He was also wondering why he was giving Henry the authority to resolve Welsh matters when he should be taking this to the council of Powys, depleted though it was thanks to Madog. Indeed, by running to Henry like this, he set a precedent for the future where Henry chose Welsh royalty. The thought galled him, but the idea of facing Hunydd was more galling if he failed to get approval. He kept the fear hidden from his men, but it ate at him, and at times, he wondered if they sensed his thoughts.

He was as nervous as a trapped rabbit as he walked towards the court with its great hall built by William Rufus to outshine any other in Europe. His palms were sweating, and his heartbeat was so loud in his ears that he felt it must be evident to everyone. He was breathless, and when he spoke, his words failed him.

The streets they navigated were filthy, with the small alleys full of rotting debris, snuffling animals, and emaciated dogs. For Maredudd, there seemed to be too many people in this place, shoving and shouting, shrieking, and jostling. He had never seen so many different-looking people: small, brown-faced men with limber skinny frames; soft-bellied, round-faced men with sharp beady eyes; tall men with bright flaxen hair and ruddy coarse faces; and women of almost every colour skin. Then there were men and women whose clothes were held together by mere threads who stole sideways glances at the Welshmen and their horses as they trudged through the sludge. Maredudd found his fingers moving instinctively for the knife he kept at his waist. In places, gangs of thugs congregated with no attempt to conceal their presence, but the Welshmen were burly-looking brutes whose meaty fists were ready to inflict a broken nose or split some lips after their miserable journey. After eyeing each other up, any potential adversaries would shuffle away with the braver ones whistling or yelling an insult from a safe distance.

After the long journey into the heart of this foreign place, they stopped in awe. Ahead was a vast cathedral. Maredudd gazed at it and shook his head. This was the great accomplishment he knew from the stories of Edward the Confessor, who had promised, while spending years in exile in Normandy, that he would make a pilgrimage to St Peter's in Rome if allowed to return safely to his kingdom. King Edward could not fulfil his promise as he found England needed his steady rule, so the Pope allowed him to renege on his oath if he restored a monastery in honour of St Peter. Edward built a Norman-style Romanesque church on Thorney Island in the middle of the Thames River. The building, known as Westminster, was consecrated on Holy Innocent's Day in December 1065, but Edward, gravely ill, could not attend. He had later been buried at the church on the Feast of Epiphany.

Maredudd knew that Edward's reign had been troubled, yet he was remembered for his piety and kindness. A legend told of the king giving a gold ring from his finger to a beggar requesting alms. Years later, two pilgrims travelling in the Holy Land were helped by a man who claimed to be John the Evangelist and who handed them a gold ring asking that they return it to Edward, who, in six months, would be joining him in heaven. As he recalled the story, Maredudd again thought of Cadwgan, his brother, who had always been so kind, and hoped that, like Edward, Cadwgan might find his way to paradise.

The group of Welshmen looked up at the massive stone edifice with its vast doorway framed by semi-circled arches, one framing another, on and on. Maredudd felt impelled to go inside. The great wooden door was open, and somewhere in the vast interior, he could hear singing, sweet voices raised in praise. He wanted to pray for strength and wisdom. At first, he stood inside the entrance wondering at the size of the enormous stone church in the shape of a cross with its generous chancel, transepts, and aisle. A multitude of candles lit up every corner.

King Edward, Maredudd knew, had fought against the Welsh, taking land from them. His successor Harold Godwin had killed the king of all Wales, Gruffydd ap Llewelyn, yet the Saxons had not been as fierce a foe as the Normans. Harold had met his end at the Battle of Hastings and, as a symbol to all of England, it was at this church that William the Conqueror was crowned. Here, Henry had married the beautiful Matilda of Scotland, an alliance to secure the north.

Maredudd looked around at the vast cylindrical pillars and imposing round-topped arches above the doors, windows, and arcades. They were built to inspire awe, and that is what he felt. He looked up as shafts of light filtered through the small windows, and specs of dust floated like a thousand stars in the illuminated air. The stone paving echoed the sound of his boots and the men behind him. He wondered how many thousands of pilgrims had worn the stone flags smooth over the years.

To Maredudd, it was as if he was in a mighty fortress, a fortress dedicated to St Peter, Christ's apostle. There was nothing so grand as this in Wales, yet close by, he knew that the cathedral of St Pauls, the east minister, in the growing city itself, would be more prominent and even more impressive. He felt humble and out of place. Even the threads in the clergy's garments glimmered from the shimmering candles and shafts of light from the heavens, so they almost appeared as angels. What foolishness had made him come to Westminster, a lowly suppliant to a mighty king? His heart fluttered again, and he thought of his wife's disappointed face and his sons' eager anticipation of his return.

Edward was buried near the high altar, and it was here that Maredudd made his way. He had heard the story of many miracles that had happened to those who prayed at the site. Some years before, the tomb of the old Saxon king had been opened to discover the body of the long, white-bearded king intact and sweet smelling, wrapped in a precious pall with a crown on his head, a sceptre at his side, a ring on his finger and simple sandals on his feet. Now a woman had laid her wan baby at the foot of the tomb, hoping for direct access to the divine to save his little life. Maredudd hoped that she would be heard.

The Welshman's mind drifted to all the holy relics stretched across the land and how miracles were performed for some who had kissed a bone or a fragment of a shroud belonging to a saint. His brother Cadwgan had said that often these relics did not belong to the saints at all but were bones of a goat or a horse, yet, if there were a bone for him to kiss here, he would not risk offending the spirits above.

Maredudd knelt on the cold stone floor and settled himself. He was a simple man who believed with all his heart that if God heard him, he would guide him. He closed his eyes and prayed: first for his brother's soul and second for forgiveness because instead of honouring him in death, he had hurried here to London. Then he prayed fervently for the right words to appeal to King Henry and that he would not be imprisoned again. His lips moved silently, and behind him, his men knelt, as mesmerised as their lord, confident that their utterings would be heard on high in such a place.

There, Bishop Richard spied on Maredudd, surrounded by his men. Candles around the shrine illuminated their faces and appeared as a tableau of devotion. The bishop had little time for the Welsh, but these strong men, in their stillness, their humility, touched him in a way that surprised him. He was not a sentimental man, not an emotional man, not even a particularly pious man for all his calling, but he felt God touching him on his shoulder. He looked at the tomb, thought of John the Evangelist sending the ring back to Edward, and was reminded that God moved in mysterious ways.

He walked down the aisle and waited patiently for Maredudd to open his eyes.

'Lord Maredudd, is it not?' he asked gently, not wanting to mar the moment.

Maredudd looked up, his eyes still glistening with the peaceful joy that had filled him in reverence and wondered that this man was at his side. He knew Bishop Richard well enough. He did not trust him but knew if he got Bishop Richard's approval, Henry's would follow. His first words resonated with the deep sorrow which filled him yet.

'Lord, Bishop, you have heard about my brother, Cadwgan?'

'I have, and I am sorry for it. He was a force of nature!'

'He was, and he will be missed.' Maredudd crossed himself, 'You have heard quickly, Lord Bishop.'

'A message came from Madog.'

Maredudd's men gasped at the name.

'His killer. A kin killer, Lord Bishop.' Maredudd felt a surge of anger as he thought of Madog killing his brother and then running straight away to Bishop Richard, but he kept his voice calm. 'Why boast of what he had done to you?'

'Madog asked that he be allowed to enter the void and provide leadership to Powys. King Henry would not countenance such a thing, so instead, he asked that we keep a promise we made to him and his brother, Ithel, for their pursuit of Owain ap Cadwgan, then an enemy, after kidnapping not only Princess Nest but King Henry's son.'

Maredudd very slowly rose to his full height and towered over the bishop.

'You have given him lands, Lord Bishop? Welsh lands?' he asked incredulously, unsure if he had misunderstood.

'Only such lands as his brother Ithel had: Caereinion, Traean, Deuddwr and Aberriw.' Even as he said it, the bishop realised that the intention of inflaming further Welsh violence by giving the lands to Madog, one relative against another, was weakly veiled.

Maredudd was disgusted but emboldened.

'Lord Bishop, he has killed his kin. This is utterly in violation of Welsh law and, indeed, Christianity. Two of his uncles lay cold, dead at his hand, yet he is rewarded?'

Standing as they were in God's House, Bishop Richard had the grace to colour.

'That is a Welsh matter to resolve,' he retorted coolly. 'Madog has given his word not to hurt any man, to give recompense to those families he has hurt, and to pay a fine to King Henry to live peaceably on his lands. Someone must rule, or there will be more violence.'

Maredudd thought carefully, and his anger emboldened him further.

'Lord Bishop, your king has pardoned Owain ap Cadwgan, and he, not Madog, is the next rightful king of Powys. I ask, as his uncle, a steadying hand, that I should rule on his behalf until his return and that I rule both his portion and that of my brother. One cannot trust the actions of Madog, whom the devil possesses. Without intervention, I fear for our country's Welsh and Norman lords.'

The bishop's penetrating ice-blue eyes took in Maredudd, who had spoken very softly yet stood straight and met his gaze with firm intent. The Welshman was not attractive but well presented, his clothes well cut, though without any rich adornments. His demeanour was of a peace-loving man driven by what was right rather than his brothers' heady ambitions and greed. He wondered if the man had the iron to take on Madog, perhaps even Owain, so the kin strife would continue. If the Welsh dispensed with the powerful men themselves, it would be all the better for King Henry.

'Let us go to the king,' he said at length, 'and I will assist you in pleading your case. You have travelled far, and I will not have you detained here longer than is necessary. If it suits you, we can go now.'

Maredudd dipped his head and indicated to his men to follow. Then, as they left the cathedral, he raised his eyes to the vaulted ceiling and silently prayed.

***

The message that Maredudd had sent to his nephew had not reached Owain. The messenger was on one boat sailing to Dublin and Owain on another sailing towards Wales. Owain, wrapping his heavy cloak tightly around him, his hood obscuring his face, had spent a gloomy voyage. Although Griffith ap Rhys had done as much as possible to lift his spirits and engage him in conversation, his efforts had been somewhat clumsy and responded to sullenly. Eventually, Griffith gave up and left him for the company of a few of his men standing with Owain's, laughing and joking. They were pleased to be going home.

Griffith returned to Owain's side as the Welsh coast approached, the cold wind whipping his hair across his face.

'It is strange that I am so close to home and feel like I do not know it anymore.'

'Certainly, a lot has changed since you were a boy, Griffith. The Normans have brought in Flemings, who breed like rats. William de Brabant came here to survey the land with no shame, as if our people were animals of the wood. He divided up the settlements, good farming land, fisheries, woods, lakes, streams, and marshes to calculate how many baronies he could squeeze his fellow Flemings into.'

'And what do the baronies do in return?'

'Nothing for the Welsh. Old William de Brabant ensured each barony had access to the coast, so they had to defend their holdings on land and sea and build their forts. They have set them up so that Roch, held by Godebert, looks out over the north of the district, Haverford controls the lower part of the Cleddau River to the west, which is Tancred's domain, and Walwyn's Castle is to the south-west. Then they refortified the castle at Rhos. St Ishmael would turn in his grave to see the activity of the Flemings in the very place he set up to encourage Welsh Christianity. Do you see what we are up against? We will be absorbed if we do not make a stand.'

'And their overlord is in Pembroke?'

'Yes, Gerald of Pembroke, Windsor, or whatever he goes by these days. Your sister's husband anyway.' He gave a mirthless laugh, 'Your host, of course.'

Griffith deftly changed the direction of the conversation, 'You did well to get rid of Brabant and to attack their holdings. Quite a few Flemings ended up on the slave route, thanks to you.'

'Not enough of them, sadly,' said Owain sourly, 'but I am not done yet.'

'Do you not have to behave now that you have been pardoned?'

'I will promise anything they want, most sincerely, smiling at them as they do to us, but what I scheme in the dark of the night will leave no one to point the finger at me. I will be cautious.'

Griffith knew that Owain had been surprised that he wanted to restore his father's kingdom of Deheubarth. Although Owain had not recognised the potential in Griffith's desire, Griffith was careful to show humility to a man who was a hero in Wales and heir to one of the most powerful kingdoms, even though Powys was currently fraught with difficulties.

'What you do here, I hope to do in Deheubarth, but first, I have much to learn. If ever I am as strong as you in men if not in reputation, I would ask that we push the Normans out together.'

Owain saw the ambition as over-reaching, but he liked Griffith. He knew he was brave and was not too proud to seek advice: something he may have done better himself when he was younger. Moreover, he was Nest's brother and there was much of her in him. Advice cost him nothing, and his father always told him to give respect to those on the way up.

'Griffith, you must ally yourself with Gruffydd ap Cynan. He is powerful, and although Henry would like to bring him down, he fears the humiliation his brother Rufus suffered at Gruffydd's hand. Henry does not like losing, and Gwynedd has been a thorn in his side.'

'I received the same advice from King Murtagh in Ireland. He said that Gruffydd is a strong strategist, very clever.'

'And in Wales, he has the most impressive warband.'

'Why would he help me?'

'He wants to see Wales unified.'

'With him as acknowledged high king?'

'Everybody accepts he is the main force in Wales. He is an interesting man. He thinks far ahead, not just what will bring a quick gain. He does not dwell so much on personal ambitions but wants a strong base for his children to build on.'

'They are but young yet.'

'He has a nest full. The first three sons are no longer young boys and have been taught to look after themselves. The eldest daughter, Gwenllian, is a rare beauty with much of her mother's looks but with a fire that comes from her father. She will be betrothed soon to ally, I am sure.'

He thought of the nubile young girl with the stunning eyes he had seen when he had been in Gwynedd, and a thought crossed his mind before he dismissed it. He was still raw from Nest's return to Gerald of Windsor.'

'How many children in all?'

'Eight. All well-educated, all well-featured. Three boys to preserve his inheritance and five girls to grow it.'

'They were good friends to my sister.'

'And they were good friends to me. I owe them a debt.'

'Your father and Gruffydd are very close, I remember.'

'Indeed they are, and together in battle, they were unstoppable. Uchdryd ap Edwin is Angharad's uncle and has led my father's warband for many years.'

'I heard tell that Uchdryd turned against your father and took money from the Normans for your capture.'

Owain laughed. 'Uchdryd? Never. He was the one that rode through the night two days straight to ensure your sister, and I were safe in hiding with Gruffydd and Angharad. Without him, I would be incarcerated now, that's for sure.'

It was hard for Owain to talk of those times, and Griffith realised from the sadness of his expression how deeply Owain was hurting. He remembered his sister Nest and Owain, a picture of happiness when they were together in Ireland. They had seemed a golden couple, destined for each other by their fathers long before. What a different land it might have been if his father, Rhys ap Tewdwr, had not ridden in haste with so few men to suppress the Normans at Aberhonddu that Eastertide so many years ago. What a different world if Owain had indeed married his betrothed Nest. Owain had rekindled old wounds in him. Even now, almost old enough to be king, Griffith still missed his warm-hearted, irrepressible father.

By the time Owain had reached Welsh soil, he had collected himself sufficiently to organise the purchase of horses for his men and food for their journey. Admitting to himself that he had behaved boorishly to Griffith, he offered to assist him in doing the same since he was a stranger in the country. Compared to Dublin, this was a tiny place where knowing who to ask was the way to get results. Having food and transport ready,

Owain looked at the sun and calculated that it was mid-morning.

'Time for us to part ways, Griffith,' he said. 'Safe journey to you and your men.'

'Thank you,' said Griffith. 'How far will you be going today?'

'I will go to my father,' said Owain. He was surprised that even though he was struggling with despair over Nest's betrayal, he was comforted by the thought that he would soon be sharing a drink of mead with Cadwgan.

'Send him my regards,' replied Griffith warmly. 'We will see each other again, no doubt. I wish you well and thank you again for the support you have always given me. Your offer to join you meant a lot to me. I am determined to get back my lands; to do that, I need to understand how to exploit the enemy's weaknesses. I will be a good pupil, though Gerald of Windsor may not know what he is teaching me.'

Owain swallowed the sour comment he would make about sending his regards to Griffith's sister and simply nodded.

'We will surely meet again, and I look forward to that reunion,' he agreed and watched Griffith with his small band trotting away towards the south and to Nest. He looked across the River Teifi longingly. How he wished he was also going south. He glanced behind him at Cardigan castle, built by Gilbert Strongbow, and spat.

Across the river, he saw the progressed construction of a priory at St Dogmaels funded by the Norman money of Robert FitzMartin and Maud Peverell, his wife. He had been told that only twelve Benedictine monks and a prior would live there, but their influence would spread. Lord Robert, who had been brought up in Devon, had inherited the barony of Kemes in Dyfed, previously part of Deheubarth, from his father, Martin de Turribus. Martin had seized the land from Rhys ap Tewdwr, Griffith's father, whose death in battle had followed his refusal to acknowledge the suzerainty of King William Rufus. Martin had sailed to Fishguard and possessed the lands between Fishguard and Cardigan with virtually no opposition from the Welsh. Owain felt his resentment rising in him.

As he crossed lands with which he was more familiar, men and women working the fields would look up with interest at the mud-spattered rider in his green, fur-lined woollen cloak, long leather boots and his party of seasoned fighters. As recognition dawned, they bowed to him solemnly, averting their gaze. At first, he was confused at their reaction, but then a sense of unease grew. What harm had he done these people? Whenever he had come this way, he had been feted as a worthy opposer of the invading foreigners.

'Something is going on here,' he said, twisting in his saddle to his men. 'Do you feel it as well?'

'Yes, lord. We will keep our weapons close.'

The men trotted on until a deep fiery sunset flared across the hillsides as they arrived at Cadwgan's llys. They were greeted similarly; people bowed and then scurried away, not meeting his eyes. They rode into the courtyard, dismounted, and Maredudd came down the stairs, his face lined with grief.

'Owain,' he said, taking the man into his embrace. 'I am so sorry!'

The cold blade of fear gripped Owain's stomach. 'What is it? Is my father ill?'

Maredudd pulled back but held his nephew's arms in a tight grip. Owain saw his uncle's face and knew. He closed his eyes and threw back his head, trying to control his anguish. The assembled riders looked on, as shocked as Owain: these closest to Owain had known his father well.

'How?' he asked simply.

'Madog. An ambush.'

Owain stared. This was unthinkable.

'My father was taken in ambush. How could that be?' For a few seconds, he clutched at the thought that this had to be a mistake, but Maredudd continued, his face as grey as death.

'Cadwgan and the other elders were going to dispense justice near the new castle your father has built. Your father had discounted any threat from Madog and was poorly guarded. The ambush was well sprung, and there was no opportunity to retaliate. It was quickly over, Owain.'

Owain shook his head, and his voice was a croak, 'No scouts ahead of them, no precautions?'

'What precautions had your father ever needed? He was Powys. He was loved in Powys. No man would think to hurt him.'

When he replied, Owain's voice was harsh and bitter. 'I will bide my time, Maredudd, let Madog feel as safe as my father did, and then I will strike. I will make his life a living hell.'

Maredudd nodded, his eyes welling. That was almost too much for the younger man; he had to breathe deeply.

'I have been to King Henry,' Maredudd said when he could speak.

Owain's eyes flicked up to his uncle with cautious suspicion.

Maredudd cleared his throat and said awkwardly, 'There will be incentive to be paid, but you will rule Powys. You are the rightful heir. I have cleared the path here, and you will have no opposition.'

Owain's eyes widened. Such an act would have put Maredudd in danger. He had escaped from Norman imprisonment, and Normans had long memories. Those five years in Henry's hands had scarred Maredudd, mentally and physically.

'I have not forgotten my debt to you, Owain.'

The words of loyalty were the final straw for Owain, and he threw out his arms to bring his uncle close to him, masking the hot tears that coursed down his cheeks.

After some time, Owain broke away, wiping his eyes on his sleeve, and it was then that Hunydd approached, dark hair streaked with silver, curtseying low with a flexibility that belied her age.

'Sire,' she said gently, 'we did not know when you would come, but everything is ready for you; everything is in order.'

Her words were comfortable, and Owain wanted to let himself be comforted.

'Come,' she urged him, her eyes darting to his grim companions, 'you and your men will be tired and hungry.'

'I should see my father's grave,' he said, though he only wanted to sit by a fire to drink himself to oblivion and then curl up to sleep.

'Your father would not see you arrive here so late in the day and not eat and rest. Tomorrow your father's grave will still be there, and you can honour him. He was farewelled by such a crowd that the mother church of St Tysilio at Meifod could not hold them all. He lies there with all the royals of the House of Mathrafal who have passed to God.'

Hunydd took Owain's arm leading him inside. Tired and shocked as he was, he let his aunt fuss over him as if she was his mother; he saw the genuinely concerned looks of his uncle, his face almost the colour of his grey hair, and at his lowest ebb, he let them step deep into his life.

Chapter 21: New Beginnings (Spring 1112)

They lay together hot and sweaty in a tumble of sheets, her long dark hair cascading over his chest. Her wideset mischievous brown eyes danced in merriment as he shook his head in disbelief.

'I cannot believe I am here in your bed,' he marvelled, and she loved his innocent honesty.

She stopped his words with her silken lips on his mouth, and he hugged her tightly.

That they had become embroiled in this passionate affair had taken them both by surprise. Hywel had left Wales empty and almost broken. He had vowed to put all thoughts of Angharad to the back of his mind, to make a new life for himself, and he had got off the boat in Ireland to throw himself into fighting King Murtagh's enemies. Murtagh was generous, and although the favour he found from the king had not gone down well with all Murtagh's commanders, his prowess and courage in battle had earned him respect.

Murtagh had given Hywel land and title but, more importantly, had allowed him to become party to his innermost secrets. This was an honour many craved but few achieved. Such swift success had come at a cost: long cold days and nights in filthy hardship as he led bands of men against the foe, sometimes against unimaginable odds. His men's lives were of paramount importance to Hywel. He was realistic enough to know that one could not overcome the enemy without losing men, but he would never put a man at a risk he would not face.

Lafracoth had always been drawn to men who flouted their achievements and wealth, who filled the room with their presence. As King Murtagh's daughter, she had known her fill of them and had married

Arnulf de Montgomery, one of the wealthiest men in England and Normandy, whose arrogance and self-belief exceeded any of them. They were still married though she rarely saw him now and was glad of it. He was a brutal husband, and for a while, she had almost lost herself as she hid her bruises and scars behind veils and long sleeves. When he came to her bed, he showed her no respect; even when she was pregnant with their child, Alice, nothing would stop the blows which excited him. Nothing. Eventually, her father, seeing her flinch from her husband, her eyes ringed red, shadowed with pain, had understood her predicament and threatened Arnulf with punishments so vile that he had fled to Normandy. Later, when King Henry had imprisoned his elder brother, Robert Curthose, whom Arnulf had supported, Arnulf fled to Foulques, Count of Anjou and Maine. Lafracoth wished that Arnulf would die somewhere in some altercation or hoped that Henry would find a way of avenging Arnulf's treachery, but Arnulf was as slippery as an eel.

When Hywel first came to court, Lafracoth sought him out for news of her friends, Angharad and Gruffydd. She had always liked him: he was so easy to talk to, but she had not been attracted to him. After Arnulf, any thoughts of lovemaking were far from her mind, and she thought she would never again seek or find love. Hywel had returned from successfully aborting one of many attempted raids by Domnall Ua Lochlainn, King Murtagh's sworn enemy. With incredible generosity, King Murtagh had been celebrating the success and Hywel's part in it. The Welshman had shied away from the thumping, pounding, and drumming on the tables and floor that had been a mark of respect for his battle skills.

Lafracoth had smiled at how modest Hywel was and how he crept away from the attention afforded him. She had felt sorry for him, alone, a foreigner just as she had once felt in England and Normandy, her Irish lilt marking her out. She had gone to him then because she felt for him in this wild Irish court full of prominent personalities. They had talked the evening away until the early hours, and she found that she was confiding in him thoughts that she had guarded until then. She rode out with him the next day. They galloped across the vast green stretches up onto hills where she pointed out rivers and lakes, holy places and places of folklore. He, in turn, had pointed out animals and birds, telling her things about them she had not known.

The next day Lafracoth had enlisted Hywel's company to visit a monastery. She saw how he admired the beauty of the building and respected the learning of the monks. Somehow, she had led him by the hand to her chamber on that third day. He had seen the marks on her body, knowing that she bore scars inside her head and, with tender lovemaking she had not experienced before, he nurtured Lafracoth's spirit while mending his own.

They both thrived, their joy irrepressible and though he felt almost guilty that he did not think of Angharad as often as he once did, Hywel allowed himself to fall head over heels in love. He knew it was wrong, but he also wished that Arnulf was dead, that she was free and not a princess. He had always longed for children, but to have a child by Lafracoth was unthinkable; her reputation would be ruined and he would not do that to her. Even if Arnulf were dead, Murtagh would use his daughter to cement an alliance with another man of power. She was still beautiful, able to have children, and highly intelligent. Such a marriage was valuable to Murtagh. They kept their liaisons secret which only fired their passion even more.

Lafracoth drew her fingers through Hywel's chestnut waves. A wisp was hanging over his eyes, and he blew it away.

'Your eyes have so many colours in them,' murmured the princess, brushing his hair away from his face with her delicate hands so she could stare at him. 'Green, two or three different shades like trees in a forest, gold flecks like autumn leaves, and even brown.'

He smiled, and she put her fingers on the wrinkles at the side of his eyes.

'You would have me look younger?' he grinned.

'No. Nothing would I change,' she whispered as she nibbled his earlobe. Then she sat back and said, 'I am not young.'

He leant forward to kiss her breast, circling her pink nipple with his tongue. 'You,' he teased her, 'are like a fine wine. I remember when you were a lovely attractive young girl, but now you are magnificent.'

She laughed and lifted herself so that she offered him her other breast. 'You do flatter me, Hywel, and I love it. You can praise me all day if you like.'

He sighed a long sigh, 'Your father wants to meet with me and some of his other advisors. He wants to attack his friend Domnall while the plague has ravished the north.'

'I do not want you to go away on campaign,' she breathed into his neck, her fingers finding an old scar on his arm and tracing the length of it.

Hywel shrugged, 'As long as Domnall claims to be the High King of Ireland because he can lead his men through Ireland without defeat, then your father will continue to fight him.'

Lafracoth scoffed, 'My father's title to High King will ever stand because he controls the three ports of Dublin, Waterford, and Limerick, and they churn out the money which makes Ireland wealthy. There is no point in being the High King of worthless land. My father is the true High King, and everybody knows it.'

Hywel turned to her and wound a long tress around his hand as he placated her, 'Your father cannot ignore him, however. He must challenge him!'

'Perhaps, but why now when I have other challenges for you,' she said huskily, running her hands down his body so that he sighed again, this time with pleasure.

***

When Howel ap Rhys, brother of Nest and Griffith ap Rhys, asked if he could come to Gruffydd's court to find protection against his enemies, Gruffydd welcomed him openly. Anglesey's position in the top west corner of all the Welsh kingdoms was valuable in that it had enough time to react to any threat but was frustratingly slow to receive news at times.

Howel's arrival in early December was a boon at the cold dark time of year.

When his father, Rhys ap Tewdwr, had died many years before, Howel had been separated from his siblings and imprisoned by Arnulf de Montgomery. Even after Arnulf and his brother had been exiled; even after Arnulf had run from his wife Lafracoth's home in Dublin; even when he had been hiding in Normandy, Howel still found himself imprisoned. He had almost forgotten what real life was like. Finally, it was decided that he should be released, but if he had any plans to produce troublesome Welsh offspring, he should be castrated first. He had hardly survived the maiming and, at times, did not want to, but he found kindness with relatives. Day by day, he recovered his strength, and his despair was replaced by hatred of his imprisoners.

At Gruffydd's llys, Howel was treated like an honoured guest, and slowly he felt his self-respect return. In Gruffydd, he found a well-tempered yet ever-burning hatred of the Normans. Gruffydd had not forgotten what they had done to his land and people before the Battle of Anglesey Sound had sent them packing back to England: he understood Howel's sentiments.

Outside, the noise of waves hurling against the beach was like a constant roar. The wind bellowed shutters rattled and banged, and loose items skidded and jangled across the courtyard. Occasionally, a hound would pace nervously around the edge of the hall and then slink back to a warm corner, ears pricked. The younger girls played board games with Susannah and Bethan while the older children joined their parents, Howel, Aeddan, and a few senior men of the teulu. They sat around the fire as it crackled and spat, flashing patterns across the limewashed walls of the hall. The smell of roasting meat still lingered even though tables had been cleared, but more prevalent was the earthy smell of ale redolent with malted grains triggering memories of summer grass and hay. Thirsty from salty food and smoke, the men drank deeply.

Like their parents, the older children were avidly intrigued by what went on outside Gwynedd and sat, eyes bright and alert, listening to the latest news of the man they loved to hate: King Henry of England.

'I find it hard to believe that even Henry would seize and capture an envoy come in peace,' said Gruffydd, his face displaying his distaste for Henry's actions.

'It is true, I am telling you. Robert de Belleme came to Henry's court in Bonneville-Sur-Touques as an envoy from King Louis of France to negotiate the release of Robert Curthose. Henry had given him a note of safe conduct, yet he was seized, tried on November 4th, and all his lands, honours, and castles were forfeited.'

The people present had no love for Belleme, whose cruelty was well known even to his wife, but the flouting of promises for safe conduct was an appalling act of deception by a king! Heads shook, and there were small tuts of disgust. A king should act with honour.

'On what charge did Henry try Belleme?' asked Aeddan, his strong but friendly face screwed up with confusion as he leaned forward to put a meaty hand up to the fire for warmth.

'Oh, Henry had concocted the charges already. First, there was a charge that he failed to attend Henry's court on three occasions. Second, he claimed that Belleme had failed to render accounts. And third, he accused Belleme of not working in his lord's interests.'

'Surely those do not warrant imprisonment!' Angharad was shocked, though she knew too well that Henry did not play by the rules.

'Especially because he should have been under the King's protection and that it is accepted internationally,' added Gruffydd, leaning back, his arms behind his head.

'When has Henry ever concerned himself with the reason for imprisoning people he believes to be a threat?' commented Howel acidly. His imprisonment was testimony to that.

A sudden draft from somewhere blew a blast of woody smoke over them, and Aeddan moved to adjust the position of a log with his thick boot.

'But has Henry not been called to justify his action regarding Belleme?' asked Gruffydd, a deep frown line appearing between his brows.

'Not at all. With everything that is happening between Henry and Louis VI of France trying to outmanoeuvre each other, Henry's breach of internationally accepted practice seems to have been overlooked. Completely!'

Gruffydd turned to his children, their bright eyes shining in the light of the fire. 'You remember we have talked about Robert de Belleme before. He was one of the most powerful barons in England and Normandy. His family are the Montgomery family, who were outrageously wealthy. Belleme became Earl of Shrewsbury when his brother, Hugh, was killed here by Magnus Barefoot in the Battle of Anglesey Sound.'

Cadwallon's blue eyes looked thoughtful, 'His family rebelled against Henry becoming King of England because all the barons had sworn allegiance to Henry's older brother Robert Curthose.'

'That's right.' Gruffydd was pleased that Cadwallon was showing interest. He was often frustrated that, as heir to his throne, Cadwallon seemed to find politics boring. Yet, Gruffydd had repeatedly drilled into his eldest children that it was essential to understand what was happening outside Wales if you wanted to form a good strategy for your kingdom. Every day he would remind them how important it was to know your enemy, and he would keep doing so!

Cadwallon continued, 'Henry won against the rebels, and Belleme handed over Shrewsbury Castle to Henry but was still evicted from England along with his brother.'

'Arnulf de Montgomery, is his brother.' His father nodded, and he noticed that Howel's face darkened at the mention of the name. It was perhaps to cover his emotion that Howel leant down to lay a hand gently on the head of a hound at his feet that had started from slumber. There was a thud as the dog's tail wagged against the floor.

'Arnulf was married to my dear friend Lafracoth, the daughter of King Murtagh, High King of Ireland,' added Angharad, her soft voice changing the direction of the conversation as she instinctively sensed their guest's discomfort.

'So, have they been fighting in Normandy against Henry in support of Curthose?' asked Cadwallon, combing back his golden waves with his fingers so they did not fall in his eyes.

'They have,' affirmed his father, 'although Belleme has changed sides several times. When Curthose was defeated by Henry at the Battle of Tinchebrai in September six years ago, Belleme was commanding the rear division of Curthose's army. Still, he fled the battlefield when the front division was losing. I always wondered about that. He tried to persuade Elias, Count of Maine, to sever his alliance with Henry, but when he failed, Bellame supported Henry again, paying him more money than you could imagine. Then a couple of years ago, in May, he was with Henry at Dover when he made the treaty with the Count of Flanders, but within months after Elias had died, he was a leading force in attempting to restore Curthose to the throne in Normandy.'

'You met him, Father?' asked Cadwallon.

'Your mother and I met him in Shrewsbury when Gwenllian was tiny,' he smiled at his daughter. 'That was the first time we had also met King Henry.'

The children, wide-eyed, wanted to ask more but resisted.

Gruffydd turned to Howel, 'What of the rebellion of the twelve Norman barons against Henry?'

'It has dwindled to nothing without Belleme.'

'And Curthose's son, William Clito, what of him?'

Howel shrugged his shoulders. 'He is living in hiding much of the time. When Curthose was defeated at Tinchebrai, Clito and his father went to Falaise, where Henry met his nephew for the first time. Henry arranged for Clito to be looked after by the Count of Arques, who was married to Clito's illegitimate half-sister. A couple of years ago, Henry sent for Clito, but, fearing the worst, he escaped to the court of Count Baldwin of Flanders, his cousin. I feel for him. His mother died when he was two, his father is imprisoned, and he cannot trust his uncle.'

Angharad thought of Howel's childhood as a prisoner, his brother hidden in Ireland, and his sister, a princess of Wales, reduced to a mistress of King Henry when he was a young prince. It was astounding that he could have such compassion. Then she thought of her husband, taken to Ireland as a child when his father had died, to protect him from those who would kill the heir to the throne of Gwynedd. He, too, was a man who had compassion.

'You came through Powys on your way here?' asked Angharad.

'My brother Griffith counts Owain ap Cadwgan as a friend. I stayed some nights there with him.'

'Griffith would know Owain well from the time he was in Ireland. He was young when I was in Ireland, but I remember him being sunny and courageous despite what had happened to your family.'

'My brother still has that personality but is ambitious to regain Deheubarth.'

Angharad looked up at her husband and knew he understood the nature of Howel's visit. Gruffydd was not willing to be drawn into anything yet.

'Have things settled in Powys after Cadwgan's murder?' asked Aeddan.

'The people of Powys still miss Cadwgan. He ruled well and justly. They have accepted Owain, who has always been considered a hero in his condemnation of the Normans and Flemings on his land.'

'Has Owain accepted Henry's terms for peace?' asked Angharad.

Howel laughed, 'Owain outwardly adheres to accepting the Norman presence but allows his teulu to conduct night raids on them. He allows

Madog to chip away at the Flemish settlements and pretends that he disapproves.'

'I am surprised that he has not sought vengeance on Madog for his father's murder,' mused Gruffydd.

'Eventually, he will, I am certain, but it suits Owain now that Madog is a nuisance to the new settlers.'

'I understand that Owain has made Maredudd leader of his warband.'

'It was an unexpected choice, but Owain's teulu is young, many of the older heads were killed alongside Cadwgan, and Maredudd brings wisdom. He also knows all the main families in Powys. Having Maredudd at Owain's side brings stability and the allegiance of those families. Owain asked me to send you his regards and is sending you some horses from his stud.'

Gruffydd frowned questioningly.

'A thank you for your kindness to him and his sister. He is hoping to visit you soon if you would allow it.'

'There was no need. He would be most welcome.'

'My brother would also like to visit you,' said Howel carefully.

'Here it comes,' thought Gruffydd, and he watched his wife tense up. Her most significant concern was war. As a young bride, she had seen the devastation and cost of life and land, which had scarred her.

'Of course,' said Gruffydd. 'He also would be most welcome.'

Gwenllian glanced at her brothers and saw their eyes gleaming as well.

***

Owain ap Cadwgan's arrival in Anglesey was met with much enthusiasm. His fame as someone who gave back the kind of treatment the Normans and Flemings meted out had spread throughout Wales. Last time, his visit

346

had been well hidden from most of the people in the llys, but there was great fanfare this time.

The whole family was outside the llys to greet him, and he did not disappoint. He was dressed in elegant finery, which Gwenllian noticed showed off his broad shoulders and tapering hips. He slid from his horse with a languid ease and walked towards them with a balanced long stride, his head high and his dark eyes unblinking.

'We meet again, sire,' said Owain, bowing deeply. Gruffydd returned the bow.

'While I am thrilled that you now find yourself on the throne of Powys, I am sorry that the world has lost a remarkable man. Your father was a close friend of mine, and the manner of his passing grieves me.'

'As it does me. When the time is right, I will avenge my father's death. It will not bring him back, and the time I have spent overseas has not allowed me to learn how to rule Powys as seamlessly as he did but I am trying to do so. My uncle, here, has been giving me good guidance.'

Maredudd blushed slightly at the praise but said nothing.

Gruffydd and Angharad smiled at Maredudd. Gruffydd noted the difference in Maredudd. As a younger man, he had been a brave enough fighter but a pale shadow of his older brothers. He had been a colourless, unattractive man with few friends and shied away from the limelight, yet Gruffydd had known him to be honourable and loyal. Now his bearing had changed: he stood with more confidence and a wisdom that told of trials faced and conquered shone through his face. His dress was simple and elegant. One thing had not changed: while he was not subservient, he had none of the occasional arrogance of the Powysian Royals.

'It is some years since we fought together, Lord Maredudd. We welcome you to our llys in more peaceful times.'

Maredudd bowed low and spoke sincerely, 'It is an honour to be here, sire.'

Gruffydd's smile was open and warm, holding the older man's eyes for a moment before returning to Owain.

'You did not have the opportunity to meet our family when you were here previously,' said Gruffydd indicating the brood behind him with an outstretched hand.

'Sadly not,' said Owain with a rueful grin, 'but I would be pleased to make their acquaintance now.'

The children were lined up, boys first and then girls. All were handsome children, as might be expected from two fine-looking parents. All had intelligent eyes, which rested on Owain. These children are a future powerhouse, Owain thought, as he looked at the three robust boys and the five attractive girls whose role would be to marry well, cementing alliances within Wales and beyond. His eyes rested on the tall red-haired daughter.

'This is my firstborn, Cadwallon,' Gruffydd introduced his heir.

Cadwallon stepped forward and bowed. He was almost as tall as his father, broad-shouldered though slim. Twinkling, almost mocking, blue eyes stared over high cheekbones. His nose was long and straight, and his mouth wide, full-lipped. He looked every inch the entitled prince.

'I would scarcely recognise you from the young prince who came to the Eryri just a few years ago,' said Owain. 'You are your father's son, I can see.'

The glance at his father to see if Owain's words met with his father's approval betrayed insecurity in the young man, and Owain wondered if he had been the same at that age.

Gruffydd beamed.

'This is our second son, Owain, named for his grandfather.'

Owain ap Cadgwan saw another tall, lithe young man, already muscular, but where his brother was fair, he had thick dark hair, penetrating hazel eyes and a thinner, more serious face.

'It is a good name. It means well born, young warrior.'

'I have been fortunate to be well born, sire, but have yet to prove myself as a warrior as you had already done at my age,' replied the young man surprising his namesake with his maturity. He noted that this young man was one to watch out for.

'This is Cadwaladr, our third-born son,' said Gruffydd.

The boy grinned at Owain impishly, and the older man saw that this fellow was allowed to get away with mischief while his older brothers were expected to shoulder responsibility.

'And your name means…'

'Battle leader, King Owain,' Cadwaladr interjected, earning a frown from his father. 'I want to be as famous as you one day.'

'Better you avoid my infamy and pursue your father's fame,' retorted Owain, winking at Gruffydd, who was scowling at his irrepressible son.

'And next, we have our princesses,' said Gruffydd. 'This is our first-born daughter, Gwenllian.'

Gwenllian curtseyed low and Owain watched the graceful girl raise her long lashes to reveal dark blue, almost violet, eyes shining up at him. She was a beauty. Her copper waist-length hair swung in waves as she moved, her complexion was flawless, her mouth full-lipped, and her smile was white-toothed. When she spoke, her voice was deeper and richer than he had expected, giving the impression that she was older than her years.

'We are all so pleased you are visiting us, sire. We all want to hear how you have flouted our foes.'

'Ah, not tales for female company, I think,' said Owain with a charming smile.

'Maybe not for my sisters, sire, but I have long been waiting to hear them.'

Owain was taken aback. He had known many women, but this young creature had disarmed him.

'And this is our daughter, Annest,' Gruffydd said as Owain was introduced to a pretty russet-haired girl with freckles. 'Then Rainaillt,' a round-faced golden-haired cherub standing next to a child who could have been her twin, a girl introduced as Marged, and finally Susanna, the youngest, a ginger-haired girl with a winning smile.

He smiled and nodded at the younger children, but Gwenllian captivated him. He turned again to look at her and saw she was observing him with a look of some amusement that caught him off balance. Behind him, Maredudd thoughtfully watched the interaction between them. Owain forced his eyes back to his hosts.

The adults moved inside the hall, leaving the youngsters to their own devices until the meal was served.

Cadwallon jerked his head towards the stables, and the four eldest headed there to sit and chat on bales of straw as they often did.

'Why do you think he is here?' asked Cadwallon.

'I think he wants Father's help to get rid of the Normans while King Henry is up to his neck in Normandy.'

'Oh please, let something wonderful like that happen,' enthused Gwenllian. 'I would gladly follow him into battle.'

Cadwallon batted his eyelids and simpered mockingly, 'I would gladly follow him into battle.'

Gwenllian glared at him. 'I can beat any of you by sword, spear or bow, yet you mock me.'

Owain put his hand up to still her. 'We have had years of this. You can beat us, but you will never be allowed onto a battlefield, and nothing will change that. We are not living in primitive times when women led troops into war. We all have dreams, Gwenllian, but we must face reality and make the best of what we have.'

Gwenllian felt as if she had been doused in cold water. She glared furiously at her brother.

'One day, Owain, I will prove you wrong.'

'Then go off into the mountains and find your band of warriors to lead against the Normans. Throw away the advantages you have been given like Owain ap Cadwgan almost did.'

'You spoke to him of being a great warrior, you hypocrite,' his sister spat back at him.

Owain considered this. 'He is a great warrior but did some foolish things. I want to be a warrior of note, and I will be, but I will think strategically like my father, know what is possible, and work within the confines of that possibility.'

'The confines of possibility,' mocked Gwenllian imitating her brother's voice, 'you are full of fancy language, but words alone will not rid us of our foes.'

Owain glowered.

'He who dares wins. Fortune favours the brave,' added Cadwaladr, stirring the pot.

Cadwallon's eyes gleamed, 'Do you like him, Gwenllian?'

The girl coloured.

'Leave her alone,' warned Owain, not liking the direction that his brother's thoughts were going.

'Do you, Gwenllian?' Cadwallon persisted.

'I do not know him. He is good-looking and famous and a man who is not afraid of taking the fight to the enemy.'

'And Princess Nest's lover,' Owain reminded her.

'Not now,' said Gwenllian hotly and too quickly. 'She has gone back to her old goat of a husband.'

'Enough!' said Owain. 'Let's go to the far end of the hall and play some board games. We can listen in on what they are talking about.'

They slipped back down onto the floor of the stable.

'I'll follow you in,' said Gwenllian. 'I want to see their horses.'

She found Owain's fine black stallion and murmured to it gently. She could see that it was a stunning, strong, wild-eyed beast that would need some handling. The saddle and bridle hanging beside the animal were beautifully crafted with silver trim showing the wealth of the Powysian royal house. She wanted to think for a moment by herself, and something thrilled inside her as she imagined herself riding onto the battlefield, side by side with Owain ap Cadwgan. Her heart began to pound, and she wondered what it would be like to kiss the King of Powys, for him to embrace her and speak words of undying love.

She brushed her dress down and entered the great hall to join her brothers. Owain ap Cadwgan's eyes were immediately upon her, and she liked it.

***

Angharad turned as she heard her husband come into the room. It had been a wonderful evening, and he had been relaxed and jovial. Her eyes sparkled in the candlelight, and he gave a wide, warm smile. He was gentle, stroking her long white neck with one finger, removing the silver combs so that her thick golden hair tumbled over her shoulders, holding her breasts as her naked back pressed against his chest. Afterwards, she lay on her side and ran her fingers through the hair that matted his chest, the flames of the fire dancing and casting shadows across the room.

'What does Owain want of you?' she asked quietly.

He wished she had not spoiled it and had just lain in his arms and fallen asleep on his shoulder. He was tired and did not want to think about how he would need to side-step all the traps that Owain and his uncle would set for him when they talked in the morning. He did not want to think about the politics of Powys, keeping Gwynedd strong, of conflict, intrigue, and strategy. He just wanted to lie there with his beautiful wife and for her to think less.

He breathed deeply and said, 'He will want an alliance. He will want to know that if Powys pushes King Henry too far, I will back him.'

'Will you?'

Gruffydd sighed again. 'There is a big difference between ruling and fighting. The man can fight, but sometimes that is just a distraction. I want to see him rule Powys, show he is capable of it, not just stirring up the hornets' nest.'

'Did you see the way he looked at Gwenllian?'

'I did.'

'Is that the sort of alliance he would want?'

'It is the sort of alliance Maredudd would want him to have.'

'She is young yet.'

'Not much younger than you were when I came to Tegeingl, but he needs to settle down before he takes a wife. He thinks like a hothead, he sleeps with half of Powys, and I am not sure she would be as valued as she deserves. I had thought perhaps an Irish, Scottish, or Norwegian marriage for Gwenllian.'

Angharad sat bolt upright, and the vehemence of what she said surprised him.

'You would send her away from Wales? No Gruffydd, she lives and breathes her homeland.'

'Angharad,' he countered gently, 'it is late, and tomorrow I need to have my wits about me. I promise you that nothing will happen with Gwenllian before we discuss it.'

He pulled her down, but her body was tense. He knew she was worrying now. He rubbed her back as if she was a child needing comfort.

If only she knew half of what he knew, she would never sleep. He tried to protect her from the messages his spies brought him from Tegeingl, from Shrewsbury, from places she had barely heard of, where men sought the downfall of the royal family of Aberffraw.

Gruffydd loved his wife with a passion that he found hard to explain. She was beautiful, intelligent, and the mother of his wonderful children, but his need to keep her fears at bay in the past had led him to make bad choices. Her absolute terror of war, having experienced the destruction of Anglesey when she was pregnant with Cadwallon, had conflicted with the pressure on him to keep his teulu happy. They were fighting men, and they thrived on being able to fight for booty. He had almost lost his way with the teulu when he had let Angharad convince him that peace at any price was the only way to rule. They had separated for a while, and those months when he took his teulu to fight in Ireland nearly drove him to a place he did not want to go again.

The king pulled Angharad to him and kissed her forehead. His thoughts wandered. The time was ripe to push the boundaries with the Normans, but Owain ap Cadwgan was wild, and he would have to contain him; otherwise, all they had worked for would be at risk. Angharad sensed that, but the support he needed from her was to allow him to do the job he had been given without needing to justify his actions. Now too, another worry was consuming her thoughts. Her children were growing up, and her daughter, their daughter, the jewel of their children, who could buy them a most potent alliance with a foreign country, might have to leave home. Was he to allow this opportunity to pass because his wife did not want her girl to leave Wales?

The king closed his eyes, and as the fire embers glowed, he drifted off to sleep. Angharad, beside him, felt fear. Her husband was strong and courageous, but sometimes she thought he did not understand the extent others would go to for their own ends. Not everybody was as honourable or kept their word, yet he believed in people. That belief made him a good leader but also made him, his family, and Gwynedd vulnerable. Owain ap Cadwgan was ambitious, and he would encourage Gruffydd to spearhead a challenge against the enemy while he would watch Gruffydd cut down, leaving Owain to claim the glory. Owain's antics had cost his own father dearly. Why would he keep his word to Gruffydd? His was not a social visit. He had not sent the breeding mares to thank Gruffydd for saving his skin. No, the breeding mares were to sweeten her husband, but for what?

She sighed and contemplated Gwenllian's future. She had almost lost Gwenllian as a baby and had been too soft with her when she grew up. There was a wildness about her, an unpredictability that could not be controlled. Suppose Owain was setting his eyes on Gwenllian as a possible wife. Would that be an alliance to their advantage, or did Owain think this was a stepping stone to rule Gwynedd and Powys after Gruffydd's time, sideswiping Cadwallon and his brothers? Was that risk worth taking rather than sending her daughter to marriage so far from her homeland that she would become half herself? Would what would surely be a turbulent marriage be better than a life somewhere as a foreigner? She could not speak to Gruffydd of these things.

In so many ways, they were true partners, but she had been cautious about politics since those awful lonely months before Gwenllian had been born when they had fought, and he had taken his teulu over the seas to Murtagh in Ireland. Thinking of Murtagh, her thoughts drifted to Hywel. She missed being able to confide in him and hearing his sage advice. She wondered how he was faring. She knew that he had often supported her views and presented them to the teulu but she had lost that backdoor to influencing policy.

Gruffydd jumped in his sleep, and she hugged him tighter. She loved him so much, but he needed to be protected from his own goodness! She thought of Hywel again and remembered his promise to her that he would never break and that if she ever needed him, he would return. Beneath her ear, she could hear her husband's heartbeat steady and strong, and finally, she fell asleep.

***

'So, what exactly are you proposing?' asked Gruffydd bluntly of Owain. His teulu leaned forward, watching eagerly, and saw Maredudd licking his lips nervously.

'A concerted effort by Powys and Gwynedd to extend our boundaries back to where they were. Where Flemings have cleared land and built villages, to make it untenable for them to farm there, to return Welsh lands to the Welsh.'

'And how do you think Henry will allow this to happen without recourse?'

'He is heavily distracted in Normandy. He has gifted our lands to his barons to clear the way for taxes into his coffers, but they can complain about our actions as much as they like; he is in no position to provide funding or support to those barons if they want retaliation.'

Gruffydd said nothing and looked at the younger man shrewdly.

'I have already been to Gronwy ap Owain and his brothers, and they will push beyond Chester.'

Gruffydd sat up at that, his eyes narrowing. So Owain had already been to see Gronwy knowing Gronwy hated him. He feared a trap.

'How is Gronwy?'

'Fat, vengeful, ambitious. He is no friend of mine, King Gruffydd; I remember he would have hounded me to my death for Henry's approval.'

'Yet you visited him first before coming to Anglesey.'

Owain shrugged, and Maredudd winced, staring at his hands.

'I needed to get assurances from him before approaching you to serve my cause better.'

Gruffydd nodded and blew out a long breath.

'And others?'

'Genillin ap Meirion Goch, Lord of Llyn.'

'He pays his renders to Hugh of Chester.'

'Who is in Normandy,' replied Owain.

'May I say something, sire?' said Maredudd, holding his hands together as if about to pray.

'Of course, speak,' said Gruffydd, his eyebrows knitting together as he waited for this man's contribution.

'People are finding it very hard in England, and there is much discontent. The king levied contributions for his daughter's marriage to the Emperor two years ago. If you remember that year was terrible for the crops, and most tree fruits perished. As a result, there was starvation and much death.'

The teulu nodded, remembering, although Anglesey had not fared so poorly.

'That year, there was an earthquake in Shrewsbury, an eclipse of the moon, and a star with a tail travelling through the heavens for three weeks. People said it was a sign that Henry was not in favour.'

Again, the teulu nodded.

'Last year, Henry spent nearly all his time in Normandy, which did not go well. War is costly; meanwhile, the winter was long, the harvests marred and murrain amongst the cattle greater than in living memory.'

Gruffydd nodded though he knew that Gwynedd had escaped this where much of England had been devastated.

'Henry can ill afford to challenge Wales. If we make moves now when the whole of England is discontent, with the death rate high from starvation and illness, and the crops poor, it puts pressure on him. Now is an opportune time to push a little.'

'What you say is true, Lord Maredudd,' agreed Gruffydd. 'England, in particular, has suffered from the weather the last two years, but this year promises to be better. I also know that Gilbert Strongbow, to whom Henry gave Cardigan, is seriously unwell. That works to your advantage because he has no energy to lead his men.' He saw them both nod. 'Before I commit to anything, I want to know that we are all truly working together, that while our resources are focused in one direction, nobody will sneak behind us to stab us in the back.'

Maredudd looked shocked, though Owain grinned.

'Fair point. So, I have a suggestion. Why do we not ally with a union? You have a wonderful daughter, and I am free and eligible.'

Gruffydd looked down, twisting his ring so they could not see his face. When he looked up again, he searched Owain's eyes.

'You have talked freely to me, and now I will talk openly to you. I had other plans for my daughter but have not put anything in place yet. My daughter is young and headstrong, yet she could tie Gwynedd to another power. I have long had a relationship with Powys and wish to still, but Owain, you are new to the power you have. You have many enemies. You have been rash in the past, and before I tied my daughter to Powys, I would want to know that one year from now, you will not be exiled in Ireland again.'

'But, in principle, you are not against the idea?' asked Maredudd.

Owain took no offence and watched Gruffydd.

'I would like my daughter to have a little more time with her family, grow up a little more, and I would like to see how Powys progresses.'

'But, in principle…' started Maredudd.

'In principle, I think it could be a good match.'

'And regarding our offensive action?'

'This is a matter for discussion with my teulu, but now we should eat. I do not know about you, but I am starving, and the smell from the spit clouds my thoughts.'

***

Gwenllian had been forbidden to practise fighting while Owain ap Cadwgan was visiting, and she felt trapped inside the llys. She had dutifully played her harp, sat with her embroidery, smiled as appropriate, and found it tedious. When Owain had smiled at her or caught her eye, however, she felt a rush inside her that she could not explain. He looked at her often, and she had to admit he was very handsome, if a little arrogant. The bards had written a song about his exploits, how he had made the mountains his home, survived against all weathers and vanquished his foes. As they sang, she felt warm inside, excited that this Welsh hero was here amongst them and that his eyes twinkled at her.

She and her brothers were up early on the second day after his arrival. It was a beautiful bright morning, and she knew she would be expected to behave genteelly all day.

'Anyone want to ride along the beach while it is so nice?' she asked them.

Cadwallon grimaced, 'I am supposed to be with Father and the teulu even now.'

He stretched and groaned. 'How they can talk about such monotonous matters all day, I have no idea! Yesterday the sun shone on my face, and I nearly fell asleep.'

'That is because you had no sleep the night before,' grinned Cadwaladr, earning a nudge in his ribs and a glower from Owain, although Cadwallon looked pleased with himself.

'I would not mind trying out one of the new mares that Owain has gifted to Father,' said Owain. 'Do you think he would let me?'

'Go and ask,' urged Gwenllian. 'He can only say no. If he agrees, will you give me a turn as well?'

'As long as you do nothing ridiculous, just keep it on the sand and avoid rocks.'

'I am not an idiot. Of course, I would take care.'

Her brother shrugged and went off to find their father.

'Are you coming?' she asked Cadwaladr.

'I am teaching Annest to do jumps on her pony; otherwise, I would have come. Perhaps we will come down to the beach at the end of your ride. She would like that. How long will you be?'

'Perhaps an hour.'

Owain was lucky. His father would let him try out one of the new mares. His sister rode on her pony with her hair loose, her face pink, and with the breeze on her skin. The beach was deserted except for the seabirds who ran along the shoreline and the little crabs scampering into holes as the tide retreated.

Owain started to canter, and the pair galloped at the water's edge, clods of sand flinging up behind them. The morning was glorious, and as Gwenllian fell behind the big mare, she felt an exhilaration. It was good to be alive. At the end of the beach, Owain stopped, dismounted, and waited for his sister, who stopped her mount in a spray of sand.

'She is fast, Gwenllian, and has a lovely nature.'

Gwenllian grinned. She was as good a rider as her brother and loved horses. She pulled herself up, and Owain adjusted the girth and stirrups.

She gave him one last beam and took off along the beach, loving the wind fierce in her face, which was slapping her hair over her eyes so that, at times, she almost rode blind. The mighty hooves thudded rhythmically below the churning sand. She pressed her knees into the mare's sides so that it bunched its muscles and accelerated. Gwenllian felt the joy of the enormous beast racing beside the waves.

Owain ap Cadwgan was sitting astride his mount on the edge of a sandy outcrop so that he could survey the area where the River Ffraw joined the sea. His light green cloak, intricately embroidered around the edges, flapped around him as he examined the site as a soldier would. He imagined boats pulling in from the sea and calculated how long it would take them from the banks further upstream to the llys to unload their men and creep up to the llys. He always regarded his surroundings as places where conflict might occur, which served him well. Two ducks flew out of the reeds, and a heron jabbed into the water to pluck a fish from the shallows.

Looking behind, Owain could see the watch tower and Gruffydd's men with clear sight. He concluded that such a thing could only be done at night, but he dismissed the thought because he did not need it. The sand began to crumble below the weight of his mount, and he turned him away sharply so that they could pick their way between the grasses and softer sand to the beach. As he looked up from the task, he saw a vision: a beautiful girl riding like the devil, her hair streaming out, catching the light like burnished gold. It took his breath away.

As Gwenllian approached the estuary, she could make out a dark-cloaked figure on a jet-coloured stallion. He spurred his horse to meet her, and her heart jumped when she saw it was Owain ap Cadwgan.

'What do you think of her, Princess Gwenllian?' asked Owain as he drew alongside her, buckles, clasps, rings and harness glinting.

'She is wonderful, sire. She glides along the sand at the gallop as if it is no effort.'

She is bred from our Welsh stock mixed with Arabian stock, which has come through Spain.'

'She is beautiful.'

The pounding hooves on the sand reminded her that her brother was close by, and she turned, pushing her hair out of her face so that the King of Powys saw the beauty of her faintly flushed skin.

'Good morning to my namesake!' said the older man enjoying his jest.

'Sire, I hope you are finding Anglesey to your liking.'

'Very much so,' said the Powysian. 'I remember it well, destroyed and burnt, yet now it looks like heaven should look to me.'

The young man smiled at the generous compliment.

'Have you also tried the mare?' asked Owain ap Cadwgan.

'I have. She is like the wind.'

'You should try this one; he has power in his legs, and you would scarcely credit. Would you like to give him a turn on the beach?'

The young Owain looked thrilled and was flying across the water's edge within moments. Owain ap Cadwgan moved closer to the mare.

'Can I help you down, lady?'

'Thank you, sire, I can manage,' she said, slipping her leather boots out of the stirrups. Owain held her then, gently lifting her body off the horse, and in a moment, he had bent his head and, not giving her time to push him away, he had pulled her towards him, finding her lips. She was breathing hard, but his mouth pressed against hers, and she closed her eyes.

At the top of the outcrop, Cadwaladr and Annest watched as Owain ap Cadwgan kissed their sister, and their brother Owain galloped away on a stallion from Powys.

Chapter 22: While the Cat's Away (Spring 1113-1114)

The four sons of Owain ap Edwin had led their men through Cheshire and returned with more booty than expected. Gronwy, of course, as head of the family, had decided how and where they would attack, and Meilyr had to acknowledge that he was an expert strategist. He had the men of Cheshire running around in circles, and it was easy pickings. Llywarch, the youngest of the brothers, had been his irrepressible self, keeping the band of Welshmen entertained on the way there and back, providing the bonhomie that Gronwy lacked. Rhydir, even more earnest as he had grown older, stayed beside Llywarch, a solid shield when his younger brother overreached.

As they rode home, Rhydir was still at Llywarch's side, but he was relaxed, and Meilyr knew that he was eager to be back with the love of his life, the ever-smiling Lleuci and their brood of merry children. Meilyr felt a tinge of envy at that. Rhydir's hair was tinged with grey now, as was his own, and Meilyr always found that surprising. It seemed such a short while ago that they were four boys sparring against each other or playing their instruments around the fire. Their father's llys, which had always been a magnet for visitors and known for the patronage of the bards, was a cold place now that Gronwy headed the family.

Gronwy, riding on his grey stallion, was delighted for once, his fat, unshaven face grinning as they greeted men and women hastening out of their homes to see who passed with horses weighed down with plunder. Lord Gronwy was feared, but he was their lord, and news had travelled fast that he had put fear into the men of Cheshire.

The cattle taken by the raiders had been driven to the mountain pastures, the hafod, along with the horses, but the Welshmen had also made off with money, plate, jewellery, and weapons. Gronwy had butchered any man who opposed him. His brothers, with no stomach for leaving children fatherless, had cut through arms or hands, making men incapacitated but had left the killing to Gronwy and his men, who were ruthlessly efficient and had taken the greater share of the booty.

Meilyr was bone weary. In truth, he had no stomach for the anguished cries, the stink of blood, the bone breaking and worse, but he would be belittled if he voiced those thoughts. You needed to measure up in the fray to gain respect as a man. His wife and family were just a few miles away, but something was troubling him that he had to get to the bottom of before he reached them. Gronwy had hinted so often during this trip that he would soon finish Gruffydd ap Cynan, and Meilyr wanted to know what he had planned. Meilyr feared his brother's loathing of Gruffydd ap Cynan and their sister Angharad. What had started as envy had become an obsession.

During the ride home to Tegeingl, while his brothers were riding together, Meilyr had held back and pulled his horse to walk alongside Gronwy's head of teulu, Wyon. The old warrior was hard-faced, tough, thick-necked, and heavy with muscle. He was reliable and used his weapons with an economy of effort. Meilyr liked him.

'We've had a good haul,' said Meilyr, 'with little resistance. No wounds on our side.'

The other man grinned, showing a mouth with more gaps than teeth. 'Surprise is the key. They did not expect us, see. They have been sitting there as fat as butter, not thinking they would face a mob like ours! Even the dogs were too lazy to come at us.'

'It is a good time now with the Normans fighting their own in Normandy,' Meilyr remarked.

'That is true right enough, and with Owain ap Cadwgan hitting them from the south and Gruffydd ap Cynan harassing them on the west, they will be feeling the pinch.'

'It might cause a reaction from King Henry, however. We must be aware of that.'

The old man gave a wheezy laugh. 'That is exactly what Lord Gronwy wants. Take what pickings we can now but weaken Gruffydd's position at the same time.'

'Weaken Gruffydd ap Cynan?' probed Meilyr to be sure.

'Yes, indeed. Just like Owain's actions weakened Cadwgan, see. When Owain ap Cadwgan visited last week, they spoke about that. See now, Gruffydd will get the blame for letting his lords run wild, and if he is finished by Henry's wrath, then that will leave a gap in Gwynedd to fill. Ha! And who better to fill it but Powys and us? Oh, yes, things will change for the better and at little cost to us.'

'Has Owain ap Cadwgan been in Gwynedd then?'

'Yes, he was here last week. Ha, Powys must be a wealthy place. Owain was decked out in such finery and the horses he had…,' he whistled.

Meilyr understood Gronwy's motivation for the raiding now. He was glad of the booty and no mistake. Meilyr's wife, Ina, was beautiful but difficult, with expensive tastes and ideas of grandeur beyond her station. Recently Meilyr had found himself struggling to make ends meet, and these raids would cover him for a couple of years. There had been astonishment that so much wealth was in Cheshire despite the bad seasons they had endured there. Gronwy's spies had directed them well.

He agonised over raising Gronwy's intentions with his brothers but decided against it. It would seem disloyal to Gronwy, who, after all, headed their family. He also knew that Gronwy's constant vitriol towards his sister and her husband had tapped away at their loyalties. That, and the fact that it would make an easier life for the brothers if the wealth from Anglesey was in their coffers.

Meilyr made a little more idle chat with Wyon and then trotted back towards the front of the group. His company had not been missed. He was sorry to have lost the close relationship he once had with Rhydir and Llywarch. Since they had all made their own homes, they had grown apart. Perhaps that is how it was with families. For many years he attempted to welcome his brothers and their families to his own home, but he knew the invitations were not returned because Ina treated her sisters-in-law with disdain. Now though, his main concern was how to prevent his sister's downfall, and this occupied his mind until they were inside Gronwy's llys with the ale flowing.

'That will teach Richard, Earl of Chester, to run over to Normandy, leaving his lands unguarded from the men of Gwynedd,' Gronwy boasted as he stretched out his legs to the fire swigging his ale.

Meilyr watched his brother, smug as a cat that had got the cream. Their relationship had changed over the years. When their father had been alive, Meilyr had largely ignored his brash vengeful brother, but since their father's death, Gronwy had flouted his power making clear to Meilyr that he could easily make his brother's life unpleasant. Meilyr paid the respect he needed to show Gronwy as head of the family, but that did not mean he had to like him. At times he detested him.

In the corner of the hall, Gronwy's wife, Genilles, sat pregnant and vigilant. Meilyr had noticed bruising on her jaw and wondered if that was his brother's handiwork. Genilles' eyes darted around, and she was jumpy. Their daughter, Cristina, danced playfully, confident and giggling, ignoring her mother's pleas to be still and quiet. Gronwy seemed to like Cristina's spirit, encouraging her flamboyance, but if he had drunk too much, even she might incur his wrath.

'I hear Owain ap Cadwgan has been visiting you,' said Meilyr casually.

'What of it?' Gronwy's eyes became slits as he regarded his brother.

If someone as important as the ruler of Powys came to visit, it would have been natural to include the other family members. Meilyr was irked at the slight.

'You kept it very quiet, is all.'

'Not at all, your brothers joined us, and we went hunting together.'

'But you did not invite me.'

'No, I did not,' Gronwy returned plainly.

'But I am good enough to bring my men when you want to raid in Cheshire.' Meilyr spoke softly, but he was boiling inside. Whilst he disliked his brother, he had been loyal to him, and this was a slap in the face. It also hurt that Rhydir and Llywarch had kept their meeting with Owain ap Cadwgan from him, another indication that the sands were shifting.

'You've done very well out of it for someone that did not bloody your weapons.'

Meilyr gripped the chair he sat in, white-knuckled, and left it a while before he replied. He had enough blood on his blade to feel overwhelmed with guilt, but he was wise enough not to argue that point. There was a hostile silence between them, seemingly unnoticed by the others laughing and reliving their adventures.

'What could be so secret that you would keep me from the company of Owain ap Cadwgan?' Meilyr persisted.

'Meilyr,' Gronwy adopted the tone of one talking to an infant, 'what I decide to do, whom I decide to meet, is none of your business.'

'I am your brother. Everything you do affects me.'

Gronwy smiled insincerely and leaned forward so Meilyr could smell his breath. He enunciated each word speaking slowly. 'A brother I cannot trust, Meilyr. I cannot trust you not to go tittle-tattling to your sister about our concerns here. Is it not time you went home to your wife? Will you not get into trouble for being out late?'

As always, Gronwy had found his Achilles heel. Meilyr, who had always preferred a quiet life, had married a woman whose tempers would fray the nerves of a saint. He had no desire to hurry home to incessant nagging and the constant reminder of his inadequacy, yet this home he had grown up in held no comfort for him.

'Brother, we all have families now, and if you play with fire, you put us all at risk.' He protested, but it sounded weak.

'I have the guts to do something that will change all our lives. Do not preach to me about putting family at risk. You do nothing, Meilyr. You just hide in your study, hoping Ina does not fritter away the last of your coin. If you had not come on this trip, you would have been begging me to help you, and you have the boldface to talk to me about risk-taking. What kind of a man are you?'

'I am a man who can live with myself, Gronwy, and I hope you can live with yourself. I may not get the thrill from shedding blood that you do or the lust to bring a man down by scheming, but our father's dying wish was that I support you, and by God, despite all your condemnation of me, I have done that! Whatever you have planned with Owain ap Cadwgan, remember that you were hunting his head only a few years ago. He will not forget that.'

'Owain ap Cadwgan is his father's son, Meilyr. He sniffs out advantage and does not hold grudges if it will hold him back. He would have done the same if the boot had been on the other foot.'

A buxom young girl edged past with a jug, and as she leaned over to pour the ale, Gronwy reached for her ample backside and squeezed. The girl turned grinning, and Meilyr looked across to Genilles, who, far from being humiliated, showed utter relief. Gronwy would not trouble her tonight.

'It has been a long day,' said Meilyr watching his brother's eyes glued to the woman swaying back towards the kitchen. 'I will take my men and leave you to it.'

His brother did not deign to respond.

As Meilyr summoned his party in the courtyard, the last vestiges of sunset were fading into the blue-black darkness of the night. Inside the llys, he could hear music, raised voices and laughter. Between the outbuildings, a figure lumbered out of the shadows, and Meilyr had quickly unsheathed his sword before he saw that it was only one of his men returning from relieving himself.

'Gave you a start, my lord,' laughed the man.

'You did that!' Meilyr laughed back good-humouredly, but he was angry at himself for appearing nervous.

'Looks like a storm might be brewing,' observed the man as they turned their horses for the gate.

'Oh yes,' thought Meilyr, 'a storm was undoubtedly brewing.'

As they rode the short, familiar journey to where Meilyr's family would be waiting for him, he felt heavy-hearted and consumed with anxiety for his sister.

***

Griffith ap Rhys brought ten of his men with him for the visit. He had sent one ahead, and as they approached the Royal Llys, the wide gates swung open, and Gruffydd was there himself with his teulu to welcome them. Angharad allowed them time to dismount and have their horses led away before she joined them. It was a pleasant spring day with the trees in bud and new growth beginning to thrust out of the ground.

Griffith turned as he heard the rustle of cloth to see Angharad in a soft green robe with dark green embroidery around the neck and sleeves. The delicate translucent veil she wore over her golden hair was clasped in place by a thin silver band. He was taken aback at her beauty and how much younger than Gruffydd she seemed. Her smile was gentle and lit up her face. He remembered that smile from many years ago in Ireland when they had met briefly.

'My sister Nest sends special greetings, my lady,' said Griffith, bowing low, and from a soft leather bag at his side, he brought out something bound in finely embroidered cloth. He held it out to her.

'For me?' she asked, thinking the youth had become an arrestingly handsome man.

'For you, my lady. My sister hopes that you will enjoy it.'

Angharad's hands moved carefully over the cloth, unwrapping the binding and pulling out a leather-covered book. She gasped, opening the present, a finely illuminated book of the Welsh saints.'

'This is beautiful,' she gasped, her eyes lighting up as she clutched it to her. 'I will treasure this gift.'

Griffith was pleased, his beam infectious. 'She also sent something for you, sire.'

He opened his bag again, pulled out a leather pouch, and handed it to Gruffydd.

Gruffydd turned his head to one side quizzically and opened the pouch as carefully as his wife had done with her present. He pulled out an exquisite silver buckle, intricately worked with a fire-breathing dragon.

The king shook his head. 'Your sister did not need to send us such fine gifts, but this is extraordinary. I have not seen the like.'

'Nest will be delighted that you are pleased with the gifts. She had as much joy in choosing them.'

A huge cry of hurrah went up from the practice yard, and Griffith looked across to where coloured pennants were hanging. The yard was filled with men, and two seemed to have finished sparring.

'They are having fun,' observed Griffith.

'We are just having a little competition amongst the men. Come over, all of you. It is warm enough to have something to eat and drink outside if you would like to watch.'

Griffith's men were eager to see and clambered to some elevated benches set up along the side of the practice yard. A sturdier construction had been set up for the royal party with soft cushions and a table close by that held drinks and small dishes of food.

Two tall, lean youthful figures made their way to the centre of the practice yard.

'Ah, the children,' said Angharad, adjusting a cushion behind her.

'This will be interesting!' said Gruffydd, leaning forward.

Both wore chainmail and helmets and carried practice swords. One wore a red sash, and the other one of blue.

Aeddan stood on the sidelines as they faced each other. He bowed at them then a small bell sounded.

'Do you do this often?' asked Griffith, watching intently.

'About once a month to revive enthusiasm and keep them on their toes.'

The two figures were moving around each other. The blue-sashed one was more strongly built, while the smaller of the two in the red sash was more agile and almost dancing.

The blue fighter saw an opportunity and lunged forward, but the red one sidestepped neatly. The blue fighter quickly regrouped and rained down blows that should have felled the red opponent but for their frustrating dodging and weaving. Then, having made no attempt to attack the blue-sashed opponent, the red-sashed one slipped a foot between the blue one's legs, swivelled and, as blue lost balance and fell, red stepped in neatly to point a sword at his neck.

There were roars of approval, and as the blue-sashed fighter retired, others came forward to try their skill.

Griffith watched as the red-sashed fighter made bigger fighters stumble like fools. He turned to Gruffydd.

'Would you mind if I tried out my skill?'

Gruffydd shot a glance at Angharad, who raised her eyebrows slightly.

'By all means. I will announce you,' he agreed, with an almost imperceptible smile playing at the edge of his mouth.

Griffith walked down into the practice yard full of onlookers, following his approach with interest.

The king stood to make an announcement, and there was a call for quiet.

'We have a special guest today who is going to join our tournament. Please welcome Prince Griffith ap Rhys, rightful heir to the throne of Deheubarth.'

Griffith waved a hand in acknowledgement and then tested the balance of the sword he had been given for the competition.

The red-sashed competitor came forward and nodded, as did he in return.

'Good luck,' he said, but the competitor said nothing.

A bell rang to start the bout, and there was tension in the air as the spectators anticipated an exciting fight. Griffith was well-built, moving with ease and confidence. He regarded his competitor carefully, noting the balance and that there seemed to be no injuries favoured. He decided to start the offensive, lunging quickly, but his opponent sidestepped cleverly. Griffith watched carefully for the foot which had tripped up his predecessor and, falling back to a balanced position, began to circle. The crowd were tense, and there was hardly a sound.

The red-sashed combatant was light of foot and quickly dipped in to strike Griffith a solid blow on his arm, almost dislodging his grip on the hilt of his sword. He feinted to the right, but the opponent saw that for what it was and was not fooled. The visitor lunged again, this time taking his sword lower to aim at the legs, but cat-like, the opponent jumped high over his lunge and struck a blow to his side, which winded him. Using all his strength, he moved forward, aiming one blow after another, but it was as if he was striking at the air, so quick was the response. He moved in close, and suddenly the hilt of a sword punched into his jaw, and he was on his back with his adversary's sword at his throat: the crowd roared.

Dazed, Griffith conceded and lifted himself off the ground, wincing, congratulating his adversary. Gwenllian removed her helmet, and her hair cascaded down as she looked up at him. He saw a breathtakingly beautiful girl with deep dark blue eyes, a gleaming smile, and the flush of the victor on her cheek. He turned to look up at Gruffydd and Angharad, who were not disguising their amusement at his shock. Gruffydd jumped down into the yard and took Griffith by his shoulder.

'I am sorry, we should have told you, but the look on your face was worth the deception. Our daughter, Gwenllian, abhors ladylike pursuits in favour of training with our warband. She challenges them all.'

Gwenllian fell into a deep curtsey which looked odd as she was not wearing a robe, and Griffith bowed in return. He felt a rush of excitement as the stunning creature's eyes twinkled with merriment, despite feeling stupid that he had not realised such grace belonged to a woman.

'It was a clever fight, lady, and I commend you. I hope I do not have to face you on the battlefield.'

The crowd whooped at his good-natured words, and Gwenllian felt a nervous tingle when their eyes met again. Griffith was a fine-looking man, and his charismatic personality was already drawing her in.

Gruffydd and Angharad drew their guest away towards the llys, leaving Gwenllian talking with the men she was used to sparring with. Griffith shook his head again.

'That was utterly unexpected,' he admitted to Gruffydd honestly. 'I am used to winning.'

Gruffydd's deep friendly laugh echoed in the hall.

'You are not the only one to be taken aback, Prince Griffith, but she is the bane of her mother's life.'

Griffith turned to Angharad very seriously, 'Your daughter is not only beautiful but an asset to any royal family. Not many women can protect themselves and their loved ones as she can. You have a rare gem.'

***

The feast that night was lively, with everyone in high spirits after the tournament. Gwenllian sat with her brothers but noticed that Griffith kept looking towards her.

'He likes you, Gwenllian,' laughed Cadwaladr. 'He keeps watching you like a sick cow.'

'Be careful, Gwenllian,' said Owain earnestly. 'You have an arrangement with Owain ap Cadwgan, do not forget.'

Gwenllian turned sharply to her brother. 'Nothing is set in stone, Owain, and I am not doing anything inappropriate.'

'You are making eyes at him,' teased Cadwallon.

'I am not,' said Gwenllian, deliberately looking away from the top table.

'Do not forget you represent this family, Gwenllian, and you need to show some decorum,' Owain warned her.

'Pffff,' spat Gwenllian, rounding on her brothers, 'you think I do not know what you and Cadwallon do when you have half a chance.'

'I might have kissed a pretty girl in a quiet corner outside when nobody was looking, but you are openly flirting in front of everyone at the llys,' replied Cadwallon, his eyes twinkling.

'I am not. And anyway, it is not just kissing that Cadwallon is interested in. Moreover, he is the heir, as he is always reminding us! I am just looking.'

'But you kissed Owain ap Cadwgan; I saw you,' Cadwaladr baited her, loving the mischief.

'You did what?' said Owain horrified.

'Just a moment,' said Gwenllian, 'he kissed me, and what was I to do? Was I to shame him?'

'You were enjoying it, Gwenllian. I watched you!' piped up Cadwaladr triumphantly.

'Well, shame on you for spying!' retaliated Gwenllian.

'And shame on him for disrespecting our family,' argued Owain indignantly. 'The man might be a hero, but he has few manners.'

'Be quiet, Owain,' said Cadwallon, 'you are becoming so sanctimonious you are like a priest. Leave the girl alone and let her have some fun.'

'I am surprised at you, Cadwallon,' said Owain angrily. 'Gwenllian is a royal princess, and if she behaves like one of your 'friends', then she will be the laughingstock of Gwynedd. Is that what you want?'

'Does it strike you as odd that it is fine for you boys to do what you like, but because I am a girl, I am supposed to behave differently? I had to fight hard to be able to use a sword, I am not allowed to swim now, and it seems that I must restrict where I look and whom I look at.'

'Be sensible,' Owain countered. 'Your future depends on how you behave, and you know it.'

Gwenllian sighed with resignation. 'And the whole family's future depends on how I behave too, it seems. I know that all too well. I can be married off to someone in Norway or Ireland, but you, my brothers, do not have to go anywhere.'

'I thought you were going to marry Owain ap Cadwgan?' said Cadwaladr perplexed.

'I told you; nothing has been arranged. They might make me marry him, or they might decide something else.'

'But I thought you wanted to marry him,' persisted Cadwaladr.

'He seemed nice enough, and at least he is Welsh,' said Gwenllian.

'Ohhhh,' said Cadwaladr, 'you were mooning about him for ages, and now you are pretending you hardly liked him.'

Gwenllian delivered a sharp pinch to her younger brother's arm, making him yelp. She did not look back at the top table again but remembered smugly that her mother had asked her to play the harp. She could stare as much as she liked then because the music would be in Griffith's honour. Afterwards, she knew there would be dancing, and surely it would only be polite for Griffith to request a dance. She blushed as she thought about Griffith holding her hand as they spun around the hall.

At the top table, Griffith was charm itself, attentive to Angharad, courteous to Gruffydd, and he had an easy way of making people laugh. He knew how important it was that Gruffydd support him. He needed to focus his mind to that end, but he could not help being drawn to the beautiful girl he had fought with. Never had he felt such a thrill as when Gwenllian had removed the helmet and her hair cascaded down in front of him. He was besotted, and he found his heart racing each time he looked at her.

Beside Griffith, his brother, Howel, felt anxious as he saw him gazing at the lovely princess. While the king was speaking to one of the bards, he grabbed Griffith's shoulder and pulled him close.

'Keep your mind on the task in hand, Griffith. She is as good as promised to Owain ap Cadwgan; you do not want to make a mess of this. We need Gruffydd's backing, and you do not want to muddy the waters by involving yourself with his daughter.'

Griffith turned as if stung, 'Owain ap Cadwgan? Nothing has been said about that. Owain did not mention it.'

'As good as, I am telling you. And why would Owain ap Cadwgan mention it to you when just a short time ago, he was living with your sister? Come on, Griffith, keep your wits about you. If you want a lovely woman to flirt with, the room is full of them, but you must use your intelligence to convince Gruffydd to further your cause. Concentrate.'

Griffith shrugged his shoulders and turned to Queen Angharad to continue a conversation they had been having about differences in Welsh and Irish customs. He knew full well that his brother was right, but the girl was spirited, intelligent, breathtakingly beautiful and the finest catch in Wales.

***

Gwenllian sank into her bed and pulled her sheet up to her chin as if it could protect her from the myriad of emotions she was feeling. The shutters were wide open so that moonlight poured in through the casement, and the chill in the air cooled her flushed face. She was so excited she could hardly close her eyes, let alone sleep. Her head spun wildly, and her heart was racing. The princess relived the moment Griffith joined her to whirl around the hall. The memory was glorious. She breathed in deeply, turning onto her side with a little sigh of joy, clasping her pillow as if it were him.

Griffith was enticingly good-looking, and the way he spoke to her made her feel as if she was the only person in the world. Gwenllian adored the way he spoke Welsh with a soft Irish foreignness in his intonations. Sometimes her father would pronounce a word that way because he had also been raised in Ireland.

When Griffith had broached his ambitions to take back Deheubarth, to march through Dyfed destroying the Normans, she had been gripped. He had the same hunger to pulverise the enemy that she had. Griffith had not dismissed her as a weak girl whose opinions were irrelevant. When she had admitted her dreams to him, tentatively at first and then with more confidence, he had nodded and encouraged her. They would have talked like that all night, but her mother came across the hall, making it clear that the evening had come to an end. Gwenllian had been completely unaware that there were few people still up, and many had wrapped themselves in the brychans, the coarse cloth blankets which kept away the night's chills.

As her mother had walked away, Griffith had leant in and half-whispered into her ear, "Will you be at the hunt tomorrow?' His lips had touched her hair, and the intimacy had intoxicated her. She had turned to search his face and found it hard not to lift her lips to his, yet she controlled herself. 'Of course,' she answered, smiling before she curtseyed, giving a hasty goodnight. She had walked away knowing that his eyes were boring into her back, her body fevered with excitement and her mind in turmoil. As she lay under the covers, her heart gave another great leap, and she turned onto her other side, relishing that moment she had with him, then turning again, unable to sleep. She could hardly breathe; her heart was pounding so.

At the other end of the llys, Griffith's mind was consumed with Gwenllian. Her eyes had mesmerised him; her lithe, sleek body had enraptured him; her grasp of political affairs and understanding of his intentions in Wales had utterly stunned him. He knew that Howel was right and that he should be concentrating on getting Gruffydd's support to move forward in Deheubarth, but his mind was in a tangle.

Gruffydd was the last to leave the hall, and he was pleased to see his wife waiting for him, her blonde hair tumbling over the white pillow.

'Come,' she said, holding out her hand. 'Do not trouble over anything tonight. Nothing can be done until tomorrow.'

'He is a persistent young man. I like him, but he is inexperienced yet. He does not comprehend the immensity of the task he is taking on.'

'Have you committed to anything?'

'No, though how long I can continue to sidestep, I do not know.'

He sat on the bed wearily to remove his calfskin boots, polished and shining. Gruffydd's blonde hair flopped over his face as he unstrapped the leather jerkin he wore over his tunic. Everything he did, he did with care. She knew that he would neatly place his clothing at the end of the bed, wash himself, and then gently come into bed beside her. He stepped across to where a pitcher of warm water and a bowl stood on a polished wooden stand. He washed slowly and fastidiously, letting his thoughts drift.

'Perhaps agree to harbour him and his men, train them, but not to join him in outright battle.'

Gruffydd snorted, 'And you can imagine how your brother will use that information to give me grief with Henry!'

Angharad considered this and knew her husband was right. If there were any opportunity to tarnish Gruffydd's good name, Gronwy would take it. She could not comprehend the hatred her brother harboured towards them both. Keeping the presence and training of a body of men from Deheubarth secret was impossible when Gronwy's eyes and ears were everywhere.

She smoothed the white sheet and bit her lip as she thought. Young Griffith reminded her of her husband in his youth, and she felt strongly that they should assist him in regaining his royal place. She thought of Nest, ousted as she had been, and the image of a young Griffith wildly riding across the country to find a boat for Ireland, knowing that his father had been slaughtered, made her shiver. How easily it could happen to their children if they were not vigilant. She pictured Gwenllian being pawed by lustful men in a stone stronghold somewhere in England; her little girls sent to be brought up by and to serve Norman families; her three boys killed or escaping, as Griffith had done, with the enemy at his heels. Then she looked at her husband, and a shudder ran through her body as she envisioned her loving husband and father of her children lying bloodied and cold. They had to be cautious, but what mother could turn away the young man whose life had been almost destroyed and yet was filling their llys with his passion for life?

'Then maybe,' she suggested slowly, picking her words carefully, her arms crossed, 'send Griffith to Llyn to train with his men there. Genillin ap Meirion Goch, lord of Llyn, is supposed to take his authority from the Earl of Chester so they can not accuse you of helping Griffith. Genillin is a great friend, and you have been good to him. He will do the favour. We can provide money, at least, horses, arms. If Henry should question you about Griffith, you can honestly say you did not give him sanctuary here in Anglesey.'

'Hmm,' said Gruffydd pensively, looking out at the stars as he played with the buckle on his knife belt. 'It might be an answer. I would need to manoeuvre carefully, but it would mean that I am not rejecting his quest for support, I am not alienating a possible future ally, and I am avoiding clear antagonism of Henry.'

She slowly unfolded her arms, gauging whether she should let the matter rest now. She was wary of seeming to push the idea too much. He gently lifted the covers, and she moved across to make space for him as he slipped between the sheets.

As always, the warmth of his body against hers was comforting. Putting his arm around her shoulders, he drew her to him and kissed her lips softly. As she lay against him, she knew his mind was still processing her reasoning as he wound her long soft hair around his hand. She slid her arm across his chest and cuddled closer, trying to expel the scene she had conjured of his lying in a pool of blood. His lips found hers once more, and as his hand caressed her breast, she responded to his touch, greedy for the safety and certainty of their union.

Chapter 23: War (Spring 1114)

King Henry was angry. Livid.

'I trusted you to keep this under control, Bishop,' he thundered.

Bishop Richard flinched, taking a step back partly to avoid the spittle which had landed on his face and partly because he thought the king might strike him.

'I have Gilbert Strongbow complaining from Cardigan that Owain ap Cadwgan is making merry with those who are despoiling and robbing his lands. I have Hugh, Earl of Chester squealing that Gruffydd ap Cynan cannot control his subjects and that his brother-in-law, Gronwy ap Owain, Lord of Tegeingl, has ravaged Cheshire and left it desolate and burnt. What is more, we have received nothing from Gruffydd ap Cynan. Nothing. Not service, despite his acclaim as a mighty warrior, and certainly not gold.'

'But this has provided us with an opportunity to....'

'An opportunity to spend money I do not have, to raise an army and march against them!' Henry bellowed.

The bishop looked down at his feet.

'I listened to you, Bishop Richard; I listened to you when you told me that the Welsh would fight amongst themselves and kill each other.'

'But they have. Cadwgan ap Bleddyn is dead at the hands of Madog ap Rhydir. Iorwedd ap Bleddyn is dead at the hands of the same Madog.'

'These were men who filled my coffers, you imbecile. And Madog, where is he now?'

'In hiding, sire.'

'In hiding, sire,' repeated Henry in a high wavering voice. 'Get him out of whatever hole he is cowering in. Tell him to wipe out Owain ap Cadwgan and the hotheads he has around him and then to finish off Gruffydd ap Cynan!'

'Of course, I can do that.'

'Yes, yes, of course you can, and then kill Madog, or he will revert to form and start the same raiding and burning that is all the Welsh are good for. Animals!'

The bishop blanched, his legs shaking.

'I will bring the whole of Wales down, and there will be not one living creature in the God-forsaken land. Do you hear me?' King Henry was white-knuckled, his face contorted with frustration.

The bishop nodded.

'I will exterminate them all, every Welshman, everyone, and I will colonise the country with all the sycophants that trail after me, pleading for land. By God, there are enough to fill Wales three times over.'

'But s-s-s-sire,' stuttered Bishop Richard and stopped abruptly as Henry swung around and glared at him.

'I will send Alexander, King of the Scots, and Hugh of Chester against Gruffydd ap Cynan with all the strength of the North. I will send Gilbert Strongbow, Earl of Strygill, against South Wales with all the strength of the south of England and Cornwall, and I will lead against Powys with all the men of the midlands.'

Bishop Richard's eyes opened wide, and he ran his tongue over his parched lips.

'Sire, the cost will be inordinate.'

Henry was still fuming, 'The cost will be recouped many times over. I should have done to Wales what my father did in the North. I should have obliterated them.'

The bishop began to open his mouth to pass comment regarding Henry's brother, William Rufus, who failed against the Welsh three times but thought better of it. Uppermost in his mind was the need to keep his own position secure.

'I will bring what information I can to aid your campaign, sire. I have built up a network of men who will help us understand what is happening inside each of the kingdoms.'

Henry scoffed. 'These men have been remarkably silent on the raids and rampaging thus far.'

'I had thought Strongbow would have the measure of Owain ap Cadwgan, and I have not been as vigilant as I might have been.'

The bishop realised that in his nervousness, he was making increasingly extravagant gestures with his arms, and so deliberately held the sides of the silk robe which covered his alb to still himself. Henry's shrewd eyes noticed this.

'He claims he has been in ill health,' said Henry more reasonably, 'but to your point, I gave him the bloody land so that he would keep these issues in check, not come whinging that it is all too hard.'

'And Hugh of Chester should have had the measure of Gronwy ap Owain.'

'Hugh of Chester is wet behind the ears. How such a lily-livered runt was whelped is a mystery. He will never be the man his father was, yet he has wealth and power we must consider.'

'I understand, sire.'

'After Normandy, this will be like squeezing a pimple; it is a victory that will send a message.'

'It should not take long, I think,' the bishop said placatingly.

Henry looked at him levelly. 'No bishop. It will not take long, but you had better focus on the task at hand. I did not put you into the position you have, to spend time on your knees. I want to come out of this blazing in glory, do you understand me? And, if I am victorious, you will be safe from incurring my wrath. Get Madog to finish off the Powysians and then turn his attention to Gruffydd ap Cynan.'

'Gruffydd will not be easy, sire. He is always well protected.'

'All it takes is one arrow,' the king said dismissively. Bishop Richard wanted to cross himself but resisted. One arrow had killed King William Rufus, Henry's predecessor. He and Henry had been hunting. When Rufus had been hit by a supposedly stray arrow and tumbled to the ground, Henry had immediately sped to Winchester to take control of the crown treasury, leaving his brother's body lying lifeless and alone. An accident, they had said. A fatal accident.

'Sire, I am grateful for the opportunity to serve.'

Henry waved his hand dismissively, and the bishop took several steps backwards before retreating through the door. The king moved towards the window, kicking a wooden stool and cushion across the room.

He looked down to see courtiers milling around below, and his eye caught an older man, purple-faced, stocky, bald, and limping while escorting a beautifully dressed woman. It was Nest. He studied her as she glided across the courtyard below. On a whim, he decided Nest's husband, Gerald of Windsor, could be sent to Cornwall to arrange assistance for Strongbow while he would keep Nest entertained. His loins stirred as he fantasised about removing Nest's robe, her sensuous nakedness. He cancelled the remainder of his day's meetings and called for a warm bath to be sent to his chamber.

***

Hunydd heard the horse as soon as it clattered into the courtyard and instinctively felt something was amiss. Maredudd was with Owain ap Cadwgan, and she was alone with her boys. She recognised her kinsman Rhydian immediately and hurried outside. It was a grey overcast day, cold and bleak, and she ushered him inside herself, ordering cawl to be brought to the hall.

'What is it?' she asked immediately. If Rhydian called on her, she knew it was for good reason.

Rhydian was a lanky young man who always seemed cheerful, but his face showed concern today. 'Bishop Richard has asked me to find Madog.'

Her eyes narrowed.

'Why?'

'King Henry is planning a campaign against the Welsh on all fronts. He is bringing in Scotland and all his forces in England. He says he will exterminate the Welsh and recolonise. It is the talk of the court.'

Hunydd blanched, crossed herself and took a deep breath.

'What does he want with Madog?'

'I do not know for sure, but I am guessing he wants him to attack Owain and then Maredudd. It would be easy for Henry to succeed with Powys in disarray, and he is heading the army against Powys himself. He needs certain victory.'

'Do you know where Madog is?'

'I know how to find him. I have found him before.'

'What is your message for Madog?'

'That he should present himself to the bishop. He will be safe. Nothing more.'

Hunydd swallowed.

'You are to take him? Accompany him?'

'I was not told to do that, no. The bishop would not want me to be seen with Madog. Nobody knows I am his man.'

'You find him, pass the message, and come back here and tell me where he is. There will be gold in it for you.'

'Hunydd, I do not do this for gold. I do it for you and your family.'

'I know,' she held his arm, 'but risk needs to be rewarded, and you are endangering your life to come to me here.'

A servant entered with a bowl of cawl, and Hunydd sat patiently as Rhydian ate it greedily, wiping his mouth on his sleeve.

'What has caused this now?' she asked, half speaking to herself.

'The earls, Gilbert Strongbow, and Hugh of Chester, have been complaining to the king. Gilbert has made it known that Owain ap Cadwgan is encouraging those ravaging Gilbert's lands, and in Cheshire, Gronwy ap Owain has also laid waste to the lands.'

'So now he wants to make a stand. He wants to look powerful. Henry, who cannot tame the Normans, is going to tame the Welsh.'

'It seems so.'

Hunydd looked outside. 'The light is going. You must be on your way. Be safe now.'

The man left, and Hunydd summoned her eldest son.

'Go to your father and tell him I must speak to him urgently. Make sure Owain ap Cadwgan knows nothing.'

It was dark before Maredudd returned home; his face anxious.

'What is it?' he asked, embracing her, and searching her eyes.

'Bishop Richard is sending for Madog.'

Maredudd looked at her questioningly.

'It seems that Henry is raising his army against us, Maredudd. He is bringing in Scotland.'

'Against us?'

'Against Wales. Against all of Wales. He is set to exterminate us all, and Madog is being set up to make it easier.'

Maredudd sat heavily on a bench, staring vacantly.

'Maredudd, we must be ahead of them. Are you with me?'

Maredudd turned his eyes toward her.

'I have a man who will tell us where Madog is. You will have to kill him, Maredudd.'

'I will not kill kin.'

'You stupid man. He will kill you, or he will lead Henry to us. There will be no safe place. Do you not realise that Henry has the most powerful army in Europe and is about to turn it loose on us all? Do you think these little wooden walls will protect us when they march across Powys? Use your sense.'

'I will capture him. I will capture Madog.'

'And then?'

'I will hand him over to Owain.'

'We need to plan, Maredudd. We must ensure everyone knows and is ready for Henry when he comes.'

'We cannot fight them, Hunydd. Their force is too great.'

'You will have to negotiate with Henry, Maredudd. You have done it before.'

'No, Hunydd, we must gather our allies together first. Gruffydd ap Cynan will know what to do.'

'Forget Gruffydd ap Cynan, save your people and never mind the rest. Henry will listen to you.'

'Hunydd, Hunydd. I know what is behind your thinking, but I am out of my depth with this; Owain ap Cadwgan will be out of his depth with this. Only Gruffydd ap Cynan has any chance of stopping Henry if he really is bringing an army.'

Hunydd looked exasperated. 'I am not going to argue with you now. First, we must eliminate the threats at home. How long do you think we have?'

'It is no small thing to mobilise a force like Henry's. They must get their men to Wales and organise food, arms, and strategy. Men will be riding all over England now, raising the army. Maybe a couple of weeks?'

'First things first, then. Owain at first light and then Madog.'

'Madog.'

***

It was May, and the world was at its best for Angharad. Solid rain meant the crops had started well, and the last few days had been warm. Gruffydd had led the hunt, and the hunters had returned laughing and happy. They had wild boar, venison, and pheasant on the table, along with delicious pigeon pie.

Angharad watched the youngsters dancing and smiled, remembering her own youth. Young Griffith ap Rhys and his brother Howel were still with them, and Griffith's energy had revitalised the llys. Men had been gravitating towards him from Deheubarth, landless men, and Gruffydd and Angharad had welcomed them.

Angharad realised that Griffith ought soon to be leaving to summon and train his men down in Llyn with Genillin ap Meirion Goch, yet there seemed no urgency to go on his part. Having solved the issue of his nurturing a creator of insurrection against the Normans, Gruffydd was also happy with the pair's company. He knew that the young prince brought with him the experience of conflict in Ireland, and his sons were soaking up the knowledge.

Angharad loved it when her husband was relaxed and easy. He was laughing with Aeddan about something that happened on the hunt but feeling her observing him, he turned. Her smile was reciprocated, and he took her hand in his.

'It is lovely to see these young people dancing,' she reflected.

'Oh, no! I know what is coming next,' he laughed.

'Please, Gruffydd. You rarely dance with me, and I love dancing, you know that.'

'What we do for our wives!' said Gruffydd to Aeddan, who gave a little cheer as Gruffydd led Angharad down onto the floor.

Cries of delight went up as they started to move in time with the others, twirling and swaying to the music as well as any on the floor.

'They look a fine couple,' Griffith remarked into Gwenllian's ear.

'Not only do they look it, but they are also!' she laughed at him.

'You were brilliant on the hunt,' he whispered, smelling her hair as he leaned in.

'You were doing well yourself until you almost got taken out by a tree branch!' she teased.

'That was because I could not take my eyes off you!' he said and instantly regretted showing his feelings so overtly. It was not the first time. Over the months, he had become close with all of Gruffydd's older children, but he and Gwenllian had formed a wonderful friendship. He watched her colour, and her silence disturbed him. Had he said too much? It was unlike her not to give some clever retort. The bard's daughter, Betsan, leaned over to speak to her, and he cursed himself as she moved away, laughing at something the girl had said.

He wanted her more than he thought possible. He could hardly sleep at night for desiring her. He would marry her in a moment but for the dark spectre of Owain ap Cadwgan. If he needed Gruffydd's help, he could not dishonour Gruffydd's commitment to Owain; if he was to regain his kingdom, he needed Gruffydd onside. He should have gone to Llyn weeks ago but found it impossible to tear himself from Gwenllian's side. If he went to Llyn, he had to think of a way of keeping Owain away from her. It was impossible.

'Hey, why the long face?' Gwenllian's brother, Owain, was at his side.

'Ah, I made a fool of myself at the hunt,' he said, covering the fact that he had been thinking about the pretty white mare Owain ap Cadwgan had sent to Gwenllian, with silver in the harness.

'You did rather,' agreed Owain solemnly and then broke out into a great guffaw.

Griffith punched him on the shoulder. 'A fine friend you are!'

'Well, you gave us a good laugh anyway!' he grinned.

Owain was still a youth, but he was as tall as his father now, broad in the shoulders and smart. He had an ease and confidence about him with the ability to make everyone feel comfortable, whatever station in life they held. Griffith found him easier company than his elder brother, Cadwallon, who sometimes tended to arrogance and was too aware of his good looks.

The hall door opened, and one of Gruffydd's men at arms rushed in. Seeing the king dancing, he went straight up to him and spoke quietly. Gruffydd's face changed, and he took long strides across the hall, hastily followed by Aeddan. Angharad's looked tense, and she excused herself from the dancing. Suddenly the atmosphere in the whole place had changed. Within a minute, Aeddan had returned and summoned each man from the teulu as well as Griffith, Howel, and the king's sons. Within ten minutes, all of them were gathered in Gruffydd's chamber.

Gruffydd stood with his back to them, facing the small brazier collecting his thoughts. When he turned, he looked straight at Griffith.

'Griffith, I have had a message from your sister, Princess Nest.'

Griffith looked concerned.

'She would have risked her life to get this message to us.'

Then looking around at his teulu and his sons, he said, 'Men, we are at war with the greatest force ever rallied by an enemy against us. King Henry and Alexander of Scotland are marching towards us, intending to kill every Welsh man, woman, and child. Henry wants to colonise Wales. Even if it costs us our lives, we must stop them.

***

Madog woke at the sound of someone talking outside his door. He grabbed the dagger from under his pillow and crossed the room. It was still dark, but he could tell from the flickering of light through the wood walls that something was happening. He opened the door cautiously and saw two of his band helping a blindfolded man off a horse.

'Who is he?' he asked, pulling a woollen cloak around his shoulders.

'He has come from Bishop Richard. We brought him up from the valley.'

'At this time of night?'

'He said it was urgent.'

'Weapons?'

'We took them off him.'

'Take his blindfold off.'

Rhydian looked around and, seeing Madog, dropped into a kneeling position.'

'Get up,' snarled Madog, 'it is too late in the night for that nonsense. What have you got to say that is so urgent.'

'Bishop Richard needs to see you, lord.'

'That man is a snake. What does he want with me that cannot wait until morning.'

'I do not know, lord, but you are to come immediately. He promises safe passage.'

'Safe passage? That is a joke, is it not? You are to provide me with safe passage?'

'You are not to come with me, lord. You are to make your own way. The bishop does not want us to be seen together.'

Madog considered this, 'What are you not telling me?'

'That is all I know, lord,' said Rhydian licking his dry lips.

Suddenly Madog leapt forward, and Rhydian felt a cold, sharp blade at his neck.'

'What else do you know?'

'Nothing!'

The blade drew some blood, and Rhydian gasped.

'There is to be a war, lord. King Henry is raising troops. He is going to march on Wales.'

'Then why would Bishop Richard want me? I cannot stand the Normans.'

'I do not know.'

'You do not know much, do you? Who else has Bishop Richard called?'

'Only you.'

'Only me? Not Owain ap Cadwgan?'

'No, lord!'

"Not Gronwy ap Owain?'

'No, lord.'

'Not Gruffydd ap Cynan, perhaps?'

'No, lord.'

'No, because those are the men with warriors enough to cause damage and hurt Henry. Not enough to stop Henry perhaps, but certainly to hurt him. He wants to kill the fly that is buzzing around him, but he wants to make sure that someone has already squashed the maggots. Well, I can squash maggots. I have done it for him before, but this time I need witnesses to the offer on the table. And I need secrecy, and for that, I am sorry.'

Rhydian slumped to the ground, his neck gaping with blood that glistened in the light of the rush lamps.

'Get rid of him,' said Madog, 'and then get everyone up. We have work to do. We are going to pay a little visit to Llywarch ap Trahearn.'

***

Hunydd had not slept all night, and from the way her husband tossed and turned, she knew that Maredudd was also desperately anxious. She had sent Maredudd to Owain as night was turning into dawn. Rhydian had not returned, and by mid-morning, she knew in her bones that something was amiss. She trusted her instinct. By the time Maredudd returned with half of Owain's warband, she was operating on adrenalin.

'What did Owain say?'

'We have agreed that he goes to Gruffydd ap Cynan, and they plan a strategy. I stay behind and start the move into the mountains. We will need everyone to go up with whatever they can carry. That means you and the household here as well.'

'The children come with me?'

'They are old enough now to…'

'The children come with me, Maredudd.'

Maredudd was not going to argue the point. He nodded. 'Did Rhydian tell you where we can find Madog?'

'Rhydian has not returned, and I feel something, Maredudd.

Something is not right.'

'Then I must find him by myself.'

'Llywarch will know.'

'You think I should put my neck in the noose? Llywarch hates me.'

'I know his wife, Dyddgu, detests Madog. Maybe I should go. You divide your men to watch the trails from Madog's land to Shrewsbury. Guard the river crossings. I will go with the children and a couple of the men to Llywarch's llys.'

'No, you get ready to go to the mountains. Dyddgu will know nothing, and even if she did, she would not tell you.'

'Women know more than you think, Maredudd. Send a man to let me know where you are. Let him come close to Llywarch's llys but not inside.'

Maredudd groaned. 'I do not like it, Hunydd. Not now when everything is turning against us.'

'Not even Madog would kill a woman, Maredudd. This needs to be done quickly.'

Hunydd dressed for riding hard. She threw a thick brown woollen cloak over herself, and the small group, including the children, made haste to reach Llywarch's llys in Cedewain. There was drizzle in the air, but it did not deter Hunydd, and they made no stop.

Dyddgu had been in the kitchen when Gwir came in to find her.

'You have a guest, mistress.'

'Who?'

'Hunydd, wife of Maredudd ap Bleddyn.'

Dyddgu looked shocked, and her hands brushed away the flour from her tunic.

'It does not pay to look too beautiful, sometimes, mistress,' said Gwir slyly. 'Perhaps pick up baby Robert and take him in with you. She has brought her children, and they are talking to your brood.'

Dyddgu drew herself up to her full height and marched past the old lady into their hall. Hunydd looked plain and drab, but she gave Dyddgu the most wonderful smile as if it was a rare pleasure to be standing in her hall. Dyddgu had met Hunydd before, but she had expected, now that Hunydd had risen in the world, that she would be arrogant and dressed in finery. Hunydd was neither.

'I am sorry to come without sending a message first,' said Hunydd.

Dyddgu heard a roar of laughter and saw Hunydd's boys playing with Cadafael and the younger children. They had a small board with ringed grooves and were trying to flick small wooden balls into dents hollowed out of the wood.

'My husband is not here,' she said, indicating that Hunydd should sit. She wondered why she had said that. 'Forgive me, you must be soaked through, let me take your cloak, and we can dry it in the kitchen. What about the children?'

She called Gwir, who took the wet cloaks, and Dyddgu asked for warm drinks to be brought.

'It is cold enough for May. Cold and wet to be riding. What brings you so far?'

'Not so far. I come to ask you a favour.'

'Me?' said Dyddgu. 'I doubt I can do you a favour given the bad blood now between our husbands.'

'Bad blood between husbands does not mean bad blood between wives.'

Dyddgu saw Hunydd smile at the children playing and warmed to her. There was nothing in Hunydd's eyes that judged the simple Cadafael. She had not once looked around at the damp in their hall nor the flour on Dyddgu's tunic.'

'I have heard good things about you, Dyddgu. You are a good mother, that I can see immediately from your children. You are a good wife, and you run a good home. You speak the truth and are not afraid to say what is on your mind.'

'Thank you. I have heard much the same about you, although your circumstances have changed these days.'

'We all live, and we all die no matter our circumstances. As a mother, my reason for being is to ensure that my children are safe. If my husband is safe, then my family is safe.'

Dyddgu started to look nervous.

'Your husband will come to no harm from mine. What Llywarch did to Iorwedd ap Bleddyn was prompted by Madog. Llywarch needed to avenge his brothers, and now all that is finished. Can I trust you?'

'You can trust me, but what you tell me will find my husband's ears: we have no secrets.'

'If you knew that your husband and my husband's lives were at stake, that a murderer was set to kill them both, would you help me?'

Dyddgu looked shocked. 'Yes, if I could. Who wants to take their lives?'

'Madog ap Rhyrid.'

Dyddgu jumped up in alarm. 'Oh my God, my God, my God. No. Not Madog, not Madog.'

The children all stopped and stared at her. Meredydd, her second son, started towards her, but Dyddgu shook her head, waved him away, and sat with her hand covering her mouth.

Hunydd was stunned, not expecting such a reaction. She leant forward to hold Dyddgu's arm, then knelt before her as tears streamed down the woman's face.

'What is it?' she whispered.

"Llywarch is with him now. They are riding to Shrewsbury.'

"How long ago did they leave?'

'You just missed them. Maybe half an hour ago.'

Hunydd jumped up, 'I will try to save your husband. Which way did they go?'

'Madog said he wanted to stay off the roads, so they were going up through the woods.'

'Can my children stay here with you, please? I must send a message. I promise I will do the best I can for your husband.'

Dyddgu nodded in shock and let the woman run out to her horse, not even bothering with her cloak yelling to her men to stay guard of the llys and protect all inside. Hunydd rode out of the llys, and as she tried to think which way to go, one of her husband's men came out of the bushes.

'Where is Lord Maredudd?' she yelled.

'Not far.'

'Take me to him,' she shrieked and then kicked her horse on for the ride of her life. When she rode up to where Maredudd and his men were hidden near a river crossing, he was shocked to see his wife, hair streaming behind her, soaking wet, her face drawn.

Within five minutes, Maredudd and his party were on their way, but before he left, Hunydd grabbed his arm and held him tight. She seemed to be struggling to say something. She knew she should send him away with what was on her heart, but it was hard for her.

'Be careful, Maredudd,' she said finally with tears in her eyes. 'Do not get yourself killed. I need you.'

For Maredudd, the words were enough. As he rode to prevent murder, he felt ten feet tall.

***

When Hywel saw the messenger from Wales and the seal, his heart started to thud. He read with trembling hands. She was calling in her promise.

'What is it?' asked Lafracoth, seeing his face pale.

'A message from Gwynedd.'

'What?' she saw the seal. 'Has something happened to Gruffydd?'

'It is from the queen.'

'I see that.'

'King Henry has raised a huge army and is marching against them. She asks me for my help.'

'No,' said Lafracoth, 'she has no right to expect your help.'

'My love, I promised her I would come if she needed me.'

'And what about us?'

'How does that change anything with us?'

'Because if you go, you will not come back.'

'My love, my love, of course I will come back.'

'Not if you are dead.'

'I am a warrior, Lafracoth. Every time I go on a campaign for your father, there is the possibility that I might not return.'

'And every time you go my heart breaks; I can hardly sleep or eat.'

'I will be careful,'

'Do not go; I am pleading with you not to go.'

'I made a promise.'

'To her. You made a promise to her.'

Hywel held her close so that he could feel her heart beating.

'What I felt for her is gone, forgotten.'

'But she calls, and you run.'

'I have to honour my promise, my love,' he explained gently.

'I need you here. Hywel. I need you here. I am asking you please not to go. Do not put her before us.'

'I have to go; I gave my word.'

Lafracoth took his hand and pressed it to her below her waist. He looked confused, but then his eyes grew wide.

'Lafracoth?'

'It is ours, and you cannot leave me.'

Hywel pulled her to him, burying his face in her hair. 'My love,' he whispered, his eyes brimming, 'our child. I cannot believe it.'

Suddenly, he broke away and held her in front of him.

'But what will this mean for you? How will you explain it?'

'I will keep it a secret until it is obvious, and then I will go somewhere else for a while.'

'But when it is born?'

'I will return to court with the adopted child of a distant cousin.'

'Your father, though....'

'I will deal with my father, but you see why you cannot go now. You are going to be a father, Hywel.'

Hywel walked to the window and looked out. She came behind him putting her arms around him and pressing herself to him. He spoke slowly, earnestly, but there was a catch in his voice.

'What kind of man does not honour his promises? What kind of warrior does not fight for his country? That is not the kind of man I want our child to see when he looks at me.'

'What kind of man leaves his lover when she is with child, no matter how much she pleads?' Her voice was thick with emotion. 'I am not sure I could forgive you.'

'Lafracoth, you know that my heart is utterly yours and now our child's. Do you think I would take such a thing lightly?'

'I am asking you again not to go. Hywel. Do you not understand the depth of my feelings? I need you here. If you go, every day you are away, with all of my heart, I will suffer, and I will feel resentful that you left me.'

Hywel closed his eyes and groaned gently, 'I have found the love of my life. Do you think I would not prefer to be with you every moment? Yet my honour makes me who I am, and if I had no honour, then we would have no love because Lafracoth, you love me for who I am. Please do not make me less of a man.'

Lafracoth started to cry. Silent sobs wracked her body, making Hywel want to weep as well. Then she stopped, sniffed, and drew herself away from him. There was a hint of iron in her Irish lilt.

'The one thing I ask you, you will not give me. The one thing she asks you, you give to her. Very well then, Hywel. You are free.'

With all the dignity she could summon up, every inch a princess, Lafracoth walked from the room. Having taken Hywel to the heights of joy, she left him plummeting towards the burning rocks of Hell.

***

Owain ap Cadwgan looked gaunt with dark circles under his eyes. He had ridden all the way to Aberffraw in haste. Despite his lack of sleep, when he saw Gwenllian crossing the hall, his face lit up, and she automatically beamed back at him.

He turned to Gruffydd and gave a wry grin. 'Is it possible that your daughter could have become even more beautiful?'

Gruffydd took a breath.

'My daughter is out of bounds, and I would be grateful if we could concentrate on the matters at hand. Unless we extricate ourselves from this mess, we will have no land, no crowns and my daughter, at best, will be sent to a Norman court like Nest was.'

Owain's smile died, 'Well, that is why I have ridden all night.'

When they walked into Gruffydd's chamber, Owain was surprised to see Uchdryd ap Edwin sitting there.

'Uchdryd,' he cried out with genuine warmth as the old man painfully raised himself from the chair and gave Owain a bear hug.

'Owain, it is good to see you. I am sorry it is in these circumstances.'

'And I too, Uchdryd, but I am glad to see you here.'

Gruffydd went to the door, and his teulu, and as many nobles as could make their way to Aberffraw, filed into the room.

'Men,' he started, 'we have on our hands the greatest threat Wales has ever known. King Henry is raising the largest army ever to penetrate Welsh lands, and he intends to destroy every Welsh person, even our babes. Some of us have seen the Normans in action before, and they show no mercy, even to the defenceless. Our threats, friends, lie not only across the border but in the heart of Wales.'

There were murmurs of agreement.

'But we are Welshmen, and Welshmen do not face the possibility of defeat with pounding hearts and shaking hands. We are born to fight to our last breath.'

There was a roar of solidarity.

'We have an inheritance, all of us. We are the land, and the land is us. Our ancestors walked these lands long before Normans, Vikings, Saxons, or Romans stepped onto our shores. Though we have kings and nobles who claim parts of this great, majestic land, steeped in story, the truth is, this land is the inheritance of all those who are Welsh. We warriors have inherited an obligation to pull together and preserve this land for our descendants. Our Welsh descendants.'

Roused, the men pounded their fists and called out their support for such sentiment. Gruffydd put up a hand to silence them.

'It will not be easy, and we will need to give more than we have ever given before, but we were born with clever brains, and Welshmen can think differently, find solutions where there seem none, and use knowledge to even out our chances. Victory will be nigh on impossible, but the Welsh have tackled the impossible before.'

Again, Welsh voices resounded with assent.

'So, the first thing we must do is to take away some of the threats that weaken us. What are those threats? First, the vulnerability of our people. We must take every man, woman, and child up into the high mountains where the Normans will fear to follow us.'

Gruffydd read the mood of the group and saw there was concord.

'This is no easy task, but it is already in motion. Secondly, we need to be united as Welshmen, agreed in our strategy. Henry's policy thus far has been to pit Welshman against Welshman, so we must forget our differences and come together as one in front of our foe. Not now should we worry about petty land disputes but saving all the land from Norman hands.'

There was a loud consensus in the group.

'Do you have any objection to my leading our worthy band of nobles?'

As one, the approval of the men was instantaneous; a mighty roar filled the room.

'Then we must use our wits and devise every possible impediment to Henry's army. We are in a good position because we have details of Henry's intentions. This allows us to prepare ambushes, attack their food carts, and use our longbows to our advantage. There is no value in hand-to-hand fighting in a pitched battle: they will annihilate us, but we can strip the land of resources they would have used and then endeavour to make Henry's efforts 'uncomfortable' for him.'

The men began to confer amongst themselves, exploring ideas, looking at maps, and bringing to the table the intimate knowledge of their lands' geography, to decide where it would be possible to inflict pain on the invading armies.

The meeting was long, but afterwards, food was waiting in the hall. Each of those present knew their duties and who they must reach out to, convince of the sagacity of the plans. They needed to work fast.

Gruffydd moved to sit next to Uchdryd.

'Well, Uchdryd, I wish you well in bringing Gronwy ap Owain into line with the rest of us.'

Uchdryd grinned at that. 'He will come to the table, Gruffydd, and I will present it as an opportunity to cement his authority over the Northeast.'

Gruffydd grimaced.

Uchdryd chuckled and sat back in his chair. 'Come on, sire, your fine speech about burying our differences also meant you.'

'We have to be aligned or Henry will finish us all.'

'Leave it to me. Gronwy is a weak link, but I will appeal to his pride and vanity. I will get his brothers onside.'

'Then you will lead your people to the mountains?'

Uchdryd gave a bark of laughter, 'I will lead them indeed, even though my old bones will protest. I thought all this riding through the night and in the rain was behind me. I was ready to settle by the fire with mead, my wife, and my hounds.'

'Not you, Uchdryd.'

Uchdryd's old eyes twinkled. 'One last adventure then!'

'Godspeed, Uchdryd.'

'And may God look favourably upon you as well!'

The old man made a point of embracing all the children before he left, and when he came to Angharad, he held her tightly.

'Thank God for Gruffydd,' he whispered. 'If any man can save the Welsh, it is him, but you will need to support him even more than you ever have. The time ahead will be long and hard. He will win the minds of the people, but you must win their hearts. Do you understand?'

Angharad nodded. This was the time to pay for her crown.

She walked out with Uchdryd and watched him haul himself into the saddle, and, flanked by a few of his men, he rode out of the llys. A cold chill ran up her spine. She watched all the others departing, her mind racing.

Last to leave was Owain ap Cadwgan, but before he set off, he crossed the courtyard to where Gwenllian was leading her mare, his eyes glinting with rising lust. Her face was glowing, fresh and healthy, her hair shining copper, her mouth soft and sensuous.

'You like your present, Princess Gwenllian?' he asked, reflecting that this young lady was indeed the most beautiful he had seen.

She blushed and looked down, 'I ride her every day, sire, and she gallops like the wind. I thank you. It was extremely generous of you.'

He moved forward and started to rub the nose of the pretty mare, gently eliciting a soft blow of contentment across his hand.

'Not a day goes past without my thinking about you riding across the sands.'

Gwenllian looked away, unsure what to say, and was glad the horse was between them.

'I hope you think of me also,' he persisted.

She looked at him squarely and gave a most delightful smile, 'Sire, my mother has invested much time and energy into trying to make me a lady. My preference, I will be honest, is to wield a sword, spear a boar, or send an arrow high to its target, but my mother firmly believes that her life's work is to create a lady out of me. What then, sire, should a lady reply to such a question?'

Owain burst out laughing, slapping his thigh.

'A superb answer indeed. Your mother should be proud, but there is much of your father about you, Gwenllian ferch Gruffydd! At a time like this, I hope your skills with weaponry are as strong as your repartee, for I warrant we face the greatest challenge to Wales we have ever faced. I look forward to continuing our conversation when we have bested Henry.'

As Griffith came out of the llys chatting to Cadwallon, his eye was immediately drawn to Owain and Gwenllian. Cadwallon noticed the lack of attention to something he was asking and followed Griffith's gaze. Griffith looked irritated, excused himself and marched over to Owain.

'Sorry to interrupt you both, but I wanted to wish you Godspeed, Owain,' he explained.

'And to you, Griffith,' said Owain, embracing his friend. 'Your knowledge of Irish tactics will serve us well, I think. I would like to hope we can do some damage to them. Do you have good men about you?'

"I do. King Gruffydd has allowed us to train with him, and they have learned a lot. They will give a good account of themselves.'

'We will need every sword, spear and bow,' said Owain.

'We will be there.'

'There are two enemies: the Normans and the high mountains. Both formidable.'

'I have already become acquainted with living rough in the Welsh mountains. I spent some time in hiding before coming to Aberffraw, and I agree with you. My eyes are open.'

Owain embraced him again. 'Stay safe, my friend,' he said, then turning to Gwenllian, who had watched the interchange with interest, he bowed. She watched as he strode over to his horse, leaping onto it quickly, and leaving with the small entourage he had brought.

Griffith tried to gauge how Gwenllian had responded to Owain, but immediately after Owain had left, she started interrogating him about what was being planned. Her questions were good ones, as reasoned as any presented at the meeting, and he was taken aback, yet again, by this young woman's competence.

When she had been called by her mother and excused herself, he tried to quell the growing jealousy he felt. Owain and Gwenllian had looked very comfortable in each other's company, too comfortable. Owain was established, was the king of Powys, and a hero to the Welsh. A good man. His friend. Gwenllian would make Owain a perfect wife, and he was stupid to think of coming between them, yet his yearning for her was clouding his every waking thought. He resolved to stop the torture. Who knew what was ahead of them? He had to take control of himself.

***

Madog, accompanied by two of his men, and Llywarch, with two of his, came out of the beech woods cautiously and started down the slope.

'I want the agreement sealed and signed,' Madog said, 'because you cannot trust that bloody bishop further than you can throw him.'

'I will have no part in the murder of Owain ap Cadwgan or Gruffydd ap Cynan. You understand that, do you not?'

'Fair enough. I will do the dirty work, but just for signing your name, I am saving you from death. You realise that, I suppose.'

'After they have got what they want, they can kill us anyway. What is to stop them?' asked Llywarch.

'Wait!' said Madog, squinting into the distance.

'What is it?'

'Horses, down there in the trees at the bottom of the slope. See?'

Llywarch looked and at first saw nothing, then branches moved slightly, and he could see something pale.

'Yes, there is something there,' he agreed.

'Back into the woods. We will make for the ridge and then come back further along.'

They turned their horses smartly and started back towards the woods, but the arrows hit true. Four men of arms fell from their mounts, leaving Madog and Llywarch unprotected. The archers appeared from the trees, arrows pointing at the two men, as Maredudd rode into the clearing, flanked by the weasel-faced Merddyn, Gethin and Gwilym.

'You are in a hurry, both of you,' said Maredudd.

'Kill me if you must, but we are all going to die anyway, so what does it matter?' said Madog.

Maredudd looked unmoved. 'There is no need for anyone else to die today.' Then he turned to his men. 'Tie up Lord Madog, if you will.'

'You are making a big mistake,' protested Madog before he was dragged to the ground, and Merddyn, who had waited for this opportunity for a long time, placed a heavy boot on his face. At the same time, Owain's men Gethin and Gwilym twisted his arms behind his back with a jerk and bound them tightly.

Maredudd looked down at him. 'I do not think we are making any mistake at all,' he said, shaking his head, before turning to the anxious Llywarch, whose mouth was agape.

'Lord Llywarch, we need a few words if you do not mind.'

Maredudd rode towards Llywarch's horse, and they reined in a little distance apart.

'I think I do not need to tell you what King Henry has planned,' said Maredudd in a calm, low voice.

'I know,' said Llywarch, 'but we have always been faithful to our Norman lords and....'

'Stop there!' said Maredudd. 'Henry has made a public announcement that he will annihilate the Welsh. Not for one minute think that it will preclude you and your family. He has more suitors for land than he has land to give, and Wales, in its entirety, would come at a good time for him.'

Llywarch said nothing but looked grim.

'We will go to the mountains where no Welshman will be an enemy of another. Are you with us, Lord Llywarch, or against us?'

Llywarch looked at Maredudd, trying to judge him.

'I helped to kill your brother, Lord Maredudd.'

'It is not in my interests to try to change the unchangeable. I believe that words can resolve most things.'

Llywarch looked back at Madog being led off, hands tied behind his back.

'What will happen to him?'

'It is not my intention to kill him,' Maredudd replied, letting out a deep sigh.

'And will he also be in the mountains?'

'I doubt it.'

Llywarch looked into the distance. 'Violence disgusts me. I will fight if I need to, but I get no satisfaction from spilling blood.'

'Nor I,' said Maredudd. 'But Lord Llywarch, you need to make up your mind.'

'Count me with you,' Llywarch said firmly.

'Make your way back to your family. I am sorry we have injured your men, but they will live. Each home you pass, explain that they must immediately make their way to the mountains with any valuables they have, what food they can bring, their livestock, and warm clothes and blankets. We will have only days to protect ourselves.'

'I will.'

'To save ourselves, we must pass the information to everyone, caution stealth, and work together.'

Llywarch nodded, 'I thank you.'

'And I you. Now make haste.'

Maredudd turned his horse, and within minutes, had vanished into the thick wood from where he had emerged.

Chapter 24: The Mountains (Spring/Summer 1114)

The Welsh defensive action was astounding. Over a few days, items of value too heavy to carry were buried, neighbours with carts assisted neighbours without, and food was collected and carted as far as possible into the mountains, then either hidden or carried on ponies. Across Wales, livestock was driven high into areas where no Norman, Scot, or Fleming could reach them. The priests became the nobility's mouthpiece, ensuring the message to flee to safety reached every home. What was astonishing was that all was done quietly, obediently, and efficiently.

Camps were set up throughout the mountains, shelters built, and, as men wielded axes, women manned cauldrons and pots and ensured a constant supply of good hearty food. The royal family was among the last to leave Anglesey.

'I will not go until I know my people are securely hidden, all of them,' said Gruffydd firmly when Aeddan urged him to make a move.

The priest, Father Luke, came to the king, his face full of concern.

'Sire, you must be safe yourself to lead your people.'

'I will see my people safe first. I left the people of Anglesey to the Normans once before, and I will not leave them again. It sticks in my craw when I think of it.'

'The Lord himself led his flock like a shepherd.'

'In this country, the shepherd comes behind the sheep, Father. I appreciate your endeavours, but I will not change my mind.'

If Gruffydd was immovable, he found his family equally so.

'I will go with you when you leave,' Angharad was adamant, 'and the children insist that they will leave only when I do.'

When, finally, the family made their way into their mountain home, everyone stopped what they were doing, and the camp erupted with cheering. Gruffydd, in his full war gear, looked every inch a great warrior. Queen Angharad looked regal, but they saw her as one of them: she had held their babies, visited their church services, and celebrated their harvests. The royal children filled their hearts with pride: the young warriors looked as formidable as their father, Gwenllian in battle dress, her long red hair twisted into two plaits, and the younger children, sitting erect on their ponies, not complaining and meeting everyone's eye.

Griffith had beheld the reactions of the Welsh to the mesmerising presence of Gruffydd and his family, and he knew he was witnessing something extraordinary. Gruffydd was in total control of his people, their adoration making him seem almost godlike as he rode through them. Yet there was no arrogance, no sense of his thinking himself superior. Their king was like the father they could trust to save them, who would have their best interest at heart. Gruffydd had told them what to do, and they had done it unquestioningly. Here was a man who had been through purgatory to make Gwynedd what it was: he had given tirelessly, cared sincerely, and protected his lands and people. Now, on this mountain, there was a general sigh of relief that their king, with his experience, wisdom, and raw energy, was among them. Griffith was humbled and awed. One day, he vowed, that will be me.

Over the following days: scouts were sent to watch the enemy's progress; messengers were sent to various parts of the mountains, where people had settled; and plans were made. Angharad and Gwenllian moved freely, offering reassurance, sitting, and participating in whatever activity people were involved with. At night, they were all gathered around the fire listening to the bards, singing, or playing whatever instruments they had brought with them. Children would wriggle on their parent's laps until they fell asleep or try to stay awake, spellbound by the stories despite heavy eyelids.

Gwenllian would inevitably find her way to Griffith's side, and they would talk and laugh as if they had known each other for years. No matter what he had resolved, he struggled to keep his passion for her in check.

From Gruffydd and his teulu, Griffith watched and learnt.

True to form, the Welsh came out of nowhere: attacking the enemy when they least expected it, doing real harm, and unsettling the troops. When the Normans made camp at night, no matter what guards were posted, the Welsh would slide in among them, set fires, steal horses, cut throats, and then vanish into thin air. Sometimes Gruffydd would lead the attacks, sometimes he would allow others to, and Griffith himself led an ambush on troops attempting a river crossing.

Working his craft alongside other Welsh lords was exhilarating for Griffith: they accepted him, he felt truly Welsh, and his urge to overcome his enemy and restore his inheritance only grew. His ambush party laughed as they made their way back through the mountains with booty and horses, although, in truth, the fine Norman steeds were inadequate for the kind of territory they had to cross.

Shortly after the triumph at the river, Griffith was talking to the king, Cadwallon, and some of the Welsh lords. Gruffydd was sharpening his sword, which always made him think more clearly. Suddenly there were cries of welcome, and Cadwallon jumped up. Griffith looked up to see Angharad drop the pot she was carrying and run towards the riders who had entered the camp, dirty, unshaven, and sweating from their onerous journey. Hywel slid off his horse, and Angharad threw her arms around him before he uttered a word.

'You came,' she said, her eyes full of tears. 'Oh Hywel, you came, and we are so glad to welcome you back.'

He felt a smile spread across his face.

Suddenly, Hywel was mobbed by the royal children, slapping him on the back, pulling him, punching him on the shoulder, and all talking at once.

Gruffydd had put down his sword, and Griffith watched him as his wife threw herself at Hywel, and Hywel's arm had automatically encircled her waist. Gruffydd had blanched, his eyes fixed, but he calmly strode across to the group, people parting to let their king pass. For a split second, there was a hush as the two men looked at each other, searching each other's faces. Then Hywel dropped to one knee, Gruffydd grabbed him by his mail and hauled him up into a mighty embrace.

'You are a sorry sight, Hywel, you and these brutes you have brought with you, but, by God, I am glad to see you. Come, man, you look like you could do with a drink and something in your stomach.'

Hywel's face flooded with relief, and his smile lit up his weary, dirty face.

Later, when things had settled in the early evening, everyone crowded around the fire to listen to the news that Hywel brought. Those who were at the front relayed messages back to those who were sitting out of earshot.

'I came on an Irish trading ship, first to Anglesey. No sign of anyone there, in fact, no sign of the Normans this side of the mountains at all,' he pointed to the West and North, and there was a collective sigh of relief. 'It was like a ghost country, eerie, not even a chicken, only the wind blowing through empty buildings. Even the boats were gone.'

'It had to be done,' said Gruffydd softly.

'Then we went onto Chester, and that is where it got interesting. I slipped in undercover as an Irish trader. They are struggling to get enough food to the Norman troops. Alexander and the Earl of Chester have set up camp at Pennant Machnwy, and Henry has moved his forces to Tomen y Mur.'

'Yes, we have been watching them. We have harried them as well.'

'The Irish sailors spread the word that King William Rufus was defeated at Tomen y Mur and that it is a haunted place. That will get to his troops eventually.'

Gruffydd threw back his head and laughed.

'That was your idea?'

'Not entirely. I remember Uchdryd did something similar when the bastards were camped in Anglesey.'

Gruffydd's face looked strained. 'I never forget what they are capable of.'

Hywel nodded. He also remembered all too well.

'There is talk that Alexander wants to return to Scotland, and he is putting pressure on Henry to make peace. His troops are anxious to get back to their land and can see no way of breaking us.'

'Well, he can whistle for his peace. As if we could trust them!' Gruffydd said stoutly to mutters of agreement from the gathered Welsh.

'Apparently, Gronwy has led the lords from Eastern Gwynedd and created havoc for the Normans. I do not like the man, but he has made their lives sheer misery. He has dug pits to prevent their carts from crossing, felled trees to block their way, dammed rivers to flood their route.'

'Yes, all the lords from all parts of Wales have been doing the same, and we are determined to stick together.'

'Henry has trouble brewing in Normandy again. He's short of coin, and his lords are squealing. He underestimated the cost and length of this campaign against you.' Hywel's words were a tonic for those assembled.

'There was talk about Madog,' Aeddan said. 'They say he was sent to Bishop Richard in Shrewsbury blind and castrated as a sign of what the Welsh will do to traitors.'

'Owain ap Cadwgan took his revenge, I heard,' Hywel agreed.

'I am glad of it. What he did to Cadwgan and Iorwedd was the act of a madman,' Gruffydd commented with sadness.

There was silence for a while, and then Griffith asked Hywel about Ireland.

'How is King Murtagh?'

'Still campaigning. He looks half-dead, but nothing stops him.'

'And Lafracoth?'

Hywel's face grew vexed. He looked down at his hands, controlling himself.

'She is well. Very much involved in the changes to the church.'

Angharad passed a look to Gruffydd.

'Well, Hywel, I think you and your men need a decent night's rest because there is work to do tomorrow, and we leave at dawn. All the men on different parts of the mountains will make an attack on the Normans at the same time.'

'That is why we are here,' replied Hywel enthusiastically, despite looking dead on his feet. Since leaving Lafracoth, he had hardly slept.

Gruffydd looked up at the sky. 'I just hope the rain keeps off, or the archers will complain about their aim with wet strings.'

They looked up at the star-studded night, and Hywel wondered if Lafracoth was also looking up. She loved the night sky.

After most of the group had retired for the night, Griffith moved over to where Gwenllian sat with her brothers. They looked serious.

'What is going on?'

It was Owain who spoke.

'Having Hywel back has dredged up some old wounds.'

Griffith raised his eyebrows.

'You will probably hear at some point anyway.' Owain turned to his siblings for their assent, and they nodded.

'Gronwy hates my parents. He is a traitorous pig. Amongst other things he did, he sent men to infiltrate the llys and spread rumours about our mother and Hywel.'

Griffith looked shocked. 'Is that why Hywel left?'

'Pretty much.'

'But there would have been nothing in it.'

'Of course not,' glowered Owain, 'it was unthinkable, but Hywel was determined that he did not contribute to the lies Gronwy was creating.'

'But Hywel is back here now.'

'Of course, he is. He is a Welshman.'

'A popular Welshman by the looks.'

'Yes, a truer man there never was.'

'After this is all over,' said Cadwallon, 'we will make Gronwy pay.'

'But he is kin?' said Griffith.

'He would kill our parents in a heartbeat,' said Cadwaladr. 'I loathe him. I almost lost my brother because of him.'

Owain's eyes flicked across to Cadwaladr, surprised at his brother's admission of concern for him.

'In fairness,' he said, 'I do not think Uncle Gronwy intended to kill me. It was me that attacked his men.'

'You should have seen it,' said Cadwaladr to Griffith. 'You know how Owain is all about doing the right thing? Well, we were feasting some poor bishop who thought he was there for a nice evening, good food and good wine, when suddenly, Owain leaps up on the table and runs, yes runs, through the platters, the wine, everything, and jumps on two men whom we found out later were Gronwy's spies.'

Griffith cocked his head to one side, eyes wide.

'Next, here comes Gwenllian in hot pursuit, her beautiful gown hitched up to her waist, flying through the venison, duck, best Welsh lamb, scattering pitchers the lot, and she is up there, with the world having a good look at her legs.'

'Cadwaladr!' remonstrated Gwenllian, 'that was not quite how it was. I thought they were going to kill Owain, and, as I remember, you were right behind me.'

'Yes, but only to pull your robe down and avoid your shame!' Cadwaladr teased, and Gwenllian poked him in the ribs.

'What happened?' asked Griffith, trying to imagine the scene.

'Hywel happened, thank the Lord,' explained Gwenllian. 'He and Aeddan jumped on Gronwy's men, but not before they had done some damage.'

'A scratch, only,' said Owain, 'but I admit I did bite off a bit more than I could chew on that occasion.'

'But what did the spies do that caused you to attack them?' persisted Griffith.

'They were spreading the rumours.'

'Nobody would believe that anyway,' said Griffith firmly.

'That's the funny thing with rumours,' said Cadwallon, 'once somebody says something like that, people keep it in the back of their minds, and suddenly the rumour becomes more plausible when that person does something they do not like. Lies are hard to counter.'

'There's truth in that,' said Griffith. 'My own family has experienced enough rumours.'

As the camp settled for the night, Griffith watched the king holding out his hand to lead his wife from the fire to their humble shelter. He was a man in his prime who garnered respect, was clearly a warrior, and had a beautiful wife and family. If someone were inclined to jealousy, he could understand how they might try to bring about the downfall of such a man, such a family.

Griffith knew that Gruffydd had come to Rhys ap Tewdwr before his father's death and pleaded with him to join forces against the Normans. Had his father understood the feelings of the Welsh and gone along with the young warrior, how different things might have been for his own family.

***

With their breath smoking in the early dawn, the Welsh made their way to the points they had agreed. Owain ap Cadwgan was in fine fettle, whistling as he prepared himself for action.

Meanwhile, Hunydd helped her husband to put on his armour. 'I do not feel good about this,' she said. 'Stay back from the fight, Maredudd.'

'Hunydd,' said Maredudd gently, touching her face with his hand, 'I am the leader of Owain's warband. I can hardly send them off without throwing myself into the fray.'

'You are the leader of his warband for your mind, not for your skill in battle,' said Hunydd.

'Thank you for reminding me,' said Maredudd. 'That is not a thing to say to your husband before you farewell him.'

'Maredudd, I just want you to use your sense. Let the youngsters take risks. I really wish you did not have to go at all, but I understand you must.'

'It will be as it has been every other time,' Maredudd explained. 'We will go in quickly, do the damage, stay out of range of their arrows where we can, use stealth to slit a few throats and then vanish into the mountains. The difference is that everybody will be doing it at the same time.'

She watched him leave, and she shivered on the inside. All day long, she busied herself with the other women at their camp, arranged for them all to pray at the time that their men would be assaulting the Normans, and

418

tried to distract herself. No matter what she did, she could not rid herself of the knot of fear that gripped her stomach. Her instinct was a blessing and a curse. When something was not right, she felt it in her gut, and an ice-cold grip seemed to be twisting her insides that morning.

Dyddgu came across to her, and they sat for a while, watching the children playing in a small stream, making dams, and catching frogs.

'They are late, coming back,' she said, biting the side of her finger.

'Not so late. They will be back before dark, though.' Hunydd squashed her own fear.

'Did you hear how big the Norman army is?' Dyddgu continued. 'Our men can chip away at them, but they can always bring more Flemish mercenaries if they want. This will drag on and on.'

Hunydd looked sharply at Dyddgu, 'We do not have much choice, do we?'

'Llywarch says that the Earl of Chester wants to negotiate for peace?'

Hunydd grabbed the other woman's arm. 'And how does Llywarch know such a thing?'

Dyddgu was shocked at such a violent reaction from someone she had begun to think of as a friend. 'When he went over to Gruffydd ap Cynan's camp to finalise arrangements for today, they were talking about it.'

'Gruffydd would never sue for peace with the Earl of Chester, surely,' said Hunydd loosening her grip.

'Apparently he scoffed at it and said you could not trust the Normans, and they could whistle for their peace.'

'There we are then,' said Hunydd with a sniff, but her brain was whirring through the information given.

Dyddgu said no more, and they stayed deep in their own thoughts until they heard the horn of the men returning.

Owain ap Cadwgan came first, grinning broadly, and the rest of the men whooped as they came in, seeking out their families.

Hunydd searched for her husband, who should have been at Owain's side, but there was no sign of him. She grabbed her sons and whispered urgently, 'Go see if you can find your father, quick.'

She ran alongside the men riding into camp, but there was no sign of Maredudd, and finally, only two or three men were trailing behind.

'I must have missed him, surely,' she reasoned, turning back towards the main camp. Then she saw her two children running towards her.

'Did you find him?'

'No, he's not here.'

She did not wait another moment. She lifted her skirts and ran towards Owain ap Cadwgan. He heard her footsteps and turned. As he saw her, his face looked grave.

'Hunydd,' he said, taking her by the shoulders, 'I am sorry. Something has happened to Maredudd.'

She thought she would faint, but he was still speaking, and she had to listen. Was he dead? Was he captured? 'Please, please God, no,' she prayed silently as she watched Owain ap Cadwgan form his words.

'Do you understand, Hunydd?' he was saying.

She shook her head. All the anxiety she had suppressed since Rhydian had brought news of Henry's intentions now overwhelmed her.

'They are bringing him up the mountain slowly.'

'Is he dead?' she stuttered.

'No, I told you, the wound will heal, but he has lost a lot of blood. He is not conscious.'

'I can sew him up,' she cried wildly. 'Where is he? I can sew him up. I can stop him bleeding. I need to sew him up.'

She felt gentle hands take her towards her shelter. Dyddgu was at her side.

'Llywarch is with him, and his men will be gentle. Rest until they get him here because you will not sleep tonight. I will get boiling water and linen. I will send the children out for moss and spiderwebs before it gets dark. I have honey and mead as well in case he should wake. Maybe you should have a little mead.'

Hunydd shook her head, but her thoughts were clouded.

'I will find the healer,' Dyddgu was saying, 'and she will be ready for him. Do not worry, Hunydd.'

'I need to sew him up,' Hunydd spoke as if in a daze, slurring her words.

'If sewing is to be done, the healer will do it. Lie down now.'

Hunydd's head spun as she lay on the makeshift bed they used. 'He will need clean sheets, and we have none,' she said. 'No clean sheets.'

Dyddgu sent someone else for the healer and returned to sit with her friend. She did not want anyone to see Hunydd like this and hoped it would pass. She held Hunydd's hand. The woman who had always seemed so capable looked frayed and vulnerable. She watched until the healer came and persuaded Hunydd to drink something, which seemed to calm her. Then the three women waited in silence for Llywarch and Maredudd to return.

***

Across the mountain, there was jubilation in Gruffydd's camp. Not a single man had been injured in the attack, and the following day, Alexander of the Scots sent the expected word that he wanted to make peace negotiations. Llywarch had arrived in the camp to bring news of Owain ap Cadwgan's attack and was pleased to see Gruffydd had stuck by his word in his adamant response to the Scots' offer. It was quite late when he arrived, so he stayed overnight.

'What happened to Maredudd?' asked Gruffydd on hearing he had been injured.

'It was a three-prong attack from our side,' replied Llywarch. 'Owain was to attack coming in from the trees and set fire to the supply wagons; I was to provide the cover with the archers; and, when Owain went in, Maredudd and his men were to go for the horses. I am not sure what went wrong, but Maredudd took his men too early, I think, and they were met by Normans, who had spotted them and were ready for them. There was hand-to-hand fighting, and Maredudd and a couple of the men were wounded.'

'Will he pull through?'

'Yes, he bled like a stuck pig, passed out on the way back to camp but was sitting up on his bed giving orders this morning as if nothing was amiss.'

Gruffydd smiled. 'It would take more than a Norman blade to put him out of action. He is an unlikely-looking warrior compared to his brothers, but he has outlived them, all the same.'

'Hunydd went into shock when she heard, but she is fussing around him like an old hen now.'

They all smiled.

'What next?' asked Llywarch.

'More of the same,' said Gruffydd. 'Give the Normans no peace. Harass them at night, then harass them during the day. We will get archers down there tomorrow night to send in some fire arrows. In a couple of days, we will return a few of their horses to them, dragging fire mats through the camp. Have you heard from Gronwy?'

'Successful so far. Uchdryd is advising him, and Gronwy is also creating chaos on his side.

'Good, I am glad of it,' said Gruffydd, picking a burr off his brown woollen tunic.

'Owain asked me to deliver something to Princess Gwenllian,' he said, pulling a small, embroidered cloth bag from under his leather jerkin.

'Ah,' said Gruffydd sighing, 'nothing has been agreed, you know, but he keeps sending her gifts.'

'Oh, I see,' said Llywarch confused. 'I had thought there had been a betrothal.'

'Something had been discussed, but I want this fighting over and done with first before we confuse issues. None of us may be alive if things go badly. Do you want me to take it for her, or do you want to give it to her yourself?'

'I said I would deliver it into her hand with a message.'

'Well, perhaps wait until you see her by herself,' said Gruffydd, not wanting to flaunt gifts in front of people who had given up so much.

***

Gwenllian was by the fire with her brothers and Griffith, all still delighted at how the previous day had gone. Griffith noticed she seemed strangely subdued.

'Are you alright?' he asked her quietly, thinking perhaps she was sad at not being able to join them when they made their attack.

'I am just a bit tired,' she said, stifling a yawn and stretching her back. 'I have been nursing a baby whose mother is sick and walking the little thing around all day so that my back and head ache.'

'You do look very pale,' said Griffith, concerned.

'Yes, I think I will turn in for the night,' she said, bidding her good nights and leaving the fire. Griffith saw her walk away, but she started to sway. He jumped up and caught her as her legs were giving way beneath her. She was shaking all over, her eyes fluttering.

He pulled her to him and held her tightly.

'I am alright,' she insisted, even though her head was swimming, and she could barely see. 'Truly, I am fine.'

'You are not fine,' said Griffith. 'You seem hot!' He put his lips to her forehead.

'You are burning,' he said. 'Here, let me carry you to your shelter.'

At that moment, Llywarch came down to the main fire, and what he saw stopped him in his tracks. Griffith ap Rhys was kissing the princess openly in front of everyone, and then he scooped her up and carried her into a shelter. He was shocked: this was not seemly behaviour. He did not see Griffith leave the shelter moments later to look for Bethan, who would care for the princess. Llywarch had already retraced his steps to the king.

'It might be better if you give this to the princess,' he said. 'I will be leaving early in the morning, and I think she has retired for the night.'

Gruffydd held out his hand and took the little pouch.

'Thank you. Do you want me to pass on the message?'

Llywarch hesitated but gave Owain's message anyway. 'Only that Owain ap Cadwgan hopes that they will be able to meet again soon once things are back to normal.'

Gruffydd nodded.

'As we all wish,' he said.

***

Hunydd had returned to her usual self, but she had had a fright. The healer's medicine had calmed her, and she continued to take it: it seemed to help her think clearly. Never before had she lost control of her wits like that, and she was determined it would never recur.

Maredudd was also recovering well, although still weak from loss of blood, and she had resolved that this would never happen to him again.

Finding a time when they were alone, she spoke to him earnestly, 'I am not going to keep on about how you should not have been in the fight, but Maredudd, you need to use your brain. You are too old for this nonsense.'

'We are at war, Hunydd,' he gently remonstrated.

'We do not have to be: at least there is no need for Owain and Powys to be in the war, I am sure.'

He gave a sad laugh.

'Do not mock me, Maredudd,' she glared at him with smouldering dark eyes. 'I know more than you think.'

What do you mean?' asked Maredudd, humouring her.

'Llywarch has heard that the Earl of Chester and Alexander of Scotland are going to Gruffydd ap Cynan with offers of peace.'

Maredudd blinked at her, surprised. 'How do you know?'

'I heard it from Dyddgu.'

'He will never agree,' responded Maredudd thoughtfully.

'What if Owain thinks he might, and what if you negotiate a peace for Owain and Powys with King Henry? Owain would not want his people trapped between a Welsh force and a Norman one.'

'Hunydd, Hunydd. What would happen then, do you think? Henry would turn his whole force against Gruffydd ap Cynan and the north. Gronwy would go over to the Normans, and most of Gwynedd would be destroyed.'

'Why do you care?' she turned on him. 'Do you not suppose that you should be putting Powys first, and if Gruffydd ap Cynan was destroyed, Powys might be able to go back to the time when it ruled Powys and Gwynedd.'

'Hunydd, enough!' said Maredudd more sharply than he meant. 'You are forgetting that Owain is all but betrothed to Gruffydd ap Cynan's daughter.'

'What I will not forget is that my husband was nearly killed. What I will not forget is that Henry never gives up. Look at Normandy. He goes back there year after year; he does not give up. If he seems to win against Wales, if we agree to a penalty payment, he gets his victory and money for Normandy. I am telling you, husband, that Henry will never give up. Think about it while you are lying there wounded!'

Hunydd stormed out of the shelter, nearly pulling the entrance flap from its fastening, leaving Maredudd to his thoughts. The cut across his chest pained him, and he felt old and stupid. He had led the men too early. He realised it as soon as he started the approach to the enemy camp. So many Normans had emerged, and he had spurred forward, trying to mow them down, to find a space. A sword had slammed into his back, taking his breath from him, but thank the Lord, his mail had saved him. As he slumped forward, clutching his horse's mane, another sword had sliced towards his neck. The horse had skittered sideways, and this time the blow took him in the chest, ripping his mail apart. Blinding pain had coursed through him, but he had gritted his teeth and tried to hold on. His men had grouped around him, shielding him. Suddenly, a rain of Welsh arrows flew over them, stunning the men attacking him and leaving a swathe of wounded ahead. He had not hesitated and veered away towards safety. If he had been younger, he would have deflected that blow with his shield, but he had been too slow. How any of them came out alive was a miracle.

He adjusted his position against the pillow and winced at the pain. He hated wearing the thick mail, which rubbed at his neck and shoulders, but it had saved him. Strangely, Maredudd was grateful he had been wounded because, otherwise, it would have been even harder to face Owain. He had let Owain down. He considered what Hunydd had said, and there was sense in it. That first time, when he had taken scouts to the fringes of the Norman camp, he had been awestruck. In the twilight, hundreds of cooking fires lit up the Norman camp. Henry's men seemed countless. How could they defeat such an army?

He did not believe for a moment that Gruffydd ap Cynan would agree to peace, and he was certain Owain, the Welsh hero, would not. Then again, what if a seed of doubt could be put into Owain's mind? No, he thought again. He is too much in love with the idea of marriage to Gruffydd ap Cynan's daughter to contemplate such a departure from the Welsh alliance.

When Llywarch returned from Gruffydd's camp, Owain was away on another foray against the foe. Llywarch had come to see how Maredudd fared. He recounted the tale of the quest for peace by the Normans and Scots, and Gruffydd's outright refusal.

'Who else knows this?' asked Maredudd in a low voice.

'Only you and my wife, Dyddgu.'

'Then I will ask you to swear that you and your wife will not repeat this to anyone else.'

Llywarch looked at him quizzically.

'It will be for all our goods,' he said. 'Will you swear?

Llywarch hesitated. Something was amiss, but he gave his word.

'Did the princess like her gift?' asked Maredudd and it was then that Llywarch divulged something that made everything much easier.

Chapter 25: Loss (August 1114)

Angharad woke with a start. It was dark, but somebody was whispering her name.

'What is it?' she asked, jumping up too quickly and throwing on a tunic and cloak as she left the shelter. Her heart started to pound, and she wondered if the Normans had found their way to the camp, but all seemed quiet.

Bethan was standing with a small candle.

'What is it?' asked Angharad, composing herself.

'It is the Princess Gwenllian,' said Bethan, 'she is sick, really sick, lady, and not in her senses.'

Angharad took Bethan's candle and started to run towards Gwenllian's shelter. She found her daughter tossing and turning in a pool of sweat, totally delirious.

'Cadwallon,' she kept muttering repeatedly, then she screamed, 'Cadwallon, behind you!'

'Shhh, shhh,' Angharad crooned. 'You are alright. I am here. I am here.'

'Cadwallon,' she screamed again. 'No! No!'

Angharad's mouth was dry with terror, her pulse racing, but she breathed deeply to calm her thoughts.

'Have you called the healer?' she turned to Bethan.

'She has been mistress and has gone back to make up some brew for her, but she fears the worst.'

Angharad's hands flew to her mouth, and a sob escaped her.

'Do not kill him. He is a child,' the girl screamed as she tried to escape the bed.

Angharad stroked her head and helped her back against the pillows.

'They have my hair, and they have betrayed me,' the girl moaned, eyes wide and seeing nothing.

'How did she get like this?' her distraught mother turned again to Bethan.

'She has been minding the baby of a sick woman, a family that came up late from near Abergele. The baby died this evening, mistress, and I think Gwenllian has caught a sickness from them.'

Angharad felt as if she had been stabbed. She tried to keep control of herself.

'We cannot have illness in the camp,' she said. 'We must separate Gwenllian, the family, you, and me from everyone else.'

Bethan stared at her, and it took a moment for her to comprehend the gravity of what her mistress was saying.

'I will need to get my things and tell Gruffydd.'

Angharad ran back across to where Gruffydd was sleeping and touched him lightly. He immediately pulled the knife from under his pillow and sat bolt upright.

'What is it?'

Angharad tried to quell the panic in her voice, tried to sound hopeful as she explained while Gruffydd hastily dressed himself. His face did not conceal the anguish he felt at her words. This was a grave blow.

Agreeing to the sense behind the precautions immediately, he carried a few of Angharad's things across to Gwenllian's shelter. She saw that his hands were shaking. He took one look at his daughter and let out a gasp. A soft-faced and grandmotherly old woman was at her side, attempting to spoon medicine into the girl's mouth. When she had finished, most of it had dropped on Gwenllian's shift as the girl's head tossed from side to side.

'She will not drink,' the woman explained, her expression grim.

'Can you do something?' asked Gruffydd.

The woman's eyes were compassionate, but she hesitated. 'We can pray, but the fever is terrible indeed.'

The parents seemed to be waiting for her to say something else, but she did not know how she could deliver such a message; this was the king.

'I am sorry,' the old woman stumbled over her words, 'I have seen many like this. I think she cannot last more than a couple of hours.'

'The sword is sharp, and they have my hair,' moaned Gwenllian.

'Oh, God!' muttered Gruffydd and then knelt at his daughter's side, speaking softly, 'Cariad, we are here with you. Nobody is going to hurt you.'

She seemed to be still for a moment. Gruffydd put his big cold palm on her forehead and closed his eyes. Then he stood and motioned to Angharad to step outside.

Tears rolled down his wife's face, and she hastily tried to wipe them away.

'I am being punished,' said Gruffydd in agony, 'I am being punished for the lives I have taken. I sent fire into Henry's camp, and now my child is burning.'

'No, no, no, Gruffydd,' his wife cried. 'Do not think such a thing. This is no punishment for anything you have done. Gwenllian cannot die. She will not.'

'I would give my life for hers,' said Gruffydd. 'Our beautiful daughter. There must be another healer, someone who can help her. She is such a fighter. This woman does not know what strength our daughter has. She gives her no chance.' The last words caught in his throat, and he looked away.

Angharad, frantic, grasped at the notion of someone else being able to do something. 'The woman who saved me when I was ill. The woman from the woods. Is she here?'

Gruffydd turned back to her sharply, clutching at some hope. 'Surely she is, if she lives. I have not seen her, but there are so many people here.'

'Yes, I have seen her,' Bethan pushed herself forward: there was no time for formalities in this emergency, 'but they say she is a druid.'

Gruffydd roared with frustration now. 'Druid or no druid, find her. Wake the whole camp if you need to. She saved our queen; she can do the same for Gwenllian. Be quick.'

Bethan did not hesitate but ran off across the camp while Gruffydd lifted the flap of the shelter to let in the cool night air. He half-pulled the blanket off his daughter, but still, she was burning like fire.

'Griffith,' the sick girl cried out. 'Griffith, do not leave!'

Angharad and Gruffydd looked at each other.

'We are here, Gwenllian,' said Angharad, wiping her daughter's forehead with a wet rag. Gruffydd almost choked to see the depth of the motherlove in her face.

'Griffith!' the girl screamed.

Bethan was quick. She returned with the woman who so long ago had saved Gwenllian's life and the life of her mother. She was white-haired now and walked with a slight stoop, but her eyes were bright, giving the impression that her years were carried lightly.

'Thank you,' Angharad said and would have spoken again, but the woman lifted her hand. She came straight to where the sweating grey-faced girl was tossing and turning. She drew back the blanket completely.

Gwenllian's shift was dripping wet. The woman felt for her heartbeat, prised apart the girl's lips to look into her mouth, and felt her forehead. The girl's parents stood motionless, waiting for the woman's words, but she did not speak.

Gwenllian yelled out something incomprehensible, and the woman took her hand. She started as a cold shiver coursed through her old body, leaving her gasping, losing her breath. The vision she had, gripped her, and she dropped the girl's hand as if it was a burning coal.

Angharad's desperation consumed her, and she grabbed the woman by the wrist, 'You are not only a healer. You see the future. Can you save my daughter? Can you stop her from dying? Will she recover from the fever?'

The woman turned slowly to the wretched parents. Her eyes were distant for a moment, glazed and fixed, but then it was as if she returned from wherever she had been. She took a deep breath, but her voice was husky.

'I can foresee some things; that is my burden. Not all things are clear; sometimes, there are different paths that can be taken. You asked me whether she could recover from the fever. Unless we get the fever down, she will not survive.'

'But she is a strong girl,' Gruffydd argued, distraught.

'I feel her strength ebbing. The fever is very bad.'

'Please,' said Angharad pleading, wringing her hands.

'There is one thing we can try, but you may not agree,' advised the woman finally, looking at Angharad.

'Anything,' said Gruffydd, and his fraught wife nodded.

'We take her to the stream and immerse her.'

'But the stream is freezing; it will kill her!' protested the agonised mother.

'It will take the heat from her body more quickly than any other way, and she might have enough strength left to recover,' the woman explained.

'We will do it,' Gruffydd overrode his wife's objections. 'We will do it! I will carry her.'

'No,' said Angharad appalled at the drastic suggestion, 'this is madness. You will surely kill her. The shock of the cold will be too much.'

Gruffydd grabbed his wife's arm. 'If we do nothing, she will die. Is that what you want? Have you felt her? Have you felt her heartbeat?'

Angharad nodded wordlessly.

Gruffydd lifted the girl tenderly, wrapped a blanket around her limp body, and carried her across to the little waterfall beside the camp. He waded into the stream as far as he could before gently lowering Gwenllian into the water. As she was submerged, she let out a plaintive cry and pulled herself into a foetal position. Angharad let out a forlorn moan and bit into her hand to see her daughter so. Gruffydd lifted Gwenllian out and submerged her again. This time she was gasping for breath and shaking violently. Gruffydd pulled her dripping body as close as he could to his, and Angharad carefully wrapped the blanket around her. Gwenllian's teeth chattered, and she shook uncontrollably as they swiftly returned to her shelter.

'You must dry her now and keep her warm,' said Gruffydd. Angharad sensed her husband trying to separate his emotional self, falling back on the safety of giving orders.

He stepped outside and found the priest, Father Luke, with Bethan. It was still dark, and the camp was still.

'Keep your distance, Father,' said Gruffydd.

Bethan, shamefaced, stepped back from the priest.

'Whatever this is, we must contain it. Bethan, the queen, and I have been close to my daughter. I am not sure who has been with the mother and baby who brought the sickness into the camp, but we must keep them apart from others, or it will run through us all.'

'Is it bad?' the priest asked, eyeing the haunted face of the king, who seemed to have aged overnight.

'It is bad,' admitted Gruffydd, his voice resonating with emotion, 'but my girl is a fighter.'

'I was there when she was born,' said the priest, and he held the despondent father's shoulder despite the warning. 'We must pray as we did then.'

'Then pray with us, Father,' said Gruffydd, dropping to his knees as if he had no strength left in him.

Inside the shelter, Angharad and Bethan had changed the bedding and put the girl into a new soft shift. The mother held her daughter as she shook, wracked by cold. The healer moved to her, held her wrist, and touched her forehead.

'Is there nothing else you can do?' asked Angharad plaintively.

The healer turned to her basket, pulling a stone jar and a spoon from a woven basket. 'We must try to make her drink this,' she said. As the stopper was removed, Angharad remembered the smell from when she herself had almost died of a fever; her stomach churned.

The healer tried to spoon the medicine into the girl's mouth, but Gwenllian's teeth were chattering so violently that she could not manage it.

'Let me try,' said Angharad. Sliding her arm behind the shivering girl's shoulders, she started to croon a lullaby. Whether responding to her mother's voice or the warmth of her body, Gwenllian seemed to shake less forcibly. Angharad gently prised her lips open, stroking her child's throat until, spoonful by spoonful, the girl began to drink. Angharad cradled her, still singing, until Gwenllian closed her eyes, and her head lolled back onto the pillow. The mother turned to the healer, alarmed.

'Is she slipping away?' she whispered.

'Now is the crisis point,' the woman said. 'We have done all we can. Her body is fighting the best it can; it is not an easy battle. If she slips away, she knows you are with her.'

'Oh God, be merciful,' Angharad prayed, moving in to listen to the ever-shallower breathing of her daughter.

Outside, Griffith had been sleepless and, getting up, had made his way across to the fire which had burned through the night. He saw the torches outside Gwenllian's shelter, and with a cold fear gripping his stomach, he ran to where he saw Gruffydd and Bethan knelt in prayer with the priest. His heart almost stopped, and he pulled at Bethan's arm.

'Stay away from me,' she said urgently. 'I might be carrying the sickness. I was with Gwenllian.'

Griffith stepped a few paces back.

'Is she dead?' He felt a wave of nausea wash over him.

'Not yet. She is very sick.'

Griffith dropped to his knees and began to pray silently but fervently.

A palest pink line stretched across the sky when Gruffydd returned through the leather flap to the little makeshift shelter where his daughter lay, white and still on her pillows. Her long red hair was damp and hung around her. There was nothing of her usual vibrance, nothing of her boundless energy: it was as if she had given up her spirit.

Angharad looked up and moved so Gruffydd could kneel beside his daughter. He held her slim hand in his and suppressed a sob as he felt her cold fingers.

'Gwenllian,' his voice was a dry whisper, 'do not leave us, Cariad. How could we do without you? Stay with us. You have your life ahead of you, and what a life it will be. It is too early to go. Stay, and you can ask me for anything. I will give it to you, I promise.'

How long he held her hand as he prayed, he did not know. He was unaware of anything else. He found himself thinking of all the times he had forbidden his daughter to join her brothers in the practice yard, how often he had berated her for being unladylike and realised how futile such concern was. He thought of her lively personality and sharp brain, how she always made him laugh; the thought of losing her was more than he could bear. He felt Angharad tugging at his sleeve and looked up. Gwenllian's eyes were open.

'Can I hear bees, Father?' she asked, her voice hoarse and weak.

'Bees?' Angharad asked as if it were a most natural question.

'No, Cariad,' said Gruffydd listening to the steady hum outside, 'that is not bees. That is our whole camp praying for you.'

***

Maredudd insisted he was well enough to go to Henry himself. He knew the risk he was taking, but he needed to do this to prove to himself that he was not utterly worthless. As he moved through the woods, he saw the extent of the Norman army stretched out across the land as far as he could see. The number of soldiers was vast enough, but the army was swollen with all the vital craftsmen and tradesmen, their wives and hangers-on who accompanied them. He urged his horse across the river shallows and tried to stop his hands from shaking.

Under the flag of truce, Maredudd was led into the old castle at Tomen-y Mur. This was an ancient place where the Welsh had had a fortress long before the Romans came, and he wished it was not here that he should meet King Henry. He was ushered into a hall where Henry and Bishop Richard sat at a wide oak table with a sheaf of parchments in front of them. Outside, Maredudd was aware of the sounds of a mighty army moving around the camp: harnesses jingling, hooves pounding, the scrape of weapons being sharpened, the sound of metal scraping against pots, and voices high and low from every quarter.

'You come from Owain ap Cadwgan,' said Henry, assessing Maredudd and finding the hollow-cheeked and grey-haired supplicant insignificant.

'I do,' said Maredudd in a low voice.

Henry, his beard trimmed neatly, bejewelled, and exquisitely turned out in a fine red tunic, looked at his manicured nails.

'And he wants to surrender?' he said matter-of-factly.

Maredudd swallowed. 'He does not!'

Henry jumped up, his face red.

'Then what are you doing here?' the king shouted, his voice ringing with indignation.

Maredudd held his ground, his stomach churning. 'I want to understand what peace looks like.'

There was a moment of stunned silence.

'What are you talking about?' said Henry in irritation. 'You know we will eventually annihilate you if you do not surrender, so peace is the opposite of that.'

'I see,' said Maredudd summoning all his courage. 'Thank you for giving me an audience, and I will let the king of Powys know.'

He made his bow as if to leave, but Bishop Richard halted him.

'Lord Maredudd, wait.'

Maredudd's heart was pounding, but he raised himself and looked Bishop Richard levelly in the eye.

'You have not come all the way here without being willing to negotiate.'

Maredudd paused for a few moments and then spoke.

'The Welsh are doing what they do best. We are well set up in the mountains with everything we need, and we are committed to each other. All the kings and lords agree that we do not want our race to be exterminated from the face of the Earth. We are a proud race and have been here long before the Normans, the Danes, the Saxons, and the Romans. Our language was once spoken all over Britain, and if one thing unites the Welsh, it is an enemy who wants to wipe us out. You may succeed eventually, but it would take years, not months, weeks, or days.'

'Get to the point, Maredudd,' snapped Henry.

Maredudd took his time. 'As I see it, you may be victorious in the end, but it would come at tremendous cost, and the money from the harvests, much of which would end up in your coffers, would be lost because there will be no harvest this year. You could bring in Flemings to farm the land, but the Welsh will not sit back and let that happen.'

Henry was staring at him, but Maredudd forced himself to go on. 'Every day your army is here, it is a cost to you, but we Welsh are as happy as swallows up in our mountain pastures. And we are united, you see. And being united feels good to us. We are singing around our campfires, as I say.'

'As happy as swallows, as you say,' said Bishop Richard, with a slight rise of his eyebrows, 'but can we just understand what you are offering us?'

'Well, it is more a case of what you can offer Owain ap Cadwgan to break the alliance of kings because, Bishop Richard, as I see it, he is now a hero amongst the Welsh and a thorn in your side.'

Henry shot a glance at Bishop Richard, and there was a slight nod.

Bishop Richard cleared his throat and took a deep breath.

'We might be generous if Owain were willing to part company from your mountain dwellers.'

'And what would you consider generous?'

'We would impose no penalty on Powys, no reparation. We would absolve Owain ap Cadwgan of any tribute he might otherwise be imposed upon to pay to King Henry. We would offer him a knighthood and the opportunity to fight with the king in Normandy, with all the honour and wealth that will come with that.'

'That is very magnanimous indeed,' said Maredudd, 'but there is the small issue of trust. How can we trust you? My brother was a very trusting soul, but then…,' he spread his hands wide.

'You insolent peasant,' spat Henry. Maredudd's mouth began to dry up, his heart palpitating. He hoped they could not see his knees shaking.

Maredudd spoke again, keeping his voice low. He turned to the bishop.

'You know what happened to Madog, who broke with Welsh trust. He was your man, I think.'

Maredudd saw the bishop's icy blue narrow eyes, and a thought crossed his mind. He pictured his generous brother Cadwgan, ambushed with all his trusted advisors, and his brother Iorwedd, burnt to death. For him, the memories were still fresh and sore. The scheming eyes held his, and he shuddered.

'You were saying, Lord Maredudd,' said the king impatiently. With an effort, Maredudd took a grip of himself.

'Can you imagine how the Welsh would view Owain ap Cadwgan, their hero, abandoning the Welsh fold? There would need to be guarantees of protection.'

'Would your Welsh hero like to come to live in my court for a little while before we depart for Normandy? Would that satisfy his concerns about his safety?' offered Henry scathingly.

'That might persuade him. I am assuming he would live as a free man?'

'Of course. I would afford him the greatest hospitality if he were prepared to embed a rift in the Welsh alliance. Other than swearing his allegiance to the English crown, he would be completely free, and I suspect you would manage his affairs in Wales while he was absent.'

The Welshman nodded and could not help but be impressed by the speed at which Henry had laid bare his plan.

'We will wait for your confirmation of our agreement then,' said Bishop Richard, 'but do not leave it too long. Our patience is running out, and no matter the cost, if we need to escalate our hostilities, we will.'

It was evening when Maredudd and his men left Tomen-y Mur, and as he made his way up the mountain, he felt sick with himself. High-flying clouds allowed a little weak moonlight to penetrate, enough to illuminate the way, but in his mind, the path ahead was only a thick fog. He tried to tell himself that what he was doing was for the good of Owain and all the Welsh kingdoms, but that felt hollow. Hunydd was right in so many ways; he did feel old and impotent. He never wanted to fight again. He wanted a peaceful life. He was not sure how he had become what he had, but here he was. What was more, he reflected, what he had told Henry about the Welsh camaraderie was true, and he would be the man to destroy it if Owain could be persuaded. Then he remembered Hunydd, a blubbering mess as he came to after he had been injured, distraught and wild-eyed. There was something so frightening about the woman he had always depended on, strong as a rock, breaking down like that. It had shifted his certainties and eaten at him.

'No,' Owain had said resolutely when Maredudd first suggested going to Henry. 'I will not betray my fellow Welshmen.' But Maredudd had worked on him insidiously, like a cancer, putting doubt into his mind until he finally agreed that Maredudd should meet with Henry. Owain could not meet his people's eye after that.

'Nearly there,' said the stout Welsh guide as he led the little group through the mountain paths.

'Yes,' said Maredudd, shrugging into his cloak as the drizzle began to fall. 'Nearly there.'

***

'You look better,' Gruffydd said, giving his daughter an encouraging smile and leaning forward to kiss her on the forehead. He was so pleased that her strength seemed to be rapidly returning.

'I want to get out in the sun,' she responded, vocally stronger than he had heard the previous day.

'Not yet,' said Angharad, 'you were very sick, and you must do things slowly. Besides, we are keeping away from everyone else for a couple of days, just until we know we will not pass anything on.'

Gruffydd looked at his wife to see if he could see any sign that she was ailing. He had not forgotten that he had almost lost her once. His eyes felt dry and scratchy from lack of sleep, but he knew his body well enough not to fear for his health.

'Is everyone else alright?' Gwenllian responded immediately.

'So far, everyone is well.'

'Bethan?'

'Tired, but she is showing no symptoms.'

'The baby died though,' Gwenllian said, her eyes filling with tears, 'and the mother?'

'Has recovered. Nobody else seems sick from that little group.'

Gwenllian seemed to retreat into her own thoughts.

'Look what Owain ap Cadwgan has sent you,' said Gruffydd, handing over the little leather pouch to distract her.

Gwenllian fingered it, and her face clouded. Then she pulled the little cords tied at the neck of the pouch and pulled out a beautiful carnelian pendant, the stone set in gold.

Angharad gave a little gasp as her daughter held the pendant up to the light.

'It is beautiful, Gwenllian,' said the mother, 'perfect for your colour hair.'

'It is very beautiful,' the girl replied, looking at the pendant but not smiling. Then she put it back in the leather bag without saying anything else. Gruffydd exchanged a look with his wife.

'Can I just sit in the sun on the other side of the flap?' she pleaded. 'I will stay away from everyone, but it would be nice to watch what is going on.'

'Maybe for an hour,' said Gruffydd. 'We can make up a seat with cushions and rugs for you, I suppose.'

'A sort of sickbed throne,' she smiled, her eyes full of amusement.

Her mother laughed, 'You are on the mend, I can see. I will get you some hot milk and honey, and maybe, could you fancy an egg?'

Gwenllian smiled. She did not feel much like eating but knew it would please her mother.

The seat-bed was set up outside, and Gwenllian, supported by her parents, moved outside gingerly. She felt dizzy and weak once she tried to move from where she had lain for the past few days. Once she was set up, though, the nausea passed, and she began to collect herself.

She watched the activities in the camp. She could see: soldiers sparring with each other; men sawing trees or hammering nails; women making baskets and cooking; and children chasing chickens and piglets. She knew some of the older children would be out setting snares for hares or tickling trout in the clear streams further down the mountains. Everyone who noticed her smiled and waved, and she was touched when Susannah brought her little charges with an armful of flowers for her. Her sisters were so excited to see her, and she wished she had a little more energy to respond to them. Susannah, sensing how Gwenllian was feeling, led them skipping away.

Her hound, Gwyll, who had been kept out of her little shelter, got up from where he had stayed faithfully outside, stretched, yawned, and put his head in her lap for her to scratch him behind his ears. The warmth from the August sun on her face began to make her feel drowsy, and she let her heavy lids close, but as soon as she drifted off, an image that had been haunting her caused her to force open her eyes.

Someone was standing in front of her and for a moment she thought it was the poor boy from her nightmare and she started. It was Griffith, his face glowing from where he had been practising with his men.

'I am sorry. I think I woke you up. How are you?' he asked, his face filled with genuine concern.

She pushed herself up a bit and pulled herself together.

'I feel as if I have been through a battle with King Arthur,' she said, grimacing.

'Will you be alright if we leave you here for a while?' said Gruffydd ducking under the leather flap. 'We can get Bethan to sit with you.'

'Let Bethan have some rest,' said Gwenllian, 'I do not need to be watched every moment, and I know you and Mother have better things to do.'

'I will stay with her for a bit,' added Griffith.

'Not too close, though,' said Gruffydd. 'Just in case.'

'You gave us all a fright,' said Griffith awkwardly when her parents had gone.

'I gave myself a fright,' said Gwenllian. 'Honestly, I did not know it was possible to feel so ill.'

'The whole of the camp was praying outside here, you know. Everyone.'

Gwenllian looked embarrassed.

'What is the matter?' asked Griffith, seeing her face.

'It makes me feel uncomfortable,' said Gwenllian. 'Especially as the whole camp did not pray for the little baby who died. Just because I was born into a royal house does not make me that different.'

'I am not going to argue with you, but it does, actually.'

'Since I have been here, I have been the happiest I have ever been,' she said. 'Remember when we were all in that glade with the little stream tumbling beside it, and we had the service and prayers there before the first attack on the Normans? That was a better cathedral than anything King Henry has built.'

He remembered the glade, how her hair had shone in the light filtering through the trees, and how, when he had passed her, he saw her eyes shining like jewels.

'Yes,' he agreed, 'this is a magic place.'

'I could live up in the mountains like this forever, living no differently from the people all over Gwynedd. Managing.'

'I love it too,' said Griffith. 'For me, this is no hardship, and having the opportunity to band together to hurt the Normans is something I have dreamed of all my life. But I want to win. I want to get my lands back.'

'I can see it can be done,' said Gwenllian. 'Look at all these people. They want to be Welsh and safe and not look over their shoulders. They will fight for that. And it will be the same in every mountain camp. All the Welsh want the Normans off our backs.'

He kept his distance, but he wanted to take her in his arms and kiss her. No matter how he tried, he could not suppress his aching for her. He knew that if she was his wife, she would fight at his side and never complain about the hardships. He had met his perfect partner, a woman beyond his wildest dreams, but she belonged to someone else. When she had been at death's door, his despair had been so great that he had bargained with God that he would give her up to Owain if she could be saved. He would celebrate her happiness when she married, but now he felt the promise to God like a stone around his neck.

***

Owain ap Cadwgan watched his uncle. Maredudd was uncomfortable; he could not meet Owain's gaze.

'They can stuff their knighthood, their amnesty, and their offer to overlook the tributes they expect from Powys. We are on the verge of breaking them, Maredudd.'

'But Gruffydd…'

'Gruffydd ap Cynan will stand firm. He is an honourable man who has done the right thing by me. I do not believe he would capitulate.'

'There are rumours….' started Maredudd, and Owain saw by the lick of his lips that he was nervous.

'What rumours?'

'Rumours that he has made an agreement with Alexander of Scotland and the Normans. Rumours that his brother-in-law Gronwy ap Owain has been putting pressure on him.'

'I can believe that Gronwy would exert pressure, but Gruffydd would never be hounded by Gronwy into making an agreement, that is certain.'

'If he had, would you not feel foolish to have forsaken a good offer from King Henry? If Gruffydd takes a peace offering, you will become an outlaw again, and Gruffydd will march into Powys with all the strength he has collected on his mountain.'

'Then I will go to see him because there is no way on this earth that Gruffydd ap Cynan would let us down.'

'No, that would make you look weak.'

Owain looked bemused, 'I do not see any weakness in going to see Gruffydd. I can gain assurance of his commitment to our alliance and, at the same time, see the fair Gwenllian.'

'Ah,' said Maredudd.

'What do you mean, 'Ah'?' snapped Owain, beginning to weary of the older man's nagging.

'Gwenllian may have turned her attentions elsewhere.'

'What are you talking about?'

'She seems to be somewhat enamoured by Griffith ap Rhys.'

Owain looked as shocked as it was possible to be. He sat down heavily.

'How do you come by this?' he asked flatly.

'When Llywarch went to deliver your present to her, he caught Griffith ap Rhys and Gwenllian together.'

There was silence as Owain processed this, his jaw clenched so tightly that the muscles were evident. Maredudd saw how he had cracked his lord's world picture of a life with a young, flawless princess.

'Send Llywarch to me,' Owain said, his voice devoid of emotion.

Maredudd bowed and went out. Owain put his head in his hands. The betrayal felt like a physical blow.

***

Gwenllian's recovery was remarkable; within a few days, she was strong enough to walk around the camp. Her mother watched her like a hawk, but eventually, even she was satisfied that there would be no relapse. At times, though, Gwenllian appeared uncharacteristically subdued.

The camp was buzzing with the preparations for a night raid, and her father allowed her to join in as he went through the plans and instructions with her brothers. She said little, which was unusual, but Gruffydd put it down to her wanting to be part of it but not being able to. As the men drifted off to get their horses and join the rest of the group, Gwenllian ran after Cadwallon and caught him by the arm.

'Cadwallon, you must be careful,' she said, looking at him earnestly.

'I am always careful!' he protested.

'No, you are not. You are wild, you do not take care, and you do not keep your guard up.' Her words tumbled out, and suddenly she was crying. She threw herself at him, circling his waist with her arms.

'Hey, hey, hey. What is all this about?' he asked, hugging her back. 'It is not like my little sister to care about what happens to me. Normally you are fighting me yourself.'

She was sobbing into his chest, and he was entirely at a loss.

'Do not worry about me, you silly girl,' he said finally. 'Father has Aeddan, Hywel and half the men-at-arms surrounding us so much that I am getting fed up with it. They are behind us, in front of us, beside us, and there is no hope of ever having a decent fight with the enemy.'

Gwenllian stopped sobbing and pulled away, wiping her eyes and nose on her sleeve.

'Just do not do anything stupid.'

'What has brought this on?' Cadwallon asked gently.

At first, Gwenllian said nothing, but he asked again. She broke away and spoke softly.

'When I was sick, I thought something had happened to you.'

A shadow crossed Cadwallon's face, but he brushed off her words.

'I remember being sick once, and I kept dreaming my face had turned into a hog's face, but I am still as good-looking as ever I was, so I would not take much notice of nightmares.'

Gwenllian gave a small laugh. 'You will be careful, though.'

He nodded. 'I will. Now let me go, or I will be too late to be part of it.'

He gave her a final hug and ran like the wind to get his horse.

She went down to where the other women and children were gathering to wave off the men and saw Griffith adjusting his stirrups.

'Griffith,' she called. He looked up, beaming.

'This night raid,'

'Yes,' he said, still smiling.

'Please, can you watch out for Cadwallon?'

Griffith looked confused.

'He is not as good as he thinks he is,' she persisted.

Griffith's eyebrows shot up.

'Do not let him hear you say that!' he joked, and then, seeing her serious expression, 'I will make sure he does not get into trouble.'

'Thank you, Griffith,' she said. 'You stay safe as well.'

As they rode out of the camp, she saw that Griffith, true to his word, had placed himself next to Cadwallon.

It was a quiet camp that night. Even though the Welsh were excellent at this kind of warfare, accidents could happen, or men could be injured or worse. It was hard to be the ones waiting for the men to return.

Angharad came to sit next to her daughter at the fire with Bethan and Susannah, all making sure that the little girls did not venture too close to the flames.

'What is troubling you, Cariad?' Angharad asked when there was a lull in the conversation.

Gwenllian wanted to unburden the awful nightmares she had had when she was sick. They haunted her such that she was waking several times a night, but she did not want to tell her mother about Cadwallon. Instead, she thought she would just let her mother know about the nightmare she had had about herself.

'I keep having nightmares, Mother,' she said. 'It started when I was sick; they will not go away.'

'What do you dream?' asked Angharad.

'I dream that I am in a meadow near a river. I am with soldiers and fighting, but I am betrayed. There is a boy: I do not know who he is, but he is important to me, and the Normans kill him. I try to stop them, but they catch me by my hair.'

She did not tell her mother how she felt the Norman sword at her neck.

'Come here,' said Angharad pulling her daughter close so that she cuddled into her. 'When I was having you, I was very sick, and my nightmares were truly terrifying, but they came to nothing.'

'They will not go away, though,' said Gwenllian in a small voice.

'Do you know, sometimes this is when we need to see Father Luke. Come, we will find him, and he will pray for you.'

Shades of pink and orange were painting the sky when the horsemen returned the following morning. Gwenllian was one of the first to respond to the sound of the horn, running to the riders.

Her father was beaming, looking every inch the warrior king. The raid had gone brilliantly. Gwenllian searched the riders and saw Griffith grinning at her. When he nodded and held out a hand to indicate Cadwallon riding beside him, she felt she could breathe again.

Cadwallon, seeing her, rode over and leant from the saddle to tousle her hair. He gave her a pretend frown, though, in fact, he had been very touched by her concern for him.

'I swear, you are spoiling it all for me just because you cannot come with us. Not only did I have Father and Aeddan and Hywel and half of Wales surrounding me the whole time, but Griffith did not take his eyes off me! Now enough of this nonsense! Here I am, you see.'

He rode back to the gang of youngsters who were already recounting their adventures to the young girls of the camp who were fawning over their handsome heroes.

Gwenllian looked to see if Griffith was among them but saw, with some relief, that he was talking to Hywel and Aeddan. Her passion for him had not abated, and she longed to feel his arms around her. Even seeing him sent shivers up her spine. She sighed. Then she went back to her shelter to lie down.

Despite the prayers, she had not slept all night, too frightened that what she had seen in her head might come to pass. But now she allowed herself to sleep deeply and peacefully, and whatever dreams she had were of woods, trees, and bubbling streams.

***

Gronwy laughed out loud when Llywarch ap Trahearn rode in to tell him that Owain ap Cadwgan had submitted to the Norman king.

'See,' he turned round triumphantly to his brothers, 'I was right all along. I told you Owain ap Cadwgan would be the first to cave in.'

'But why?' asked Meilyr.

'In part, something to do with a fractured promise of betrothal with Gwenllian ferch Gruffydd,' explained Llywarch.

Gronwy edged forward in his seat.

'I did not know they were betrothed.'

'Not officially, but there was definitely some understanding.'

'So, what happened?' asked Rhydir.

'She seems to have cast her net towards Griffith ap Rhys.'

'What do you mean?' said Meilyr.

'I saw them together, very cosy, and he carrying her into her shelter,' said Llywarch.

'She would not do that!' countered Meilyr, aghast at the insinuation.

'I saw it with my own eyes.'

'Like mother like daughter,' said Gronwy grinning. Meilyr wanted to punch him.

'So where does that leave us?' he asked Gronwy.

'I go to the Earl of Chester and sue for peace. Then I will lead Henry's troops to Gruffydd's camp and do Gwynedd a favour.' Gronwy was as cool as if it was the most natural thing in the world.

What is this?' said Uchdryd, lifting the flap to Gronwy's shelter and coming in.

'Owain ap Cadwgan has gone over to the Normans,' said Gronwy with a leer.

'By my oath, what is the matter with the man? We had them. We had them where we wanted them.' Uchdryd was incensed.

'So, I will sue for peace with the Earl of Chester,' continued Gronwy smoothly.

Uchdryd's eyes widened for a moment, and then he clapped Gronwy on the back.

'No, Gronwy, if you go to the Earl of Chester, you will most likely lose your lands,' said Uchdryd quickly. 'I will go to the top. I have a good relationship with Bishop Richard. He is a pragmatic man. You stay here in the mountains until we are sure you will be safe.'

Gronwy looked hard at his uncle. 'I can take Chester's troops to Gruffydd's camp and bring Henry Gruffydd's head as a gift.'

'Gronwy, Gronwy,' his uncle spoke softly. 'Who do you think would get the reward for that? Not you. Chester would. We must outplay them, Gronwy.'

Gronwy made two fists and pumped them in silent jubilation as he imagined leading the people of western Gwynedd down from the mountains and instating himself into Gruffydd's royal llys at Aberffraw. Suddenly he jumped up, his eyes wild as another thought occurred to him.

'We need to be quick, or Owain ap Cadwgan will betray their position and get in before me. He craves to head up Powys and Gwynedd, but Gwynedd is mine now. I have waited long enough.'

Uchdryd put up his hand to still his nephew, and Rhydir looked at his uncle with concern.

'It may be too late, Uncle. If Owain has fallen in with Henry, surely the first thing he would do is to wipe out Gruffydd and his teulu.'

Gronwy's eyes registered horror as he heard Rhydir's words. He grabbed his uncle by the arm.

'There is no time to be lost, Uncle. Take Meilyr with you to offer as a hostage.'

Meilyr started, his stomach sinking, his mouth agape.

'No, indeed, you are right, Gronwy. I will ride with Meilyr to Henry and the bishop now with a few of my men,' said Uchdryd at once.

'Tell them I will deliver Gruffydd's head. Remind King Henry that Gruffydd's children are too young to take the throne, so there will be a vacancy. Henry will want some nominal Welsh figurehead to keep the people in check.'

Uchdryd nodded vigorously, 'Quite right.'

'Make sure he understands that until now, our family has served the Normans well, and after Gruffydd, I am the most senior in Gwynedd.'

'Most certainly.'

'Make sure he realises that our family is reliable, respected, and that Owain would not be a steady ruler if that is how the wind blows. The man is wild and has always rebelled against the Normans.'

'Of course,' said Uchdryd. 'Leave it with me, Gronwy. I will vouch for your character and suitability to rule Gwynedd.'

Gronwy looked sceptically at Uchdryd but saw the man was serious. Meilyr looked sick, and while Gronwy smirked again, the other brothers seemed dubious. They did not like Meilyr being offered as a hostage. Rhydir and Llywarch exchanged glances, but neither said anything.

'I will not live at Aberffraw,' crowed Gronwy, 'it is too isolated, but Caernarvon would suit me.' Then, turning to Meilyr, he said. 'Whatever happens to Gruffydd, you need not worry; I will look after my nephews and nieces, and my lovely sister.'

'Do not worry, Gronwy, I have always got on well with Henry,' said Uchdryd. 'He will listen to my words about you. I liked Gruffydd, but I am an old man without time for sentimentality, and it is important to think of the good of all the Welsh.'

'Then Uncle, you and Meilyr make haste before other people get any ideas,' said Gronwy, glaring at Llywarch ap Trahearn, who looked perplexed at what was happening and how he had unexpectedly incurred Gronwy's wrath.

Meilyr bowed his head as if acquiescing, but it was hard to contain his anger. He left Gronwy quickly before he could say something he would later regret. The betrayal of his brothers felt like death to him. Not for the first time, Meilyr agonised at his inadequacy, his weakness, and his inability to speak out and act on what he believed to be right. Duty to the head of the family had been drilled into him since childhood, and although he despised Gronwy with every fibre of his being, he had no more autonomy than a leashed dog.

The mountain camp was merry, with children playing and men laughing and joking as they attended to their tasks, but Meilyr was oblivious to anything but his despair, his powerlessness. He crossed the camp to say farewell to Ina and his children, explaining that he was to ride to King Henry with his uncle. He was too humiliated to elaborate on his brother's willingness to offer him as a hostage if Henry required it.

Ina tried to insist he changed into the best clothes he had with him and was excited by the prospect of her husband meeting with the Norman king. He knew his internal fury towards her at that was out of proportion at a time when he feared for his own life and those he was betraying. He fought to repress the built-up resentment for his shallow, grasping wife, who had looked at him with reproof when he had grunted that he would be wearing his mail.

With a heavy heart, Meilyr hugged his children too firmly so that they squirmed: at this pivotal moment, he was even failing to reach them, and he had no words for them that they would remember with fondness later.

Meilyr saddled his horse and sat mounted at the edge of the camp, waiting for Uchdryd. He was numb. The horse seemed to sense the change in him and whinnied and fretted. Meilyr patted his neck and took a handful of the beast's mane in his hand, gripping it tightly. He could hardly believe that Uchdryd would abandon his old friend, Gruffydd ap Cynan, so willingly, and he struggled with the thought of what would happen to the royal family.

Hearing hooves pounding behind him, he turned. Uchdryd, his white hair flying as he rode swiftly across the camp, was actually smiling.

'Christ knows, I am too old for this,' complained Uchdryd as he pulled his horse alongside his nephew.

Meilyr's ire was visceral, 'I thought better of you, Uncle,' he spat out.

Uchdryd just trotted on in stony silence so that Meilyr had to spur after him, bringing his horse between his uncle and the men accompanying them.

They rode a descent until they reached an area well out of sight of the camp. Uchdryd told his men to wait and rode ahead with Meilyr. When he turned to his nephew, Uchdryd's eyes blazed. He was uncharacteristically furious.

'Meilyr,' the old man's tone was curt and cold, 'After all these years, I am disappointed you would doubt me. Do you not see that I had to prevent

Gronwy from liaising with Chester.'

Meilyr struggled to understand, 'But you are betraying Gruffydd and Angharad.'

'Use your brains, lad. I ride to the Norman camp to convince Henry that Gruffydd is a better bet to raise his tributes. Better than putting in any Norman, Fleming, or other Welshman who will have the lands in ruin within two twelve months. Everybody can see how Gwynedd is prospering under Gruffydd, and I am going to use that to Gruffydd's advantage, but you must make Gruffydd consider peace.'

Meilyr looked at his uncle with shock, and then his expression lightened.

'Me?'

'Yes, you. If anyone can persuade Gruffydd to submit to Henry, you can.'

'He will never do it. They have got Henry in a bind.'

'They had Henry in a bind until Owain capitulated. You need to smooth the waters on the mountain, and I need to smooth the waters with the Normans below. Christ knows if I can pull it off.'

Meilyr took a moment. 'What will Henry demand, do you think?'

'It will cost Gruffydd more coin than he can imagine, but it will save lives and lands,' Uchdryd continued. 'Gruffydd will rage, but he is not a fool.'

'And if he will not sue for peace?' said Meilyr.

'I have confidence in you, Meilyr. He will listen to you. Remind him that victory is sometimes merely when there is no death, and the people are safe: money comes, and money goes. He will understand.'

Meilyr shook his head at the immensity of his task.

'Tell him you have been speaking to me and that I will convince the conniving bishop of the sagacity of keeping things as they are. And be honest with him about Gronwy. I will not always be there to keep the fox from the hens; you must be the voice of sanity in the future.'

Uchdryd pulled his cloak around him and looked back towards his men. Then he looked at Meilyr. 'I will send two of my men with you. These are treacherous times.'

'But Gronwy?'

'Gronwy will know no different. I will send word, and we will ride back and face him together, whatever happens. He will not know where you went this day. If I do not send word, save your skin as best you can.'

Meilyr nodded.

'And Meilyr?'

'Yes, Uncle.'

'The future of the Welsh will depend on you convincing Gruffydd to think of the bigger picture, not some self-sacrificial act. I know the man.'

'Thank you, Uncle,' said Meilyr feeling the weight of the task he had been given. 'I am sorry for doubting you.'

'Godspeed, Meilyr, and may luck be with us both.'

Uchdryd twisted in his saddle with a wince, and his gloved hand summoned his riders to join him down the steep mountain track.

***

It was a hot, lazy afternoon. The mountains of Eryri soared into a cerulean blue sky, the racing streams glistened, and insects buzzed and chirped in the undergrowth. From early in the day, the fighting men had been practising their skills, endlessly repeating the exercises which would someday save their lives and help them to take others. Now they performed the many small tasks which kept them safe. Some sharpened their weapons and repaired spear shafts or bows; others cleaned the mail they had taken from adversaries or tried to adjust the neck where it chafed against skin more used to the softer leather jerkins they commonly wore. Older children had been given simple tasks to search for eggs, watch animals, or use nifty fingers to help the women making twine or weaving. Many women had been cooking and baking, so beautiful aromas drifted across the camp from pots and makeshift bread ovens.

A simple church had been built, and Angharad sat with Father Luke and a few other clerics discussing a simple drama that the older children would perform for the younger to celebrate the lives of some of the Welsh saints. Her attire was simple on the mountain, and she wore darker colours which would not show the dirt. Today she wore a finely cut brown tunic with green embroidery at the neck and sleeve and hardy leather boots polished until they shone. Her four youngest daughters played freely with the other children. She dressed them similarly in plain woven cloth, cool enough for the hot weather but hardy enough to withstand paddling in the stream or chasing around in the bushes making dens or pretend markets. She looked up to see Susanna scrambling after her older sisters and friends, with Susannah, plump and cheerful, trailing them like a mother hen.

Gruffydd, dressed in a finely woven green tunic, his long kid boots stretched out in front of him, leant against a boulder surrounded by his teulu, who had congregated on a grassy mound in the middle of the camp. There was a sense of informality as they were planning their next moves. Things had been going well for them, and they were happy. Gruffydd was relaxed, making sure that everyone had a voice and that his sons and Gwenllian had a chance to learn, particularly from the older warriors. He also wanted to help his children understand the importance of making his men feel valued. Gwenllian, who had recovered well, sat silent but intently listening as Hywel put forth an idea.

'If we dam the stream above their camp and divert it, we could cause enough consternation for them to come to investigate. We could hide archers in the woods and let them fly as they came through.'

'It might be dangerous for the men doing it though; that's the only thing,' commented Aeddan and then, with a wink, 'mind you, if we could dam enough water, I would like to flood the bastards and their camp. Give them a taste of Noah's trials without a rainbow.'

The men laughed, seeing the joke, and when they stilled, Hywel continued.

'Aeddan is right to be concerned, but I still think we could pull off if we chose the right place where the archers can cover us from all sides. I have a couple of places in mind.'

A horn sounded, the sign of someone approaching. Gruffydd turned and saw Meilyr with two horsemen riding into their camp, scattering chickens and goats. Gruffydd leapt up with athletic grace and waved welcome before excusing himself from the group and striding across to his brother-in-law, who was dismounting.

'Meilyr! Welcome.' Gruffydd beamed. 'You have come at a good time. We are just planning our next attacks. There are some interesting proposals. Come share your wisdom with us, but first, you and your men will need something to eat and drink. You have ridden hard by the looks of you.'

Meilyr looked awkward.

'What is it, man?' asked Gruffydd, immediately sensing something was amiss and noticing the strained look on Meilyr's face.

'Sire, we should speak privately.'

'Sire? Then you bring me bad news.'

Meilyr said nothing but turned to Uchdryd's men to tell them to feel free to rest.

Gruffydd led Meilyr to the privacy of his tent.

'What has happened?'

'Treachery,' answered Meilyr, his mouth dry.

'Gronwy?'

'Yes, he is a threat to you, but the main threat has come from Owain ap Cadwgan, who has been seduced by King Henry to abandon the cause.'

Gruffydd's eyes opened wide with disgust, and his face turned chalk white. The breach of trust hit him like a punch to his stomach: his body tensed as a wave of nausea engulfed him.

'We had them, Meilyr. We had them. What was he thinking?' he said softly.

Meilyr elaborated on what he knew and what Uchdryd was doing. Gruffydd listened without interruption, but his face became increasingly downcast. When Meilyr had finished, Gruffydd raised his head skywards and said nothing for a while as he allowed the implications of the news to sink in.

'Well, Meilyr, we take this to the teulu now and let them know what is afoot.'

'Gruffydd, please,' said Meilyr dropping all formality, his voice breaking with emotion, 'to fight on would mean certain death for you.'

Gruffydd turned and gave a sad smile. 'You give me such little chance against the enemy, Meilyr?'

'Against the greatest army ever assembled against Wales, against the treachery of Owain and Gronwy. Even you, whom everyone acknowledges as the greatest warrior in the land, cannot beat those odds. Your family, your people, will be decimated.'

They had almost reached the group of warriors laughing heartily at something Aeddan had said. Hywel looked up as the two men approached and, seeing the look on his king's face, raised a hand to still the men. Gwenllian turned to discern what had changed the atmosphere so quickly, and, seeing her father's expression, her heart sank. She caught his eye, and he said quickly, 'Fetch your mother and the clerics, and you and your brothers round up all the main men from each family and settlement.'

'What is it, Father?' asked Cadwallon, standing up immediately.

'I will explain when all the representatives of Gwynedd are here,' said Gruffydd.

Within twenty minutes, the principal decision-makers of Gwynedd had been gathered; the air was thick with tension. Gruffydd stood, one foot resting on the rock and surveyed the men and few women before him. His voice was controlled and effortlessly powerful when he spoke.

'Over the last weeks, we have shown the Normans that we are no easy prey for their greed. We have experienced comradeship together, suffered hardship, loss and pain together, but most of all, we can be proud of what we have achieved together.'

He paused, and the only sounds were of the children playing in the brook, the gurgling waters and the bird call.

'Every man, no matter his station in life, has contributed to piercing the armour of the greatest foe Welshmen have ever faced. We in this camp have stood firm, resilient and eager to continue to war against injustice. Today, we must decide, together, how we continue because our friends on the other sides of the mountain have deserted us, and we now stand alone.'

There was a gasp of horrified fury, then outcry as the news hit home. Angharad grasped her brother's arm, her face draining of colour as he nodded, confirming that what Gruffydd was saying was correct. Gwenllian gave an anguished cry and shouted, 'Father, we cannot give in.' Her sentiment was taken up by many others who now stood to show their vehemence and make sure their voice was heard.

Gruffydd put up his hand, and the crowd stilled.

'I have no doubt we can damage the Norman force though it would take time and sacrifice, but I think all of you know that we are certain to be betrayed by our own: those we called brothers and friends. For their own benefit, they will lead forces to our camp; we will not be able to sleep, rest or hide. Our people will be maimed or killed, and our lands taken from us. Our only means of protecting ourselves is for me to parley with King Henry, meet terms agreeable to him, before our Welsh enemies do his job for him.'

Again, there was an outcry. Gruffydd gave them time, then he raised his hand again, and the hubbub died down.

'What lies ahead is not certain, but of this I am sure: should you decide that we make terms and, in so doing, save lives, there is no cowardice in that. It is cold common sense that drives us, not fear. This is the hardest decision I have ever grappled with, and I will be guided by you but know that I am no coward hiding from conflict. If the price of your lives and lands is my head, then so be it. I will give it willingly and be proud that I could do something worthy of such a fearless people.'

There was nothing in Gruffydd's face or demeanour to suggest the turmoil he felt, his fear for family, friends, and his people. He had immediately recognised the heart of the issue and given them the solution. Now he would wait while they discussed and argued but came to their own conclusion. After a short pause, he spoke again.

'You should discuss this honestly without any fear of reprisal. We have not long, I think, but I will retire to spend a couple of hours with my family. When I return, you must have decided a course of action, and I will abide by that decision whether it is to fight on, in which case I am happy to lead you, or it is for me to make terms, in which case I will ride from here to Henry's camp later in the day.'

Angharad was praying silently, her heart close to breaking, her hands gripping the sides of her tunic to stop the shaking. Cadwallon was angry, but he knew he must contain this in front of the gathered people of Gwynedd. His father was a hero, a warrior who had brought these men to the brink of victory, yet he was allowing the men of Gwynedd to decide on their future. Fury coursed through him, but he kept his face expressionless.

The crowd was vocal, and the atmosphere charged. Owain felt numb and empty. The father, whose love for him had given him the confidence and security not often afforded to a second son, was facing the greatest challenge of kingship. His father's life was at stake, and yet he had seen greatness: his father had behaved with honour and integrity. Owain realised this was a pivotal moment in all their lives: one which had come as unexpectedly as a silent assassin's blade. He looked at his brother

Cadwallon, whose eyes were as cold as flint, and recognised the sign of suppressed anger. Cadwallon, Owain knew, was already planning revenge.

Owain glanced across to his mother, stoic beside a haggard-looking Meilyr. What torment she would be going through, and Owain promised that he, too, would have revenge no matter how long it took. Then his eyes flicked towards Gwenllian, stony-faced but with hands clenched in tight fists by her sides, standing beside his younger brother, Cadwaladr. He remembered the blood pact made long ago in an ancient oak: not one of them would break it. Then his mind conjured his gloating Uncle Gronwy, his perfidy twisting in Owain's stomach: they would need no blood pact to make Gronwy pay for his actions.

Cadwaladr wanted to throw himself into his father's arms and cry, but he knew it would not be seemly. With a visible effort, he kept his face masklike, sat straighter, and kept his feelings in check. He would not let his father down by being less of a prince.

Gwenllian knew that as soon as she and the family were together in private, she would rail and beg and plead for her father to continue the fight. They had come so far, yet their own Welshmen had failed them, their own kin. Her eyes were welling with tears, but she choked them back, breathing deeply to steady herself. She dared not look at her siblings or her parents.

Gruffydd turned to his family and Meilyr, motioning that they should follow him to the shelter he had used as his chamber during their stay on the mountain. They walked away a dignified group, their bearing slightly stiff yet regal, only their pale faces betraying something of the anguish they felt. Susannah and Bethan ushered the small girls towards their parents and then respectfully retired as Gruffydd lifted the leather flap that served as a door, and he and his family disappeared inside.

EPILOGUE

Anglesey in August was hot and sultry. Fields of wheat and barley stretched across the landscape in some places almost to the water's edge, gleaming and waving atop cliffs and below woods. Back on their land, some farmers were already bringing in the harvest, which had suffered little during their sojourn.

The fishermen were back on the seas, which stretched further than they cared to venture. They stayed close to shore, but the sea was teeming with good catches as if stored up in their absence. The fishing communities had every hand salting and preserving.

The little lime-washed churches were being well used and provided places of safety and solace. Angharad wondered at the normality of it: had everyone already forgotten what had so recently passed?

Hywel stood next to Angharad, looking out across the Irish Sea. Her eyes were dark-circled, her face drawn, her long hair braided tightly beneath a flimsy veil.

'Gruffydd did everything he could,' Hywel consoled her. 'Circumstances conspired against him, against Gwynedd, against Wales.'

Angharad sighed, and when she raised soulful eyes, he saw them well with tears. 'If we had gone ahead with Gwenllian's betrothal to Owain ap Cadwgan or if I had worked harder to repair the rift with Gronwy, then maybe things would have been different.' Angharad spoke as a woman tired of weighing up what could not be.

'You cannot blame yourself. Not for one moment.' Hywel soothed her.

'It haunts me, Hywel.'

'You have to look to the future now, not look back.'

Angharad looked at him and held his arm, 'You are a wonderful friend, Hywel. Your support means so much to me, and I will miss you.'

Hywel coloured. 'I have done little.'

'You came. Hywel. Thank you.'

'I wish it had ended differently,' he admitted.

He wanted to hold her to him. He knew he still loved her, not in the intense, passionate way he loved Lafracoth, but she still drew him to her as a wave pulls the sand on the shore. Yet this love was a more honourable love that he stored in his heart.

'Say my farewell to everyone,' he said, turning away to gather his horse's reins. 'I have enjoyed being here with you all again though I wish the circumstances had been different.'

'Are you sure you do not want to say goodbye yourself rather than slipping away?'

'It is hard enough as it is.'

'Then you should stay.'

Hywel gave a half laugh.

'If only it were possible to live in two worlds at the same time.'

'Are you ready then?' A deep voice sounded from behind them.

Hywel turned and smiled, 'I am ready.' He swung himself lithely into the saddle, turned back once to bow to Angharad, and rode with Gruffydd down to the port to meet the boat which would take him to Ireland.

'Thank you again, Hywel,' Gruffydd said, 'you know there is no need for you to leave. There is always a place for you here.'

'I know,' said Hywel, 'but I promised Murtagh I would return, and I must respect that promise.'

Gruffydd hesitated for a moment and then said, 'Angharad thinks you might have found someone special over there.'

'I did, but I am not sure she will be waiting for me. I will find out soon enough.'

'Anybody I know?'

Hywel gave a mirthless laugh, 'I seem to be attracted to other people's wives. It is not intentional. It just seems to happen.'

Gruffydd's face clouded.

'She has not seen her husband in years, and he was vile to her,' Hywel explained.

'Oh, Hywel. Why can things not be simple for you?'

'Are they simple for anyone?'

'Probably not.'

They rode on for a while in silence.

'I wish we could have pulled it off against Henry,' Hywel said.

'Nearly did, except for Owain.'

'Yes, it was a blow that.'

'I blame Maredudd. I heard that he fed Owain all sorts of rubbish about me coming to an agreement with the Scots,' said Gruffydd, his expression sour.

'Rumours,' said Hywel, grimacing, 'they make things even more complicated.'

'This will not be the last we hear from Henry, you know. Once he has sorted out Normandy, he will be back at us again.'

'And we will ride against him again.'

'Perhaps.' Gruffydd's voice was almost whisper.

Hywel turned and looked earnestly at the man who had been his lord for so long.

'You are ever too hard on yourself.'

Gruffydd shrugged.

'It is a fine day for the crossing, at least.'

'It is.'

'Thank you, Hywel,' Gruffydd reiterated, 'do not ever hesitate to come home.'

Hywel's smoky gelding tossed his head and snorted in protest, seeing the quay ahead.

'I will never forget you,' said Hywel, 'any of you.' He slid off his horse and blindfolded him for the walk up the plank to the ship.

Gruffydd dismounted, and the two men embraced.

The king waited and watched as Hywel's ship pulled out, then stood on the quay, lost in reflection.

He had come so close to killing the Norman threat, so close. He should be proud of that. His teulu had made the right decision, although they had insisted that Meilyr be the go-between for Gruffydd rather than Gruffydd riding to Henry himself. That had touched him. If he had, it would have meant certain death: it would have been Henry's vengeance.

The settlement with King Henry had been more costly than he could afford, and now, after years of hard work to make Gwynedd thrive, he was back to worrying about money. It was not a pleasant experience. Yet, it was a small price to pay for the safety of his family and people.

He heard hooves behind him and saw Griffith ap Rhys riding too fast down to the quay.

'Damn! I missed him,' the young man exclaimed as he saw the ship in the distance. 'I meant to say goodbye, but I was out riding and lost track of the time.'

'With my daughter?' asked Gruffydd.

'Yes,' said Griffith and then began impulsively, 'Sire, I have been meaning to ask you ….'

'Do not,' said Gruffydd. 'Not yet. I nearly lost her. I am not ready for her to go anywhere yet.'

'I almost lost her too,' exclaimed Griffith vehemently, 'and I love her.'

Gruffydd turned his head and looked at the young man, long and hard.

'Does she know?'

Griffith hesitated. 'I do not know. I have not told her.'

'Does she love you?'

'I do not know, but perhaps in time.'

Gruffydd said nothing for what seemed an eternity to the ardent suitor.

'I am not saying no. I like you, Griffith, and I am supporting you, as you know, but she is young. I have committed to you, but your future looks uncertain. Had we beaten the Normans, you would have stood more of a chance. You are quick with your sword and words, and everyone is charmed by you, but you will need more to make it to be King of Deheubarth. You will need a strength that has not yet been tested. Besides, with the position I now find myself in, I may need to make an alliance.'

'You would marry her off to someone against her will?' Griffith protested.

'I have the right to marry my daughter to someone who can provide for her every need,' Gruffydd replied.

Griffith flinched at the note of iron that had entered Gruffydd's voice.

'But you would not marry her to Owain ap Cadwgan? Not now?'

'Not if he was the last man on Earth,' said Gruffydd.

Griffith still looked crestfallen, but he would not give up.

'But you are not saying no.'

'I am not saying no.'

'So, I can court her?'

'Is that not what you are doing now?'

'She does not see it like that. She treats me like her brothers.'

Gruffydd laughed, his eyes knowing.

'Griffith, women are complex creatures. Never underestimate what they understand.'

Griffith looked at him earnestly, and the king draped his arm around the young man's shoulders.

'Do you want me to go to Llyn?'

'Maybe not yet,' said Gruffydd. 'We are getting used to you here, but do not always be in such a hurry.'

As they rode back into the llys, they could hear Gwenllian's laughter as she raced her brothers to the practice yard, where the men were doing what they did best. The fighting and time in the mountains had made Gruffydd's men lean and strong, and he knew they were unmatchable. Angharad was sitting against the wall, her eyes closed and her face to the sun. The younger children were sitting on the grass under the apple tree with Susannah and Bethan, playing with lambs that were really too old to be kept as pets. Gruffydd smiled. It was a time to be content.

THE END

www.historiumpress.com

www.historiumpress.com/arianwen-nunn